PROMISE OF RAPTURE

There was a seeking look in his eyes now, a tremor at his lips. She caught her breath as his lips came onto hers and pressed, gently and tenderly. Her own lips moved under his and they kissed.

"Hester . . . Hester . . ." he whispered as she held him. He stroked her hip. "It's all right if I can't wait . . .?"

"Don't wait!" she half sobbed.

"Hester, little Hester!" he gasped, her name coming onto her cheek with his breath.

"What . . . is it . . . Master Phil?"

"Call me Phil, never master again . . . Hester . . . sweet Hester . . . I love you!"

His voice broke with wonder. "I *love* you! Love you the way a man loves the girl he marries!"

BLACK IVORY

Saliee O'Brien

BANTAM BOOKS
TORONTO · NEW YORK · LONDON
NEW YORK

BLACK IVORY
A Bantam Book / April 1980
2nd printing

ISBN 0-553-13021-8

Published simultaneously in the United States and Canada

Bantam Books are published by Bantam Books Inc. Its trade-
mark, consisting of the words "Bantam Books" and the por-
trayal of a bantam, is Registered in U.S. Patent and Trademark
Office and in other countries. Marca Registrada. Bantam
Books, Inc., 666 Fifth Avenue, New York, New York 10019.

PRINTED IN THE UNITED STATES OF AMERICA

In memory of my parents
Benjamin F. Griggs
Lillian M. Griggs

BLACK IVORY

Part One

❖

The Rape
1857

Chapter One

❖

Hester awakened as the first faint blush rose in the sky. Outside the window of the cabin a breeze stirred, carrying with it the perfume of the snowy white blossoms of the cottonwood trees.

Something was going to happen today, Hester thought, as she struggled to wake up. Something wonderful.

A sense of being fourteen seeped through her. Astounding, she thought, and wondered what astounding was. It was the word that Granny Myrtle had used to describe her.

Hester was the lightest-skinned slave at Thornton. When she sat on her father's lap and he held her with his powerful arms, she would stroke his skin, wishing her own was the same velvety, bottomless black. Or that it was like her mother's skin, as shiny as coal. Briefly, she wondered about the strain of white blood her mother bore. But she had the same large brown eyes they had, and of this she was fiercely proud, for it tied her to them as securely as did their warm and protective love.

She thought of Granny Myrtle, an old woman of seventy-four, rich with wisdom. Many years ago, she had worked in the big house and had learned the right way to talk; she could even read and write and figure a little, having learned from the master's young daughter, whose nurse she had been.

Granny had said her piece about Hester when Hester was a little baby, and now it was a legend in the Quarters. "You got a miracle baby, a blessin' straight from the Lawd God!" she had told Hester's parents. "I don't know why He chose you for such a gift, but He did it, and you should thank Him all youah lives."

"De house slaves call her white niggah," Hester's father, Sam, had said. "If othahs do it, Hester be treated bad."

"I won't allow it," Granny had declared. "No pickin' on this baby! Mastah Thorne, he come to the cabin and named her like he names all the suckahs. He say white niggah then?"

"No. But I don' know he rightly seen huh."

"He saw. He's not a mastah who misses nothing. Fact that he named Hester and didn't claim you been with a white man, Lela Belle, shows he's satisfied Hester is youah natural-born baby."

"We got to raise her good," her father had said.

"You will, Sam. The Lawd God, He'll help you. It's a sign you lived right, Him givin' you a beautiful chile. All of us will watch ovah her and see that she don't suffah no harm from her beauty."

They all do love me, Hester thought now, filled with that story she had heard so often. She gazed at her pink fingernails, which her mother said showed that she was healthy and that her blood was rich.

Now fully awake, her mind jumped to the Big Thing. So eager to hear the outcome of last night that she was suddenly trembling, she scrambled out of her bunk and pulled the blanket up, tightly and neatly. She stripped off her mended nightshift, folded it and put it under the pillow, and then she ran, naked, across the board floor to the wash shelf.

Above the shelf hung a cracked looking glass her father had salvaged from the trash at the big house. She watched herself in it as she bathed from the tin pan, using the soap her mother made and being careful, on this important day, to wash everywhere.

She noted the changes that had recently occurred in her body. Where she had been flat, she now had what her mother called titties. They were full and round. She had a tiny waist, her belly was flat, and she now had curved hips.

After drying herself, she put on her clean daytime shift. She didn't mind that it hung above the knees, but it was too tight in the bust, which bothered her.

Her hair, which hung halfway down her back, was tangled. Her mother wouldn't let her plait it, so now she pulled the brush slowly through it. Auburn was the word Granny Myrtle used to describe its color. She said there was a glint like the red of fireplace coals deep in it. As Hester brushed, the top and sides fell into waves and the ends sprang into the big round curls her parents were so proud of.

Sometimes, looking at their hair, cut close in tiny black ringlets, she wished hers was the same. She wouldn't even mind that it was auburn if it could be that easy to take care of. Carefully, she tied her troublesome hair back with a string.

The excitement, anticipation, and dread she had been trying to hold back flooded over her, and she hurried into the kitchen. It was deserted. Mush was bubbling in the iron pot at the fireplace, fatback was sizzling, and coffee was simmering. The double bunk was made up. The table was ready.

She went to the door, then glanced up and down the street. There was no movement: everybody was inside, eating. Mammy and Pappy had gone to tote water, that was it, she thought. Usually Pappy toted after supper, but last night he and Elmer and Jase had gone to the big house, and even when the bed bell had rung, they hadn't come back. Hester had thought she couldn't go to sleep, but she had been so tired from working in the field all day that, excitement or no excitement, she had been asleep the instant her head landed on the pillow.

She stirred the mush and turned the fatback. A few drops of sizzling grease hit her in the face, and she wiped them away, then ran back to her room to scrub her face with her wet washrag.

Her mother and father were coming through the door when she got back. Neither of them said a word as they set their wooden buckets on the shelf. Both were unsmiling, yet looked at her with tenderness. Hester couldn't tell what had happened last night, not from their faces.

"Hester—chile," Sam said, his voice deep and beautiful. "De mastah, he say no."

Hester's look flew to her mother, who had tears in her eyes. They weren't making a joke.

"She need to be tol' like you tol' me las' night, Sam," Lela Belle said. "Do it while we eat, so we won' be late to de field or you to de anvil."

Sam nodded, then smacked one fist noiselessly into his other hand and turned away. It was as if he couldn't bear to look at his daughter, as if he blamed himself.

Hester's insides seemed to twist. It must have been awful. Maybe the master got mad at Pappy and Elmer and Jase because they talked like field slaves. Well, she wouldn't have Mammy and Pappy change their talk, not even as much as she had changed hers. They wanted better for her than they had had, and they had asked Granny to teach her to talk better, and that was fun. But Granny had never tried to teach Mammy and Pappy. They were perfect, Hester thought, and always there, just like the cabin and her own room.

Hester helped her mother get breakfast on the table. As they sat and ate, her father recounted what had taken place the night before.

"Elmer an' Jase an' me, we walked to de big house," he began. "Axed dat fat Aurora-cook to tell de mastah we was axin' to talk on a important mattah. Aurora, she tried to chase us off, an' he heard her screechin', an' him an' young Mastah George an' his cousin, Mastah Phil, dey come out on de back gallery an' stood lookin' down at us. . . ."

Chapter Two

❋

There were lanterns hung along the back gallery of the mansion, and they shone on Thorne Wabash, the master of Thornton, and the two young men with him. Light spilled onto the three slaves who stood below them, their faces upturned.

Thorne Wabash was the most important man in Warren County. A slender and perfectly built man, he had dark brown hair parted on the side and drawn forward. At each temple he had a streak of white going up like a horn. His eyes were dark brown and keen under white, thick eyebrows. By his stance, it was obvious he was furious.

"What's this?" he demanded. "No field hands are permitted at the big house!"

Sam and Elmer stood unmoving. Jase shifted from one foot to the other.

"Well!" snapped Master Thorne. "Speak up!"

When none of the slaves responded, Thorne turned to his stepgrandson and future heir, George Drummond. "See this?" he asked. "On your first evening from New Orleans! I apologize."

George, twenty, was strong and muscular. He had dark brown, wavy hair that curled down over his temples. He wore an ivory sack coat with a handkerchief in the pocket and narrow plaid trousers.

"George?"

"I see, Grandfather. It's their nature." His mouth took on a mean cast. "They're—pushing."

Thorne turned to the other young man, his stepnephew, and George's cousin. "Phil?"

Philip Bennett was eighteen. Blonde, with intensely

blue eyes, he had strong, patrician features, and his mouth was firm but kind.

"Maybe they have a real need, Uncle Thorne, sir," he said, calling him uncle though there was no blood relationship between them.

"Hmm. Why didn't you come up with that, George?"

"I didn't care to speak out of turn, Grandfather," George replied, not quite succeeding in keeping an edge off his tone. "I'm not the master, sir."

"Not yet, true." Thorne turned back to the slaves. "What is it? I presume one of you is spokesman?"

"Yas, suh," ventured Sam.

"Well, Sam, talk."

"I ain' de one, suh. Jase, he's to talk, 'cause he got de mos' suckahs an' he talk good. We come 'long to show we's in it, too. If mastah be so kin' as to lissen."

"Hold it!" ordered Thorne before Jase could speak. "How many of the people are involved in this?"

"All of us, Mastah Thorne, suh," Jase quavered.

"When did it start? When did you discuss it?"

"We talk fo' mos' a yeah, Mastah Thorne, suh," said Sam. "Yestahday in de fiel's, we decide dat Elmer an' Jase an' me come to de mastah, an' Jase, he talk, it bein' 'bout dem wif suckahs."

"What's suckers got to do with it?"

"Dey de ones involved, Granny Myrtle, she say, suh."

"So. Granny's behind this?"

"No, mastah, suh. We go to her an' ax, an' she say Mastah Thorne want dis to be de bes' plantation of all, an' it our duty to talk to him, 'case he ain' 'sidered it hisself, bein' so busy."

Thorne made a chopping motion with his hand. "Out with it!"

"It dat we got so many suckahs we bin talkin' dat mebbe de mastah, he git a teachah to come learn 'em to read an' write an' add. Jus' on Sunday, when dey ain' no work."

There was silence. Thorne's body became rigid.

"I couldn't be more—astounded," he said, through clenched teeth, "if my *pigs*, roaming the woods, were suddenly to come to me—against all rules—and demand that I get a teacher for their young!"

Jase, Sam, and Elmer stood speechless. Elmer nudged Jase, but Jase was trembling.

Thorne looked at George and Phil. "Did you ever hear of such a thing, that a man's *stock* wants a *school?*"

"Some plantations do run schools for the black children, sir," Phil ventured.

"None around here!" George snorted. He glared at Phil. "Don't you think you're pretty fresh to say such a thing to my grandfather?"

"Maybe I am fresh, sir," Phil said. "You know better than I how plantations are run."

Thorne's fierce look deepened. He gave a brief nod. "What do you think your suckers can do with books?" he snapped at the slaves. "Will it make them plow a straighter furrow, chop cotton better, pick it faster?"

"No-no, mastah, suh," stammered Jase. "Dat ain' de reason."

"What *is* the reason?"

"Uncle Thorne," Phil interrupted, "don't most parents want things for their children? Can't it be that some black children want to read, *need* to?"

"You're very young, Phil, or I'd hold you to account for that question. However—" He glared down at the black men, who were gazing miserably at the ground. "Do any of *your* suckers want to read?"

Sam forced himself to speak. "My Hester, Mastah Thorne, suh, she learn' f'um Granny Myrtle, an' she yearns fo' mo'. It a hungah in dat lil' wench, mastah, suh. Seem like nothin' but books'll sat'sfy it."

There were a few seconds of silence, and then Thorne spoke. "Answer me some questions. Speak together, for there can be but one answer. Now. Your cabins, are they tight-built, up from the ground, whitewashed every year?"

"Yas, mastah, suh."

"Every week, do you get your cornmeal at the corn-crib? Do you get a peck for every full slave, and your three or four pounds of salt pork or bacon at the smoke-house, and proper shares for your suckers?"

"Yas, mastah, suh."

"Do I sometimes give you salt?"

"Yas, mastah, suh."

"Do I occasionally give you milk and molasses? Do I give each of you a piece of wasteland at the back of my own property so you can raise vegetables to eat and to sell?"

"Yas, mastah, suh."

"Do I permit you to have Sunday to work your garden and later buy from you at a fair price your extra vegetables so you'll have cash with which to buy knicknacks for yourselves?"

"Yas, mastah, suh."

"Do I furnish you, at times, with coffee, sugar, poultry, and beef?"

"Yas, mastah, suh."

"Do I furnish each buck in the fall with two shirts of drill, a pair of woolen pants and a woolen jacket, and in spring two cotton shirts and two pair of cotton pants? Do I, in the fall, give each wench six yards of woolen cloth, six yards of cotton cloth, a needle, a skein of thread, buttons, and in the spring six yards of cotton shirting and six yards of cotton cloth similar to that for the bucks' pants, with suitable yardage for the suckers?"

"Yas, mastah, suh."

"Do I give each black, worker or sucker, one pair of stout shoes every year, and a heavy blanket to each cabin every third year?"

"Yas, mastah, suh."

"When one of you falls ill, beyond Granny's potions, do I bring in my own physician to dose you and make you well?"

"Yas, mastah, suh."

"Do I allow a preacher to exhort you quarterly?"

"Yas, mastah, suh."

"Do you have a dance every quarter?"

"Yas, mastah, suh."

"Do I take care of my other stock—my horses, cows, mules, pigs, and chickens?"

"Yas, mastah, suh."

"Do I take better care of my slaves than of my other stock?"

"Yas, mastah, suh."

"Do you have any complaints?"

"No, mastah, suh."

"You're treated well, lack for nothing?"

"Yas, mastah, suh."

"Yet you do come to me with a complaint."

"No complaint, mastah, suh."

"Do you deny that you asked for a teacher, a luxury I

do not supply to my other stock? Do you deny that con-
stitutes a complaint?"

The slaves shifted uneasily. Sam and Elmer glanced
sideways at Jase. His lips trembling, he spoke. "We don'
mean it fo' complaint, mastah, suh. It a—*reques'*. Sam,
he got dis wench dat hungahs to read, an' Elmer, he got
one—an' Jase got a wench an' a buck bof wants to read.
Wif Mastah Thorne sech a good mastah, keepin' his people so fine an' healthy—"

"You thought you could impose on me. That you could,
eventually, with book knowledge, rise against me! Did
you stop to think, before you came here, that I'm a firm
master? How long has it been since I've had a slave
thoroughly whipped? Tell me that—you Jase, you fast-
talking buck!"

"It—it bin ovah a yeah, mastah, suh."

"It's been eighteen months, and you were the one
whipped. For laziness." Thorne's voice was thinning on
every syllable, his rage increasing. "Now you come to me
with insurrection, and that I will not tolerate."

"Mastah goin' have Jase whip', suh?" Jase half-whis-
pered.

"I don't like to whip. I don't permit my mules, even, to
be lashed unless they won't move at all. I don't like to
mark up my stock, but sometimes it's necessary. This
time it's vital."

"Good for you, Grandfather!" exclaimed George. "Are
you going to put only Jase to the lash, or all three of
them?"

"All of them. George, go inside and send the butler,
send Old Dewey, to the Quarters. Have him bring two
trusties—Brutus and Buck."

As George disappeared into the house, Phil faced
Thorne. "Can't you let them off this one time, sir? They're
so frightened, I don't think they'll ever—"

"Young man, you're a family connection only, not an
heir! No harm has come of this yet, and I'm going to
see that none does. There's the seed of insurrection here,
and I'm stamping it out before it grows."

It seemed like forever to Sam that he stood there between Elmer and Jase, whose teeth were chattering. Suddenly he knew the master was staring at him.

"You, Sam."

"Yas, mastah, suh."

"You don't seem to realize that I've been exceptionally good to you and Lela Belle. I've kept you in spite of the fact that you produced only one sucker in fourteen years and that a freak-skinned wench. If she had looked mulatto—which I won't have on the place—instead of some freak mixture of inheritance factors between you and Lela Belle, I'd have sold you all."

"Yas, mastah, suh."

"I decided to keep you only because I didn't want to bother about finding a new blacksmith and another wench who can work a plow so well."

"Yas, mastah, suh. Thank you, suh."

"Sir," Phil said, his jaw stiff, "could you compromise?"

"How's that?"

"Two of the wenches, Hester and Jewell, I know them."

"So?"

"They're very intelligent. I was thinking—well, I've been told that Mr. Barry Millhouse's bookkeeper, who lives at Elmhurst, was tutor to the Millhouse twins years ago and stayed on to do the bookkeeping. If he could teach just these two wenches, they'd make you good house servants, able to speak properly and with intelligence."

Thorne made a chopping motion. "The master who permits his darkies to read and write has trouble. No darky will be educated at Thornton. There'll not be one of them with the knowledge needed for rebellion. Hear that, George," he warned the other young man, who had returned and stood listening. "Ah. Here come the trusties. Listen well now, both of you. Learn to deal with blacks."

The old, white-haired butler who had gone on the errand to the Quarters now scurried into the house as the big, muscled trusties came to a stop behind Sam's group.

"You Brutus, you Buck," Thorne ordered, "will put Jase in the jailhouse. There'll be a whipping in the big stable tomorrow night. Jase will take sixty lashes."

"Mastah—*suh!*" screamed Jase. "Jase can't *stan'* no sixty lashes! He too thin, he too—"

"Lazy. Sixty. Every slave will be there to see. You also, George—Phil. Object lesson. You're both fortunate. You, George, because you inherit and you, Phil, because you dream one day of buying land for yourself."

"What about the other two, Grandfather?" George asked excitedly. "Is Jase to take the lash for all three?"

"They all pay. It's cotton planting time, and Sam has to keep the mules shod and mend plows. He'll get ten lashes. Elmer will get ten. He's needed behind a plow."

"But why sixty for Jase, sir?" Phil asked. "He won't be able to work for a long time."

"Small loss. His punishment will be remembered— and discussed—by the slaves for years to come. The memory of it will keep all of them in their places."

George grinned. "Why wait? Why not whip them now?"

"Waiting gives all the darkies time to think—and dread. It adds to the impact." He turned to the slaves. "Sam and Elmer will sleep in their own cabins. They will do their regular work tomorrow. If they don't work better than usual, they get two extra lashes. After the whipping, they heal two days, then back to work."

Now, in the little cabin, Sam finished his account.

Lela Belle was crying, tears running down her face. "Yo' ain' nevah bin whip' befo'!" she said.

"I ain' nevah step' out of my place. Elmer neithah. He kin stan' ten lashes—me, too. But Jase—" He shook his head. *"Sixty!"* he whispered. "At forty lashes, an' dat's not as many as sixty, I seen—" He broke off.

Thinking of her father being whipped, Hester felt tears slide down her cheeks. Sam and Lela Belle took her into their arms at the same time, and they stood, locked together.

"Ah got to warn yo' ag'in, honey," Hester's mother sobbed. "Aftah de way Mastah George act lately, you stay close by de Quarters, an' in de fiel's. Stay far f'um Mastah George long as he around."

"Dat's right," her father agreed. "I don' like how he look at yo'."

"He looks at Jewell, too. He looks at all the wenches."

"Dey ain' de same," insisted Lela Belle. "Ain' nothin' like yo'. Mind me, now."

"Yas," Sam said. "Leas' touch f'um any white man or any buck, yo' run an' yell. Evahbody in de Quarters has pertected yo' since yo' born, an' always will!"

"Why I got to be so careful?" Hester asked. "Jewell doesn't have to, and she's fourteen!"

"She ain' got titties like yo' got, honey," Lela Belle said. "She mo' a lil' wench, yet."

Obedient as always, Hester promised. She felt heavy-hearted. Part of it was that there would be no school, but the big trouble was, she thought, that Pappy and the others had to take the lash tonight.

Their flesh would be cut by the strap and it would bleed and fester and they would suffer. All because she'd wanted to learn books. Heaviness and grief filled her at what was going to happen. There was no way to stop it. The master of Thornton had spoken.

Chapter Three

�֍

The field hands moved out into the fields in frightened silence. Even the young children, who were left with Granny Myrtle, weren't running around or crying for their departing mothers.

Sam squeezed his daughter's shoulder, then turned off for the blacksmith shop. Hester and her mother walked on with Elmer and Hattie, both of whom managed plows.

To keep from dwelling on what was to happen tonight, Hester forced herself to think of other things. Staring at the ground as she walked, she pictured Thornton, which she loved. Once she had stolen through the orchards to the far end of the long, grassy driveway and looked up its oak-shaded length to the tall, white-pillared house with the veranda across the front. Then she had run home before someone at the big house spied her.

Next she thought of the four streets of cabins comprising the Quarters. They were a good distance behind the big house, hidden by the wall of cottonwood trees. Behind the Quarters stood the overseer's square white house, both stables, the smokehouse, the corncrib, the hogpen, the harness shop, laundry room, blacksmith shop, and the jailhouse.

Beyond all this, on every side, spread acres and acres of planted fields, stretching to the ends of the sky. In the pastures horses, cows, and mules grazed, and in the swampland two hundred hogs ran loose to fatten.

Jewell broke into her thoughts by moving close and gripping her hand. Jewell's hand was sweating. They glanced at each other, then away. Both their fathers were to get the lash.

Jewell, Elmer's daughter, was as tall as Hester, but flat-chested and knob-kneed. Her skin was dull black, and her hair was in pigtails.

"It's all ouah fault!" Jewell whispered hoarsely.

"What you mean?"

"If we hadn't axed ouah pappies to ax fo' a school— but we did, an' they did and now look!"

Hester felt like she was choking. Jewell was right; Hester had been trying to push that thought out of her mind by thinking about the plantation.

"It *is* our fault," she acknowledged sadly.

"There ain' no way we can undo it, Hester!"

"If we go to the master. Just turn right now and go to the big house and *tell* him—"

"They won' let us *neah* the big house!"

"We'll *sneak* and tell him! It wasn't our pappies, and it wasn't Jase. It was you and I, wantin' to learn more than Granny's taught us. We could beg him to whip us, instead. He'll believe us—he's got to!"

Hester's voice had risen without her realizing it, and she was heard by all the trudging slaves nearby. Suddenly Hattie and Lela Belle were right beside Hester and Jewell, each with an arm around her daughter.

"Hush!" Hester's mother whispered. "Stop dat talk! It *ain'* yo' fault. Yo' pappies an' mammies bin wantin' books fo' yo' since you was born! Yo' pappies would of axed even if you two lil' wenches wasn't so eagah fo' books!"

Relief washed over both girls. Their eyes met, and there was understanding. By even being born, they had gotten their fathers into this trouble.

But we can't blame ourselves for that, Hester thought. It would be better to pin her mind on the work that lay ahead.

Now, with the cottonwood trees in bloom, was the only time to plant cotton. She had helped put in the early vegetables during the freak January thaw, and already the cabbage, greens, spinach, and onions were thriving. The second planting of peas and lettuce had come in February, and she had worked at that. And at St. Valentine's, in the dark of the moon, she had been in the gardens planting potatoes and later, in the light of the moon, the leaf vegetables.

They walked a bit faster. Here was their part of the

field. It was a big stretch of land, and there were thirty mule-hitched plows waiting to turn the earth.

The size of Thornton never ceased to amaze Hester. The plantation had two hundred slaves, of which one hundred twenty-five went to the fields. There were also a cook and seven house slaves, four mechanics—blacksmith, carpenter, wheelwright, harness maker—two laundresses, two seamstresses, two stable servants, one cattle tender, four hog tenders. one teamster, one midwife and one nurse—Granny Myrtle. There were, in addition, three trusties, two hoe-gang drivers, and one plow-gang fore-man.

Boys and girls in their early teens, like Hester and Jewell, were counted as quarter-hands. The twenty wom-en who left the fields four times a day to nurse their suckers were half-hands, expected to do half the work of a prime field hand.

Hester's group stopped. Her mother gripped the han-dles of her plow, slapped the reins on the back of the mule, and slowly, the mule began to move. Lela Belle bore down on the handles, and the plow dug in, cutting deep, making a furrow.

Jewell, clutching her seedbag, followed Lela Belle. Carefully she dropped seeds into the new bed. Hank, a strong-built boy of fourteen, followed Jewell, stroking the soil over the seeds with his hoe. Hester came last, on hands and knees, smoothing and patting the dirt so it would lay just right over the precious seeds.

She felt the sun on her back, warm and good. She loved the fields, the mules, the loam. Above all, the loam. No matter how mean the master was, this warm, loose dirt was a part of her.

Carrying a whip, the gang driver walked along a far line of workers. Periodically he cracked the whip, al-lowing the lash to fall lightly upon a shoulder. It wasn't needed, not today, for the people worked steadily, si-lently, refraining even from their usual working songs.

The water toter appeared. This was Cindy, Jase and Sippy's oldest, who was built on the square lines of her mother. Cindy, who was ten, carried the wooden bucket of water on her head. She set the bucket on the ground, filled the calabash, and gave it to Hester.

Cindy's wide brown eyes seemed even bigger today.

She looked as if she might cry, but if she did, the driver would give her a taste of his whip.

Hester drank, then returned the calabash. She and Cindy didn't talk. There was too much wrong. Cindy moved on.

As she turned again to her work, Hester spied the overseer, Boss Murray. He was on horseback and was riding toward her furrow. Hester willed that he go deeper into the field. She willed that this time, with three whippings to give tonight, he wouldn't look at her the way he always did.

Instead, he rode right up and jumped off his horse as if he owned the plantation. He was forty-five years old, a tall thick-built man. Looking at him, Hester thought that the way his muscles stood out, he could squeeze a mad bull to death with one hand.

"You," he said, his voice rough. "Stop."

Hester moved along, pretending not to notice. He hadn't said her name. Maybe she could escape his attention.

"You." The voice was rougher. "You white-skinned wench. Stand up."

Stiffly, to control the trembling inside her, Hester got to her bare feet.

"Look at me, white nigger."

She forced her eyes up but looked just past his small, dirt-colored eyes.

"I got a private thing to say," he whispered. "Not to be blabbed, 'specially to her." He jerked his square head toward Lela Belle, who was plowing on, her jaw stiff.

Hester swallowed. Her throat and mouth were dry.

"I warn ye. 'Less ye want yer mammy to git some rawhide. Understand?"

"Yes, sir, Mister Murray."

"That's more like it. Stay still, wench."

She stood, stiffer than before, and he stepped around so that his broad figure hid her from her mother and the others. The people working in other lines kept their eyes on the ground in fearful silence. The overseer put out his hands and grabbed both her titties. He squeezed until it hurt, then he twisted, first one direction, and then the other. Hester held her breath against the pain, against screaming.

When he let go, he said, "Nobody saw. You'll tell nobody. Will ye, white nigger?"

"N-no, sir."

She felt like she might throw up her breakfast. What did this devil want?

"I've had my eye on ye. I could jest take, but the master'd not like it. But I got a way—a deal. I'm doin' ye the honor of offerin' ye a deal."

Her heart felt like it was in her throat.

"I aim to play with them tits," he whispered. "Yer goin' to let me—secret—between the two of us. Here's the deal. I'm the one to whip yer pappy tonight, and I'll let him off easy. Ye kin see I speak true because he won't git no deep cuts."

She stared at him. She couldn't imagine why he had hurt her like that and why letting him do it again would make him not whip her father hard. She would do anything for Pappy, she thought, but there was something wrong with this.

"Whippin's tonight," the overseer growled. "Yer payin' later. Shows I'll keep my word. Ye'll see fer yerself that he heals fast."

It sounded like it made sense, but she couldn't say yes. Nor could she say no—not when it lay in her power to help her father.

"Say yes," hissed the overseer.

She stared and swallowed.

"Then say no."

Not knowing what to do, she shook her head.

"I got my answer," he said.

He mounted and rode along the line, yelling at Lela Belle to plow faster, Jewell to drop the seeds better, and Hank to be quicker with the hoe. And then he rode off into the field.

Trembling, Hester patted the soil. She had no idea what he would do. She glanced along her row of fellow workers. None of them had seen or heard what had happened, or they would be stealing looks at her. And Mammy would ask right out, she thought, and try to get at the facts.

After a long time, Jewell muttered, "Maybe the mastah won' really give Jase sixty whole lashes. Maybe he wou' rub salt an' lemon into the cuts."

"He'll do it," Hank said. "De mastah is hard. My pappy's bin a fiel' han' sixteen yeahs, an' he say he nevah know de mastah to be anythin' but hard. Granny

Myrtle say it. An' my mammy, bein' head laundress an' in an' out of de big house, say it. She's heard him say wif his own mouf dat his word is law."

"He's just plain mean!" Hester cried softly. "What's more, the master will teach Master George to be as mean as he is! Meaner, because Master George has always been mean!"

"Mastah George young," Jewell said. "If we could git him to talk to the mastah, he might change them sixty lashes."

Hester considered. None of the slaves could ask such a thing of Master George. Maybe Master Phil would, of his own goodness, speak to Master George and he, in turn, to Master Thorne. Because Master Phil had tried to speak there at the very first—Pappy had said so. Her heart glowed, thinking of Master Phil.

They fell silent as they worked on. The vast quiet of the many people, who usually sang as they toiled, put an ache through Hester. At last, under her breath, she began a song of her very own, making it up as she went, as they always did, using the field hands' kind of words, unlike the way she herself spoke.

"I got a pappy . . .
"I got a pappy . . .
"He goin' be whip . . .
"He goin' be whip . . .
"He goin' take de lash . . .
"De lash . . . lash . . . lash . . .
"I got a pappy . . .
"I got a pappy . . ."

On she sang, louder now, and Jewell and Hank took up the song. Then Lela Belle added her thick voice to theirs, chanting the words, the easy, true, heartbreaking words, and their joined voices, drifting on the rising, wailing lament, covered the great field until every slave and hoe boss and water toter was singing.

And for every one of them each word was a drop of blood from the heart.

Chapter Four

First to enter the big stable where the overseer waited were Thorne, Wabash, George Drummond, and Philip Bennett. George had asked to see the preparations beforehand, and they went directly to the area of operation.

The stable had strong oak posts running down the middle of the carriage section, which was empty now and lit by lanterns. The floor was strewn with fresh straw. There was a wooden bench on which several buckets stood. Three newly made whips, each with a fourteen-inch buckskin cracker at the end of a tapered leather plait, were laid in a precise row beside the buckets. There were also three empty milk crocks, each with a thick white rag in it.

"What do you think of it, George?" Thorne asked.

"It's impressive. What's in the buckets?"

"That's the pimentade for rubbing the cuts."

"That hurts, doesn't it?" asked Phil.

"Right smart. Lets the buck know he's been whipped and starts the healing process at the same time."

"What're the crocks for?" George asked.

"To pour the pimentade into," Thorne explained. "We have a fresh batch. Made from my pa's recipe. It stings like fire. I'll give you a copy, George. Cayenne, salt, and lemon. You can see there's a set of everything for each buck. There's no stinting on this any more than there is on anything at Thornton."

"Are the people really going to watch?" asked Phil.

"Indeed they are. I've got to be the law here. The time's come when telling them I'm the law isn't enough. This"—he gestured about the stable—"is the only way to hold off eventual insurrection."

George nodded, smiling. Phil, feeling sick, looked through the wavering light toward the open double doors. Beyond was blackness. As he inhaled the cool March air, he wondered if he would smell blood.

Two black, powerful figures, naked to the waist, came through the doorway. These were Brutus and Buck, the trusties. Behind them a silent line of slaves moved out of the night and into the stable, lining the outer wall beyond the bench, then folding back until there were three rows.

Thorne and the two young men stepped to a spot just behind the bench. Hester, rigid with determination to make no sound, stood crushed between her mother and Sippy. Hattie and her children were just beyond Sippy's brood.

"Begin, Murray," Thorne ordered.

The overseer tramped to the doors. Immediately three strong, towering black men marched in and took their places at the buckets of pimentade.

The overseer returned, gripping the big-linked chain that joined Sam, Elmer, and Jase. Naked, they inched along in leg irons, holding their chained wrists before them, staring at nothing.

Murray stopped. "Ye want 'em spanceled, Mr. Wabash?"

"Certainly."

Murray unlocked the irons. The trusties stepped forward to help. Neither Sam, Elmer, nor Jase uttered a sound. There was no plea. Their only movement, nearly impossible to detect, was their long, slow breathing.

Murray clamped the chain of Sam's leg irons to a post, then locked Sam's hands around the post above an iron brace. The trusties did the same with Elmer and Jase.

Hester could feel the combined, painful breathing of her people, who formed a sorrowing, living wall. She felt the pain of her own breath, closed her eyes, then opened them. She had to watch, she thought. She owed it to Pappy and to Elmer and Jase.

Murray and each trusty grabbed a whip. They advanced on the spanceled slaves and took position, their feet apart. The overseer stood ready to lash Sam.

Thorne spoke. "As I count, crack down with the lash

in unison. Make each blow harder than the one before. Don't cut the buck Sam's male parts or Elmer's. With Jase, lay every stroke where it goes. After the count of ten, you will rest.

"At that time, you three bucks at the bench pour on the pimentade. Don't be stingy with it. Sam and Elmer will remain spanceled until Jase has taken his sixty lashes. You will stop to rest at the end of each ten strokes. You will use the pimentade on all three during every rest.

"We stop after sixty. At the end, pour all the pimentade over them—sluice them off with it so it'll get into every cut."

He stopped speaking, and silence filled the stable. Then he lifted his arm and let it drop. *"One!"*

The whips swung up and back. Then the buckskin crackers whistled down upon the naked backs. Motionless and silent, the men took the blows.

Hester reached for her mother's hand. Their fingers clung.

"Two!"

The whips slashed the men's backs, and the ends held in flesh and had to be torn away. The tense and miserable watchers moaned.

"Three!"

Lela Belle tried to pull Hester's face against her, but Hester resisted. If Pappy can take the lash, she thought, I can watch! She knew already, from the trails of red across his back, that the overseer was whipping him as hard as the trusties were lashing Elmer and Jase.

After the first ten strokes, the waiting black men fetched the pimentade and sloshed it over the cut and bleeding men. They poured with care into the deepest cuts, so that it would go into the broken flesh and burn with the fire of hell. Only now did the victims groan.

The whipping recommenced. Now only Jase was left. Sam and Elmer remained shackled to the post, immobile. At each count of ten, when the trusty whipping Jase rested, more pimentade was poured on the bleeding backs of the three men.

Near the end, the cries of Jase winged into the night. The sobbing breath of the people became a constant, sighing moan.

"Fifty!"

The buckskin made its song and slashed across the welter of cuts. This time Jase sagged until he hung by his wrists.

"Sixty!"

After the last lash, Thorne shouted, "Pimentade! Pour it all on him, drown him with it!"

When the pimentade was gone, Thorne ordered, "Murray. Examine him."

The overseer unlocked Jase's manacles, lowered him to the bloody straw, and shook him by the shoulder. He yanked the man's head so that it lay face up. The lanterns glinted on the open eyes. Murray felt for Jase's pulse, then wiped blood off Jase's chest, and put his ear against it. Standing, he wiped his hands on a rag one of the trusties gave him. He called to Thorne. "He couldn't take it, sir."

A muted wail rose from the group of slaves.

"Sam and Elmer can go to their cabins," Thorne said. "Two days off to heal, then back to work."

"Yes, sir," Murray said. "Where ye want us to bury the dead buck?"

"Why do you think I ordered thirty hogs put in the fattening pen this morning? Throw that"—he gestured toward Jase's body—"into the hogpen."

A hush hung over Thornton and over the fields. No song, not even the whipping chant, rose from the grieved and laboring people. Sam and Elmer lay in their cabins, and their wives toiled in the fields. When they returned that evening, Sippy and her children were gone, sold downriver. It was as though Jase had never existed.

The people stayed to their cabins, thinking only of going to bed early to wipe what had happened out of their minds with sleep.

Hester was restless. After her father's wounds were treated, she asked her mother if she could go outside.

"Whut fo'?"

"To breathe. Theah's a little breeze."

Reluctantly, Lela Belle gave permission. Hester wandered down the deserted streets to the big oak behind the blacksmith shop. She sat down at the base of the tree.

It was there that Phil Bennett found her. "I've been to your cabin," he said. "Your mother said you'd be here."

Hester's heart jumped. She was frightened—not of him, never him—but that they might be found together.

"I came to tell you, Hester. I told your parents. I tried to get Uncle Thorne to call off the whipping. He got angry, and George laughed. Uncle Thorne threatened to cane me, eighteen or not, if I didn't shut up. I'd have taken the caning if it would have done any good."

"I hope you won't get caned for coming heah."

"I won't. Uncle Thorne's got what he wanted—execution."

"What's 'execution,' Master Phil?"

"It's when someone is put to death for doing something bad."

"But Jase didn't—"

"Uncle Thorne sees it differently. Hester, ever since that day—"

Before he could finish, there was the sound of footsteps. It was Thorne and the overseer.

"What's going on here?" Thorne demanded. Murray was scowling.

"I came to tell Hester that I was sorry about what happened, sir."

"What are you, a milksop?"

"I hope not, sir."

"Thank God my grandson isn't like you!"

Phil remained silent. Hester stared miserably at nothing.

"Murray," Thorne ordered, "lock the wench in the jail."

"Yes, sir. Anything else?"

"Let me think."

"Hester hasn't done anything, Uncle Thorne, sir."

"She's met you, a young white master, in secret. That means one thing only. Next, if I let her off, she'll be after George."

"Are you going to punish Sam again—or Lela Belle, sir?"

"Sam's had his lesson. They're as good darkies as I own. But this one—she's always been a freak. This, with you, goes beyond all limits. I'm selling her off, as I should have done years ago."

"If I leave Thornton, will that settle it, sir?" Phil asked quietly.

"Definitely not."

Hester dared a glance at Phil. In the starlight he looked pale.

"I think I should leave, sir," Phil insisted.

"No! George needs your company. Just stay away from the Quarters. Murray, take the wench along now."

"Right away, sir!" he said, smirking. He grabbed Hester's arm, hurting it, and propelled her away from the oak, away from Phil.

A sick feeling came over Hester. Master Phil was her only white friend in the world, and fear told her that she had lost him forever.

Boss Murray yanked Hester along the street toward the jailhouse as the master and Phil returned to the mansion. Thorne's words about selling Hester rang in her ears. She would not let him do it. Determinedly, she set her bare heels in the ground and twisted under Murray's grasp.

Murray jerked her to face him and grabbed her other arm. His hands were like iron; they dug to the bone. She fought him, but he gave her a vicious shake.

"Want a clout on yer head?" he snarled.

"Master Thorne didn't say to handle me rough!"

"He don't give a damn." He gave her another shake. "Come along proper, or ye'll find out what trouble is."

He started propelling her from behind, one hand clamping each of her arms. She jerked and tried to dig her heels in again, but it was no use. He only pushed her harder, making her stumble.

At the jailhouse, he rammed a knee into her buttocks and lifted her by the arms, putting her on the step. Before she could even try to yank again, he had the door open and threw her across the room so hard she hit the far wall. Quickly he slammed the door shut behind him and locked it.

The jailhouse was utterly dark. Terrified, Hester huddled against the wall, unable to see Boss Murray but aware of his presence.

There came the sound of a match being struck. Murray lit a candle on a shelf. In the wavery light, Hester could see two board bunks, one small barred window, and bare walls.

Murray smirked at her. "Ain't this better? Ye standin' like a decent wench, us carryin' out our deal."

"We've got no deal!" she cried.

"We got one. I told ye if ye'd let me pleasure myself—
I even give ye a sample—that I'd hold back on the lashes
I give yer pappy."

"You didn't hold back! He was cut as bad as Elmer!"

"But no worse. I only matched the trusties, blow fer
blow. If I'd used my power, yer pappy'd be cut so bad
it'd take him weeks to heal up."

"That's a lie!"

"I run a risk fer our deal," he snarled. "If the master
ever knew I was holdin' back my strength, I'd be in
trouble. I cut yer pappy just enough to satisfy the master, but not enough to let ye out of yer deal."

"I didn't make a deal! I never said—"

"My say is enough! What the overseer says—the white
overseer—a wench has got to do! She got no choice. I
could've broke my word. I could've showed the master
how much better at whippin' I am than the trusties. I eat
crow fer ye, an' I aim to git my reward!"

Too scared to move, Hester stared at his evil face.
She could hardly stand up, but somehow she had to get
out of this.

"Take yer shift off," he ordered.

"No!" She edged away, along the wall.

He followed, grabbed her shift at the neck, and tore it
down the front, right through the hem. The garment fell,
leaving her naked. She stopped and grabbed it up, but
he snatched it and threw it across the room. "Come here,
into the light, so's I kin see!" he ordered.

"No!" She moved another step. Maybe, if she was quick
enough, she could claw his eyes, dig them right out of his
face and throw them on the floor.

But he came at her so quickly and struck her wrists so
hard that her hands went numb. Then he gripped one
breast in each hand and pulled her away from the wall.
She held back, but he dug in so cruelly that she had to
stumble toward him. Her breasts were on fire; her arms
were numb to the shoulder.

Grinning, he let go and struck her wrists again. Rage
and terror were blended with pain. She wanted to kill
him, to sink her teeth into his windpipe, and bite it
all the way through, then watch him fall dead, dead and
bleeding as Jase had bled.

She dived at him, and his fist took her in the stomach.

Doubled over, she hung in an infinity of pain. She was unable to resist at all when he scooped her into his arms and threw her onto the board bunk. She wanted to spring up, to attack, to flee, but in reality she didn't stir, she couldn't move.

He stripped off his clothes. His chest was wide, and his body was covered with hair from collarbone to his jutting male part. His shoulders were wide, and his arms bulged with muscle.

He came at her grinning, spittle at the corners of his mouth. Just as she thought she could move, he gave her another blow in the stomach. "That'll hold ye!" he gloated.

He couldn't wait any longer. He moved to her, his part ready in his hand. He came onto the boards, straddling her legs, crawling up. She willed herself desperately to move, and her legs did stir, but then he came ripping inside her, and she screamed. Only once did she scream, however, for the rest of the awful, endless time, he kept a hand across her mouth so hard that she could hardly breathe.

Chapter Five

After he was gone, she lay in the darkness and wept from pain and fear. Yet in her agony, she was concerned about whether or not the master would cane Phil.

She lay, sobbing quietly, thinking of how kind Phil had always been, and let memory take over.

She remembered that from the time they were ten and eight, Master George and Master Phil had spent each summer at Thornton. They were given the run of the plantation. Hence, they spent hours in the Quarters, playing with the slave children. They came to know Hester. At first they marveled at her white-skinned freakishness, but eventually they accepted her as they did the other slave children.

One day, when Hester was eight and the boys were fourteen and twelve, George strutted up carrying paper and ink. Hester spied the boys, and leaving the group with whom she had been playing kick stick, she raced to them.

George waited, his cousin beside him. Phil was smiling, but George had a mean look on his face. But that was natural, and Hester was used to it. To get along with Master George, Hester knew you played how he said, even when it made you mad inside.

"What's them?" Hester asked, looking at the paper and ink.

" 'What is that, Master George, sir?' " he corrected.

"Yes, sir. What is that, Master George, sir?"

"Don't you know anything? It's paper and pen and ink."

"We goin' to play wif 'em, Master George, sir?"

"Playing is tiresome. Even with Phil, and he's white. It's boring to endure nigger games with suckers."

"Hester's not a sucker," Phil said.

"She's a sucker until she's twelve and a quarter-hand! Haven't you learned anything about a plantation? She's nothing but a white-skinned nigger sucker!"

Hester stiffened her jaw and blinked. She never could get used to the way Master George talked.

"You needn't say those things!" Phil cried. "They're mean, and if Uncle Thorne knew—"

"He doesn't care! He speaks that way himself! It's the way a master does!"

Hester shifted uneasily. She swallowed. She didn't know where to look or what to do. They were talking about her as if she weren't there.

"Hester's a good little girl," Phil said. "I like to play with her."

A good feeling swept over her. Master Phil was nice. He always said good things and made her feel happy.

"She's not a little girl! She's a nigger!" George shouted. "I'm going to draw her picture to show at school. They won't believe my grandfather's got one like her."

"I didn't know you could draw pictures."

"I can do anything! Hester. Sit on that stump. Phil, keep the suckers chased away. When I finish drawing Hester, I'll draw one of them and color him black to show the difference."

Hester sat on the stump, her legs dangling. and didn't move, not even to wiggle her toes when they itched. Scowling, George drew on his paper, while Phil stood to one side. Once he smiled at Hester. She wished she dared smile back, but Master George had said not to move, not a muscle.

When he finished, George had a small boy stand beside Hester, and he drew the boy. He showed the completed picture to Phil. "What do you think of that?" he demanded.

Phil took the paper and studied it. "You can tell that Hester's white-skinned and the sucker's black," he said. "You can see that her hair curls some. But one leg's bigger than the other."

"You saying it's bad?" shouted George. "If one leg's bigger, it's because she's got one leg bigger than the other!"

"She has not! Just look and see!"

But George wouldn't compare Hester's legs to those in his drawing. He rushed over and shoved the paper at

her face so close she could hardly see what was on it.
One leg really was bigger. And it showed the difference
between the color of the boy's skin and her own. She
wished she could hit Master George for what he did and
said.

"It doesn't even look like her," Phil said.

"It'll do! I don't need to draw any better!"

"C-could I draw a picture, too, Master George?" Hester asked timidly.

"Certainly not! No darky can draw! Where did you
get such a crazy idea to ask such a thing—tell me that!"

"G-Granny Myrtle. She showed me how to write my
name in the dirt. She learned me to count and write
numbahs with a stick. Can you write numbahs and lettahs
on paper with ink, Master George?"

"Of course."

"W-would you let me see you do it?"

"No! I don't perform for any darky!"

"She let you draw her picture," Phil said.

"She's got to do what she's told. I don't have to give
her ideas Grandfather wouldn't like. Come on—I'm
through here. Let's go back to the house."

They raced away, but not before Phil gave Hester a rueful face and flung out his hands. Then he smiled at her and
was gone.

The next day he came alone to the Quarters. He had a
ball and asked if she wanted to play.

"Yes, Mastah Phil. Can the othahs play, too?"

"Sure. After we talk some."

He tossed the ball, which was fairly large. She caught
it, tossed it back, and he caught it easily.

"I was angry yesterday at the way George treated
you," he said. "He uses proper manners up at the house,
but not at the Quarters. I told my father once, and he
said a gentleman uses good manners everywhere."

"That's what Granny Myrtle say—says."

"The nurse? That fat old wench?"

"Yes. My pappy says she's wise from livin' so long."

"George said that once she worked up at the house."

"She he'ped—"

" 'Helped,' Hester."

"Thank you, Master Phil. She helped take care of Miss
Rosalie, a long time ago. That was Master Thorne's
daughter that got married and nevah came back."

"She's George's stepmother, you know. Uncle Thorne hates her—he disowned her long ago. That's why he's putting George into his will."

"What's a will?"

"It gives Thornton to George when Uncle Thorne dies."

"Oh. Miss Rosalie, she learnt—"

" 'Taught,' Hester."

"She taught Granny Myrtle to read and write and figuah and talk good."

"You like to learn, don't you, Hester?"

"Oh, yes, Mastah Phil!"

"What's the next best thing you like?"

"It—something I nevah done."

"You can tell me. I'll never let George know."

"He gets awful mad."

"He and I get along. He's bossy, and when it doesn't matter, I let him boss. When it does matter, I just laugh it off and do things my own way. So go on—tell."

"I hanker to see inside the big house," she whispered.

"You've lived here all your life and never were inside?"

"Once I went to the end of the driveway and looked up and saw how it is from the front."

"Why? Why haven't you been there?" he cried, and she could tell he was shocked.

"Mastah Thorne don't 'low darkies from the fields to step into the grounds of the big house. It's a rule."

Phil went white. Even his lips paled, and he was shaking a little. He was mad. It was the only time she had seen him mad, and it frightened her.

"You just come with me!" he cried.

She held back, but he gripped her hand and pulled her along. She had to trot to keep up with him. "I'll get you into trouble!" she protested, running and stumbling and stubbing her toe.

"No, you won't! We won't even be seen! Uncle Thorne and George went to Warrenton, and the servants are all busy. We'll keep to trees and bushes."

They ran, slower now, more evenly, their footsteps quiet. They stole through the rose garden, across the driveway, up the broad steps, and across the veranda.

Phil opened the door, drew her close, and let her peer inside. She saw a long hallway covered with ruby red carpeting and a red-carpeted stairway rising from it. On the wall opposite the staircase was a narrow table with a white top, a silver vase of roses on it, a big looking glass above it, and a red chair on each side.

Inside the house there was movement, and they fled back across the veranda, down the steps, past the driveway, through the garden, and to the Quarters.

Now, aching on the hard bunk in the jail, Hester was no longer sobbing. Remembering Phil was a comfort, and she kept thinking of him to forget what Boss Murray had done to her. She dwelt on last summer, when she was thirteen and Phil was seventeen. All summer, the good feeling between them had deepened.

Hester knew a hidden spot that she thought of as her lake room. The plantation creek, which meandered, made an extra turn that went nowhere, but flowed back, eventually, into the main body after forming a tiny lake that was like a room. Its floor was sun-sparkled, shade-dappled water, its roof the sky, and its walls the great live oaks. Nobody came here but Hester. To her knowledge, nobody else knew about it.

Because Phil was the only white person who had ever been kind to her and she wanted to repay him, she told him about the lake room and asked if he would like to see it. He smiled and accepted.

When they reached Hester's secret place, Phil stood silent, looking at the tiny lake, at the sky, at the oaks hung with moss, and at the flower-studded grass.

"Can we sit down?" he asked. "Can we just sit and enjoy it?"

"Of course, Master Phil! That's why I showed you!"

"Do you come here often?" he asked. He broke off a blade of grass and played with it.

Hester sat cross-legged, facing him. "I come here all the time. Nobody knows it's heah. Or if they do," she added to be honest, "they nevah come. Even Mammy and Pappy don't know 'bout it."

"Maybe they'd like it, too."

She sighed. "I reckon not, Master Phil. It's kind of a long walk, and they're tired when they're done with work."

"When I get my plantation," he said, gazing about, "I hope it'll have a lake room."

"Are you an heir, too, Master Phil?"

His laugh was tinged with sadness. "Nothing like that. I'm going to have a plantation, but I'll have to earn my own money and buy it."

"I thought youah fathah was rich!"

"He's very well off, but we live in an expensive manner. He's disappointed that I'm not going to be an attorney like himself and live the same."

" 'Attorney,' Master Phil?"

"A man who knows the laws. Who settles arguments between other men and gets paid for doing it." He smiled. "It's not for you to worry your head over."

"But I need to know! I need to learn!"

"Well, that's what an attorney is. And I don't want to be one. I want a plantation."

"I s'pose Thornton's the biggest plantation in the world."

"It's big enough."

"How'll you make money to buy a plantation, Master Phil?" she asked softly. She couldn't quit staring at him. How like the sun he was, she thought, how good to look at. He was as beautiful as her lake room, more beautiful.

He picked a flower and tickled the end of her nose with it. "That'll take explanation, the way you want to know everything in the world."

"Yes, Master Phil."

"Do you know what an actor is, what a stage play is?"

She nodded. "Granny Myrtle told us. She said Miss Rosalie went to a play. People get up on the—the—"

"On the stage, a raised platform."

"And they play-act, pretend to be somebody else than who they are, and othah folks sit and watch. Sometimes the actors make folks laugh, and sometimes they make them cry. But it's all make-believe."

"That's what I'm going to do—be an actor and travel. I'll watch for plantations and even just farms. I'll find a place I can buy."

"Play-actors travel, Master Phil?"

"Many of them do. I'm going on showboats."

At her wide-eyed, questioning look, he explained what the showboats were and how they plied the rivers, tying up at various spots to present their dramas. He described the way a showboat looked, inside and out, and she held her breath most of the time, amazed at this marvel.

He noted her absorption. "You do learn every scrap you get a chance to!" he exclaimed.

"Oh, yes, Master Phil!"

"Don't ever stop learning. Getting an education is one of the most important things in life."

"Like getting a plantation, Master Phil?"

"Like that. It's worth whatever it costs to get it. Remember that always."

She nodded solemnly. "Like when I found Master George's book undah the tree and tried to copy the lettahs in the dirt?"

He nodded. "You got a whipping for that, I know. Uncle Thorne made your pappy hit you five times with the strap. Because George said you'd stolen his book, when you'd only picked it up from where he'd left it."

"I was goin' to put it back, Master Phil."

"And you got another five whacks when the overseer caught me teaching you to count by fives," Phil said regretfully. "I got off with a tongue lashing."

Hester stared at the wild flowers she had picked. She blinked tears away. There was no sense letting him see how those things still hurt.

He said, "Look at me, Hester. Into my eyes."

"It ain't—isn't propah, Master Phil."

"It was all right when we were children. It's no different now."

Slowly she lifted her eyes to his, and he gazed back and smiled, and his smile was warm and filled with kindness. She felt a strange inner warmth that she couldn't put a name to, as well as a sensation of being gently tugged closer and closer to him. She had never had such a feeling and didn't know whether to push it away or accept and treasure it. It seemed that he, too, felt the mysterious pull. Lost in the dazzling blue of his gaze, she wondered, dreamily, how it would be to nestle in his arms.

"You see," he said, "it's right for us to look. Your eyes are so beautiful, so brown and big, and the way those auburn brows and that hair—" He broke off and gazed at her, and his gaze seemed to stroke and caress her. Then his eyes blazed a deeper blue, softened, and dots of sunlight flickered in them. "Bless you, Hester," he whispered, "bless you!"

She leaned closer, and he enfolded her, and they kissed. His lips were warm on hers. At first her lips trembled under his, then strengthened and returned his kiss. She could feel the wild beating of his heart. Gently he moved his hands down along her breasts to her waist. Still kissing her, he laid her down on the bed of wild flowers. Hester felt, deep inside, a budding warmth that seemed ready to flower into full bloom. He was lying on top of her now, and through her shift, she felt his secret part hard against her thigh. Her breath quivered, and their kiss broke.

It was then that they heard footsteps. A fallen branch snapped, and they sprang apart, straightening their clothes. By the time the man came into view, Hester and Phil were sitting at a distance from each other.

The man was tall, strongly and gracefully built. He had sunny hair and blue eyes, and Hester knew instantly he was Phil's father.

"And who is this I find you with, son?" he asked, his tone friendly.

They stood, Hester's knees threatening to buckle.

"This is Hester, sir. From the Quarters."

"Ah, yes. That Hester." His eyes pierced her, but not unkindly. "I'm Master Neal, Master Phil's father," he told her.

"Y-yes, sir," Hester stammered, looking just past him. In spite of herself, she dared a glance at Phil. He had a piece of grass in his hair, and his cheeks were flushed. She knew that her own hair was mussed and that her face was burning the way it did on the hottest day in the field.

"My son used to play with all of you in the Quarters," Neal Bennett said.

"Y-yes, Master Neal, sir."

"Where are the others now?"

"At the Quarters, sir," Phil replied.

"And—?"

If he noticed their disarray, Hester couldn't tell. He looked calm and sure of himself.

"We came here alone, Father," Phil explained, "because this little lake is Hester's secret room. She offered to show it to me, knowing I won't tell."

"And now it's not entirely secret," Mr. Bennett said. "I found it, just tramping about. I presume, now that I've stumbled on this spot, there in't an inch of Thornton I haven't covered by horseback or on foot."

"That's what I'd thought about myself, sir," Phil said. "Until Hester brought me here."

"And what do you do in this place, Hester?"

"I sit heah and—love it, Master Neal, sir," Hester replied. Her voice shook some, because her heartbeat was shaking her body. There was no way to tell whether Master Neal had seen her and Master Phil kissing. And no telling what would happen if he had.

"Don't bring a young master here again, Hester," Mr. Bennett said kindly. "Or any buck, young or old. Keep your secret room secret."

"Y-yes, Master Neal, sir."

He turned to his son. "Walk to the house with me, Phil. Now that you've seen the room, I'd advise you not to return and risk betraying its existence."

Phil said, "Yes, sir." Then, with a look at Hester, he started away through the trees with his father. The older man was speaking, and in the silence a bit of what he said drifted back to Hester.

". . . have any dealings with wenches here or anywhere. Stay to your own race."

Hester felt suddenly bereft. She sank to the grass and sat trembling. What she and Master Phil had done had been so wondrous she had never wanted it to end. But now it was not to be, ever again. She wept a little, remembering how his arms and lips had felt, and she knew that she wanted to be with him like that, close and warm and happy—forever.

Chapter Six

Hester could no longer concentrate on her happy memories. She felt blood oozing between her legs, the sting and burn of her breasts, the pain in her stomach. Even her arms hurt to the elbow from the way Boss Murray had hit them. She longed for her parents—for their arms, which would hold and comfort her, and for their rich, crooning voices, their enveloping love.

She crept off the bunk and in the darkness felt around over the floor, searching for her torn shift. At least she could wrap it around herself. The cloth would feel better than the wood on which she had to lay.

She was on hands and knees, searching, when she heard the sound at the window. She stiffened. Was it Boss Murray? Would he do all those awful things to her again?

"Hester!" came a rich voice so low it was almost a whisper. It was Pappy!

"I'm heah!" she answered, low. She moved, as fast as her hurting body would permit, to the window, climbed onto the bunk, and grasped the bars. It was a dark night, but there were stars. She could make out two figures.

"Pappy—!" she quavered.

"We heah," he whispered, his hands on hers. "We wait an' wait, den we look fo' you, fo' de longes' time!"

"We dassn't go to de mastah or Boss Murray," whispered Lela Belle, her hand on her daughter's arm. "We thought of de jail, but dassn't come soonah less de mastah fin' out an' put yo' to de lash 'cause we come."

"We didn' tell nobody yo's missin'," Sam said. "It dang'rous fo' dem an' fo' yo'."

"So we go visitin' to de cabins, wifout tellin', to see if

38

yo' was theah," Lela Belle continued. "Yo' wasn't, so we waited fo' Boss Murray's house to be dark, an' den we come heah! We sorry it took so long, darlin'!"

"Tell whut happen," Sam said.

Clinging to their hands, sobbing, Hester told them everything. Both Sam and Lela Belle began to sob.

"And Master Thorne, he said he's going to sell me!" she wailed. "Oh, Pappy—Mammy—I can't be sold away from you!"

Their sobs rose, then quieted. "We be heard," Sam warned. "We got to be quiet. Yo' not goin' be sold. Wait—we be back."

In their cabin they lit a candle stub and faced each other. "Set down, Sam," said Lela Belle. "It time to salve yo' cuts."

"It time to save ouah chile," he said, but he sat.

Lela Belle wiped his back and sides gently with a damp cloth, then spread the salve over the criss-crossed wounds. He sat rigid, his jaw like iron.

She closed the container with a rag stopper, set it on the table, and put other cloths with it. "Now we talk," she said.

"We dassn't tell Mastah Thorne whut Boss Murray done to Hester."

"No. Boss Murray white."

"We could try."

"No. De mastah'd have yo' put to de lash again, mebbe like Jase. Me, too. He a mean man. We dassn't 'pend on him."

"We can't let Hester be sold. She ouah chile, ouah only chile."

Lela Belle put her face into her strong hands and wept. Her great heart tore and bled with wanting to save her child, to keep her safe, to heal her after the grievous things that had been done to her. "Whut we do?" wailed Lela Belle, choking on her tears.

Now was their safest time, Sam believed, their only moment for thought. "We got to run," he decided. "We got to git Hester out of de jail an' run. All of us."

"She lock' up, Sam. Yo' all cut from de whippin'. Yo' can't run."

"I kin do whut I got to do."

"Folks see yo' back."

"I'll covah it wif my shirt."

"De shirt'll stick to de cuts. Dey'll hurt like when de pimentade went on. Folks'll see de shirt stick an' wondah, an' git us caught!"

"Whut yo' want to do, den?" he demanded angrily. "Let ouah Hester lay in jail an' dat Boss Murray—"

"It a chance we got to take. He mebbe not be able— two or three nights in a row—him not so young, an' he abuse Hester three times tonight. One mo' day, Sam. Take one day to heal, den tomorrow night—"

"We ain' gamblin' wif ouah chile! We go now!"

Lela Belle wept again. "It all ruint!" she moaned. "We happy heah, yo' de bes' blacksmith in de county, me good at de plow, an' Mastah Thorne talkin' 'bout gittin' a fine buck to marry Hester to!"

"Dat all change now. We bin lucky, but we los' ouah luck when we let Hester go fo' her walk tonight. She de bes' loved wench in de Quarters, but not all of ouah people kin save huh now. We got to do dat."

"Whut yo' want me to do, Sam?"

"Pack dat cornpone an' fatback. Put de salve in de bundle, too. Put on youah shoes an' bring mah shoes and Hester's."

"Wheah we run to, Sam?"

"No'th."

"Wheah to, Sam?"

"I knows wheah de neahest Undahground Railroad way station be."

"Whut's dat?" Lela Belle asked, packing swiftly.

"It white folks ag'in slavery whut he'ps slaves run no'th wheah dey kin be free. Belong to no white mastah. Belong to 'demselfs."

"We got a chance?"

"Bettah dan mos'. 'Cause Hester's skin is white. She kin be de white lady travelin' no'th, an' we'll be huh slaves. When dat comes, we be free, 'cause we no'th an' we belong to ouah own Hester."

Lela Belle finished making up the bundle, adding a tin cup. It was a small bundle, and she tied it with strips of cloth, then looped them over her neck so the bundle hung between her shoulders. She carried the shoes in her hands.

Sam nodded approval and reached for his shirt. Lela Belle put down the shoes for the moment and held the shirt, which was his old, soft one, and he slid his arms into the sleeves. Lela Belle pushed his hand aside when he would have buttoned it, and she buttoned it so deftly that he could scarcely feel the movement of the shirt on his wounded back.

Lela Belle picked up the shoes, then blew out the candle flame, and they tiptoed to the door and across the stoop. Silently they followed the path to the blacksmith shop. Here Sam, who knew where every hammer, horse-shoe nail, file or other tool lay, took the best file, which he had sharpened and not yet used, and they went to the jail.

They sensed Hester at the bars, but it was too dark to see her, and she made no sound. Lela Belle passed Hester's good shift and her shoes through the bars to her.

Carefully, the motion rubbing his shirt against raw flesh, Sam raised the file high and inserted it between two bars, resting it against the bottom of the one to his right. He waited. All was silent except for the cry of a nightbird and at a distance, the croaking of frogs. Sweat beaded his brow.

"Stan' watch," he breathed to Lela Belle. She moved into the darkness.

He pushed the file, grinding it against the bar. It made a growling noise. He ground his teeth against pain, against noise, and pulled the file back and forth. The sound filled him, though he knew it wasn't really loud.

Hester, her shift and shoes on, stood scarcely breathing, aware of how her father's back was hurting. She listened, trembling, to the file eating into the iron. She hated Master Thorne for the whipping Pappy had suffered and for the need to run.

Sam pressed his great strength to the task, pain eating into him the way the file ate into the iron. Sweat covered his face and ran down his neck and under the shirt. It seeped into cuts and found crevices in the salve, stinging the raw cuts like pimentade.

His jaw set, he filed harder. Once he stopped to feel the bar. He was more than half through it. He worked on, in strong, unvarying rhythm, his ears filled with the grating sound.

The bar parted suddenly. He laid the file on the ground, gripped the end of the bar and pulled, trying to force it out. The bar didn't move.

Sodden with sweat, his shirt was stuck to his back. He pulled again, the cords of his neck rigid, pain shooting everywhere. He spraddled to give himself more leverage, threw all his power into his shoulders, pulled, and the bar moved slightly. It was not enough. He would have to file through the top of the bar. Ignoring the pain he felt, he took up the file again.

It was harder now because he had to stand on tiptoe to reach the top. It put the file at a different angle, and it made more noise. He threw greater power into each stroke, power he hadn't known was there, and the file bit and chewed.

Suddenly Lela Belle was at his side, quietly warning him that the noise was greater. He grunted once, to tell her that it didn't matter, that he had to get the bar out.

At last the bar gave and clattered onto the bunk inside. Sam froze. There was no sound, no stir. Pushed for time, he had to assume, rather quickly, that the noise hadn't been heard. He felt the space and thought Hester could get through. She was right there, standing on the bunk, and she had one foot out already. He turned her sideways and pulled, and felt her squirm and push and gasp. At last he pulled her through.

Hester couldn't stand alone, so Lela Belle supported her, letting her rest against her. Sam gripped the file, his weapon now, and waited for a moment.

"She able to walk?" he breathed.

He sensed Lela Belle's nod. He moved then, leading them east, along the backs of the buildings, passing behind the blacksmith shop, beneath the big oak tree there, and on.

They overtook him. "Yo' got to rest," Lela Belle whispered. "Den we run. We got to find a hidin' place."

"No. We got to keep goin'." And then he fell.

They got him up, and they all stood listening. There was no sound.

"I know a place," Hester said softly.

Still they waited. When they hoped it was safe, they moved on until they reached Hester's secret place. Here the oaks, the willows, and the cypress trees embraced and hid them. Exhausted, they fell to the dewy grass beside the lake. There was no sign of pursuit.

Lela Belle brought Sam water in the cup. She and Hester drank from the edge of the lake. Then Lela Belle opened the pack, spread more salve on Sam by touch, drew his shirt together, and buttoned it in the darkness. Hester helped put his shoes on his feet.

"Wheah we going?" asked Hester.

Sam told her about the Underground Railroad.

"Wheah is it?"

"East an' no'th. Fifteen miles. It wif folks on a farm."

"How did yo' find out?" Lela Belle asked.

"De grapevine. De farmer man was once a ovahseeah on a plantation an' didn' like de way slaves was treated. He joined up wif othahs det feel de same."

"Yo' certain dey he'p us, Sam?"

"Dey ouah on'y chance. We got to git theah."

After a very short rest, they started. Hester led them around the lake to where it went into the creek, and they waded for what seemed miles to kill the scent in case dogs were put on their trail.

After they left the creek, they walked for hours, stopping only infrequently. Once they ate some cornpone and fatback and drank water from another creek, which they then waded eastward.

Night faded and daylight came, dim at first, then too bright. They kept to timber. Once they glimpsed a farmhouse and outbuildings and detoured, backtracking, to get around it unseen.

After this detour, Sam veered north, partly because the way station was north and east, and partly because there was a seemingly endless stretch of timber through which they could move unseen. They waded every creek they found for as long as they could, always listening for the sound of dogs.

The rest periods became more frequent because Sam could barely drag his feet along and Hester was nearly as sore and weak. But they kept going, each step that many more inches away from Thornton, that much closer to the way station. At one rest period, Hester asked what would happen at Thornton when they were missed.

"De mastah, he'll get othah mastahs an' trusties an' dogs. Dey'll track us an' try to catch us. Dat why we got to move ev'ry minute. To covah dem fifteen miles. Le's go now, we rested enuf."

It was noon when they heard dogs behind them at a distance. They ran, stumbling, toward a farmhouse that they could make out ahead and that Sam believed was the way station.

"Is that really it, Pappy?" panted Hester, stumbling in her waterlogged shoes.

"I hope to de good Lawd God!" Sam gasped. "Way we has—traveled—mus' be fifteen miles. An' dat house is white an' de bahn red!"

"But de dogs!" gasped Lela Belle. "How'll dey save us f'um de dogs trackin'?"

"Dey got a way, dem white folks got a way! Dey allus saves de slaves! Dey got hidin' places dat no dog kin smell out—all we got to do is git theah!"

They broke from the timber, the barking of the dogs louder now, into the open, moving as quickly as they could past a cow, a horse, chickens, toward the house. A tan mongrel came rushing and barking, and then a burly man in work clothes came out of the house, a rifle in his hands. He had faded hair, a hard, tanned face, and squinting eyes.

"Stop!" he yelled, pointing the rifle.

Sam, Lela Belle, and Hester stopped short.

A burly woman with stringy black hair came out and stood beside the man. "What you doin' on our place?" she screamed. "Set down to dinner and look up and what do we see? Niggers!"

"Runners!" spat the man.

"Ain' dis de way station?" Sam cried.

"No, it sure as hell ain't!" bawled the farmer. "This is the Donahue place—Elmer and Samantha Donahue, knowed by all! We wouldn't have no part of them undergrounders! No better'n niggers theirselves! Where'd you run from, nigger?" he finished, hurling the question at Sam.

"Jus' let us go, suh," pleaded Sam in a desperate voice Hester had never heard him use. "We'll nevah come back, nevah bothah yo', nevah—"

"Shut up—let me listen!" ordered Donahue.

Sam quieted. Hester could see how rigid he was. She

wished they could turn and run, but they didn't dare, not with that rifle.

"Dawgs," said Donahue, of the growing sound. "Them's dawgs!" He motioned with the rifle. "Turn—march! To the barn!"

They did as he said, and he followed, pointing the rifle at their backs. At one side of the barn he opened the door of a lean-to shed and herded them inside.

Hester saw a pile of oats and a pile of unshelled corn. A mouse scurried out of sight. The door slammed shut on them, and the latch clattered into place.

Livid with fury, Thorne Wabash pursued his runaway slaves. When he caught them, he made them walk the fifteen miles back to Thornton, mollified somewhat by George's enthusiastic approval and that of the neighbors who had come along for the chase. But he was irritated by Phil's attitude.

"Why not let them ride, Uncle Thorne?" Phil asked. "They won't be any good to you if they're sick."

"They'll be more than sick when I finish," the older man said.

Sam, Hester, and Lela Belle walked, limping.

Thorne spoke seldom after his neighbors rode on home, but he considered and weighed. He decided not to make an example of these slaves as he had done with Jase. He wanted to keep Sam and Lela Belle because they were two of his best hands. But he wanted them cowed and grateful not to be sold away. He decided they would be a different kind of example—punished by the master, turned into reformed runners, slaves for the others to emulate.

It was night when they arrived at the plantation, and Thorne had Sam and Lela Belle taken to the stable and spanceled. He left a trusty to guard them and Boss Murray to get things ready. Then, George and Phil trailing, he went to the jail, where two trusties had taken Hester.

Thorne and the two young men stood inside while the trusties boarded up the window opening. One trusty nailed a layer of boards outside the window, and the other nailed a layer on the inside.

The light was dim, for there was only a candle burning, but Hester saw the triumphant, mean look on George's face. She noticed that Phil looked sad.

Thorne Wabash closely watched the boarding up. He wasn't going to have Hester put to the lash because he didn't want her marked. He intended, he announced, after she was jailed for a spell and tamed down some, to sell her off. He gave her a hard look. "Should have done it before now," he added.

She caught his look, which frightened her. The boards on the window frightened her. Boss Murray terrified her. He would come again tonight, after the plantation was dark. He would do what he had done before, worse.

Desperate, believing all was lost anyway, she cried out to Thorne that Boss Murray had raped her. She told him everything, and long before she had finished, she was sobbing. "It was rape, Master Thorne, sir!" she cried. "I told my mammy, and she said that's what it was!"

She saw a sharp look cross the master's face. Phil, near the candle, was very white. "How will you deal with that, sir?" he asked.

"Negroes are born liars, Phil. But I'll warn Murray off this wench. I don't want her used."

When the window was finished, Master Thorne told the young men to come along, and they all left. Hester heard the key turn in the lock outside and the trusties exchange a few words. They were to take turns guarding the jail.

She blew out the candle because if she didn't she would be punished for letting it burn down. Weak from all she had been through, she lay on the board bunk. Tears covered her face, and she wiped them away. She had to think how to keep from being sold, to stay here with Mammy and Pappy.

While Hester was desperately trying to think of some way to persuade Master Thorne not to sell her, he and the others had returned to the stable. Here, with Thorne, the two young masters, Boss Murray, and two trusties present, Sam was given five more lashes. Lela Belle was given ten lashes that would mark her for life.

After warning Murray not to molest Hester, Thorne Wabash went off to bed, satisfied.

The next morning, he mounted his gelding to ride his fields. Feeling pleased, even gleeful, over his handling of the runners, he kicked the horse into a gallop and put him at a hedge. The gelding jumped low, scraping through the top of the hedge. He stumbled, throwing Thorne Wabash, then raced on.

Thorne Wabash lay on the ground with a broken back.

Chapter Seven

George, as heir presumptive, immediately started giving orders, the first one being to call the doctor, the second to cut the recuperation time for Sam and Lela Belle. After that, he sent a trusty to post the notes Phil had written, summoning both George's father and Phil's parents to Thornton.

Doctor Cline arrived, driving his litle rig. He was in his late sixties, a slight, white-haired man with piercing, ice-blue eyes and a face as kind as his nature. He wore his usual black trousers, sack coat, and narrow tie. Leaving his black hat on the marble-topped table in the downstairs hallway, he climbed the steps to his patient.

George walked a step behind him, relating what had happened. At the door to Thorne's bedchamber, the old doctor told George to wait downstairs.

Thorne Wabash lay in a haze of agony. He knew the doctor was there but gave no sign and spoke no word. His fury, however, was by no means wiped out by his misery.

His mind was in a turmoil. It was his back. Just let it not hurt so, and he would be all right. He could handle any runners. In the redness of pain, through which he heard his own groans and low cries, he planned another public whipping. He would make those damnable slaves hurt the way he was hurting. Maybe give Doc Cline a taste of it as well, if he didn't let up feeling along his back, which was on fire, and stabbing it, seeming to grind its parts together fiendishly.

Doctor Cline, unaware of what was going through his patient's mind, examined him carefully. "Thorne," he said quietly. "Thorne, you hear me?"

"Yes, damn you—quit pounding my back!"

"I won't touch it again. It's broken in two places," the doctor said in his blunt but kindly manner.

"Fix it—damn you!"

"All I can do is have you rest."

"You mean to say—you can't cure it?"

"Think, Thorne. You know what a serious thing a broken back is. Leslie Farnsworth—"

"He—died—you old fool!"

"It was a very serious break. And he wouldn't rest."

"Worse—break—than mine?"

"About the same."

"You're saying I'm going to die—damn you!"

"Rest, I said. You want the truth."

"You can—be wrong."

"You do have a chance, Thorne. Complete rest."

"How can I rest—pain. Give me something!"

"Laudanum. I'll give you that."

"Give me plenty!"

The old doctor administered a dose, then wrote out directions, which he set on the table, along with the bottle. He turned back to his suffering patient. "Thorne," he said, "I've known you for years. I feel it's my duty to speak. I know that George is to be your heir. But have you had your attorney draw up a will?"

"Damnation—hellfire. That's the second time you've said I'll die! Well, I won't—hear me? No attorney!"

"Why not? You'll do it eventually to make sure that George and not—not someone else inherits."

"No! You keep an heir wondering—let him worry."

"Do as you please, Thorne," the doctor said. "But stay quiet. Rest. Sleep. I'll come every day."

Hester, in the jail, knew nothing of the master's accident, nothing of the lashes Sam and Lela Belle had been given.

The jail was so dark that she couldn't tell the difference between day and night except that sometimes it didn't seem quite so black. Boss Murray brought food and water twice a day, and when he opened the door in the morning, she got a blinding flash of sun, and that was the only light she saw. He didn't step inside, didn't speak, and didn't empty the slop pail, the stench from which filled the room.

When she had been fed four times and there was no sign from her parents, she knew they had been whipped. On the third night, she heard a scratching at the door. Hester ran to it and laid her ear against the wood. The scratching came again.

"Who is it?" she called softly.

"It Mammy. Yo' all right, baby? Yo' bin rape ag'in?"

"No, Mammy. Wheah is Pappy?"

"He bin whup—he mis'rable. But he healin'. I healin' fastah."

"Oh, Mammy!" wailed Hester.

"Shh—I goin' now. I dassn't come back. We love yo', baby!"

Hester said she loved them, too, but didn't know whether her mother heard, for there was no answer. She knew that her mother was gone, and she prayed she wouldn't be caught.

George's father and Phil's parents arrived. They took turns slipping into the sickroom, where Thorne lay on his bed and groaned and cursed. His one comfort was laudanum, which dulled the pain and enabled him to doze for brief periods of time.

He snarled at his visitors. He swore in the presence of Wanda Bennett, Phil's mother, then refused to apologize. After he finished berating her, she fled, joining the others in the library.

"How did he treat you, Aunt Wanda?" George asked. "Did he curse?"

Wanda looked distressed, but even so younger than her forty-five years. She smoothed back her blonde hair, and there was a glint of tears in her eyes.

"I'm afraid he did," she admitted.

"He swears at everybody, Mother," Phil said.

"Even the doctor," put in Neal, walking over to her and holding her protectively.

"That's right," put in Seth Drummond. "George took me in earlier, and it wasn't pleasant." Seth Drummond, also in his mid-forties, strong and muscular and with tawny blonde hair, bore a resemblance to his sister Wanda. "Don't let it bother you," he said to her. "The poor man doesn't know who's in his room, doesn't know whether he's cursing a man or a lady."

"He said he knew. But then, who can blame him?"

She wiped away a tear. "He's in torture, he's going to be in torture. Neal, darling, people do recover from broken backs, don't they?"

"Occasionally, dear. Occasionally."

"He'll fight," Seth put in. "Thorne will fight. He'll swear and blaspheme his way out of it if he has to."

"If only Rosalie could—Seth, do you think—?" Wanda appealed to her brother.

His mouth tightened. "Only if he asks for her. She has that much of Thorne in her. She'll not crawl."

"We've had enough talk," George cut in. "Father, I think you and Uncle Neal should ride over the plantation. Take a look around and give me your opinion."

"Our opinion about what?" Seth asked.

"Whether things look as good as I think they do. Whether Murray's doing his job right, and if the slaves are working well."

"I don't know that we have the authority, son."

"I'm giving it to you. I'm the heir."

"Your grandfather may not appreciate it when he finds out," Seth replied.

"He'll commend my initiative, if ever he hears about it. I want you to go. That'll be in my favor if he does find out, because I've asked the advice of my elders. Oh, I know all of the old gentleman's foibles!"

"George!" Seth admonished. "That's not respectful! If your mother—"

"Stepmother."

"She'd be shocked. She's given you a fine upbringing. Don't kick aside all she's done."

"We can ride out and look," Neal said. "Under the conditions, George feels responsible, and we both know Thorne would be very angry if some detail was overlooked."

"That's it!" George said. "That's what I can explain to him if he ever—and it's the truth!"

Phil gazed at his cousin. For the first time he recognized that George's selfishness went beyond youthful matters. He was trying to take over the plantation now, with the master still alive, with the will still unwritten. He watched George quietly. How would he get around that will business, should Thorne not recover?

In the days that followed, Phil was a silent observer. Thorne was still in agony, still crying out, demanding more and more laudanum, and every day George was giving new orders to the overseer. His father and uncle had found all running well, but George unearthed new faults, all of them minor, and ordered them changed.

Phil wandered about the plantation and even through the Quarters. He passed the jail but refrained from calling out to Hester, lest he get her deeper into trouble. He learned that Lela Belle was behind the plow again. Sam was still in his bunk, his back raw and festering.

Apparently the two older men hadn't come into the cabin during their inspection. This troubled Phil, and because George was in charge, Phil went to him about it. "The buck who ran away," he said, "Sam. Uncle Thorne had ten lashes laid on top of the ten he'd had already."

"What of it?"

"I understand he's to go back to work Monday."

"That's right."

"He can't, George. You stand to lose a prime hand if he does."

"Who asked your advice? But since you know so much, what do you think I should do?"

"Hester's locked in the jail yet."

"Where she belongs."

"She's wasted there. If you'd give Sam a week and put her to tending him, he'll heal as strong as ever. Then you can put her back into the fields."

"Grandfather wanted her locked up. He was going to sell her."

"Do as you like," Phil replied, his heart in his throat. "I just hate to see you risk losing one of the best hands on the place. A blacksmith, at that."

"I'll do what I want!" he snapped. George strode outside, looking for Boss Murray. He ordered him to unlock the jail and went with him to do it. As Boss Murray unlocked the door, the stench hit them in the face. George stepped back.

"What pigsty is this?" he snarled.

"I don't empty no slop fer no white nigger," mumbled the overseer. "Mister Wabash didn't say to."

"I'm saying it now. Any time niggers are locked in here, you get a trusty to empty the slops. Hear? You go fetch a couple of trusties right now to clean this place up and air it out!"

"Yes, sir," muttered Murray. He turned and walked away.

"You—Hester—come out!" ordered George.

Barefoot and dirty, she stepped through the door. Her face was streaked from crying and the dust of the bunk. She blinked in the strong daylight.

"Go to your cabin," George said. "Clean yourself. Take care of Sam so he can work."

"Yes, Master George, sir."

"I'm doing you a favor. The master wanted you sold. I'll keep you on—if you behave. I expect you to be grateful."

"Yes, Master George, sir." She looked at him, then away. He had the same look in his eyes that Boss Murray had had.

Still, it was right for her to be grateful, she thought. Master George had some good in him to let her out of jail. She had been trying to think how to make it possible to stay at Thornton with Mammy and Pappy, and here was her chance. Just to work hard, not run away, and be grateful.

"This gratitude is to be for life, or however long I want it, wench."

"I undahstand, Master George, sir," she murmured. "I'll be like you say. I'll work, nevah run."

Even as she promised, she became afraid that he would want what Boss Murray had taken. Then she thought of Phil and knew, if such a problem arose, he would influence his cousin. She would just have to tell Master Phil, she thought, and he would fix it.

It wasn't until she was back home in the cabin, tending her father's ugly wounds and cleaning herself up, that she learned of the master's accident. That explained why Master George had let her out of jail and why he had said she could stay at Thornton. He was the heir. He was taking charge. Master Thorne was surely dying.

Lela Belle, when she came from the field, verified this. "Mastah George, he be hardah dan Mastah Thorne," she added.

Sam groaned, sitting forward to ease the pain of the weals and cuts. "We got to work hardah, fo' sure," he said.

Hester didn't worry over this. She felt sorry for Master

Thorne, who must die. But she was so happy to be with her parents, the three of them having supper together, she couldn't worry.

Boss Murray stopped by at times and looked at Sam's sores. He said another week would see them healed. George never came, nor did Phil. Word drifted down from the big house that the master was still very sick but that he was improving.

One afternoon Hester bathed, put on her one good shift, and combed her hair and tied it back with a clean black tape her mother had sewn for that purpose. After making sure that her father was feeling as comfortable as possible, she told him she was going to her secret room to pick flowers for the cabin.

"It's time for those pink little rose flowahs to bloom," she said. "I'll put some in a mug on the table."

Outside, she thought she saw George pass by, two streets away in the Quarters, and she slowed down. When she got to that spot, all the streets were deserted. If it had been Master George, she thought, he had gone into one of the cabins.

She walked silently on bare feet, anxious to leave the Quarters behind. She longed to run, but that would draw attention if some slave was in a cabin, so she kept to a walk. Only when she was well away from the Quarters did she run. As soon as she reached the timber, she slowed down and walked again. At last she reached her lake room, as lonely and peaceful as ever. The grass was studded with pink flowers, and she dropped to her knees, then lay flat, burying her face in them, breathing their sweetness. She wondered how it would be if she could somehow put this wonderful smell into a bottle and keep it in the cabin and sniff it whenever she wanted to.

"Roll over on your back!" ordered a sharp voice. "Spread your legs!"

Startled, she sat up. George was standing in the pink flowers. As she started to get up, he lunged, knocking her flat. He was laughing now, a keen, whinnying sound. She struggled to get up, but he held her, one hand bearing down fiercely on each shoulder. She twisted, and he straddled her. She tried to roll, but he held her with one hand and worked at his trousers.

Hester screamed, her voice carrying over the tiny lake. They were rolling and struggling, when they heard the sounds of someone running through the woods. George let her go, and she scrambled to her feet, straightening her shift. George was trying to get his trousers closed, but a figure came plunging out of the timber and into him, head down, striking him in the belly. It was Phil.

They rolled, punching, and kicked, first one on top, then the other. They fought to their feet. George brought his fist up from the hip and smashed Phil's nose. Phil put his head down and aimed for George's belly again, but George sidestepped, and Phil almost sprawled on his face.

He turned fast enough, though, to meet George head-long, and now it was Phil who sidestepped. George crashed to the ground but was up so quickly that Phil, who was coming at him again, slammed into him so hard that Hester heard their bodies thud. Now they circled and danced. They punched methodically, in the ribs, the back, the belly, the jaw and face.

Suddenly Phil drew back his arm, then brought it forward, cracking against George's neck with the edge of his hand. George dropped to the ground where he lay for several moments. Slowly he sat up, his face twisted in rage. Plainly, he was beyond fighting any more.

"You followed me here!" he accused Phil.

"You followed Hester! I saw what you were going to do!"

"She's nothing but a wench!"

"If Uncle Thorne finds out—"

"How's he going to find out? Think he'll believe you over me?"

"I don't have to tell. He has his ways of knowing."

"I'm running Thornton now, remember!"

"Only for him. He can sit in a chair now. He has a cane. He'll walk."

"So. What he doesn't know won't hurt him."

"I promise you," Phil said, between clenched teeth, "that if you lay hand on Hester again, I *will* tell Uncle Thorne."

"What you'd better worry about is what we're going to tell all of them about your nose. And my eye and jaw!"

"That's your department, George. You're the one with something to hide."

"No more than you!"

They glared at each other, and for one awful instant Hester thought they would fight again. Then George shrugged. "Hell, we'll say we fought on a dare," he said. "That it was a draw."

"And a lie. I bested you. And it wasn't a dare."

"Would you rather raise a stink and have my grandfather roaring mad? I say keep it private between us."

Phil looked thoughtful. Then he nodded. "Agreed," he said. Then, to Hester, "It'll be better if you stay in the Quarters."

"Yes, Master Phil, sir."

The young men turned and walked off through the timber. When she could no longer see them, Hester picked some flowers, because she had told her father that was what she was going to do, and then she hurried to the cabin. She knew that things would never be the same between the cousins and that it was her fault, and this saddened her.

Thorne Wabash, after all his agony and cursing and laudanum, after his miserable, sleepless days and nights, had mended and was going to live. He could now walk up and down the stairs very carefully, could sit in a straight, hard chair and from it run his plantation. He could not, as yet, mount a horse, nor did he wish to.

On learning that George had taken charge during his illness, that George had given orders and seen to it that they were carried out, he was pleased. He even came to accept Hester's having been freed from jail. She had settled down, George reported, as had Sam and Lela Belle, and all three were exemplary slaves.

George had proven himself, Thorne thought. When he got around to it, he would have his will drawn up and sign it, making George his heir. In a year—or two. There was something about a man's actual execution of his will that was like writing his own death warrant. It could wait.

Chapter Eight

Hester thought often about Phil, the way he had saved her, his kindness, and his handsomeness. She couldn't forget how it had felt, last summer, to lie in his arms and to kiss him. She longed for it to happen again but knew it never could.

He didn't even want her to go to the secret room. That was for her own safety, but she yearned to just the same. It was doubly precious now, for she could sit among the flowers, gaze at the tiny lake, and remember how it had been with herself and Master Phil.

There came a day when Thorne and George went to pay a call at Rose Hill, the plantation of Guy Kirby. With George gone, Hester seized the opportunity to visit her secret room.

Sam was back working in his blacksmith's shop, Lela Belle was in the field, and Hester had not yet been ordered to work. This might be her last day of freedom, the last time at the lake. She told her father, who knew nothing of George's assault, where she was going. He warned her not to stay long.

In her wilderness room, there were blue flowers now, mingled with the pink, and Hester sat cross-legged at the edge of the lake, the blossoms feeling soft against her legs.

She had only been there a short while when Phil rode out of the timber, dismounted, and tied his horse. He came toward her, his face anxious. "Hester!" he exclaimed. "You promised!"

"They said Master George was gone, Master Phil, sir."

He sat down near her and lounged on one elbow. "It's safe enough, I suppose. But you haven't been coming here?"

"No, Master Phil, sir. Only now."

He nodded, the serious look vanished, and he glanced around. "It's really the loveliest spot I ever saw," he said. "That's why I came." He became serious again. "How have you been, Hester? Has Murray— or George—?"

"No, Master Phil, sir. Mister Murray looks and grins a bad way, but that's all."

"Uncle Thorne warned him. He warned George. And me."

"Do you know, Master Phil, if the master is going to sell me off?" This fear was constantly with her.

"George let slip that he'll probably keep you."

Relief flooded her, and she began to tremble. He noticed the trembling.

"It means so much to you, Hester?"

"I want to be with my mammy and pappy."

They talked on. He told her the plot of a play he had seen. He said he was going to join a showboat company the next summer. He described the kind of farm he might be able to buy.

When she made mistakes in speech, he corrected her and she thanked him. He bemoaned the fact that George knew of this spot. "If he didn't, I could bring books here and teach you," he said.

She felt her eyes shine, and her heart went faster. To have him teach her would be next-best to being in his arms.

"But," he continued, "it isn't safe. He'd be sure to catch us. And then Uncle Thorne really would sell you. But don't give up. Somehow, some day, you'll get the chance to learn. And when it comes, grab it. Promise me that?"

She nodded vigorously. She dared not speak or she would cry.

Before he left, he promised to let her know the next time George left the plantation. They could meet here if she didn't have to be in the fields.

"I'll at least teach you to speak properly," he said.

The following week, Guy and Vera Kirby of Rose Hill gave a dance in honor of the eighteenth birthday of their only daughter, Eve. The entire Thornton contingent arrived at Rose Hill in a new carriage.

Thorne Wabash carefully descended from the carriage and, walking slowly, led the way to the mansion, and the others followed. The house was tall, white, and pillared and surrounded by trees. Light showed in every window, and laughter sounded from within as they crossed the veranda. Phil wished himself anyplace else. He hated dances.

A grizzled Negro butler admitted them to the hallway, where the Kirbys, their daughter, and a girl Phil didn't recognize were lined up to receive the guests, who then moved on into the great double rooms. Gus Kirby was portly, red faced and jovial. He wore a smile meant to last the evening, pumped their hands, bade them welcome, then passed them on to his wife, a tall, thin, pale woman in a full, ruffled gown. Her handshake was limp, and her voice almost a whisper as she said, "You know my daughtah, Eve." He remembered her from years past.

She was tall, slat-thin, very pale. Her features had a bony look, and her lips, which were quite red, were thin. Her best feature was her hair, which was golden and which she wore smooth and parted, with a knot at the back.

"Good evening, Phil," she said. "You remembah me?"

He smiled. "It's been a few years, with you traveling summers," he said, "but I remember."

"Aren't you going to admire my gown?" she demanded. "Everybody else has!"

He looked at the gown, trying to remember things his mother said about fashion. Eve's gown had a low-cut, tight-fitting satin top that revealed her bony neck. The skirt, which he knew was held out by hoops, was covered with rows of lace ruffles that were the same pale blue as the gown. "Charming," he murmured, hoping this response would be acceptable.

Eve gave him a smile and introduced him to the girl standing next to her. "Leloi Roper, of Whitehall," she said. "You remembah her, too, of course."

"Yes," Phil agreed, scarcely remembering, for this girl, too, had been traveling in the summers. He put out his hand, and firm, warm fingers pressed his. Her hair was blonde, too, but with red in it, and her eyes were midnight blue. Her features were smooth and pretty, and her voice was pleasant.

"It doesn't mattah if you don't remembah!" she declared. She tilted her head. "We know each othah now," she chuckled, "and that's good enough! I'm celebrating my birthday with Eve," she said. "We're twins, in a way. Same birthday, only I'm nineteen, and she's eighteen."

She was a year older than he was. But that didn't matter. They were near enough in age to be friends, and he had a feeling they were going to be friends.

Phil drifted into the double rooms and mingled with the people gathered there. George edged up to him and muttered. "Don't hang around Eve. She's mine."

Phil stared. He would never have thought George would be attracted to Eve Kirby. His cousin compounded his bewilderment by muttering, "Leloi Roper's the one for you."

"What is all this?" Phil asked.

"The plantations! Don't you keep up with anything? They both inherit! I'm going for Eve because Rose Hill's bigger than Whitehall. Add it to Thornton, and you've got real land!"

Before Phil could respond, the Negro band, situated on a dais, struck up. The gentlemen, who had been writing their names on the dance cards that fluttered from the wrists of the ladies, now claimed their first partners.

George had almost filled Eve's card with his name. As they glided and turned among the other dancers, she coyly protested what he had done. "You've simply got to give up some of youah dances with me!" she said. "It's my duty to dance with every man heah, me bein' guest of honah!"

"I'm not giving up one dance. We belong together."

"And just why, bold man?" she asked, flirting.

"We match," he replied, a smile on his lips. "Thornton and Rose Hill. Our coming together fast is natural."

He saw color rise in her cheeks. But she wasn't displeased. Rather, she was excited. He knew that by the way her flat bosom rose and fell. He read her nature in that moment. She was as smart as he was, as eager and acquisitive. He was so sure of himself that he threw caution aside. "Will you marry me?" he asked, his face close to hers as they executed a sweeping step. "We've known each other forever."

Eve stared at him.

"Will you?" George pressed. "May I speak to your father? Now—tonight?"

Her eyes narrowed. "This is very sudden, George."

"Not at all. I've thought of nothing else since we called on you that afternoon. When I saw you then, I knew you'd make a wonderful wife."

Her eyes gleamed. "What kind of husband will you be?"

"The best. I'll manage our two plantations better than any planter in the county."

Her eyes were mere slits now. "You don't say you're in love with me."

He stared, dumbfounded at this oversight, then recovered. "But of course I am! The day we called, I came to see how you'd turned out, if what I felt for you years ago had lasted."

"And?"

"It's the same," he lied. "Only more so."

They waltzed on, her eyes now closed. After a moment she opened them and looked into his. "Then I consent," she said. "I'll marry you."

He didn't waste a moment. He rounded up his father, his grandfather, and Eve's parents. Bewildered, they gathered in the library, and he closed the door.

When they returned to the dancing, all but George and Eve looked dazed. They stood just inside the ballroom and waited for the number to end.

When it did, Guy Kirby lifted his hands and called for attention. The rooms fell silent. "I have the honah," Kirby announced, "on this most happy evening, to tell you some pleasant news. Not only is this my daughtah Eve's birthday, but she has just consented to become the bride of Mistah George Drummond! Friends, congratulations are in ordah! It's not every day that two plantations such as Rose Hill and Thornton are united or every day that two such young, fine people plight their troth!"

There was subdued applause, and a few squeals from the girls. This was followed by a general movement toward the engaged couple.

Phil, who had just danced with Leloi, gazed at her, stunned. She smiled. "Aren't you surprised?" he asked.

She kept smiling, and he thought how pretty she was, how sweet natured. He wondered what she and Eve had in common aside from being neighbors and almost the same age.

"No, I'm not surprised," she said. "I've known Eve all my life. I know how she is, and I helped draw up the guest list for tonight."

"What does that mean?"

She continued to smile. "I shouldn't tell," she said mischievously—and waited to be urged.

"She's going to be my cousin," he insisted. "What about the guest list?"

"She and her mothah discussed the prospects of every unmarried man invited." He waited. "Don't you undah-stand, Phil?"

"No, I don't. Or don't want to believe the implica-tion."

"It's true, though. Eve wants to get married. But she can't marry a poor man and won't let herself be married for her inheritance alone. She's nevah made a secret of that. So"—Leloi made a small gesture—"she decided, even before the invitations were delivered, that George was the best prospect."

"Then why did she invite me? I haven't a prospect on earth!"

"Because youah George's cousin. What do you think, Phil? Has she fooled him, or has he been thinking the way she has?"

He grinned, then sobered. "George won't object to her having Rose Hill," he conceded.

She sighed, then smiled slightly. "Maybe it's best for them. Both feeling the way they do about owning land."

"And every girl does want to marry," Phil ventured.

"Every girl?"

"Well, I thought—I assumed—"

She laughed. "No girl wants to be a spinstah! I want to marry, but for love, not the way Eve is doing."

"Isn't she in love with George at all?"

"As much as she can be with anybody. She likes his mannah, says he's bold and will get what he goes aftah. And, as we know, his being heir to Thornton won't lessen that love."

The dancing resumed, and Phil sought out his next partner. It was considerably later when George got him into the library. "How are you getting along with Leloi?" he asked. "I see you dancing with her. And talking a lot."

"We get along fine. She's a pretty girl."

"Lovable?"

"Y-yes. Why do you ask?"

"As if you didn't know! Make love to her! Propose! Sweep her off her feet! Tonight, while it's in the air!"

"Why should I?"

"Your future, you fool! She inherits Whitehall!"

"So I understand."

"Well, what's holding you back?"

"I've the same as just met her. These things take time."

It was too soon. The idea was too new. He didn't know Leloi well enough to propose, much less marry her. It felt wrong.

"I'll tell you one fact," George said, disgusted. "If Whitehall weren't smaller than Rose Hill, it'd be Leloi I'm engaged to now."

Phil held his tongue, and they rejoined the others.

After that evening, the two couples were together frequently. They went for drives, to Warrenton to spend the day, and on many picnics. They always had a pleasant time.

George and Eve seemed to be happy. They held hands openly and called each other "dear." Sometimes George daringly kissed Eve on the cheek in front of the other two.

Phil enjoyed the outings. He and Leloi found much to laugh about and were never at a loss for something to discuss. In fact, Phil realized, he and Leloi were the ones who kept the atmosphere gay for the engaged couple, who were inclined to fall glum and silent despite their hand holding.

Often he thought of Hester. He had had no opportunity to meet her at the lake, for his time was filled. Besides, she had been put back to field work, so there would have been no grammar lessons anyway.

George kept insisting that Phil marry Leloi, arguing that it would be natural, then, for them to pool the resources of their various plantations. "We can make more money that way," he declared.

Phil laughed it off, and finally George stopped pressing the matter. Instead, he spent time closeted with his grandfather. They seemed to be planning something, but

George didn't mention what it was, and Phil didn't ask. When his father was included in the talks and began to look thoughtful and announced he was going to prolong his visit another week, Phil waited for him to speak. When he didn't, Phil held his counsel, as he had with George.

It all came out one day when William Roper, his wife Mary, and daughter Leloi appeared at Thornton. They were ushered into the front parlor, where they took seats. In addition to the Ropers, all those at Thornton were present—Thorne Wabash, Neal and Wanda Bennett, Seth Drummond, George, and Phil.

Leloi sat beside her mother on a sofa. Mary Roper was a pretty woman, an older version of her daughter. William Roper was tall and thin with hair starting to gray, and a pleasant mouth.

"Speak out, William," Thorne said. "Let's get this matter settled."

"It seems unfair to have called an audience," Roper began slowly. "It would be less of a strain if Phil and myself and his father were to speak in private."

Phil straightened in his chair. This sounded ominous. He didn't like the smug look on George's face. He felt the hair on the back of his neck stir. Seeing regret on his father's face, the hair stirred again.

"Nonsense," snapped Thorne. "We're like a family in this community. Rose Hill, Whitehall, Thornton. That makes this discussion a family matter and is why I demanded that you, Neal, not speak to Phil in advance."

Roper cleared his throat, then glanced from Phil to Leloi. "The two of you," he said, "have spent a great deal of time together these last weeks."

"That's right, sir," Phil agreed. "We've been with George and Eve. And we've had good times, haven't we?" he finished, his eyes on Leloi.

She looked as puzzled as he felt. "Yes!" she exclaimed. "I've had more fun than I evah had!"

"We've refrained from questioning Leloi," Roper continued. "We've waited for you to speak, Phil."

"About what, sir?" Phil asked. But he knew. He looked at Leloi. She was scarlet.

"Your intentions, Phil," Roper said, his pleasant mouth firm. "I've permitted you to court my daughter long enough, I believe, to be informed of your intentions. Your father and uncle feel the same, to say nothing of my wife, her mother."

"Papa!" Leloi cried. "Please!"

"I have no 'intentions,' sir," Phil replied soberly. "I've never treated Leloi as anything but the greatest lady. We are friends."

"You deny you've been courting her?"

"I've been her escort in a group of four, sir."

"Oh, please!" cried Leloi, her scarlet face even redder. "Phil and I aren't like George and Eve! We haven't been courting! We've just been going around with them because we have fun togethah!"

"Darling," wailed Mary Roper, "you needn't covah up for him!"

"If you have tampered with this young lady's affections, son," Neal Bennett put in, "your mother and I want to know it. I apologize for not speaking to you earlier, alone. But if you've led her on, even unintentionally, led her to believe your association would lead to a proposal of marriage—"

"Look," Phil said, deeply serious. "I like Leloi. I'm even fond of her—as a friend. I've had no thought of marriage."

"Nor I!" cried Leloi. "I'm fond of you, Phil, but I told you at the very first I must have love to get married! And that's what they're getting at—marriage! But I don't love you!"

"Nevertheless," put in Thorne Wabash, "you have, Phil, put this young lady's reputation under question because you've been seen in her company so frequently. I suggest the two of you announce your engagement. At once."

"The idea!" cried Leloi. "I won't do it!"

"Considah your mother's feelings, daughter," said Roper. "Consent to an engagement. Continue your pleasant times with George and Eve until their wedding in late summah. It's possible you'll both change your minds."

The meeting ended with an angry, weeping Leloi and a grim but courteous Phil agreeing to a semi-engagement, one which could be rumored, but not formally announced.

After the group dispersed, Phil accosted George. "You had a hand in this," he accused.

"I admit it. One day you'll thank me, cousin. Tell me—what *have* you been up to? Playing the fool or playing it smart?"

"I don't know what you mean."

"What's wrong with Leloi? Seriously."

"Nothing. She's a lovely girl."

"Well, there's plenty wrong with Eve. But that's not stopping me."

"George! She seems—"

"She has a sharp tongue, for one thing."

"I've never heard it."

"She keeps it under control—except when we're alone. And she wants her name on Thornton, right with mine!"

"What's wrong with that?"

"Thornton's being left to me, not her. And her father is leaving Rose Hill in her name, and she won't add mine."

"That makes you even, as I see it."

"The man should own everything! Or he'll not be master in his own house!"

Phil shook his head.

"Why *don't* you marry Leloi?" George asked fiercely.

"Because we're not in love. That's the true reason."

"Fool! I thought you wanted a plantation!" snarled George, and went striding from the room.

Thoroughly depressed and angry, Phil had a horse saddled and galloped over the roads until both he and his mount were exhausted. When he went to bed, he was still in a defiant, reckless mood.

Chapter Nine

Once again, with George gone to Rose Hill to ride its acres with Guy Kirby, and Hester not to be seen in the field or the Quarters, Phil went to the secret lake. He hoped to find Hester there and to explain why he had not been able to make good his promise to teach her grammar. He didn't actually expect to find her, but it seemed to be his only chance.

She was sitting among the little wild flowers she loved, and when she heard him ride to the edge of the timber, she looked up apprehensively. Then, seeing who it was, she smiled, and he could see the gleam of pleasure in her great brown eyes even before he covered the space between them.

"This is my first chance to come," he said, his excitement over being with her increasing. "George went to Rose Hill alone today—I've been going with him other times."

Her smile softened. "I know, Master Phil. They said he rode off alone."

"How did you get out of field work?"

"I was ordered by Mr. Murray to help Granny Myrtle with the suckers."

"Then why are you here?"

"Granny Myrtle told me to go play. To come back later."

"What if Murray misses you?"

"She'll tell him the truth. He won't do nothing—"

"Won't do *anything*, Hester."

"Thank you, Master Phil. Mr. Murray won't do anything to Granny Myrtle."

Relieved, Phil dropped to the flower-studded grass beside her. "I've missed you, Hester," he said.

"Me, too, Master Phil. What you been doing, sir?"

"You know that George and Eve Kirby are to be married in late summer?"

"Yes, Master Phil. They talk about it in the Quarters. It was—romantic—Granny Myrtle said, the way Master George proposed right at the birthday dance. Will you tell me about the dance, Master Phil?"

He told her every detail. He described how the carriages had been met by stable slaves, explained about the receiving line, spoke of the great double parlors filled with yellow and white roses and soft music, and he told her about the guests and explained the dance card each lady wore fluttering from her wrist. He related how Guy Kirby had announced the engagement. But he said nothing of the way George had spoken to him concerning Leloi Roper.

"Did you have fun at the dance, Master Phil?" she asked, her heart warm at the wonder of the scene in which he had lived and moved, happy that he would share the evening with her thus.

"I enjoyed it more than most dances," he replied. He realized that had been because of Leloi.

"I'm glad, Master Phil."

"But I don't like dances, really." He frowned slightly.

She couldn't understand how it could be two ways. "How could you like the dance and not like it, Master Phil?" she asked teasingly, hoping to make him smile.

He was silent for a bit as if he were trying to decide something. Not answering her question, he said instead, "It's George and Eve. They bother me."

"How, Master Phil?"

"You know George inherits Thornton and Eve inherits Rose Hill."

"They'll be very rich," she said softly. Their vast wealth stretched beyond her comprehension. Master George would be the richest man in the county when he inherited Thornton, then for him to marry Miss Eve, who was also to inherit a large plantation—it was completely beyond her grasp. It was like the kings and queens Granny Myrtle told her stories of.

Phil remained unsmiling.

"Where will they live, Master Phil?"

"At Thornton. Uncle Thorne says it's time for a woman to run the house properly. My mother agrees."

Hester thought that sounded right. But Master Phil didn't seem happy over it. He was gloomy about something, and she had no idea what.

Although he was master and she was slave, she could no longer endure the feeling that he was troubled, so she asked softly, "Master Phil, what is wrong?"

He looked at her for a long time before speaking. When he did begin to talk, he spoke in a murmur, quickly and honestly, his eyes never leaving hers. He said that, in his opinion, George and Eve were marrying to get two plantations instead of one each. He said that he did not and could not believe they loved each other at all.

"And they—should—love each other, Master Phil?"

"I think so. I know marriages are arranged, but it's better with love."

Her heart glowed. Her eyes shone. Even troubled, he still looked like a sun god.

"In the Quarters," she said, "the master says which buck marries a wench. Mostly." His frown deepened. "Did I say something wrong, Master Phil?"

"What makes you ask?"

"You act—troubled."

"I am troubled," he said so openly that it frightened her. He was talking to her like she was a white girl, not a slave, and she didn't know how to respond or what would happen if Boss Murray, by some evil chance, found out. She pushed the thought from her mind. This was Master Phil, and he was unhappy, and if she could help him back to his own sunny self, she would do it, no matter how much trouble she got into.

"There's another girl in the neighborhood," he was saying. "Her name is Leloi Roper, and she's to inherit her father's plantation, Whitehall."

"That's a big plantation, Master Phil. My pappy knows about it."

"Yes, it's quite large. The thing is, since George and Eve have been engaged, they want to go about, and Leloi and I have gone along as chaperones. You know what chaperones are?"

"Granny Myrtle told me, Master Phil."

"I've been with Leloi so much that her father asked my intentions, whether I plan to marry her."

Hester's stomach turned. She had never thought of him marrying. Suddenly she wanted to cry.

Phil talked on, softly. "It's crazy, the whole thing! Leloi and I don't love each other and never will! Yet, in spite of both of us, our fathers and Uncle Thorne insist that we let word seep out that we're engaged! This is to protect Leloi's good name, which is fair enough. But they expect that we'll change. And George keeps after me. He wants me to marry her so we can form some kind of big power in the county with our three plantations!"

"Then you don't have to marry her, Master Phil?"

"Indeed not! I've got to be nice to her," he explained, "and squire her about until after George and Eve are married. Then we'll just drift apart because, for one thing, I'll be going home to New Orleans."

She gazed at him, unexpectedly beginning to shake. How nearly he had been lost to the unknown white girl with the big plantation! But she felt impelled to speak of the land, he wanted land so much. Maybe, no matter how awful it made her feel, he should take this chance. "If you like Miss Leloi, Master Phil," she forced herself to whisper, "maybe—and you'd have the land you want."

"I'll not marry for land," he said firmly. "I'll get my own land, and I'll marry for love."

They discussed this. Their voices, already whispering, became even softer. Without realizing it, they had moved nearer and nearer to each other.

He was close beside her now, still on his elbow. With his free hand, he ran his fingers lightly along her arm, and the touch sent a shiver of delight down her back.

He shifted so that his upper body was above hers and he was supported by both elbows. His frown was gone. There was a seeking look in his eyes now. She caught her breath as his lips touched hers, gently and tenderly. They kissed, a long, lingering, trembling kiss.

Tendrils of delight wound all through her body. There was a delicious tickling inside her, and when he would have moved his lips away, she followed with her own, and he sighed, and their second kiss joined itself to the first.

Tearing his lips free, he murmured her name, changed position, and reached to take off her shift. Lying on her back, she lifted her hips so he could draw the shift up, over her head and away, and she heard his gasp when she lay naked under the sun.

"Unbelievable!" he exclaimed.

As she lay there, he stood up and quickly took off his clothes. He was indeed a god as he came to her, nude, his skin golden in the sun.

He lowered himself over her, and her arms lifted and drew him close. Her heart was beating so fast it felt like a trapped bird under her breast; the hair on his chest was soft against her, and the delicious inner tickle increased and left her breathless.

"Hester—Hester—" he whispered as she held him. He stroked down her hip, lower, then lifted himself slightly. "It's all right—if I can't wait—?"

"Don't wait!" she half-sobbed.

He entered her with the smoothness of velvet. She pressed upward, and he began to move, making sobbing noises, and she both clung to him and moved. Her breath came in short gasps as they moved together, fitted and welded, and the sun poured down on them.

There came the moment, the one short tick of eternity when they stopped moving and simply clung, winging through space into a new and perfect heaven. Hester was bursting with glory; it was throbbing and singing deep within her, coursing through her veins, tingling in her scalp and down to her toes. She gripped him, wanting it to go on forever, but then he was falling away, to his side, but keeping her in his arms so that she lay coiled and curled the length of his body.

"Hester, little Hester!" he gasped, his chest heaving against her breasts. "There's—something—ever since we were children! I didn't recognize it until—now!"

"What—is it—Master Phil?" Hester asked, her breathing uneven.

"Call me Phil, never master again. Hester—sweet Hester—I love you!" His voice broke with wonder. "I *love* you! Love you the way a man loves the girl he marries!"

Before she could speak, before she could say that she loved him, too, he came into her again. And again they moved together, their bodies cushioned by the earth, by the grass and the silken flowers, and Hester clung to him and partook of his love in a whirl of wonder. This was love, this was what it was. This body to body, heart to heart. The bliss, the perfection—they were love.

After another miraculous kiss, Phil reached for Hester's shift, then gently lowered it over her tousled curls, drawing it down over her body. Then he dressed swiftly, and Hester, watching, saw his face turn grim.

He sat near her in the flowering grass. "I ran an awful risk, darling. We might have been caught."

"But we weren't." Her voice quavered.

"Thank the fates. Now. We've things to say—this moment, because I may not get a chance to see you alone before we go back to New Orleans."

The thought of his leaving, ever, was like a stab. Trying not to show the hurt, she nodded agreement.

"We've got to face reality, Hester. First, I'm engaged to a girl I must not hurt."

"Of course not—Phil."

"Next, I'm white. You're not white."

She bowed her head. There was nothing she could say. Facts, bare facts, were defeating them.

"We can overcome everything," he said firmly. "Leloi and I mean to break our 'engagement,' anyway. And she won't mind, but will be glad for me when I tell her I've found love."

"But the othah, Phil. The othah."

"Simple, when you analyze it. You can pass for white anywhere. I'll just buy a farm in the north. We'll get married, and no one will ever know about you!"

Gazing into his blue eyes, Hester felt her heart break for him and for herself. But mostly for him—he was so certain, so eager, so wonderful. She wanted to believe he could bring this miracle to pass, she longed to be his wife, but she knew it could never be. He was white, and she was Negro. God himself couldn't change that.

He kissed her, then left, and she watched him ride off, his head high, to make and carry out future plans that included her. Hope sprang, died, sprang again, then died when she thought of the white masters. There was some way they would keep Phil from doing what he meant to do, she was sure of it. Tears filled her eyes, and she could no longer see Phil as he rode further into the trees.

Before Phil could manage a private talk with Leloi, Eve had driven over to Whitehall with an idea she couldn't wait to discuss. She drew Leloi into the rose garden so they could sit among the roses, which she considered romantic, and speak in privacy.

Leloi, a bit puzzled because since her engagement, Eve hadn't come over often, sat and waited to hear what this was all about.

"As I told you in the house," Eve began, "I've had this perfectly wonderful idea! It'll make my wedding perfect, if you'll just do it!"

"I will if I can, Eve. What is it?"

"Promise! Promise this instant!"

"Not until you tell," Leloi said, and laughed. "You used to catch me that way when we were little girls, but no more, Eve Kirby! You've some sort of plot in mind!"

"The most delicious plot! You'll adore it!"

"I'm waiting," Leloi said. The preliminaries didn't encourage her.

"Well, it's simply earthshaking, Leloi, honey! I only had the idea last night and could hardly sleep, it kept me so excited! I pictuahed us having a double wedding—George and me and you and Phil!"

Leloi was speechless.

"What do you say, darling?" demanded Eve. "Isn't it wondahful?"

"But you know Phil and I aren't formally engaged, Eve! You know why our parents let out word quietly that we're—well, semi-engaged. That it's because they thought my good name was in dangah! And even if—even then, I just couldn't make a switch and say to Phil, 'Let's get married with George and Eve!' Not even then could I do that! It would be forward and unladylike."

"That's not the way you do it, silly! You act warm and soft and let Phil see that youah falling in love with him—"

"But I'm not falling in love with him! I just like him, and that's way different than love!"

"You just let him think it, that's all! Then he'll do the askin'!"

"Eve!"

"That's the way I've worked it with George!"

"It's dishonest! If you don't really and truly love him—"

"Not so dishonest! Instead of running the risk of marryin' some fortune huntah who's aftah Rose Hill or ending up being a spinstah with a plantation on my hands to run alone, I'll have a smart husband and *two* plantations! And you will, too, if you do like me, 'cause Phil's so crazy about land that if he married you, he'd keep buyin' more land, and you'd be richah!"

Leloi could only stare. She had suspected her friend's mind worked in this manner, but now that she had proof from Eve's own lips, she was stunned. It seemed to her that Eve was gambling with her own future.

Eve seized upon Leloi's silence for agreement. "Ouah double wedding'll be the biggest social event Warren County has evah seen!" she exulted. "No, not a word! The less you talk and the more you *think* of the advantages, the bettah you'll undahstand it must happen my way! And Phil's so *handsome*! I vow, if it wasn't that he's to get Thornton, the biggest plantation in the county, I'd nevah have used my charms on George! I'd have won Phil foah myself!"

It took more than an hour for Leloi to convince Eve that she absolutely would not try to make Phil propose and that there would be no double wedding. In order to part in a friendly manner, she did agree that their foursome would continue, if Phil was agreeable, until Eve's wedding, knowing well that Eve would keep up her persuading at every opportunity.

At approximately the same hour, George, carrying out his promise to Eve, was trying to get Phil to agree to a double wedding. They were sitting together on the front veranda of Thornton. Phil, who had only his love for Hester and their future in mind, was exasperated to find himself caught up in such an insane discussion. Still, he had to endure it, to get it over with so he could ponder his own affairs.

"What's wrong with a double wedding?" George demanded after Phil had curtly refused.

"One obvious thing, which you well know. Leloi and I are 'engaged' just for the look of things. It's not a bona fide engagement. Even the families know that."

"I ask you again. What's wrong with Leloi?"

"Nothing. She's a fine girl, a real lady."

"Isn't she pretty enough for you?"

"Far prettier than I deserve," said Phil, thinking of how he had seduced Hester, who was beautiful.

"Work on her, then. Court her. She'll not be able to resist. Eve'll work on her, too."

"I can't, George," Phil said, holding onto his temper.

"What's bothering you so much? Don't want to be my neighbor? Because of the fights we've had?"

"Those were only boy stuff. No."

"What, then?"

"Love!" Phil replied, letting his anger through. "Leloi and I aren't in love and never will be!" He was suddenly angry at being pressed to marry Leloi Roper, to have a double wedding, to live on a plantation that belonged to his wife, not to him.

But George wouldn't let go of the subject. "Love!" he scoffed. "You don't even know what love is! I'll wager you've never kissed a girl, never gone to one of those houses in New Orleans, even! You've got a long way before you find out about love!"

"Oh, no, I haven't!" cried Phil, goaded beyond all caution. "I know about love, real love, and I've found the girl I'm going to marry! It's she or no other!"

"Is that right?" taunted George. "And just who is this make-believe girl?"

Phil was reckless beyond all caring. "Hester!" he cried. "I'm going to marry Hester, and all hell can't stop me!"

George's mouth fell open. He glared at Phil. "Nigger Hester—the wench?" he grated.

"She's as white as you are!"

"You want to marry Nigger Hester!" yipped George. "Wait until Uncle Thorne hears this!"

Chapter Ten

Phil knew he had to talk to his uncle before George did and made his accusations and ugly implications. When he sought his uncle, he was told that the master had ridden, carefully, into the fields with Mr. Murray.

Immediately he rushed to the stable and ordered a horse saddled. The boy was so slow that Phil waved him aside and, in a frenzy of haste, finished the task himself.

He rode across the fields at a gallop, the growing crop and the toiling slaves a blur. He had no idea what he was going to say to his uncle, what words would come, but he had to sway and convince him. It was impossible, but it was a thing he must do because Thorne Wabash owned Hester.

He met his uncle, the overseer, and George, who had managed to get there first after all, riding back toward the plantation house. George had a triumphant expression on his face. His uncle and the overseer looked grim. A pang of near despair went through Phil that his cousin had gotten to his step-grandfather first.

"Go on ahead," Thorne ordered Murray. "Get along with it!"

Then, as the overseer put the whip to his horse and galloped away, the older man turned a cold-blooded look of fury on Phil. "Not a word out of you!" he grated. "I'll hear no 'explanation,' no argument!"

"Uncle Thorne, you must! I realize it's unusual, unheard of, but I love—"

"Quiet," ordered Thorne viciously. "Understand. I'm angry, but I don't blame you! It's the wench."

"Hester isn't to blame! I'm the one who—"

"Quiet, I said! I'll listen to none of your talk, not a word! I'll do what I should have done fourteen years ago, and that'll be the end of it!"

Though Phil persisted, Thorne only grew angrier. Phil gave up finally, knowing the only course that lay open to him.

He would abduct Hester. They would run away together.

Even as he came to this conclusion, moments before he got back to the house, hours before he would be able to steal through the darkness to Hester's cabin, Boss Murray had his iron hand around Hester's arm and was marching her out of the field, away from her mother and the others.

When Lela Belle came stumbling after them, crying out, asking what was wrong, he slapped her so furiously she staggered backward and sat, hard, among the cotton plants. "Whut she do, Mr. Murray?" Hester heard her mother cry as she herself was yanked, stumbling, along. "Whut my baby do?" And when he didn't answer, she came running again. He hit her again and forced Hester into a trot and then a run.

Hester's heart pumped with fear at being torn from her mother and rushed away. Somehow the master must have found out about Phil and her. She was afraid for Phil. What would Master Thorne do to him? Would he put a young white master to the lash? Would he send him away, never to return? Was she not to see Phil again, ever?

They passed the blacksmith shop, and now it was her father who tried to question Boss Murray. What had his little girl done, where was she being taken? Boss Murray grinned, spat, but did not reply. He pushed Hester along, and she could only cry out, the words trailing behind her, "Pappy—oh, Pappy!"

And then she was in the jail again, the boarded-up, locked jail. Without a candle. She sat on the bunk and wept for Phil and for her mother and father. What trouble had she brought on them by loving Phil? Why was it so wrong to love him?

As she sat weeping in the jail, Boss Murray was riding at top speed for Warrenton, seeking out two brothers, itinerant traders, said presently to be in the town, finding them, telling what he had been ordered to tell. Before he left, a deal had been made.

Hester didn't sleep all night. She could hear the pacing of a guard outside and knew it was one of the trusties. Thorne was making sure that she couldn't run and that Phil couldn't get to her.

She twisted and turned on the bunk and wept. She knew that the master would sell her now. She felt a vast emptiness, an aching sense that she was nobody bound for nowhere.

After countless hours, she heard the clank of chains and the murmur of voices. Instantly alert, she stood and waited.

The key turned in the lock. Boss Murray, carrying a lantern, came in. Behind him followed Thorne, George, and two square-built, roughly dressed white men. They had tobacco juice at the corners of their mouths. Their skin was sun darkened to the point where they were browner than many of the slaves at Thornton.

"This is the wench, gentlemen," Thorne said to the men. "The one who wants to marry an innocent white boy!"

"And he doesn't know what's happening now!" sneered George.

They looked at her. One of them had an eye that stayed at the corner of its socket. Hester was terrified.

Boss Murray raised the lantern so that it shone on Hester. At the master's order, he grabbed the shift and pulled it up to her chin, revealing her naked body. She fell back a step, and he jerked her back, the shift cutting into the nape of her neck.

"You see, gentlemen," Thorne said, "she is as described. White as alabaster. The only white wench to be found in these parts."

"Jest look at that, Lee!" rumbled one of the men.

"I got eyes, Bawley," growled the other one. He grabbed one of Hester's breasts in one rough-skinned hand and squeezed. He ran his palm along her buttocks, felt her legs, and then rammed a finger up her woman part. Hester winced, humiliated and frightened.

"She ain't no virgin," the first man said.

"Hell, man," Boss Murray put in, "she ain't been busted but once. She's a prize."

"That will be enough, Mr. Murray," Thorne said. "Drop her shift. Well, gentlemen, is it a deal?"

Boss Murray let the shift drop at last. Hester was

shaking so she could hardly stand. But she had to stand, and she forced herself to keep her chin lifted.

"Since she ain't a virgin, three thousand's high."

"You knew in advance she wasn't a virgin," Thorne said quietly. "You'll have no trouble getting five thousand for her, not with her looks."

The traders mumbled together. "Deal," said the one called Lee. "Bring 'er along outside. We got twenty to twenty-five miles to cover today with them lazy critters, an' stop to buy others slaves to fill out our coffle while we're doin' it."

Hester, panic-stricken, broke for the door. One of them, George, she thought, shot out his foot, catching her below the knee, and she fell, her face hitting the boards. Hands wrenched her up, slapped her, first on one cheek, then on the other.

"Don't mark 'er up, Bawley," warned Lee. "She's our prize. Here, Mr. Thornton, is yer three thousand."

"Please, Master Thorne!" Hester cried as she saw him accept the money. "Don't sell me away! I won't do wrong! I'll work hard—keep away from Master Phil—just let me stay!"

The master didn't reply. He just put his money into his pocket and stood there, cold and unrelenting.

She tried again for the door. This time the blow came between her shoulders, and she staggered, barely maintaining her footing. She thought of Phil, wildly, that he knew nothing of this, that it was being done while he slept.

"She's got to be tamed," said one of the traders.

"Trip tames 'em," said the other one. "Let's put 'er in the middle."

"Quietly, please," Master Thorne said. "I don't want my darkies roused."

"You keep yer mouth shut, wench, or I'll clout you in it," warned the man named Bawley. "Understand?"

Wordless, she nodded. Then, with a trader gripping each of her arms, she was shoved and half-lifted through the door, down the step, and across to a stand of trees. Here, by the lantern light, she made out a line of Negroes, both men and women, chained together and crouched in silent, spiritless waiting.

Bawley held her while Lee stooped at the center of that captive line. "Stick 'er in here," he said. "Put 'er in the middle where she can't do no mischief. She rounds us out to a even dozen."

Bawley ordered her to kneel on the ground. With five men ready to grab her, if she tried again to escape, she knew she could not get away—not now. So, kneeling on the ground as ordered, she watched sullenly while a chain was looped around her right wrist. She noticed it connected with the chain around the left wrist of the woman beside her. Then her left wrist was chained to the wrist of a tall, thin black man.

"They's play enough in that chain that you can git yer hands to yer mouth," Bawley told her. "And so's you kin tote this—hold yer hands out."

She did so, and he handed her a leg iron. It was heavy and had a length of chain that the trader fastened onto her wrist chain. "Tote it days, wear it nights," he said.

Lee and Bawley moved along the coffle, testing chains. Then they ordered the slaves to stand. Holding the leg iron in both hands, Hester staggered getting up, but the skinny man fastened to her steadied her. She whispered her thanks, and he warned her not to talk.

Lee went to the head of the coffle, his whip ready, and Bawley took up position near Hester, warning her that the first wrong move would bring the whip across her shoulders. At the end of the line followed a cart, driven by a white man called Zeke.

"Whip marks heal," Bawley said, still on the subject of Hester's punishment, "so don't think you kin do what you want because you don't look black. Ye've got pure nigger blood and a nigger heart, and that makes you scum like the rest of these niggers."

The slaves moved at a brisk pace, chains jangling. Hester was barefoot, and she tried to say goodbye to Thornton with the soles of her feet. She memorized the feel of the soil, the brush of grass, and sought for but did not find the silken touch of flowers. She kept doing that so she wouldn't weep aloud for her parents or for Phil.

By noon they were on the hard and beaten road that hurt her feet because of the unexpected sharp stones. She looked along the line of the coffle as best she could, and noticed that all the slaves were barefoot.

All that day they walked along the road. Under the hot and beating sun they walked, always at a brisk pace, whips cracking when any lagged. Twice they stopped at farms, and at each the Baker brothers bought a slave. One big man with a scar on his face and one plump woman with an ugly mouth. There were now fourteen in the coffle. At each farm they were allowed a drink of water but no food.

Hester was so tired she could hardly move, but she had to move, and briskly. She was so hungry it felt like her stomach was stuck together. She hadn't eaten since breakfast the day before.

At dusk the traders took the coffle off the road and into the trees. They ordered the slaves to sit, then locked the leg irons on them. Hester, whose feet were bleeding, felt the drag of iron on her aching ankle and thought it would be a relief to scream. But she didn't even moan. Only a sigh passed her lips.

The woman on her right looked at her kindly. She was about thirty, rather scrawny. She had a plain face but kind eyes. "We kin whispah some now, honey," she whispered. "It's allowed, jus' a bit. Youah feet'll toughen."

"I thought they were already tough from the fields and going barefoot," Hester whispered.

"De fiel's ain't de road. I'se Bitha. Who you, honey, an' whut you doin' in dis coffle? You a white girl!"

"I'm Hester, and I'm only a wench. My pappy and mammy are blacker than anyone in this whole coffle."

Bitha stared. She leaned across Hester to the tall, thin man and whispered the information. She introduced him. "Dis is Ratio. He a good walkah, got callous on he feet, like me. Like you git soon. He got white blood, you kin see it."

Hester looked at Ratio. He appeared to be half white.

"Dey feed us now, Hestah," he whispered. "Dey feed us good, breakfus' an' suppah. Dey keep us healthy 'cause we got to walk so far. Dat's whut de cart wif dat othah white man is fo'. It ouah meals."

Soon the white men passed along the coffle, which fell quiet, and passed out the food. There was cornpone and fatback and mustard greens. It was all cold but had been well cooked and seasoned.

Hester ate hungrily. When she had eaten everything

given her, she was almost satisfied. There would be more in the morning, then again tomorrow night. She wouldn't get so hungry again, and for that she was grateful.

Now they were ordered to sleep. They lay flat on their backs, chains clanking as they moved into position. They were on grass, but the ground was hard and lumpy under Hester's aching body, and she wished she could turn over. She whispered to Bitha, asking how that could be done, chained this way.

"Stay still 'long as you kin, Hestah chile," whispered Bitha. "Dat's how we do. When we can't stand it no moah, de one in mis'ry whispahs to de one nex' to 'em —you whispah to me or Ratio, whichevah side you want to lay on, an' dat one whispah to de nex' an' on down de line, den evahbody turn ovah at de same time."

"Even if they don't want to?" whispered Hester.

"Dey want to. We all git tiahed bein' one way. When we turn, de white man whut's time it be to keep watch, walk 'long to make suah we ain't tryin' to run. But dey let us turn fo' de same reason dey let us eat an' drink, so's we keep well an' healthy. Ratio, now, dey give ext'ry cornpone 'cause he skinny an' dey want him not to git worse."

Hester whispered her thanks and lay quietly. It would take a good deal of turning and twisting to get comfortable on the ground, and it was out of the question to make the whole coffle turn and twist with her. Besides, the traders would never permit that—they would put their whips to use.

Before she knew it, exhausted and sore, she slept.

Days crawled past. Miles crept behind them. The small toe on each of Hester's feet split, bled, festered, then began to heal. They went south, toward a place Hester had never heard of, called Natchez. The traders bought more slaves. Now the coffle had twenty chained beings walking their twenty miles a day, carrying their leg irons, eating what they were given, whispering the bit they were allowed to the one on either side, and this only when they bedded for the night, sleeping wherever they were told.

They traversed rutted country roads. They trudged past great plantation houses set far back, slave cabins, fields being cultivated, crops being harvested, towns at a distance. There was no end to it.

The sun grew fiercer, and the heat spread everywhere, dulling the air, eventually making it heavy and sickening from moisture. Even the nights were hot. Near morning, rain would fall, cooling them, but the sun, when it rose, brought another smothering day.

Hester tried to count the days, but she couldn't count very far, and she was so tired she couldn't remember, finally, whether it was twenty days they had been on the awful journey, or more or less. The heat grew hourly. They were not allowed to really bathe when they came to a stream, only to kneel in the water, chained, and drink and throw water over themselves.

Hester was now so bone-tired that she seldom thought consciously of Thornton, though the ache for her parents and for Phil was as much a part of her as the calloused feet on which she dragged her weary way.

At Natchez, deciding they would get a higher price for their wares in New Orleans, especially the white-skinned wench, the traders shipped their coffle like cattle. Thus it was that, on the keelboat, still chained and always in the leg irons now, Hester had her first chance to rest.

With rest came the return of her ability to think, to recognize fact. She knew that the traders meant to sell her for five thousand dollars and that it was a great deal of money. Bitha told her she had heard them discuss that figure.

"It dat you so purty, Hestah, chile," she whispered. "You whut dem rich white gent'mens pay anythin' in de world to git. Dat really why de tradahs not sell us in Natchez. Dey know dey git moah fo' you in New Orleans, an' mebbe fo' de res' of us, too."

By the time Bitha stopped whispering, Hester understood, with utter heartbreak, that Phil's plan to marry her was indeed a hopeless dream. She was bound for the slave block.

Chapter Eleven

The morning after Hester had been sold, George gloatingly told Phil that Hester had been sold downriver. Immediately Phil went to his father, who, with his mother, was still at Thornton. He confessed his love for Hester and asked that Neal Bennett help him find her.

"And buy her for you?" asked his father, shocked.

"That's right, sir. I'll work. I'll repay you."

"You know how your mother and I feel about bed wenches. How can you ask such a thing?"

"I don't want her for a bed wench, sir. I want to free her and take her someplace where we can be married. To another country, even."

Neal Bennett visibly held his breath. At last he whispered, "I simply cannot believe it!"

"There's more you must believe, sir," Phil said grimly. "I've a plan that's been in the making for years. You'll not like it any more than you like my love for Hester."

"Out with it!" his father said abruptly.

Staring his father in the eye, his own eyes unflinching and ungiving, Phil outlined his plan to become a showboat actor, to buy a farm, and to build the farm into a plantation. "Somewhere, sir," he finished, "either in this country with Hester as my wife, or in some other. But with Hester, and no other."

"You are to study law, my boy. Nothing else!"

"I am no longer a boy. I am a man. With my life carefully laid out."

"You'll study law. You'll come into my firm. You'll do as a proper son, an only son, does—follow in his father's profession."

"Sorry, sir," Phil returned. "In my case it isn't possible. I regret disappointing you, but I must live my life in my own way."

"Your mother—"

"No such plea can move me, sir."

"Have you stopped to think what even knowing this wild notion will do to her?"

Later, when she was told, the news sent Wanda Bennett into such wracking tears that she swooned. When father and son had brought her out of it, she laid trembling hands on her only son and pleaded, "Phil—Phil, darling! I know you think you love the wench! I'm sure she is, as you say, a beautiful, bright child! But a child, too young for—even if—and you're only—"

"I'm eighteen. I know my mind."

"Not when you want to marry a wench, you don't know your mind!" Neal Bennett exclaimed, glaring at his son. "We're leaving at once. There's a boat due for New Orleans at noon, and we're going to be on it, all three of us."

Phil accepted the decree for reasons of his own. Hester was gone from Thornton, had been sent, George gloated, downriver. That meant she would be sold at the marketplace either in Natchez or New Orleans. It was possible that she might be sold at some point between, but with her skin so white, her beauty so pure, she would bring a higher price in a city.

Consequently, angry, worried, and silent, Phil boarded *The New Orleans Queen* with his parents without undue protest. He stayed apart from them and from all passengers as the steamboat moved downriver, its first stop, for two hours of loading and unloading, to be the city of Natchez.

The instant the gangplank was lowered, he was down it and away from his watchful parents. He heard them call out as he ran, but he only went faster.

He might be in time. If Hester had been brought to Natchez, her boat would have arrived only a day earlier, and she would be in the slave pens. How he would manage to buy her, he had no idea, for he had less than fifty dollars in his pocket. But he would think of something.

He reached the slave market. It was virtually deserted. No sale was in progress, nor were preparations being made for one. He sought out the manager of the stockade, who had a bare little office a short distance from the sales block.

He was a broad, wide-cheeked man with unruly hair and squinting eyes. His chair was tilted back, his great boots on the table that served as a desk.

"What kin I do fer you?" he asked in a gruff tone, bringing his feet to the floor, the chair legs making a sharp sound as they, too, met the boards.

"It's a wench you may have in the stockade!" Phil panted. "I need to know if she's there!"

"Place is full of wenches—and bucks. How'm I to tell one from t'other?"

"This wench is different. You'd remember. If you see them all."

"I see 'em. Examine 'em before they go into the stockade. What's so diff'rent 'bout this wench?"

"She's fourteen years old, sir—"

"Lots of them that age—and younger—and older."

"If you'll let me finish, sir! Her skin—she doesn't look like a wench. She has skin whiter than most white girls, and her hair—it's only curly, not wiry, and a deep red color!"

The man whistled and shook his head. "You bet I'd remember her!" he exclaimed.

"And she's pretty—she's beautiful!"

"Why you so excited? Want to buy her?"

Phil, painfully aware of his lack of funds, nodded. He couldn't buy her, of course. He would have to resort to his original plan of somehow abducting her.

"Ain't that a shame?" drawled the manager, his eyes mocking. "There ain't no such wench in this stockade. Only wish there was. She'd bring real money, and when that happens, I get a commission from the auctioneer—fer takin' extry care of extry fine wenches."

"You're certain, sir? If you'd let me into the stockade, just let me look—"

The man lumbered to his feet. "You'd best git along, young sir," he said. "There ain't no such white-skinned wench here. I'd tell you if there was; I'd spread the word. We'd have an auction to remember!"

Convinced that the man was telling the truth, Phil managed to thank him and departed. He ran all the way back to *The New Orleans Queen,* anxious now not to be left behind. He had to reach New Orleans quickly and go to the stockade there.

He was only vaguely aware of his parents or what they said as, he reached the deck. The steamboat bell rang; the boat began to move. Phil stood clutching the rail so hard his knuckles were white, willing the steamboat to go faster.

They had no sooner docked in New Orleans than he was off and away, taking only an instant to excuse himself to his parents. He was aware of their worn faces, of their feelings of disappointment and worry, but Hester and what happened to her was so much more important that he forgot them as he raced toward the market.

Here he had no better success than he had had in Natchez. They did let him into the stockade and even permitted him to speak to the slaves chained to posts. Hester wasn't here, nor had any of the Negroes seen or heard of her.

He attended the next auction. He was almost glad when Hester didn't appear on the block, for he would not have been able to bid on her if she did.

Again he asked his father for a loan and again was turned down. Politely, he listened to the ensuing lecture, and the next day went to the auction again. Daily he went. Hester was never brought out.

He decided, eventually, that she had been taken to Natchez after he had left that city. Using his spending money, which his father continued to furnish, he bought an upriver ticket and returned to Natchez.

He stayed a week, until his money ran out, then returned home. He cursed himself for not having forced George to tell him in what manner Hester had been taken away from Thornton, whether by coffle or boat. Miserable, he tried to measure time and miles, to figure out whether she had been taken to Natchez or New Orleans at all.

At last, failing to uncover the least trace of her, he did the only thing he could do. He got a job playing the juvenile lead on a shabby little showboat called *The Dixie*.

Working, traveling the rivers, he would save his money. He would look for Hester every inch of the way. And he would find her—somehow, he would.

Part Two

✖

The Slave Block

Chapter Twelve

The stockade was a sweltering hell filled with sweating, moaning slaves chained to posts that lined not only the outer walls but the open area that they enclosed. Four slaves were chained to each center post, two to each wall post. The walls were high, with open slits near the top to admit air. The floor was packed dirt. Four armed guards stood at the closed, barred door, alert, ready to shoot.

Hester had never seen so many people in one spot. When they sat with their legs stretched out, very little of the dirt floor was visible. When they lay down, their bodies were intertwined, and the stench of their sweat mounted and filled the stockade.

Hester suffered an inner tremor that wouldn't let up. The auction was tomorrow morning; her coffle had been brought into the stockade late this afternoon. They had been fed and watered, and now it was night, but the place was lit by lanterns so the guards could see.

Hester's one comfort was that she and Bitha were padlocked to the same post by the ankles, arms blessedly free. Bitha put both arms around her. "Don' be so skeered, baby," she whispered. "Lay down in my arms—dat's it. Git to sleep. Come day, things do git brightah."

"What's the slave block like?" Hester's voice quavered.

"It jus' a platform made out of wood, chile. It only a place fo' us to stand so de white gentlemen kin see whut we look like."

Hester let out a sob. Bitha's arms tightened, and Hester forced back the next sob. She mustn't be a bother; Bitha had troubles of her own.

"Jus' do whut dey say do," Bitha whispered. "Be quiet

on de block an' quiet when de new mastah buy you. Do whut he say. Yo' so purty no mastah goin' pay a big price, den treat you mean and mark you wif de whip." She drew Hester closer still. "Cry now, baby, cry on Bitha. Den tomorrow it all out an' you kin stand whut you got to stand. It all right, cry fo' bof of us."

Silently, Hester let the tears flow. She pressed her face against Bitha's neck and wept until she tasted her own tears on Bitha's skin. Bitha patted and patted. Her arms were so tender. Next to Mammy's arms, to Pappy's, to Phil's, she thought, they were that tender. Drained, she gave a great sigh and fell into restless sleep.

In the morning, they were fed and given water again. Bitha smiled at Hester, and Hester managed to return the smile. Now that day had come, things weren't really any better. They were worse, for she was going to the block and she was stiff with terror. But she wouldn't let Bitha know. Bitha had helped her last night; now she was on her own.

The guards opened the double doors, and daylight flooded in. "On yer feet!" bellowed the head guard.

There was a stir and wave of motion, the clank of chains, and every black was standing. Silent. The stench of their sweat rose, blotting out the morning freshness that came through the doors.

There was a swivel of heads toward the open doors. Hester looked, too. A short, fat man in light gray trousers and white shirt waddled in and stopped, his glance sweeping every inch of the stockade. He was red faced and sweating and mostly bald, his remaining brownish hair plastered with sweat. His belly hung over the top of his trousers.

"You niggers!" he bellowed in a fat, deep voice. "I'm Mr. Fisk. I'm the auctioneer, and I got to sell off every one of yer worthless black hides today! The buyers are gatherin', and some'll come in here and examine what we got to offer."

His eyes lit on Hester, and he walked to her, then around her, a smirk on his face. "Yer the one them Bakers was braggin' about!" he grunted. "Behave yerself when you git on the block, hear?"

Wide-eyed, Hester swallowed and nodded.

Fisk turned away and raised his voice. "First nigger

gives trouble gits five lashes on the spot, then gits sold to whoever'll have him! Understand that! Eh?" He glared about.

Hester nodded again. She saw a few more nods, but not one slave dared to answer Mr. Fisk in words. Bitha's hand stole to hers and pressed, and Hester pressed in return. Bitha didn't risk a whisper, just the one slow, warm squeeze of her hand.

Now buyers came into the stockade. They wandered from slave to slave, ordering them to turn, feeling their muscles, looking into their mouths. Five or six men looked Hester over. When the first one, a slit-eyed, tall man, stopped in front of her, she was so frightened she could hardly breathe.

"How old are you?" he demanded.

"F-fourteen, master, sir," she mumbled.

"What's that? Speak out!"

She repeated the words.

"Hmm," he grunted. He flipped up her shift, whistled low, then pinched a breast. He dropped the shift.

"You had any suckers?"

She shook her head. "No, master, sir," she said, making her voice as steady as she could.

He raised her shift again and looked at her back. This time he pinched one of her buttocks so hard she felt it to the bone.

"Ever been put to the lash?"

"No, master, sir."

"Hmm. Not a troublemaker, eh?"

"No, master, sir." She would not mention the escape attempt.

"Open your mouth," he ordered. "Wide."

She did, and he poked at her teeth.

"Shut it now. You ever get sick?"

"No, master, sir. I'm healthy."

"You speak well for a darky."

As he walked around her, she remained silent, miserable, more scared than ever. Glancing at some of the other slaves, she saw that they were miserable, too, their faces drawn and worried. A pang of longing went through her for her parents. For Phil.

The slit-eyed man pinched her other breast so it felt like it was bleeding, then finally wandered off to look over another, very black, girl. Hester willed it that he had decided not to buy her. Any master, she thought, any master but him!

She thought the same about all the men who looked her over. She stood rigid while they lifted her shift, while they squeezed and pinched, while they felt her legs and prodded her teeth. Although frightened, she was also angry at the indignity she was forced to suffer.

Even as the buyers finished in the stockade, the auction began. Slaves were led out by their chains, one or two at a time. Mr. Fisk could be heard above the noise of the crowd of bidders.

A guard came for Hester, unchained her, and yanked her toward the doorway. She looked frantically at Bitha, who made a kissing motion with her lips, and that was their farewell.

Outside, on a square platform in the middle of an open space, were Mr. Fisk and a male slave Hester hadn't seen before, who was being bid on. All the area was filled with white gentlemen, some watching, nodding a bid now and then, others milling about. They were all hot and sweating. They made jokes and called out to each other, but a large number kept their attention on the auctioneer, and Hester knew these were the serious buyers. She tried to look at their faces, but they blurred. Fear went through her. Which one would buy her?

Mr. Fisk was singing out the bids like music, the words running into each other smoothly, and it was both a fearsome and exciting song. "Thousand—thousand and five hundred—six, who'll give me six—six—six—give six —seven—seven—thank you, sir—eight—who'll give me eight—eight—eight—all right, gentlemen, *sold!* Sold to Mr. Seth Wilson for one thousand seven hundred dollars!"

As the man was claimed by his new master and taken to one side, Hester felt the guard unlock the chain from her ankle, then grip her arm. He shoved her up some steps and onto the block. Terrified, she stood rigid. She needed to swallow but could not.

"Here, gentlemen," Mr. Fisk said in his carrying tone, "is the prize of the year! Offered to you now, before you git hot and tired! You've all heard about her, some of you seen her in the stockade, and now here she is fer all to see—the white-nigger wench! The beauty and pick of every slave ever born!"

Looking at all the men staring at her, Hester had a thought that filled her with panic. All these men, all of them, were her masters.

"One thousand!" shouted a voice.

"Not yet, gentlemen, not yet! You got to really see this one! Look at her, study her, then make yer bid!"

Hester felt, rather than saw him bend, and as he came up, he yanked her shift away, over her head, then flung it aside, and she stood naked on the block. A moan ran through the crowd.

"Turn, wench," ordered Mr. Fisk. "Turn as slow as you can so's every man here kin see you from every angle."

Terror stricken, embarrassed beyond belief, she drove herself to move with infinite slowness. Her mind was numb, even her feelings were numb. She hadn't known that pure fear could do that.

"Fourteen years old, gentlemen!" cried the auctioneer. "In the first fresh bud of womanhood! Skin white as alabaster! Hair such as you've never saw—no nigger wool here! Nothing but beauty—beautiful face—perfect tits— perfect butt—perfect legs! You kin see fer yourselves, gentlemen, that there's many years of enjoyment here fer the lucky highest bidder!"

A cheer went up, and crude remarks were shouted. Hester didn't hear the words, but the tone went through her like a knife. She was covered with goose bumps and began to tremble.

"She a virgin?" a voice yelled.

"I ain't found out yet, but I will now!" shouted Mr. Fisk. "Spread your legs, wench!"

Still trembling, Hester did as he said. The auctioneer rammed a finger up her private part, then pulled it out. He wiped it on her breast, then gave the nipple a hard pinch.

"No virgin!" he shouted, "but she's tight as one! Better, being broke in to some extent. Won't be no yellin' and cryin' when a man pleasures hisself. What am I bid fer a starter for this little lovely?"

"Two thousand!"

"Don't forget she's no virgin!" shouted someone. "Two thousand, one!"

"Who cares about virgin?" boomed the auctioneer. "She's diff'rent—a white nigger! Alabaster! Three thousand—do I hear three—four—four. Do I hear five—five, do I hear five one—five one, five two—five two—do I hear five three—going once for five two, going twice —*sold,* for five thousand two hundred dollars!"

Les Crane, forty, here to buy an assistant seamstress for his cotton broker employer's wife, edged close to the block. He was manager of the brokerage and, being a good judge of blacks, did nearly all of Edward Dalton's slave buying.

This beauty was no seamstress, but she could fill a lack in Edward Dalton's life. Crane, aware that his employer had an octoroon mistress in a house on the Ramparts, was equally aware that he rarely got to her because of the close watch his frigid, jealous wife kept over him. With this new wench installed in the servants' quarters at Woodlawn, the New Orleans home, his employer would at least have the means of much needed relief at hand.

After paying the auctioneer in cash, he took Hester's arm, gave her the shift, waited until she got it on, then led her to the ground. She ventured a glance at him.

He looked kind, with dark, soft hair and a smiling face. A tinge of relief went through her.

"Come," he said, "I'll take you to your new master."

Her heart went numb again.

Chapter Thirteen

❖

The kind man who was not her master guided her to a carriage pulled by fine black horses and driven by a liveried slave. The kind man, who said he was Mr. Crane, helped her to the high seat beside the driver.

"This is Tench," he said. "Tench, this is Hester. She's to help Nell with the sewing. If she has any questions about the city or Woodlawn, answer them."

"Yas, suh, Mr. Crane. Tench will answah."

Mr. Crane got into the carriage, and Hester, on the high seat, braced herself and closed her eyes as the carriage turned. The height made her dizzy, but she managed not to sway or fall.

The carriage moved along, and she rode with her eyes still closed. This was the first time in her life she had been in a town or a city, and she was frightened. She asked no questions. She could tell when the carriage turned a corner, for she had to catch her balance. There were sounds of horses' hoofs passing, the snap of a whip now and then, the command of the driver of some other carriage. Still she didn't open her eyes lest she lose her balance.

Once Tench said that over 160,000 people lived in New Orleans. She caught her breath. She hadn't known that such an overwhelming number of people even existed.

The carriage slowed, then stopped.

"Here we are," Mr. Crane said.

Hester opened her eyes. They were on a street lined with buildings. Many had signs on them. Though she couldn't read the signs, Hester knew they designated the type of business conducted in them, because Phil had

97

told her that once. She gazed about. Even from this spot, the city was so big its size was impossible to accept.

"What place is this?" she asked Tench when the carriage stopped.

Mr. Crane answered. "This brick building right here," he said, indicating the awesome, two-storied structure, "is the Dalton Brokerage Company, owned by your new master, Mr. Edward Dalton."

As he spoke, a slave boy came hurrying out the door.

"Run get the master," ordered Mr. Crane. "Make it fast."

The boy grinned, mumbled, and left.

Hester sat scarcely breathing, staring with unseeing eyes at all the business establishments as she waited for her new master. Would he be mean—an ogre? Or would he be kind, like Mr. Crane? Or would he be like Boss Murray? She shivered.

Soon a tall, handsome man in his mid-thirties came out of the brokerage. He wore tan trousers and a brown coat.

Hester looked sideways at him, careful not to meet his eyes. His hair was auburn, like hers, only redder. His skin was very white, with a sprinkle of freckles on his nose. His mouth was firm and unsmiling, but not mean.

He stood on the sidewalk and looked her over. "This is the buy you made for me, Les?" he asked. His voice was firm and, though not saturated with kindness, sounded friendly when he spoke her name.

"That's right, Edward."

"She—" The new master gestured.

"She's a white nigger. Fourteen years old. I doubt she can sew. But she can learn. I blew the whole five thousand on her, the money you gave me for a sewing wench and a buck for investment, plus two hundred more. I figure"—he gave the master a keen glance—"if you don't want to keep her, you can have Nell smooth off the rough edges, dress her up, and get six thousand. We both know men who would jump at the chance. A wench with that skin and hair, those looks!"

Now it was the master who gave his manager a keen glance. "You did the right thing, Les," he said. "Take her to Nell."

This time, as the carriage rolled, Hester kept her eyes open, although she didn't really see what they passed, for she was too intent on staying erect to look at houses, though she noticed lacy ironwork, high walls, greenery, and colorful blossoms.

The new master was going to keep her. Would he do the awful thing to her that Boss Murray had done? That Master George had tried to do?

The carriage turned through wide, lacy iron gates into a flagstoned courtyard lined with magnolia trees. Hester gazed at the familiar gray trunks, the big, dark-green, shiny leaves, at the great, creamy blossoms that Phil had said measured eight to ten inches across. She breathed in the fragrance, the good, drugging sweetness. Looking up, she wondered if these were sixty feet tall, like Phil said they often grew.

Mister Crane got out of the carriage and ordered her off the high seat. She scrambled down as fast as she could; it was with relief that she felt the solid flagstones under her feet.

"Follow me," Mr. Crane said. "I'll take you to the Quarters."

The Quarters were in a separate, long, low building at the back of the estate. He took her almost to the end of this building, looked in at the open door, and spoke. "Nell. The master has bought you a helper. She's fresh from the slave block."

A lean, tan-skinned woman of fifty appeared. She wore a starched blue dress and matching tignon and had a kind face. On first seeing Hester, she looked astonished, then broke into a friendly smile. "Help I can use, Mr. Crane," she said, her voice soft. "Step up, child, so I can see you."

Hester almost smiled in return. But she was still too frightened, too awed.

"I'm Hester," she said timidly. "I can sew a little. My mammy taught me what she knows."

"I'm going now," Mr. Crane said. "I'll leave word for the mistress that the new wench is here."

"Yes, suh," murmured Nell. "Thank you, suh."

She drew Hester inside. The room was very clean, furnished with a cot, a dresser, two chairs, a wash shelf, a long looking glass, and a big table. A half-made garment was draped on one chair and a length of yellow material was laying on the table, along with scissors and a pin cushion.

Nell looked at Hester closely. Hester felt hotness in her cheeks and knew they were red. She firmed her chin. She had to get used to being stared at.

"I sewed this shift," she volunteered, touching it. "It's dirty from the trip, but the stitches show."

Nell examined it carefully. "The stitches are perfect," she decided. "You know how to use a needle. Next, you got to learn to cut a dress and put it togethah and fit it. There's lots of dresses and lingerie and shirts to be made heah. The mistress needs new dresses all the time, and so do the little missies, two of them. And there's mendin', too. You'll have to learn that. How to darn."

Hester nodded. A yearning for her own family, for Phil, surged through her. She wished she could make clothes for them, not fine dresses for her new, unknown mistress.

Nell filled the wash basin with water. "You got to get clean," she urged. "The mistress may come down to take a look, and if she was to see you. . . . Take off that shift and soap youahself. I won't look. I'll be gettin' out an undahshift for you and a pink dress the mistress gave me and then it shrunk. It shouldn't be much too big for you."

Beginning with her hair, Hester washed thoroughly. She poured panful after panful of water into the slops, offering to fetch fresh water to refill the bucket and pitcher if Nell would show her where to get it.

"Latah," said Nell, thrusting garments at her. "Dress now. Use my comb. It's got wide-apart teeth, but it'll do. No telling when the mistress'll come. I got to warn you, Hester. She don't like a purty wench, so look as plain as you can." She helped Hester into the pink dress and tied the belt to make it snug at the waist, then clicked her tongue softly. "You too purty with that pink against youah skin. Just keep youah place with the mistress. Say 'Yes'm,' to ev'rything."

"What else can I do to please her?" Hester asked anxiously.

"She won't fuss 'bout youah stitchin'. Ev'ry stitch is so tiny and even and exactly like the ones beside it. She's very particular 'bout that. And you have to fit ev'ry garment perfect. Above all, be polite to Mastah Edward, but not friendly polite. The mistress had one kitchen wench who only *smiled* at the mastah sold."

"I'll remember," Hester said solemnly.

"Follow me," Nell told her and went out the door. She led her into the room next to her own. It was a cubbyhole with one window, a cot, a chair, and a washstand. It was as clean as Nell's room.

"It's little, but it's private, with its own outside doah," Nell pointed out. "I s'pose the reason they didn't make a doah between this room and mine was they needed the space for furniture. Only they nevah put much in."

"It's fine," Hester said. "I'll keep it clean. Do you think that will please the mistress?"

"It's only what she demands. Keep to my room and this room and go no fa'thah in the big house than the kitchen. We all eat theah."

They went back into Nell's room, and Nell began to show Hester the dress she was working on. They had their backs to the door and were bent over the material on the table, when the strident voice brought them erect.

"Nell! Is this the way you receive the mistress?"

"Excuse us, Miss Mildred, please, ma'am," apologized Nell. "I was just showin' Hester how to cut—"

"Hester! That's a fancy name for a wench! Step out, away from the table, so I can see you!"

Tremulous, Hester obeyed. Her one glimpse of the mistress showed her to be a woman of thirty-five, fully her husband's age. She wasn't much over five feet and was on the verge of obesity, her body lumpy even in the artfully fashioned dress she wore.

Her hair was straggly, though she wore it in the latest fashion, in a knot behind and curls in front of her ears. Her eyes were faded blue, and her lips were full but not gentle.

When Hester stepped into the full light of the doorway, the mistress gasped. Her eyes pierced Hester. "You don't look like any wench!" she snapped. "Your skin is nearly white, and your hair has no kink, even wet!"

Hester inclined her head. "I suppose I'm a freak," she said. "Some call me that, Miss Mildred, ma'am. Because my mammy and pappy are black as night."

"My husband—did he bid for you?"

"No, Miss Mildred, ma'am. Mr. Crane came to the slave market. He bought me."

"Has the master seen you? Has he?"

"Yes, Miss Mildred, ma'am. For a moment only. Mr.

Crane took me in the carriage. On the high seat beside Tench."

"Keep out of my husband's sight! Completely!"

"Yes, Miss Mildred, ma'am."

"And stay away from the house slaves. Don't even speak to them when you eat. And go to no room but the kitchen unless I send for you! I'm giving orders that you're off limits to all the male slaves. Understand?"

"Yes, Miss Mildred, ma'am."

"I have my reasons! Is that clear?"

"Yes, Miss Mildred, ma'am."

"And they're sound reasons. A wench like you—you're born for trouble! Make none for me, or you'll pay dearly for it!"

Chapter Fourteen

✻

At supper time, Nell took Hester to the kitchen. Here, stiffly proper, she told the gathered servants Hester's name and status. They stared openly and nodded. Hester's cheeks burned. Next, Nell spoke the name of each servant to Hester, her proper tone a reminder that she, the new slave, was under orders to be friendly with none of them.

Hester murmured and nodded, memorizing names swiftly. There was Horace, the butler; Hannah, the cook; her helper, Lura; Docia, the bitter-faced personal maid to the mistress; Sukey, the upstairs maid; and Cass, the downstairs maid. There was also Tench, the driver, and Varon and Finch, who tended the grounds, and Flo, nurse to the children.

They all ate quietly, with a minimum of conversation, none of it directed to Hester, though a few of the servants, after the first amazed stare, looked at her kindly. She knew, since no word was addressed to her, that they had had their orders from the mistress. She resented this, and it also saddened her.

Back in Nell's room, the seamstress gave Hester a nightshift. "I got three," she said. "This is old, but it's mended right. You can wash it out days, wear it nights."

Hester took the garment. "Thank you, Nell," she said. "You don't think the mistress would mind?"

"She don't care what I do with my old clothes. I get plenty to make ovah from her. When she gets tired of something, she lets it hang in her armoire for a long time, then gives it to Docia or me. I cut them down and sew them. We both keep neat that way, and she don't fuss."

Hester suppressed a sigh.

"What is it, child?" asked Nell. "What wrong?"

"The mistress. She doesn't like me. She really did tell the servants not to talk to me, didn't she, Nell?"

The older woman nodded.

"But why? What did I do wrong?"

"Youah diff'rent and youah purty. Miss Mildred is a very jealous lady. She won't 'low no purty wenches near the mastah. You saw her personal maid, that Docia. She got a face like a horse and that tooth stickin' out."

Hester realized then that never, under any circumstances, must she be in the presence of the master. At least not when the mistress could be aware of it.

Later, alone in her cubbyhole, turning on the hard cot, she fretted. How could she avoid the master if he had bought her for a bed wench? What if he came to her now, tonight? She'd have to do what he wanted. He was the master; he had paid over five thousand dollars for her. Remembering Boss Murray and Master George and even Phil, remembering the rough hands on her at the slave market, she became convinced that the master would come into this room at any moment. And if he did, what would happen if the mistress caught them together?

She waited, staring through darkness toward the door, listening carefully. There was only the stir of the night breeze through magnolias, the cry of a night bird. But the master would slip quietly along; she wouldn't hear or know until that door opened and he came in.

But he did not come, and eventually she fell asleep. When she awakened the next morning, she felt relieved. At mid-morning, Docia appeared as Nell was showing Hester how to set a sleeve. Her voice was as harsh and bitter as her face.

"The mistress wants both of you in her rooms," she announced. "Bring the green dress and the yellow. Even if it's only basted." Not waiting for Nell's response, she went away.

The mistress's rooms were a bower of gold and blue; the sitting room was furnished with white-painted, graceful furniture covered in gold. The carpet was blue, the drapes at the long, jalousied windows a rich blue brocade with gold roses embossed on them. The bedchamber decor was the same, but with a wide bed and two great armoires.

"One for the mastah's clothes and one for the mistress's clothes," whispered Nell.

Both rooms were unoccupied. Neither the mistress nor her maid was visible. Nell cleared her throat discreetly.

The mistress, clad in a flowing blue silk negligee, appeared in an open doorway on the far side of the bedchamber. "Clean the bath, Docia," she ordered as she moved toward Nell and Hester. She gave Hester a cutting look, then said to Nell, whose arms were filled with the garments to be fitted, "What took you so long? Do you think you can make your mistress wait all day for a simple fitting?"

Though they had half-run to get here, Nell replied meekly. "We sorry you had to wait, Miss Mildred, ma'am. The dresses are only basted, so we took care to get them heah in good condition."

"So. Well, lay them out on the bed! I want to settle this white-skinned—what's your name, wench?"

"Hester, Miss Mildred, ma'am."

"You're not to wear that pink dress. Not another time."

"I won't, Miss Mildred, ma'am. I washed my shift this morning. When it's dry, I'll put it on."

"I won't have slave-block clothes at Woodlawn!"

"Miss Mildred, ma'am," ventured Nell, "theah's that green-sprigged dress you gave me. We could fix that."

The mistress's look pierced Hester, who flinched at the hatred in those pale eyes and stood very quiet.

"No. Color makes her flamboyant. She's not to have any dress I hand down to you. There's that brown cotton material in the storeroom we haven't known what to do with." Nell's eyes widened; she looked as if she were going to speak, but said nothing.

"Well, do you know the material?"

"Yes, Miss Mildred, ma'am. But you did say—" Nell hesitated, then plunged on, "that it was too drab for anyone at Woodlawn."

"No more. This—Hester—needs toning down. Make her two shifts, not dresses, of the brown. And two tignons. I want that hair covered at all times, understand?"

"Y-yes, Miss Mildred, ma'am."

"You understand, too, wench?"

"Y-yes, Miss Mildred, ma'am."

"Now. Studs. White men. Are you a virgin?"

"No, Miss Mildred, ma'am," Hester murmured.

"Speak up! Why aren't you a virgin?"

"I was raped, Miss Mildred, ma'am."

"Likely story! Who raped you?"

"A white man. The ovahseer."

"Who else?"

"Nobody else, Miss Mildred, ma'am. Just the one."

She would never tell of the sweet encounter with Phil, not if she died for it. Besides, he hadn't raped her. She had gone to him joyfully and would again if only it was possible.

"Take this robe off me, Hester!" snapped the mistress. "Help Nell put the green dress on me!"

"Yes, Miss Mildred, ma'am," Hester murmured and carefully put out her hands. The silk of the robe was the first silk she had ever touched, and even in her frightened state, she thought the feel of it was wonderful and laid it very carefully on the bed.

They worked at the fitting, which lasted an hour, the mistress displeased with this, angry at that, demanding that the waist be nipped in more when her own abundance of flesh prevented any such thing. Hester marveled at how Nell pretended to obey the order, and the mistress thought the waist had been made smaller when actually it was unchanged.

Hester was tired beyond description from rushing to carry out every order, from making certain she answered the mistress properly, trying to avoid provoking one of her hateful, cutting remarks. By the time she and Nell were permitted to take their sewing back to Nell's room, the mistress had half-convinced Hester that she was not the least bit pretty.

As for Mildred Dalton, when her husband came home for his noon meal and went into the bathroom to wash his hands, she was pacing the sitting room of their suite, waiting. She had not mentioned the new wench last night, nor had he. But now she was informed. And she was ready.

As he came into the room, he asked, "Shall we go down now?" Then he got a full look at her face and frowned slightly. "What's wrong now, Mildred?" he asked, and there was a weariness to his tone.

"That wench you bought, that Hester!"

"I told you several nights ago I was sending Les to the slave market, Mildred. To pick up a helper for Nell."

"I don't believe that's what she's for!"

"It's the God's truth."

"How much did you pay for that white wench?"

"She's Negro. Les paid five thousand two hundred."

"Five thousand dollars?" she shrieked. "For an apprentice seamstress?"

"When Les saw her, he realized what an exceptional buy she was and put aside the thought of a seamstress. Hester is an investment. I can sell her and show a sound profit."

"You don't mean to sell her, I know you don't!"

"I may well do so, Mildred."

"Then sell her now—tomorrow—today!"

"Not quite that soon, Mildred. I want her to be a fine seamstress first, and to mature a bit. By the time she's sixteen, or even fifteen, I should be able to realize six thousand dollars on her, even more."

"You'd sell a seamstress who was that fine? You'd rob me of her services, me, your wife? You know how I try and try to get that lazy Nell to make me the best-dressed lady in New Orleans! Then, if we get a really good seamstress, you mean to take her away from me!"

"We'll keep her, Mildred. If you want her."

Her eyes flashed. Her lips thinned to a line. "Now the truth begins to come out!" she cried. "You're keeping her for your bed wench, isn't that it? That's why Les bought her, and that's why you're keeping her!"

"No. No, Mildred." In his own mind he didn't intend to touch the girl, appealing though she was. In fact, he couldn't imagine doing it.

"How do I know what you'll do?" she accused. "She's an animal, they all are. And you—you're so bed-crazy, so anxious. If ever I catch you, that's your last breath!"

"You'll catch me doing nothing wrong, Mildred," he said quietly. "If you discharged your wifely duties, such a thought would never enter your mind. You haven't so much as let me kiss you in—"

"All you want from me," she screamed, "all you've ever wanted, was my dowry, a mistress to run your house, and a son to inherit your brokerage!"

"Companionship, too, Mildred. I want that."

"Don't tell me! Well, I've faced death twice for you! I've given you two beautiful daughters, and now you'll have to wait for your son! Wait until I can gather courage to face death again!"

"I know you had hard labors, Mildred. But the doctor says—"

"Fiddle on the doctor! What does he know? Did he ever bear a child? Did he ever suffer the agony, look death in the face? I'll be my own judge of when I'll do that again, not the doctor, and certainly not you!"

Edward shrugged his shoulders. "Shall we go down to our meal?" he asked again. "Francie and Anita will be wondering where we are."

They descended the stairway in silence, his hand under her elbow. The dining room, decorated in glowing wine and mahogany tones, was dominated by a huge, oblong table.

Francie, eight, and Anita, six, were standing behind their chairs. They looked almost like twins when they smiled.

"Mama! Papa!" they piped. "You're late!"

"That we are," Edward agreed. "And we ask your pardon. Horace," he continued, speaking to the butler, "you may seat the mistress and then the young missies."

They sat at table chatting, the little girls talking of their dolls and wreaths of flowers they were going to weave tomorrow for doll necklaces. Edward looked from one to the other, smiling and responding. Mildred, her face a bit less cold now, listened, too, but there was an underlying air of disapproval about her.

"I must bring up a serious topic," she said finally, glaring at Edward, who was laughing with the girls. "It's more important than dolls and necklaces. I want my daughters to have a tutor."

"A tutor!" Edward exclaimed. "They're ready for books, that I agree, but what's wrong with a good school —Miss Hathaway's, for instance? I thought you were favorably impressed with it."

"As schools go, it's the best, Edward. But I want a man's influence over them so they'll learn to be at ease with men, and all the teachers in the schools are women. They'll learn more from a tutor and learn it better. He'll have only the two of them claiming his attention, and they'll progress faster. Later, they can go to college."

"No tutor."

"Either they have a tutor, Edward Dalton," she hissed, disregarding the stricken look on the little girls' faces, "or I'll go home to Natchez, and you'll have nothing! Nothing at all—no family!"

The little girls began to cry and ran to Edward and clung, one on either side. They sobbed and begged for a tutor and pleaded not to be sent to Natchez and leave him. As he tried to soothe them, his mind was racing.

Mildred's parents were the wealthiest people in Natchez. They had never thought him good enough to be their only daughter's husband, and he knew they would delight in taking his family and keeping it. He would seldom, if ever, get to see his beloved children.

"Very well, Mildred," he said, coldly angry, "a tutor it is. But I select the man. You will agree to that?"

She considered. "Subject to my approval," she said.

"It will take time to find just the right man," he warned, "but you have my word I'll be as prompt as possible."

Relieved, he knew he would keep his beautiful little daughters until they married. And he would still have his other life, his haven of love besides. . . .

Chapter Fifteen

Ten years ago, faced with the opportunity of marrying Mildred Vannice for her two-hundred-thousand-dollar dowry, for her social standing and the prestige of her Natchez parents, Edward Dalton knew he could wed her but could never love her. Try as he would, he could find not one lovable quality.

She was twenty-five, his own age, and she was a fiercely moral woman, completely capable of managing a large establishment, of entertaining, of rearing a family. Unhandsome, she still managed to shine brilliantly and coldly in society. To give her just due, he was not her only suitor, though he was the youngest.

She considered her three older suitors, then looked long and hard at Edward, who was handsome, who did own a cotton brokerage, and who had the ability, given money, to expand the brokerage into a very lucrative concern. So she decided on him. Once decided, she recklessly promised him sons, and he arranged to marry her, assuring himself that a man had to look to his future.

Inwardly he was rebellious that love was missing from the upcoming union. He yearned for softness, tenderness, and devotion. Quite deliberately he decided that, to be a success, to carry his business to its heights, he must fill this need. And, the situation being what it was with Mildred, the love he found must be a true love and must remain in the background, permanent and secret.

There was but one way to accomplish this. Numerous white men in New Orleans kept quadroon mistresses, or placées, in little white houses down on the Ramparts, near the waterfront. These girls were the offspring of mulatto beauties who had enjoyed the lifelong devotion of

wealthy white protectors. They reared their daughters
carefully, trained them for love, and taught them to serve
a man and to make him happy in bed.

Before a man could win one of these placées, he had
to enter into an agreement with her mother by which he
undertook to set the girl up in her own house. He must
support her, make her independent for life, and free any
children born to them. In return, he got the love of the
girl, her devotion, and complete fidelity. Edward determined to make this type of arrangement for himself.

Periodically, the mothers presented their daughters at a
ball given at the Orleans Ballroom. There young white
gentlemen came, finely dressed, either to seek placées
or just to enjoy the sight of so many exquisite beauties
in one place.

Edward went to the ball alone. As he entered, the
place was alive with light, soft laughter, and throbbing
music. The bottom floor was divided into reception and
card rooms. In the privacy of these rooms, a gentleman
discussed the girl of his choice with her mother, came to a
financial agreement, and closed the transaction.

A wide stairway led to the ballroom. The ballroom, he
discovered, was long and somewhat garish, with a tall
ceiling and, leading off along the sides, balconies from
which could be seen the gardens behind the St. Louis
Cathedral. Great crystal chandeliers hung low, their
brightness reflecting in the polished dance floor. There
were statues in wall recesses and original paintings hanging
on the walls, which were paneled with fine wood inlaid
with mahogany.

The orchestra was on a dais, and the dance floor was
alive with impeccable white gentlemen and the perfectly
gowned, beautiful quadroon girls Edward had come here
to see. Their mothers sat around the sides of the room.
They were beautiful, all of them, even those in their
older years. They were elegantly dressed and wore the
jewels lavished on them by their protectors, fathers of
the young girls being presented.

Edward moved along the edge of the ballroom, looking
at each girl. His pulse was racing. This was the night,
perhaps the very moment, in which he would make his
choice, and it must be the right choice. It was a reckless
thing he was doing, he knew that. But he also believed
that, from among these beauties—all of whom moved

with grace and delicacy, their lovely faces mirrors of purity and their trembling lips seeming to promise what he must have—he would pick the right one.

In fact, almost immediately there was one he began to single out. It was her utter, perfect grace when dancing that first caught his attention. Then, forcing himself to discount the pure and innocent smile with which she favored her partner of the moment, he looked at her and then at others, but always back to her.

She was a whisper tall, perhaps four inches over five feet, and she looked to be about nineteen. She was wearing a filmy, white gown. Her figure was perfect, slimmer than the others, a trifle more shapely in the bosom. Her skin was as white as his own, and her hair dark blonde with a deep, gentle wave. Her features were gentle and pleasing. Except for a trace of broadness at the cheekbone, she could have passed for white.

He stood against the wall, ready to move in on her. She must have sensed him for she glanced up and her great brown eyes met his. This girl was white, this dream of a girl, was the only one among all the beauties that he wanted for his own.

He restrained himself from going onto the dance floor and taking her from her partner. He waited until the number ended and the man returned her to her mother, a comely matron with diamonds and a streak of gray in her hair. Then he approached them and introduced himself.

"I'm Edward Dalton, madam, mademoiselle," he said. "I own a cotton brokerage in the city."

"I know of the Dalton brokerage," said the mother. "I know of all the business establishments, and their owners. I am Dorothea Ançoine. This is my daughter, Clio."

"M'sieu," murmured the lovely Clio.

"May I have the next dance?" Edward asked properly.

She curtsied, smiled, and he noticed there were dimples at the corners of her lips. He put out his arms, held her, and she was like a feather. Their steps fitted the music, fitted together, as if they had been created to do so.

"You're no quadroon," he murmured.

"My mothah is quadroon, m'sieu. I am octoroon."

That very evening, he got Clio's shy consent to be his, conversed with the mother, and reached an agreement. In another week he had bought the little white house on the Ramparts that the mother selected and Clio approved, and he was waiting impatiently for her to move into it.

The first time he went to her was in early dark. He walked, as he would later walk from Woodlawn, afraid that Tench might let slip to Mildred that he had driven the master to the Ramparts. Mildred, with her sharp mind, would suspect instantly, and there would be hell to pay. No, to walk was insurance. He would establish now, before he and Mildred were married, that he enjoyed a solitary after-dinner stroll. Mildred would come to accept it.

It was dark when he reached the little house. A candle burned in every window. He leaped up the steps and worked the knocker. He had to wait a second only. The door swung open, and he entered their house, locking the door behind him.

Clio was wearing a muted gold silk robe that gave her eyes almost a golden cast. Her hair was loose, curling gently about her face, reaching her hips.

Edward's loins caught fire. There was no way of hiding his state, though he tried. She mustn't think he was an animal, a beast of the fields, that he had a purely carnal desire for her. He longed to whisper tender words, to give her vows that he would never break, but he could only moan, "Clio—oh, darling!"

"I undahstand, m'sieu," she whispered. "My mothah told me of how it is with a gentleman the first time. There is no need to wait, even to speak. Not now—not yet."

She took his hand and led him into the bedchamber, a simple, peaceful room in blues and whites. The bed was already turned down.

"Now, m'sieu," she whispered. "I should like for it to be now, when you are eager."

Somehow he got out of his clothes and dropped them on the floor. He faced her, his need revealed, wondering if she would be afraid of him, not knowing how to deal with it if she was.

"I am happy, m'sieu," she murmured, "that it is you I am to love."

Her brown eyes clung to his, then slowly moved down his body, saw his need, and returned to his eyes. "Now," she whispered, her tone a kiss, "come to me now."

She moved her shoulders, and her robe slid off and lay in a golden pool. She was naked, her skin white and soft.

Her breasts were even fuller than he had dreamed. The area around the nipples was pale pink, the nipples tiny and unawakened. Her body was exquisite.

She moved to him, pressed against his jutting figure, and sighed. He picked her up and carried her to the bed. Then, uttering a cry that might have been heard on the street, he drove into her.

He was aware of her gasp, of the tightening of her arms. He was aware when she began to move, slowly at first, then faster, meeting his plunges, going faster when he did, slowing when he slowed, reaching the peak with him, clinging there until it seemed his chest would burst.

He rolled to his back, holding her. Her breath was shaking, her hand, which lightly stroked his chest, unsteady. She kissed his neck and rose on her elbow and put her lips on his in their first kiss, and they drank of each other until they had to break apart to breathe.

"I love you," he murmured, and it was the truth. "I really love you."

"And I, m'sieu. Always. From the night at the ball when first we met. I began to love you then. To look at you was to love."

Edward had had Clio for one month before his marriage. He told her about Mildred and tried to explain the dowry, how he needed it to make the brokerage prosper, how it was expected that he establish his bride in a fine home.

Clio hushed him before he got well into his explanation. "I know those things, m'sieu, my love. From when I was a small girl, my mothah spoke of them. You need feel no regret, no guilt. It is thus our society is formed. I want only to be youah placée, to love you all my life. You must live youah othah way. When you want me, I'll always be in this house."

The wedding took place in Natchez. Henry and Evelyn Vannice gave their only daughter the finest wedding that city had ever seen. If Mildred had been taller and only a bit less plump, she would have looked regal in her white wedding gown. As it was, she looked her best, which was more than passable. Her gown was very smart, she wore flashing diamonds, and she held her head high and smiled the evening through.

But when they were alone in their chamber at her parents' plantation, the touch of regality vanished. She became very white, and Edward knew that she was afraid. He was on the verge of being sorry for her, but then he recalled Clio's warmth, her readiness, her delight, and his heart hardened toward his bride.

He felt no desire for her. His one wish was to get what must be done over with. He hoped to heaven that he could impregnate her tonight, that the offspring would be a boy, an heir, and that he need never touch her again.

"My mother told me what to expect from you!" she snapped before he so much as unbuttoned his coat. "I hope you won't be a complete beast!"

"You undress first, Mildred," he said, making his tone kind. "That way you won't have to look at me any longer than necessary."

"I don't want to look at you at all!"

"Then why did you marry me?"

"Every girl has to marry—you know that! But the part my mother—the vile, coarse part—can be kept under control. If the man is willing. Like Papa."

Edward almost smiled. He knew for a fact that Henry Vannice kept a bed wench and that when he tired of one wench, he took another. Either his wife knew nothing of this or chose to shut her eyes to it, as so many women did.

He looked keenly at Mildred. She would not close her eyes to any infidelity.

"And don't think I'm ignorant!" Mildred continued, turning her back to him. "Here. Unbutton me. I've heard talk about men having bed wenches. I won't stand for that!"

"I have no bed wench, Mildred," he said. Clio was his love, his heart. He finished unbuttoning the dress, then helped her out of it. She began to pull off her other clothes, yanking at them.

"No need to hurry so," he told her.

"I want to get it over with!" she snapped. "Mama says the first time's the worst. And to be bare or the man'll tear your clothes off."

She got out of the last, inner shift, peeled off slippers

and stockings, and stood revealed. Her skin was white, smooth, chubby enough to be dimpled, but her breasts were small and flat. The overall effect was lumpishness and dimples, except for the flat breasts. The triangle of hair at her thighs was thick and curly.

That curl put the first tinge of desire into him. He began to take off his clothes, hurrying, so as not to lose it. He glanced at her face. Her eyes were squeezed shut so as not to see him naked.

At last, he was ready. He took her arm and led her, wordlessly, to the bed. She stiffened when he urged her down, but she let him arrange her, straighten her legs, even push them apart. As he bestrode her, he closed his own eyes and imagined Clio, her soft, receptive beauty, her sighs and gasps and murmurs, and the feeling in his loins grew.

"Don't talk," he whispered to Mildred, still imagining Clio, desperate that the illusion not be shattered. By some miracle, Mildred said nothing, just took a deep breath and held it.

It was then that he made his thrust, hard and fast, hurrying so he wouldn't lose the ability. Mildred screamed. The scream made him leap to greater size within her, and he began to move. She was dry, tight and dry, and there was pain for him as he moved. But he kept at it, his hands pressing her shoulders, silently urging her to move, but she lay rigid, and suddenly, without pleasure, he broke within her, and it was over. He withdrew.

She was weeping angrily. "You hurt me! You might as well have taken a knife and—"

"It does hurt the first time," he said, remembering the way Clio had gasped. "It'll be better after this. You'll even get to like it. Women do."

"Not ladies! Ladies hate it! I hate it! I'll always hate it!"

She did continue to hate lovemaking. As for himself, in order to be husband, to beget an heir, he cultivated that feeling the curl of the hair at her loins never failed to rouse. The dimples in her body began to help and imagining Clio in his arms finished the job.

Edward's male need also helped. At first, when Mildred made frequent visits to Natchez, he was free to go to Clio nightly. When Mildred's visits all but ceased, he cut down his trips to the Ramparts to protect what he had there. Twice a month was all he could risk going to Clio. His naturally strong passion, fed by Clio, built his need until he was not only willing but at times desperate to ease it with his wife.

She humored him perhaps twice a month, never failing to say, after it was over, that it was only to give him the son she had promised. She did, after much coaxing on his part, begin to move stiffly when he moved, and thus he sometimes achieved a measure of relief.

When he went to Clio, their love was a flood, a living, pulsing abundance of joy. For a week after being with her, he was at peace, but then the craving began, and he had only Mildred to turn to.

Ned was born to Clio a year before Francie was born to Mildred, who created a great uproar over her agony and fancied bout with death. Tom was born to Clio a year before Anita was born to Mildred, who again suffered loudly and told everyone, including the doctor, how nearly she had died.

Clio bloomed after childbirth and became more beautiful. Mildred looked her usual self afterward, although a bit plumper each time.

Ned and Tom were handsome boys, small replicas of their father, even to the sprinkle of freckles across their noses. Watching his sons grow, Edward felt the irony that his wife had given him only daughters, while his placée had given him only sons. He desperately wanted Ned to inherit but knew that it was impossible. The boy had the makings of a good businessman and, like his brother, showed not one Negroid characteristic, not even a hint of the cheekbone that betrayed Clio's blood.

He devoted much thought to the future of his sons before he spoke to Clio. One afternoon, when the boys were at the school to which he sent them and he had slipped away for a talk with Clio, he divulged the plan he had made. "Darling," he began, "our sons are white. They will be white men."

"They've got the othah blood, darling."

"It doesn't show, it will never show. Not in them, not in their children if they marry white. They *must* have a good life, you agree to that?"

"Of course, my love! You and ouah boys—that is my world!"

"I've planned it carefully. I'll send them to London to school as white boys. There they'll be like all the others. They'll grow up white, and they can enter any profession."

Clio began to weep. Edward took her into his arms and held her, rocking gently, as if she were a hurt, beloved child. "I know, I know. I'm taking your sons away from you."

"No, my dearest!" she sobbed. "Nevah that! What you plan is for them, so they can have fine lives, so they won't have to live on the Ramparts any more, so they can go anywhere in the world and be looked up to. It's only—"

"It's that we lose them. They can never come back, even to visit. They don't know of the blood now and never will. When we put them on the ship, they'll be going out of our lives. You can't even write to them, or they to you."

"But how will we know about them, my love? They're only little boys. Tom is only seven!"

"In England boys go away to school at that age and seldom see their parents. Our boys will be only a little less well off in that respect. I'll correspond with the school officials, the letters will come to my office, and I'll destroy them after you read them. We'll know how they're progressing. We'll continue this until they've finished college."

"And aftah that?"

"They enter life as fully trained, educated white men. I'll settle money on them in a London bank immediately. They'll have a financial start, and they'll do well."

"But won't they remembah?"

"At first. But the memory will fade. Years from now, they'll be told we've passed away; I'll have my attorney apprise the school of our supposed deaths. That will complete their freedom from black blood."

Within a month, they sent their sons to London under the care of a tutor. The tutor knew nothing of Clio, and the boys promised, bewildered, not to mention the Ramparts to him or anybody else, ever, and Edward knew they would keep their promise.

The boys had been gone a week when Edward stole to Clio one afternoon. His objective was not to make love, for there was no time for their slow, tender form of lovemaking, but to give her a bit of company. She was lonely without her sons and was in the midst of painting the woodwork of her little house when he arrived.

He told her about Hester, who had arrived a few days before—her age, her white skin, her beauty. He told her the exorbitant price he had paid and mentioned Mildred's reaction.

"Poor little slave girl," Clio murmured. "You really think she could pass for white?"

"As easily as Ned and Tom."

"What a pity she can't have the same chance they have!"

"Agreed."

She looked thoughtful. "M'sieu—"

"Yes, my darling?"

"Would it be possible, now—if we hurry? It's been a month since—"

"I don't want to mar our pleasure by hurrying," he said. "Maybe I can make it next week. Mildred is suspicious again. I think she senses, after all these years, that I have someone. She can't sleep nights now. She takes laudanum, but not enough to make her sleep all night. It isn't safe to risk coming to you. On top of that, she's got the idea I bought Hester for a bed wench!"

"M'sieu—darling!" Clio cried. "That's the very thing! Take this child for youah bed wench! You won't hurt her —youah so gentle. And youah wife won't permit you— and you are able to come to me so seldom!"

"Ridiculous! Unthinkable!"

"Not so, my love!"

"I want only you."

"Which makes me happy, my beloved. But it makes me very unhappy to know that you are deprived, you who need love."

"It wouldn't be love with Hester."

"But it would be comfort you must have," Clio urged. "It would please me that you don't have to be deprived."

"I'd be untrue to you."

"But—with youah wife—that's not untrue."

"That's mostly to get an heir—when she'll permit it. And to keep up the semblance of marriage."

"You are good to her, darling. You've given her a fine

house, you've doubled her dowry money, and redoubled it. She has fine jewels, beautiful gowns, she's a leadah in society."

"You've let me give you no jewels, Clio."

"You are my jewel, m'sieu. You've earned the right to some happiness. I want you to have Hester when you can't come to me. I want it truly, with my heart. I beg you to do this out of love for me!"

Moved beyond discretion, scant though his free time was, he took her into their bedroom. They stripped quickly. Their love had never been sweeter, faster, more intense; they scarcely missed their cherished preliminaries. This, for now, was perfection.

When he would have gotten up to dress, she held him. "Promise, love."

"Promise what?"

"That when you are in real need, you'll considah Hester."

Groaning, he kissed her deeply. "All right," he said at last. "I promise to consider only."

Chapter Sixteen

✦

Each night Hester lay on her cot listening, dreading, fearing, resenting. Would this be the night the master came to take his pleasure? Would he be cruel, or would he be gentle? Would he, please God, be just a little bit like Phil? She tossed for hours, wondering, longing for home.

But mostly it was Phil for whom she yearned. New Orleans was his home, and despite uneasiness over her situation, she felt quiet joy over that. They were in the same city; the same sun shone on them, the same stars. She had no idea where his house was, how to learn its location, or get to it if she did find out. For now, the knowing that she was in the same city with him comforted her.

If he knew where she was, he would buy her. She didn't know whether he had enough money, but somehow he would get it. She considered asking Nell if she knew the Bennett family but gave up the idea. She was a slave wench, and a new one in this household at that. If she was found asking such a bold question, even of someone as kind as Nell, it could bring trouble.

For now, being in the same city with Phil had to be enough. Somehow, someday, she would find him. She knew that Nell and the others went about the streets on errands; she, too, would eventually be sent from the house to fetch something. Then she would search for Phil.

Meanwhile, she sewed the brown garments the mistress had ordered her to wear. All day she stitched. And at night, always, she lay in bed waiting and fearing, until she fell asleep from exhaustion. And still the master did not come. She began to hope he never would.

The first brown shift and tignon were finished. Hester had cut the garments and sewn every stitch, Nell keeping an eye on the work as she stitched the two gowns for the mistress.

"You bettah wear the brown to suppah," Nell told her. "It's done, and the mistress will only be maddah with you if she looks into the kitchen and sees you still in youah old shift. Heah, I'll help you. The quickah we get you changed, the bettah."

She helped Hester out of the old shift and tossed it aside. Then she took up the new, coarse brown shift and lowered it over Hester's curls. As the rough material slid down her nude body, Hester felt Nell guiding her to the long looking glass the mistress sometimes used.

Hester stared at her reflection, amazed. The garment lay smoothly at the shoulder, clung to her breasts, and hung in folds to midcalf. The brown seemed to match her eyes, to make them look wider and more lustrous.

"It's bettah on you than the pink was!" Nell exclaimed. "It makes youah skin even whitah! There ain't nothing can spoil youah looks, child! Hold quiet, now. I'll put the tignon on you this time."

She swept Hester's hair to the top of her head, twisted it into a knot, and tucked the ends in so they would hold. Swiftly she took the head cloth and wound it into a graceful tignon over Hester's hair, then tied the ends and poked them up under the edges. Hester stared at the folds of the headdress, at how it seemed to make her into another person.

Nell clasped her hands. "You look like a—a queen!" she crooned. "That tignon makes youah face like it was carved out of marble, it's so white! I don't know what the mistress will say. She didn't like it because you was so purty in the pink dress. We can only hope she don't see what I see!"

Dazed, Hester stared on into the looking glass. She really was different. She looked grown up, like a new girl. She wondered whether Phil would like her in the brown shift, or if he would choose the pink dress, which she was forbidden to wear.

When she walked into the kitchen with Nell, she kept her eyes downcast. Even so, she felt the others staring at the change in her. When she ventured to look up, one or two of them nodded then glanced away, but she didn't feel hurt. They were following the mistress's order not to be on friendly terms with her.

As she ate, her unhappiness grew. At Thornton, her beauty had been admired by all the slaves and mentioned freely. It was even accepted by the white master, who made no effort to force her to hide it. But here the mistress wanted to make her plain and ugly, and, though Nell said the mistress was jealous and didn't want the master to see any pretty wench, it seemed impossible that Miss Mildred, with her fine house and her silken clothes, should take a dislike to a mere slave, the newest and lowliest one of them all.

It was the next night before supper that the master came, at last, to Hester's cubbyhole. He didn't stride in as he had the right to do, but stopped and tapped at the side of the open door.

Hester, who had been adjusting her tignon at the cracked bit of mirror Nell had propped on the wash shelf, spun to face him, blood seeming to drain from her heart. She hadn't expected it to be like this. She had thought he would come in the deep of night, when she was on her cot, when the mistress and all the household were asleep. Yet here he was, with the house astir, come to claim his rights.

As he stepped inside, his smile vanished. "You're frightened," he said, in a wondering way. "You're afraid of me. Why are you afraid, Hester?"

She tried to move her lips, to speak, but she could only stare into his auburn eyes, straight into them. She was so startled that she forgot a slave must never meet the eyes of a white person. She tried again to speak, then shook her head.

His face changed, and he looked understanding. "I didn't come to demand anything of you, Hester. I only want to see for myself that you've settled in, that things are going well for you." She gulped, swallowed, nodded. "And the sewing? Are you doing well?"

"N-Nell says I am, Master Edward, sir," she stammered. She touched the shift with her fingers and tried to say she had made it, but could not. She was so beset by a mixture of fright and relief that she could scarcely stand properly before him.

"The outfit you're wearing. It's downright—striking. Did you make it?"

"Y-yes, Master Edward, sir."

"Everything is all right with you? You get enough to eat, the other servants treat you well?"

"Y-yes, Master Edward, sir." She couldn't tell him that the mistress had given orders for the other slaves not to associate with her and that her only allowed companion was Nell, and only because she had to learn sewing from her.

Edward Dalton stood a moment longer, studying Hester. He noted her stunning beauty, her shy and frightened manner, her pure female allure, which was clean and natural. He felt his loins tingle and realized how seldom he had been able to be alone with Clio these last months, and that it had been three months since Mildred had permitted him to come to her.

He murmured something to Hester about being a good girl and learning to sew, then made his way back to the house, up the stairs and into the suite he shared with Mildred.

Wearing a purple robe, Mildred was seated at her dressing table, turning her head this way and that, peering into the mirror. "That front curl, Docia," she snapped at the hovering wench. "It doesn't lay right. Fix it."

She held very still, and Edward stood very still, until Docia had arranged the curl to Mildred's liking. When that was done, Docia fastened a diamond-crusted ornament in the middle of the looped knot, then held a hand mirror so her mistress could see the back of her head.

"Finished?" Edward asked.

He was burning so that he even found Mildred's hair exciting. He thrust his hands into the slit pockets of his trousers.

"At last!" Mildred agreed. "What do you want, Edward? Don't you see that I still have to finish dressing?"

"Go downstairs, Docia," he ordered. "To the kitchen. Tell Hannah you're to have your supper now. And take your time eating it."

"Yes, master, sir," said Docia, her protruding tooth showing. She hurried out.

"What are you doing?" Mildred demanded shrilly. "I need her!"

"You're not dressing yet, I hope, Mildred."

"Have you lost your wits? We're due at the Wilsons'. I don't know what you're talking about!"

"About your being wife to me. Now. This moment."

"And ruin my hair? Really, Edward, what has come over you?"

"A desire for my wife. Is that so wrong?"

"At this particular time, when I'm dressing for an important dinner, it's sinful, Edward Dalton!"

"It's been three months, Mildred. I can wait only so long."

"Are you threatening me? With another woman? Me, your lawful wife?"

"You know I'm in my office all day. You stop in often enough."

"You'd better be there!"

"And I'm home every night. You know that, too."

"I don't know what you do when I have to take laudanum."

"You wake in an hour, two hours. I'm always here."

"What's this supposed to make me do? Throw myself on the bed and tear up my hair?"

"Docia can fix your hair."

"What about that white wench of yours? Why don't you pour your filth into her? Nothing makes her look decent, not even that ugly brown!"

"And if I should do as you say?" He spoke quietly, but his fists clenched to keep from grabbing her, from shaking her until her hair fell, from throwing her onto the bed and raping her. Maybe that was what she needed to turn her into a wife—a vigorous, husbandly rape. No, that would only make her more angry and vicious.

"You touch that white wench, you touch any wench or any loose woman, any woman at all!" Mildred screamed, her eyes glittering. "If you do that and I find out, she'll pay, you'll pay, you'll wish you'd never been born!"

Seeing Mildred's twisted, vicious-looking expression, Edward's desire subsided as suddenly as it had sprung to life. "Ring for Docia," he said. "We'll be at the Wilsons' on time."

Even as she flounced over to the bell pull he knew that, for some time to come, he would have to stop even his five-minute visits to Clio. At times, even now, as he went about town, he had the sense of being followed. Mildred wasn't above following him or having him followed. He dared not let her find out that Clio existed.

Chapter Seventeen

✽

A week later, at breakfast in the kitchen, there was murmuring and whispering among the servants, as well as the usual covert glances at Hester to make certain they were divulging nothing to her. However, after breakfast Nell told her everything as they cut out and basted a dress for the mistress.

"Miss Mildred has took the little missies and went to Natchez," Nell said, positioning her scissors and cutting into the fabric carefully. "This has to be slow, see, Hester, so as not to pull any of the threads of the brocade. Miss Mildred makes a big fuss over one pulled thread, thinks it'll end up ruining the whole gown."

"I'll remember," Hester said. "When you let me cut brocade, I'll be awfully careful."

"No telling how long the mistress'll be in Natchez, but we got to work as fast on this gown as if she was home. Though I don't think she'll be back the next few days. She was called away by sickness. Her mothah—weak heart."

"That sounds bad," said Hester, who knew little about such ailments. "Is she going to die?"

"I don't think so. She's had spells befoah. She rests, and likes foah Miss Mildred and the little missies to be theah. Seem they help her get well."

Hester felt sorry for Miss Mildred and her mother. She knew how sad she would be if her own mother had a weak heart.

Nell finished cutting the bodice pieces and left them spread on the end of the table, and Hester stood to work, carefully basting, her lower lip between her teeth. Now she thought only of her job; Nell said basting was very im-

portant to the fitting of a gown. From time to time, she
even left her own task of cutting gores for the skirt to
trace out where Hester must leave room across the back
so the roll of flesh between Miss Mildred's shoulders
wouldn't show.

At supper that night, Edward sat at the table in relief,
eating slowly, drinking more wine than usual with his
meal. At last he was free to go to Clio, to spend hours
with her every night Mildred was gone. He would have
been on the Ramparts now, but this was the first Thursday of the month, the night Clio had asked his permission,
since the boys had left, to have supper with her mother.
Sometimes she even spent the night and part of the following morning with her.

After supper he sat in the library, sipping wine, waiting
for time to pass so he could go to the Ramparts. His
hunger for Clio built steadily. He felt a bit fuzzy-headed
from the wine, but it was a pleasant feeling, and he knew
Clio wouldn't reproach him.

He arrived at the little house shortly after eleven. Clio
was usually back at this hour, and he hoped that she
would be there now. The house was dark, however, and
he used his key, letting himself into the small, peaceful
rooms. Even when Clio wasn't in them, he could sense
her. Thinking to wait in darkness, he sat in the armchair
she kept specially for him. Then, deciding it might startle
her to come into the dark house and find someone there,
he lit a candle and sat watching its flame, gazing foggily
about at the outlines of furniture, happy just to be here.

Clio kept no wine in the house, no spirits of any kind.
She didn't use them herself, and he had told her he had
no need of them when he was with her. Now he wished
he had a bit of wine to help fill the waiting.

When she hadn't come by midnight, he knew she was
sleeping at her mother's home. Disappointed, miserable
with need, knowing it was the wine, his thoughts turned to
Hester, beautiful Hester. He pondered how Clio had insisted that he make use of Hester, that he consider it. He
sat brooding, and at the back of his mind, he could hear
Clio urging, "Go home now, m'sieu. Go to her now, calm
her fright. Aftah being with you one time, she will no
longah be afraid."

Cursing his weakness, he started home. He was very
careful to walk steadily, pleased to find that he could do

so. The closer he got to Woodlawn, the more anxious he
was to arrive. He expected Hester would be asleep, that
he would have to waken her, and that this would add to
the fears that he must allay.

Hester, however, late though it was, sat in her nightshift in her cubbyhole making tiny, even stitches in the
second of her brown shifts. She held the work very near
the candle, meticulously making each stitch tiny and even.

"Miss Mildred ordahs that every stitch on every garment, slaves' things, too, be perfect," Nell kept telling her.
"Any minute, she'll catch hold of a dress a wench has been
wearing a month and examine the stitches and all the work
as close as if they was her own. She examines them while
I make them, too, and latah, while in use, to see how
they standin' up to being worn."

"Hester," said a voice from the open door, interrupt-
ing her thoughts, "Hester, the beauty. What are you doing
up so late? Surely Nell doesn't drive you like this?"

She started, and the needle went into her thumb. As she
pulled it out, blood welled, standing in a big drop. Instinctively she put her thumb into her mouth to keep
blood from getting onto her work.

She couldn't speak. This was it. The master had come
to take her. Even by candlelight she saw that jut of his
trousers. Her heart moved into her throat, and she began
to tremble.

The bleeding thumb still in her mouth, she watched
him. He was pale and sweating, a bit unsteady and smell-
ing of wine, but he seemed kind enough. She watched
him cross to her and let him pull her thumb out of her
mouth.

"It's still bleeding," he said. "We can't have that. Hold
still, little Hester. I'll fix it."

Trembling, she let her hand rest in his as he drew a
handkerchief from his pocket, unfolded it with one hand,
then wrapped it tightly around the thumb. "Sit still," he
said, then broke off a length of sewing thread and tied it
around the handkerchief. "There. You won't get blood on
your nightshift. Or on the cot."

He took her sewing from her lap, held it to the candle,
and looked at it closely. "Very neat," he said, putting it
down on the table Nell had gotten for Hester.

"You know why I'm here, Hester, so late at night?" he
asked. Numbly, she nodded. "I mean to have my way,

understand. I'm not a beast. I hope I'm a gentleman and promise to behave as such. Do you understand that—is it getting through your fright?"

Again she nodded. She felt far away, not in this place at all. It seemed that she was dreaming. This couldn't be real. She had lain on her cot so many times waiting for this to happen that now she couldn't believe it.

"Just do as I say, Hester," the master told her. "I won't hurt you. Just don't—resist. This is the way things go between the master and a wench, and it can be very good for both of them. Speak, can't you, Hester? Just say my name, so I'll know you are friendly."

"Y-yes, Master Edward, sir," she stammered. She knew he was telling her the truth and knew that he would be gentle. But the terrifying fact remained. He was going to take her as she wanted only Phil to do. And in obeying— she had to obey the master—she would be untrue to Phil.

In the instant he put his hands out and lifted Hester from the chair, Edward Dalton had a fleet, sad thought of Clio. Clio, who had pleaded with him to do this. His desire flamed. It was as if he held both his beloved placée and this enticing white-skinned girl at the same time, as if they were one and the same. The same in passion, he thought groggily, never in love.

He stood her on her feet. "I'm going to take off your nightshift," he said. "You won't be frightened—will you?"

Her eyes were wide, but because she must, she shook her head.

He pulled the shift off over her head, then tossed it. It landed atop the shift that she had been sewing.

Her eyes were on his face. She couldn't keep them away, she had to read what was there. If cruelty showed, she must brace herself against hurt; if only desire filled him, she would prepare herself to accept it.

He laid his palms on her shoulders, stroked lightly down, over the curve of her breasts, along the insweep of waist, around the flowing curve of her hips. His palms were firm, and his touch set up little sparkles on her skin. Her trembling grew, increased by the realization that his touch was pleasant.

"Your skin," he murmured. "It's so soft!"

"Y-yes, Master Edward, sir," she stammered, knowing that she had to make some response, that if she stood wooden and silent, she might displease him.

"Stay right there, stand as you are, so I can enjoy you," he ordered, his tone so low that it wouldn't carry beyond this room, though the door was still open.

Even as she had this thought, he closed the door. Then he faced back to her and began to take off his clothes. He was very quick about it. Proper behavior or not, she was impelled to watch.

He was superbly built. There was a scatter of auburn hair on his chest, thickening down the front, ending in a broad arrow above his male part. She felt his eyes on her private spot, and she felt she was blushing from face to toe. He was so needful of a woman that her breath caught.

He took the two steps that separated them, pulled her to him, and held her so that every inch and angle of his body followed every curve and line of hers. Holding her lightly and, she recognized, despite fear and reluctance, tenderly, he ran his fingers through her loosened hair slowly and repeatedly.

"You're a marvel," he whispered, "a miracle."

His body braced hers, cradling her, and her outward trembling eased. The inward trembling, however, increased as his touch became urgent, his breathing faster, the prod of his maleness harder. She smelled the wine he had drunk and wondered if it would, before this encounter ended, push him to the edge of cruelty.

"Hester, little Hester," he whispered. "You're not a virgin?"

"No, Master Edward, sir. I was raped."

"This will be no rape. Do what I say, and you'll find it even pleasant."

"Yes, Master Edward, sir."

"You will—cooperate? Do what I say? I don't want to just throw you on the cot and have it over, fast and furious."

"I'll co—co—"

"Cooperate, Hester."

"Thank you, Master Edward, sir. I'll cooperate."

He turned her to the cot. "Lie down. Rest your hands on the sheet near your head. Spread your legs, just a bit."

Stiffening against the trembling, she did as he said. By the time she had arranged herself, she filled all the space. She watched him, unable to control her eyes, and looked him full in the face. He was handsome even now, when she was so scared. He didn't smile as he stood looking down at her. His auburn eyes roamed all over her, up and down. His mouth was tight but not cruel, his features immobile, intense.

New fright swept her. This slowness, this savoring? Would it make him worse than Boss Murray? Would he turn fierce, tear at her, because he had waited beyond endurance?

She rolled her head from one side to the other. She almost moaned. Uncertain as to whether her movement was fear or the stirring of passion, Edward came onto the cot, bestriding her. Because he couldn't wait another moment, another instant, not even to reassure her, he guided himself into her with one smooth, swift thrust.

She was hot and tight and moist, her body rigid. He forced himself to hold back, not to move, not yet, not wanting to frighten her still more. He held his breath, making his body rigid, forcing himself to wait.

"Relax," he whispered. "I'll move, I have to move, I can't wait. You move, too. It'll make it easier for you, better for me—for both of us. That's what makes the pleasure—moving."

She had scarcely time for the flashing memory of how it had been with Phil when the man atop her groaned and began to plunge slowly, deeply, in and out. Because she must obey, she moved when he did. She matched herself to his lead. He plunged faster now, harder, moaning constantly.

At first, wine-befuddled and half-mad with need, with holding back at the very threshold of relief, he pretended that Hester was Clio, that he was making love to his placée. Then he forgot that fantasy because Hester's movements were different—clumsy and seeking, inept and innocent, yet exciting beyond description. She was new, alluring youth, and he came to the very peak of passion and hung there, unbreathing, aware that she had reached no heights, had felt no joy.

Afterward, as they lay entwined on the narrow cot, he whispered, "Did I hurt you?"

"No, Master Edward, sir."

"Will you let me—again—tonight?"

"If you wish, Master Edward, sir."

"I do wish. For myself and for you. I want to give you pleasure as well as take it."

"Thank you, Master Edward, sir," she murmured. And

wished for her beloved Phil. She wanted only for the master to leave.

But he remained, cradling her, one hand roaming her body. She was rigid again, and he continued stroking her, patting her, until she relaxed and lay quiet, feeling safe with him.

This time he entered her slowly, ever so slowly, and she found the sensation not unpleasant. As soon as he moved, she responded to please him, and as their matched thrusts built, the last vestige of her fear was gone.

At the end he moved very quickly, and she matched his speed instinctively. Briefly, from deep within, she felt the hot pulsing sensation she had suffered with Boss Murray, but suddenly it turned into the delightful sensations she had known with Phil.

As before, she lay in the master's arms, and he stroked her, and she felt no dislike of it. But she was ashamed for what she had done with him—and the pleasure she had felt. In some ways, especially in his gentle manner, the master reminded her of Phil. Thinking of Phil, she grew more miserable for what she had done. She had betrayed him. The misery deepened as she realized she must continue this way whenever the master wished.

She had no sooner thought this than he took her the third time, with fervor he had held back before. Again that hot flood rose in her, and she was swept to the edge of ecstasy. Tortured by love for Phil, she knew she was caught. She had to surrender to the master. She had no choice, none at all.

Thus she gave reluctant consent when he asked if she would receive him again. "I'll do whatever you want, Master Edward, sir," she murmured.

"And like it as well as tonight?"

"Yes, Master Edward, sir," she said, burning with shame that she was probably speaking truth.

He got up and began to dress. Then, finished, he helped her into her nightshift. "After this, I'll take precautions," he said.

"Precautions, Master Edward, sir?"

"I'll see to it that no sucker comes of our lovemaking. That's a promise."

His words struck like a blow. Why, she might have a baby inside her! There had been Boss Murray and Phil and now the master! And only Phil's child would she welcome, although she would not want his child growing in her now, for the master might sell it away from her, all she had of him, even as she had been sold away from Mammy and Pappy.

Chapter Eighteen

The following night, ashamed that he had permitted wine and desire to take him to the very young Hester, Edward went to the house on the Ramparts immediately after supper. He would have preferred to dine with Clio, but it was safer to appear at his own table for meals, even when Mildred was out of town. His habit of a long after-supper walk had long been established, so, his mind easy, he departed after dessert. He covered the streets between Woodlawn and the Ramparts at twice his normal speed. Clio was waiting. She came into his arms the instant he closed the door. When she lifted her face and would have shared one of their long, sweet kisses, he turned his face.

"What is it, love?" she asked. "What's wrong?"

"I was here last night. You were with your mother."

"Yes, love. I knew you'd been here; there was your cigar smoke. So I believed, hoped, you'd come tonight. And now you have."

"But with a guilty heart," he said, again evading her lips. "Don't, my darling. I have no right to kiss you. Not yet, not until you know."

"Tell me, m'sieu, love. So I may have my kisses."

He blurted out how Mildred had been called to Natchez, how he had drunk too much wine and, after leaving the Ramparts, had gone to Hester. "I took her three times," he finished. "Once wasn't enough."

"Of course it wasn't enough, my love!" Clio exclaimed, and there was the faintest hint of laughter in her tone. "It's been months since you've been able to make love to me, and you're a man who must have love, much, much love! You did only what I begged you to do, and I thank

134

you for it. It gladdens me that you didn't have to suffer during the night, and it makes me doubly happy that you came to me tonight."

"But I should have waited for you, Clio!"

She pulled his head down, placed her lips against his, kissed him, and murmured, "It was the wine, and it was youah need! We'll not speak of it again. And you are to go to Hester any time you have the need."

He groaned, taking her kiss, pressing until he was kissing her teeth. "It's you I want, only you!"

She pushed back, and a note of alarm came into her voice. "She didn't please you, this wench? You didn't enjoy her?"

"She pleased me, and I enjoyed," he said grimly.

"Then it must continue, my love. When you can't come to me, when youah wife won't—you must use this wench. She'll soon learn how fortunate she is to have you even once in a while!"

He swept her into his arms and carried her to their bedroom. And the glory they experienced surpassed any they had ever known.

As Hester sat uneasily sewing in her room, not knowing whether the master would come so soon again, her monthly time began. Gratefully she put on the clean, folded rags she used for this purpose, knowing there would be no baby.

When she grew so sleepy she couldn't hold her eyes open, she folded her sewing and laid it on the table. She put on her nightshift, blew out the candle, and went to bed. She scarcely had time to wonder if the master would come, for she was so tired, she fell into a deep sleep.

Every night she waited, but he didn't come. Each time she lay down on her cot it was with relief but also with worry that tonight he would come, or tomorrow night, or the one after that. Maybe he had another bed wench, she thought. Maybe he liked the other wench better than he liked her. She hoped so. As long as Miss Mildred was in Natchez, she reasoned, the master was free to go to any wench he chose. She wished she could ask Nell questions, get things clear in her mind, but she dared not, for Nell might know, from the tone of the questions, that the master had been to bed with her. And that would never do, for Nell might accidentally let it slip and the information eventually would come to the ears of Miss Mildred.

Miss Mildred, in turn, would surely have Hester whipped and maybe even sold. She went weak at the thought. She couldn't bear to stand on the slave block again. Never again. If the master ever does sell me, she thought, please God it will be to some man he knows, a thing between gentlemen. Or, please, please God—to Phil!

Mildred arrived home sooner than Edward had expected. He couldn't risk sending Clio word of this, but when he didn't appear at the little house, she would understand that his wife was again at Woodlawn.

On her first night home, they dressed for supper together.

"Your mother is really on the mend?" he asked, buttoning his shirt. "This attack wasn't as severe as the others?"

"That's right. Actually, it wasn't a real attack. Just the vapors. Why do you ask?" she demanded. "Wasn't two weeks long enough for us to be away? Didn't you get your fill of carousing?"

He smiled grimly. "Your jest isn't in good taste, Mildred."

"It's no jest! I don't trust you an inch! Well," she continued, lowering her voice so that Docia, who was emptying bath water in the next room couldn't hear, "I'm going to test that out tonight!"

He looked at her and raised his eyebrows questioningly.

"I'm going to bed with you tonight, Edward. To see if you're able to perform. Or if you've worn yourself out on fast women—or wenches!"

"You'll find me fully able to oblige," he countered, glad now that Clio's monthly time had prevented lovemaking these past nights and that he had not gone to Hester.

"Hmmph! There's more. You needn't take precautions tonight. I've decided to oblige you often enough to become enceinte one more time. But one only. If I do bear a child, and it's not a son, you can expect no more sacrifice on my part."

Edward's pulse quickened, not at the prospect of bedding Mildred, who now had no appeal for him, but at the possibility of getting an heir. A white heir, who could carry on the name of Dalton and, in years to come, expand the brokerage, open branches in Natchez, even in other cities.

"Well?" Mildred spoke sharply. "Haven't you anything to say? Is this the reception you give the woman who bears your name, the wife who is offering to face death for you still again?"

He went to her, held her, then kissed her twice, as warmly as he could manage. Given the fact that she was Mildred, taking into consideration the coldness of her nature, she was, actually, being as magnificent as she considered herself to be.

"What brought you to this wonderful decision?" he asked, kissing her again. He tried to keep his mind off Clio's lips, to give Mildred her due.

"Papa, in fact," she replied. "You have him to thank, as well as me. Now that he's older, he wants our son, when he's grown, to inherit all his holdings and run them, along with the brokerage."

So. There lay the kernel of the matter. Greed. He put Mildred out of his arms as soon as he could, and they went down to supper. Here she broached the subject of a tutor again.

"I'm screening men daily," he told her. "It won't be long now. I'm about to finish arrangements with one man who is a bit worldly but wonderfully intelligent and educated. He can give the girls a touch of sophistication."

Mildred smiled, actually smiled. "About that Hester wench," she said next. "I'm giving orders tomorrow to send her on sewing errands."

"But she doesn't know her way about the streets, Mildred."

"She'll learn. I want her to go into shops, see the materials, get acquainted with their quality. I don't approve of the—worldly—look she has in those brown shifts, but they do reveal that she has a flair. I'm getting her sandals so she won't disgrace us going barefoot to the shops. She can study the fashion dolls. And she'll see ladies, not just myself, and observe the cut and fit of their gowns."

"You really do think she'll learn to be a good seamstress?"

He had scarcely thought of Hester since the night he had spent with her, for he had had Clio It was only now that he felt a tingle in his loins over Hester.

"Yes, I do," Mildred said. "I intend for her to be my private modiste. I know talent when I see it. She's already draping and pinning fabric on me—designing gowns—and when she's learned to cut and fit, she'll be a marvel. Some of the modistes are going to want her, but you're not to sell her, Edward, regardless of the price offered, not even if you can double your money."

"Whatever you say, Mildred," he agreed.

And he was amenable, not because of Hester's sexual availability of which he had no intention of availing himself, but because Mildred was willing to give him an heir. Whatever her reasons, she was willing, and he knew she was frightened. If having her own modiste would make her happy, she was to have the modiste.

At midnight, after supper and an almost friendly evening, he bedded Mildred. He was gentle with her, and she didn't complain. She even moved when he moved, and he dared to pierce deeply, deeper with every thrust until, at the end, when he expelled his seed, he hoped it would shoot into every crevice and take root.

He was ready to repeat the act the following night, but Mildred was cross and restless and would not permit any bed activities. She turned and tossed, murmuring that she was sure she was enceinte and would die, then saying that last night must certainly be a failure, and next month they would have to try again.

"Why not next week?" Edward asked boldly, risking her displeasure. His thought was to save his seed, couple with her weekly, and perhaps thus increase the likelihood of conception.

"I'll not subject myself to that indignity more than once a month!" she snapped. "It's a sensible way, too. We'll know exactly when the—act—took place and know from that when the baby will be born."

He had to accept this, or she would give up the whole idea.

She began to have trouble sleeping again. Every night, against Edward's protest at first, she took laudanum drops and fell into a sleep that grew fitful, and then she would wake, tossing and complaining.

She went to the doctor, who forbade increasing the laudanum. The doctor, taking Edward aside, suggested that a nightly bout of love would help Mildred sleep naturally, but when Edward repeated this to her as delicately as he could, she went into such a frenzy she almost called off trying to produce an heir at all, and Edward quickly backtracked.

"It's too much to ask of you," he agreed honestly. "You're the one to be enceinte and give birth. It's only right that you say when we make our trys to get a son."

Regardless of their plan, her suspicions of him hadn't lessened. Hence he dared not visit Clio, either on his nightly walk or for five minutes during the day, lest he be followed. The days and the nights passed, and Edward's seed formed in him, and he was tormented with need for Clio, who, above all women, could assuage it.

He managed one very brief visit to her on his way to the brokerage in early morning. Actually, he let Tench drive him to the establishment, and then, when the coachman had turned the corner on the way back to Woodlawn, he hurried on foot to the house on the Ramparts.

Hurriedly, he explained the situation to Clio. He told her, for the first time, how he had had the feeling that someone was following him about the city. "It's probably my guilty conscience," he said, grinning.

"It might not be, love."

"The upshot of it is, my darling, that it may be weeks, even months, before—"

"Befoah you can come to me. Even like this. It's all right, deah love. The time will pass. And theah is the one thing you can do for me."

"Anything—anything," he agreed.

"The Hester wench."

"Unthinkable! I'm still ashamed of the one time."

"But there won't be the wine now, m'sieu. You'll be completely youahself."

"Even so."

"Are you afraid, love?"

"Afraid of what?"

"That you may come to love Hester?"

He groaned and took her into his arms, covering her face with kisses. "You are my love," he said. "You are my love for life."

"Then there is no dangah. This you must do for me, love. You will go to Hester for love of me."

Some nights later, after Mildred was asleep from laudanum, throbbing with need for Clio, Edward stole through the dark and sleeping house to Hester's room. The door

was open, and he stepped into the black cubbyhole, drawing the door softly shut.

He knelt beside the cot. "Hester," he whispered against
her cheek. His lips brushed her skin, and he tasted salt;
she was sweating lightly.

She woke with a start, and he put his lips on hers to
keep her from speaking. He kissed her lips and stroked
her cheek. He could feel her quivering.

"It's I—Master Edward," he whispered. "Don't be
afraid."

"I'm not afraid," she whispered.

"I'm sorry to come so late, to wake you, but it's the
only way. I must wait until the household is settled."

"Of course, Master Edward, sir."

"Take off the shift," he whispered, loosening his robe,
under which he was naked.

"I'm ready, Master Edward, sir," she whispered.

Quickly he was on top of her. As he entered her, he
noted that she had spread her legs. She began to move before he did, and this he found exciting. Within seconds, he
had reached the peak. Only just in time did he withdraw,
letting seed shoot where it would, just so it wasn't into
her.

Before he entered her the second time, he asked for a
towel, and she got it and laid it at hand. His second burst
was harder, longer, fiercer. Hester, brought to the verge,
lay throbbing and reaching for what she had missed. But
she was grateful to the master; she understood, now, how
he would protect her from bearing a child.

Nightly he visited her, for nightly Mildred resorted to
laudanum. Once when over his protest, she took half
again the usual dose, he considered a flying trip to Clio
but gave it up.

This night, as usual, he went to Hester and eased himself. Instead of leaving at once, however, he lay with
her on the cot, and they whispered together. "You're being sent to the shops?" he asked.

"Yes, Master Edward, sir. The mistress took me around
them the first time and introduced me. Now Nell sends
me every day for something we need or the mistress
wants. She tells me the name of the street and of the shop,
and I ask at some of the shops when I get lost, and I do
find them all. The shopkeepers are kind to me because

Miss Mildred is such an important lady. They let me touch all the materials and other things."

"You're doing well, then. How do you like New Orleans?"

"It's beautiful, Master Edward, sir. But it scares me, it's so big. The houses are so fine with patios and courtyards and so many trees and shrubs and flowers. And the fences and gates and balconies—I know theah iron, but they look like lace."

She ached to ask him, in this moment of closeness, if he knew the Bennett family and where they lived. If he knew Phil. But she dared not. He would want to know why, and she couldn't tell him.

Phil had described the lacy ironwork to her back at Thornton. Now that she had seen it, she wished that her father could see it. Being a fine blacksmith, he would be able to do work just as beautiful, she thought.

Now the master was speaking of a tutor he had engaged to teach his daughters. She listened raptly.

"He's a handsome, personable man," the master said. "Highly educated and will, I'm convinced, do Francie and Anita a world of good. If only we can keep him any length of time. He's a restless fellow, likes to be on the move, and I don't know whether he'll be content."

"You mean he'll teach the little missies to read and write?" breathed Hester.

"And spell and do sums and study Latin. You'll probably see him every day when you go upstairs for the mistress's fittings. He'll be here mornings, have dinner with us at noon, then go to his place near the waterfront."

Hester almost blurted out her own desire to learn. Because she and the master had become friends, she almost asked to be allowed to sit in the room and listen while the girls learned. If only she could listen, she could learn. But remembering what had happened at Thornton when her father and the others had asked for a tutor, she held back the words. Besides, she remembered, she had to spend mornings with Nell, learning to sew.

She noticed that the master was staring at her. Now he picked up the candle and held it close to her face. "Something's wrong," he said. "What is it, Hester? Did I hurt you tonight, was I rough?"

"Oh, no, Master Edward, sir! Youah never rough!"

"Something's wrong," he insisted. "Tell me. I command it, Hester. I don't want you troubled and worried. Are you having to work too hard, too many hours? Is that it?"

"Oh, no, Master Edward, sir! I love my work!"

He waited. "Well," he pressed, "out with it."

Timidly, not daring to look at him, she confessed her longing to study books, to sit in the room, off in a corner, listening to the tutor instruct the little girls.

When she finished, he was silent for a heartbeat. Then he stroked her hair in a warm and comforting manner and kissed her on the brow. "I'd be willing for you to have lessons right along with my daughters," he said. "But the mistress—she has her heart set on your becoming her own private modiste. That is an education in itself, and she is making it possible. She'd never consent to the other."

"I undahstand, Master Edward, sir," Hester murmured, disappointed even though she had known that it was impossible. "Thank you kindly, just the same."

He kissed her on the lips, lightly but with a comforting touch, and then he left. She stretched flat on the cot, bitterly disappointed, even though she understood and appreciated the reasons why she could not have what she longed for. She wouldn't let herself cry.

Chapter Nineteen

Beau Kidd was a young, strikingly handsome thirty-six. The rent on his waterfront room was paid a month in advance, but he spent as little time as possible in it. His taste ran to rooms in the St. Louis Hotel, but his luck at cards had deserted him temporarily, and he was low on funds. So low that he didn't have the fare to travel up to Pittsburgh on one of the luxury steamboats.

Highly educated, once a practicing attorney, he had tired of the dry routine of law and turned to the lure of gambling, at which he was talented, and which got into his blood and drove him to the tables nightly. The gambler's life entranced him, and by the time he was thirty, he spent all his time on steamboats plying the rivers between Pittsburgh and New Orleans, flirting with unattached girls, flattering married women, often getting one, who was traveling alone, into his bed.

At first, when Edward Dalton introduced himself and stated his objective—that he was seeking a polished tutor for his small daughters—Beau had laughed. Then, seeing that this stranger, a man of means, was utterly serious, he stared in quiet astonishment.

Edward Dalton gazed back openly, studying, liking what he saw. The attorney turned gambler was six feet tall, slender-built but strong, and fashionably dressed. His skin was very white, his features so handsomely even they looked to be sculpted. His mouth was firm and unrevealing. He was worldly, suave, and intelligent. He had none of the earmarks of the usual tutor.

"You're serious about this matter," Beau Kidd said at last, and his voice was quiet.

"Entirely serious, sir."

"But you know nothing of me. Yet you would take me into your home and permit me to associate with your small daughters."

"I've made inquiries, Mr. Kidd," Dalton returned. "You come from a fine New Orleans family, you were a success at law, you're an intellectual genius. That you turned to gambling is none of my affair."

Beau Kidd smiled. "You doubtless know," he said, an innate charm coming through, "that my luck at cards has been running against me and I need funds."

"Something to that effect, yes. I'll pay you twice what a tutor usually gets, provide a room in my home—"

"I prefer to keep the room I have. I might later move into the St. Louis Hotel."

"As you please. I'll provide your noon meal—the classes will be mornings only—and you'll have afternoons and evenings to do as you please."

"What I please to do is find a card game ashore or on one of the steamboats that might have the card room open. You'd not like for your children's tutor to so occupy himself."

"What you do in your free time is your own affair," Dalton said. "You conduct yourself as a gentleman, of that I've made certain."

"I'm tempted," Beau Kidd said. "I confess I'm—astounded—that you'd offer this post to a riverboat gambler. For two small girls to associate with such a man—frankly, most people would consider it detrimental to them."

"I trust you," Edward Dalton said simply. "My objective is that they not only learn books but how to conduct themselves with a man of the world. I consider this extra preparation and insurance for the future. As you know, we are very active in society."

"I see your point," Beau Kidd said reflectively.

"My wife is in accord. I've taken the liberty of discussing you with her."

"This has come as a surprise to me," the gambler mused. "And not at all unwelcome, I might add. However. There is the time element."

"We'd want you to stay as long as you would, sir. I'd appreciate your agreement to be engaged on at least a yearly basis. I realize that, once you get some money ahead—"

"A stake," the gambler cut in. "The salary is stake enough that I can indulge in cards. However, should my luck turn and run high, it would be a temptation to board the first upriver boat."

"That's why I ask for the assurance of a year at a time," Edward admitted.

Suddenly Beau Kidd smiled. "Agreed!" he exclaimed, his voice warm and almost eager. "Even if my luck turns. If it turns while I play ashore, I'd be taking a real gamble if I started on the boats again. I'll not start that until I have a really large stake. You can depend on me, Mr. Dalton."

The following Monday, Beau Kidd arrived at Woodlawn in a hired carriage. He had won money the night before and thus could arrive at his place of employment in style. He was half-smiling, amused at the incongruity of becoming a tutor. Beau stepped lightly down from the carriage, paid the driver, and regarded the house.

It was very large, having four massive columns across the front and galleries running from one side to the other across both the ground floor and the second story. There were iron lace balconies at the upstairs windows, repeating the grape and leaf pattern of the gates.

A butler showed him to the library, where Mildred Dalton was waiting with the little girls. She greeted him regally, smiled coolly when he touched his lips to the back of her hand, introduced his pupils, and left them together.

Beau Kidd spent the entire morning telling the wide-eyed children about travel to Pittsburgh by steamboat. He described that faraway city and promised them that if they learned quickly, they could read even more about it. And then, because they were so bright and eager, he found himself promising to tell them a river story every day on which they did their lessons properly.

By the end of the first month, he found himself enjoying the situation. Mornings with Francie and Anita flew past. Being an extremely passionate man, he often spent his afternoons with one of the cleaner, prettier waterfront girls whom he paid to come to his room. In fact, this was why he had declined the offer of a room at Woodlawn. He wanted privacy, a place to bring his women.

Doubtless there were nubile wenches at Woodlawn— he had glimpsed two rather plain ones—but he had never bedded a wench, having an aversion to intimate contact with them. In any event, things were working out to his advantage.

He seldom used a carriage, the long walk between the waterfront and Woodlawn providing him with daily exercise. He was satisfied with the flatness of his belly and the overall strength of his body and meant to keep himself fit.

One day as he was leaving Woodlawn, the goodbyes of his young pupils still in his ears, he made for the small gateway that led to the street. His objective was to select the prettiest girl he could find and engage her for the afternoon.

As he went onto the sidewalk, he saw ahead of him a slender figure in brown with a brown tignon on her head. Hearing his footsteps, she turned, and he discovered that she was no servant, regardless of the shift, the tignon, and sandals. Her skin was white, her eyes a soft, deep brown.

For an instant he didn't know what to do or say. She had stopped, pressing herself against the wall to give him room to pass, and he, Beau Kidd, who had frequented the finest ballrooms, didn't know what to do.

Instinctively, he stopped. "Good afternoon," he said.

"Good afternoon, master, sir."

"You," he inquired, feeling his way, "are from Woodlawn?"

"Yes, master, sir. I'm Nell's helper. She's the seamstress."

"You're the white-skinned wench!" he exclaimed. "The one they all talk about, even Francie and Anita."

"I—yes, master, sir, I suppose I am. My name is Hester."

He looked at her, bemused. She was the most beautiful girl he had ever seen, she was as white as he was, and she was a wench. He wondered, swiftly, if he could get her to his room. She was black of blood, true, but it didn't show, and her beauty and what he could swear was purely innocent allure blotted out his aversion to wenches. To this wench, at any rate. Even though he suspected that Dalton used her, he decided that he, too, would have her sooner or later.

"I'm Master Beau Kidd," he told her. "The tutor."

She inclined her head. "I know, Master Kidd, sir," she murmured. Though she hadn't looked full at him, Hester

saw enough that she was awed by his handsomeness, his
assured manner, and his fine clothes. She even noted his
open admiration of her and felt her cheeks burn. Then she
recalled that he was a tutor, and that enhanced him further still.

"It's ridiculous for us to just stand here," he said.
"Where were you going?"

"Nell is sending me to a shop on Royal Street, Master
Kidd, sir. To match some thread," she replied.

"Run along, then," he told her. "I'm certain Nell wants
you back promptly. As for myself, I feel like strolling. So
you go first."

She gave him a small bow, then murmured, "Thank
you, Master Kidd, sir," and went running to the corner,
where she turned toward the shopping area. He walked
along slowly, toying with ways of getting her into his bed.

Now that she had seen him, had actually spoken with
him, Hester was more entranced than ever that such a
tutor came to Woodlawn five mornings a week. She recognized the same qualities in his speech as those in Phil's
and Master Edward's, which made her long more deeply
than ever to just listen—even one time—to lessons in
the library.

There came a morning when the mistress decided to do
the shopping herself and take Nell along, leaving Hester
behind. She would also stop at the brokerage, she
announced, and bring the master home for dinner.

Their departure was like a gift to Hester. The mistress
frequently went to the brokerage, but those trips were
short, and she never took Nell with her. Today she would
be gone much longer.

Hester waited to make certain they didn't come back
for some forgotten item. Then, silent, on bare feet, she
passed the kitchen. Horace was there, polishing silver. Hannah was making a cake, Docia was tidying the mistress's
rooms, and the other maids were turning out the remainder
of the second floor.

Like a shadow, Hester flitted to the library, put her
hand on the door knob, and waited. She laid her ear
against the wood but could hear nothing.

Holding her breath, she turned the knob, ever so slowly
opened the door a crack, and listened. Now she could

hear their voices, but not the words, not clearly. She pushed the door a bit further and stood quaking and listening.

"Rose," she heard one of the little girls say.

"Close your book, Francie. Keep your finger in to mark the place. Now spell the word, spell rose," said the tutor.

"R-o-s-e," Francie spelled distinctly. "Rose. That's an easy one, Mr. Kidd! Why do we have to spell easy words we already know from reading the book?"

"Because people sometimes forget how to spell a word," he said pleasantly, "even easy ones. And educated people never spell any word incorrectly."

"R-o-s-e—rose," whispered Hester, at the door. "Rose," she said aloud, softly.

There was a sudden silence in the library, a sense of listening. Hester held her breath. Had they heard her? Oh, why had she been so foolish?

"Take your spelling books," the tutor said now. "Turn to page nine. I'm going to step out of the room for a moment. When I come back, I want you to be able to spell all six of those words."

Hester turned to flee, but he was out the library door, pulling it closed behind him, before she had gone three steps. "Wait!" he ordered, speaking low.

Quivering, she stopped, her throat stiff and dry. He put a hand on her arm, drew her into the front parlor, and closed the door.

She had never been in this room. She had a confused impression of pink and blue and crystal and white marble and many cushions. Of too much of everything.

The tutor let go of her arm. He regarded her soberly. "What were you doing at the library door, little beauty?" he asked.

"L-listening, Master Kidd, sir."

"Listening to what?"

"To the spelling lesson, Master Kidd, sir."

"Why?"

"B-because I like it, Master Kidd, sir. I—I'd like to learn books."

"But you have no way to learn. Is that the trouble?"

"Yes, Master Kidd, sir. Wenches can't go to lessons."

Beau gazed at her, reading her fright. So, he thought,

she is starved for learning. "We can remedy that," he said. "I'll teach you."

"T-thank you, Master Kidd, sir, but Miss Mildred would nevah allow it. I'm to learn to be her private modiste. That takes all my time."

"I'll teach you in secret, Hester. If you pay me."

"I haven't any money, Master Kidd, sir. There's no way I can get any."

"You're not a virgin, are you?" he asked.

"No, Master Kidd, sir," she said, confused and bewildered.

"Master Edward—does he—?"

She dropped her gaze miserably. Her whole body burned.

"So. The lessons—and the payment—both must be secret," he said. "You get time away from Woodlawn, as I hear it from the little girls, to go about the shops. How often?"

"Three aftahnoons a week, Master Kidd, sir. It's part of my training, Nell says."

"Splendid. You'll be taught books, and you'll pay for it without money."

"H-how, Master Kidd, sir?"

"I'll meet you at the riverfront. Take you to my room. So you'll know where it is. I'll get you books. Once a week, I'll instruct you in them. And once a week—twice, if you can manage the time—you'll pay me, right after your lesson. How does that sound?"

"I don't undahstand the paying, Master Kidd, sir."

"A simple matter, my pretty. You go to bed with me. For a short time. I teach you books. You give me pleasure."

She felt herself blanch.

"Isn't that a fair exchange, Hester? For something you want so much? Isn't it?"

Chapter Twenty

Stunned, Hester looked straight into his hooded gray eyes. They gazed back, steady and unrelenting.

"Have you found any other way to get an education?" he asked.

"N-no, Master Kidd, sir."

"Do you think you'll get another opportunity—ever?"

Wide eyed, she shook her head. Her mind was in turmoil. It flew and darted, turned back upon itself, then flashed along another path. Would she betray her love for Phil if she willingly, by her own decision, made this arrangement? Yet Phil himself had told her to get an education in whatever manner she could.

Master Edward. Suppose he found out? What would he do? Sell her on the block again, have her whipped, or keep her and turn rough and spiteful? If she made herself sweet toward him, showed more passion, maybe he couldn't tell that she was letting another man use her. Or maybe he wouldn't care. After all, she was only a slave.

"If you're worried about your master," the tutor said as if he had looked into her mind, "he'll never know. I'll protect you from having a sucker—I'm as anxious to avoid that as you should be. I assume Dalton takes precautions?"

Her face flaming, she nodded.

"What's your decision? The offer is simple, but I'll repeat it. You come to my room. I instruct you from books. Perfect your manner of speech, which is already good. You'll learn to read, write, and do sums. After each lesson, I have my sport with you. You understand clearly?"

"Yes, Master Kidd, sir."

"Well, is it yes or no?"

"Could I—think about it?"

"There's no need for that. Either you want an education, or you don't want it. So make your decision right now."

Through no conscious volition, her mind filled with the vision of books and the wonders they held, she felt herself nod agreement. The decision was made. She swallowed miserably.

"Good wench! You'll not be sorry. I find I'm an adequate teacher, to judge from the speed with which the little girls learn. I believe that you're almost as intelligent as they are, and certainly more anxious to learn."

His words sent elation through her. Phil would want her to have the education, oh, he would! He would even understand the bed part.

"This afternoon," the tutor said. "Do you go to the shops this afternoon?"

"No, Master Kidd, sir. Not until tomorrow."

"At what hour?"

"Right aftah noon dinner, Master Kidd, sir."

"Splendid! I'll leave here a bit later tomorrow. You wait, just outside the wall. I'll lead the way, a square ahead of you, to my room. You'll see where I enter. Wait a bit—three or four minutes. Then, after you've looked around and made certain no one you know has seen you, tap at the door. My room opens onto Chartres Street."

"But the shops, Master Kidd, sir? How will I go to the shops?"

"Damn! You've got to know the way to my place. Tomorrow I'll give you a short lesson, one you'll not have to pay for. Then you can hurry to the shops—they let you in at that hour, the siesta hour?"

"The important ones do, Master Kidd, sir. Miss Mildred is such a good customer."

"So, you'll do what you must at the shops quickly. Our arrangement is going to require delicate timing; you must always get back to Woodlawn when you're expected. Otherwise, you'll be in disfavor, and it could even lead to your actions being discovered and the loss of my own employment."

"Oh, Master Kidd, sir!" Hester whispered. "It sounds very dangerous!"

"Not if we're careful. We'll allow one hour for both lesson and payment. Can you manage your errands that one day a week and get back to Woodlawn on time?"

She considered. "I can run very fast. I'm told to take my time in the shops, being careful not to bother the shop-keepers."

"What has this to do with timing?" he asked, his eye on the door as though he suspected someone might come in.

"I'll take less time in each shop," she explained. "And I'll run very fast."

"You'd better not run at all. It's certain to draw attention. Just walk as fast as you can and take short cuts."

"Yes, Master Kidd, sir."

"Tomorrow, then," he whispered. "Go back to the Quarters or wherever you're supposed to be."

"In my room, Master Kidd, sir. Sewing."

"Sew, then." He went to the door, glanced up and down the corridor, signaled to her that it was safe, and then he disappeared. She escaped to her room, which seemed like a haven now, and began to stitch. Her fingers trembled so that her stitches were uneven, and she had to pull them out and start over.

When he came through the gate, she was waiting. He walked briskly along the sidewalk and past her as if she didn't exist, and she lingered, fiddling with her sandal strap, until he had gone a full square.

Then she followed, taking note of the streets they traversed, the corners they turned. As always, though intent on learning the route to Beau Kidd's room, she observed the homes she could see and tried to look into the walled courtyards of others. And with every house she passed, she wondered, Is this where Phil lives? If he came through that gate now, what would happen?

As she often did, she toyed with the idea of one day asking some slave the location of the Bennett home, but again she gave up the idea. She dared not bring shame on Phil; the very slave she asked might gossip and say there was a white-skinned wench looking for Master Philip Bennett, and he would be embarrassed before his friends and incur the anger of his father. For Phil, she realized unhappily, might no longer love her as she loved him. The idea made her so heartsore she rejected it. Phil would never stop loving her.

Beau Kidd had gotten too far ahead. She had to trot a bit to close the space. Then she fell into the fast walk that kept her at the proper distance.

Woodlawn was on St. Charles Avenue, from which they had turned onto Eighth Street and continued, street after street, passing some of the shops Hester would visit later. They crossed Rampart, Burgundy, Dauphine, Bourbon, then turned onto what must be Chartres. They went two squares, and Beau Kidd stopped at a tall brick house painted buff, opened a door, and went inside.

Hester dawdled, glancing in all directions. Though there were some white people passing and a number of slaves, she saw no one she recognized.

Even so, her knees were unsteady when she tapped at Master Kidd's door. He opened instantly, drew her inside, and locked the door.

"My room, you see, is plain," he said. "But it suffices for the short time I spend awake in it."

It was a small room, though larger than her own in the Quarters. There was plain carpeting, clean drapes, a dresser, an armoire, a table, and two chairs. And the bed, neatly made.

She felt herself blushing about the bed and turned her back to it. In so doing, she caught Beau's eyes as they flashed hungrily over her.

"Sit at the table, Hester," he said.

She did so. He opened a drawer in the table and lifted out a small, worn book. She saw paper, a pen, and ink in the drawer, and her pulse quickened. This was it! This was the moment in which her education was to begin! She was almost gasping with excitement and had to breathe deeply and steadily to calm herself.

He pulled the other chair up beside hers, opened the book, and spread it on the table. There was the picture of a child's bright red ball on the first page, and below it letters.

"Have you learned your letters?" Beau Kidd asked.

"Only in my own name—Hester, Master Kidd, sir. Granny Myrtle taught me to write them in dirt. She taught me to count to fifty."

Beau Kidd put one finger under the letters in the book.

There were four of them. "What does that word say, Hester?"

"Ball!" she whispered in wonder. "It says ball!"

He pointed to the opposite page on which was a picture of a small boy. There were three letters under it.

"Boy!" Hester cried. "It says boy, doesn't it, Master Kidd, sir?"

He gazed at her in surprise. "You *are* quick!" he exclaimed. He returned to the first page and indicated each letter in turn. "B-a-l-l. That spells ball." He moved the finger. "B-o-y, that spells boy. Now. Let me hear you spell them."

Frowning in concentration, she pointed out each letter in the word ball and spelled it correctly. Then she did the same with the word boy.

"Perfect!" Master Kidd exclaimed. "Do it again. Read the words, then spell them. After that, close the book and see if you can spell them from your mind only."

She obeyed, and he laughed. "I never saw such a quick study! Not that I've had much experience. Not with a wench—" He shook his head. "Remarkable!"

He took out a pen, ink, and paper. He dipped the pen into the ink, printed two words on the paper and blotted them carefully. Then he pointed to the first word. "What does it say?"

"Boy," she replied promptly. "And the other one, ball."

"I'll make you an alphabet," he said. "You've grasped these words so quickly without it that—but you need the alphabet."

"Alphabet, Master Kidd, sir?"

He began to write. "The letters," he explained. "Words, all words, are made up of letters. You can hide this paper in your tignon. Then, when you have a chance, study the letters."

"That's the same letter that's in boy and ball," she cried as he printed the letter B.

"Splendid!" he said, writing more letters. "I'm certain that it's most unusual for an untrained mind to pick out that similarity at the first lesson. You can search the alphabet as you study and find the other letters in boy and ball."

She marveled at how fast he wrote and how clearly. She identified the letters used in the words boy and ball and learned their names. He read the letters from A through J to her and had her repeat them until she had them memorized, which she did quickly.

Then he folded the paper and gave it to her. "When you study these, knowing them by memory will help you to identify them. Next week, I expect you to recognize each one when I write it by itself."

Smiling, she secreted the paper in her tignon.

Beau took out his watch and glanced at it. "How quick you are. We did all this in half an hour! It's a pleasure to teach you!"

Hester was so excited over her first lesson that she felt guilty about accepting it free. Haltingly, she told him so.

She caught the glitter in his eyes, saw them travel her form, and could all but feel them looking through her shift. "We made a bargain," he reminded her. "I was to give you one lesson free."

"But the lesson was so fast," she said, "that there's as much time today as there will be othah days for me to— to—"

"I'm so taken by your beauty," he said, "so excited by your sparkle and enthusiasm that I stand ready to be paid. Agreement or no agreement."

"I'm willing, Master Kidd, sir," she whispered.

She took the folded paper out of her tignon and laid it on the table. He was undressing as she unwound the tignon and hung it on a chair. Swiftly he draped his garments on the other chair and turned just as she pulled her shift off, her auburn hair tumbling far down her back.

For an instant they stood looking at each other. By God, he thought, what a wench! He started toward her, ready, but he didn't forget to snatch up a towel on the way.

Looking at Beau Kidd, Hester decided he was more handsome than anyone in the world but Phil. She let Beau push her onto the bed, but the thought of Phil almost made her cry out that she couldn't go through with it. But then she believed that Phil would want her to keep her word, to pay her way, though he would not like the manner in which she was doing it, and she prayed to Phil, even as Beau was positioning her, Forgive me—please forgive me. . . . And then the prayer vanished.

"Get on your hands and knees," Master Kidd directed. "Buttocks in the air."

She was clumsy about it, but he helped her until she

was arranged to his liking. She gasped when he thrust into her woman part from behind; it felt different than it had felt before.

"You don't have to move," he said. "Just hold steady."

She tensed, set her jaw, and held her breath. She strained against the mattress to keep her position, but time after time his lunges almost pushed her onto her face. He began to groan and murmur, to thrust faster and harder, and then she felt him withdraw, and she dropped to the bed, rolled onto her side, and saw that he was clutching the towel.

"Superb!" he gasped. "Magnificent! Now—that didn't take long, and I'm still—we have time for one more. This round, you sit on me."

Bewildered, she watched him lie flat, the soles of his feet on the mattress, his knees spread. His part was big and stiff, and at this she marveled; Master Edward needed to rest between times. She wondered if this ability made Master Kidd more manly, stronger.

"Straddle me—no, facing me," he directed. "Now, let me enter—that's a good girl." He moved beneath her and groaned. "Next, we play a game," he continued. "I'm a stallion, and you're a horsewoman. You bounce up and down, careful to keep us linked, and I gallop and buck. You have to hit hard on the downthrust to keep us together. Now—start!"

They went into wild, hard motion. At first the bounce and upstroke hurt her, but gradually she began to get used to it. Again he was groaning, even cursing, and this time, before he pushed her away and reached for his towel, that sudden, inner hotness that was so wicked with anyone but Phil took her, and she moaned with it.

"Wash up if you like, though there's no need," Beau told her. "You're clean as you were when you came into this room and always will be."

She dressed rapidly, then began to wind the tignon around her head. When it was tucked in, she hid the alphabet paper in it. "I thank you for the lesson, Master Kidd, sir," she said. "And for—" Her face burning, she motioned to the towel on the bed.

"Oh, that," he said carelessly, reaching for his clothes. "There'll be no black suckers born with the features of Beau Kidd. Not even yours, lovely as you are. I'll not mix my blood with Negro blood."

Curiously, though there was logic in what he said, this hurt. What a cruel thing to say, she thought. And, though it was to her benefit even more than to his, she wished he had made no more of it than Master Edward did, who followed the same practice and for the same reason.

Chapter Twenty-one

✳

At Thornton, during these months, Eve, George, and Thorne Wabash waged a ceaseless power struggle. It was Eve who made the first move, and that on her wedding night.

Tight-lipped, she had given a semi-ardent George access to her body, keeping her nightgown on, permitting him to fold it to her waist. When he pierced her treasured virginity, she whimpered and clutched her fists on his back but let him have his way, lying rigid, moving not so much as a toe.

When it was over, he lit a lamp—she had demanded darkness for his bestiality—and she winced and looked away when he would have stared into her eyes. She wasn't crying—at least he didn't have that to cope with—but she was no happy bride.

"You didn't like it, did you?" he asked, getting back into his nightshirt.

"It was horrible—nasty!"

"So you're one of those."

"What do you mean by that, George Drummond?"

"That some women hate what goes on in bed. And you sure don't act as if you like it."

"It's horrible!"

"You'd better not deprive me. I won't tolerate it."

"I'll do my wifely duty! But nothing can make me like it! So don't try!"

"If that's the way you feel," he grated, "why put up with it?"

"Because we need heirs, that's why!" she spat. "We need at least two sons!"

"Why two?"

"One to inherit my plantation and one to inherit Thornton! And maybe a third son to inherit other plantation land we'll buy! The Drummonds will be the most powahful plantahs in the state of Mississippi, and I'll be the one who made it possible! In this bed!"

"We'll get the power," he snarled, "but it will be my brains and my ability that does it. Not your ability to push out sons the way a wench in the Quarters pushes out suckers! One son is all we'll have. I don't like the nasty little brats, and one is all I'll put up with!"

"I don't like them, either!" she cried, her eyes wild. "But we've got to have them to be a powah in the state! I plan to turn them ovah to mammies to raise—I don't want them in my sight any more than you do!"

George, who had achieved some pleasure from Eve on this night, considered her plan to have two or three sons. It took only brief thought. He would not have screaming brats infesting Thornton. One heir, that was all. He kept silent about this; if he debated the question with Eve, she might get hysterical or even swoon, and he didn't want that kind of uproar.

She would find out in time. After his heir was born, he wouldn't touch her in bed. It was as simple as that. Let her berate and carry on and demand if she wanted to lower herself; he would be adamant.

It was at breakfast the next morning, which they took with Thorne Wabash in the dining room, that Eve made her second move. She frowned sharply when she saw the older man take his usual place at the head of the table, with a place set for her at his right and one for George at his left.

Thorne caught the frown. "What's wrong with you, Eve?" he demanded.

"Nothing, suh," she said shortly, and laid her napkin across her lap.

"A bride doesn't frown on the first morning of her marriage," he pressed. "I must know everything that goes on in this house. So speak."

"Well," she snapped, "if you must know, I'm surprised that George isn't sitting at the head of the table, with myself at the foot, as befits the mistress of the house."

"Eve!" George exclaimed angrily. "Remember who you're speaking to!"

"My grandson is right, young woman," said Thorne Wabash sternly. "He isn't the master here yet, nor are you the mistress. When you are—when I'm no longer in existence—then George will sit at the head of this table and you at the foot. Not one moment before."

"You owe Grandfather an apology!" George said fiercely.

"I meant no harm," Eve said clearly. "If I'm anxious to take my propah place as mistress of Thornton—you said you want me to oversee the running of the house, suh— it seemed to me that the seating should be propah."

"It is proper," Thorne said coldly. "Now. I suppose you have other things on your mind—being a woman, and with the duties of directing the house slaves. Out with them, here and now. I haven't the patience to be confronted with a constant stream of minor irritations such as this."

Eve inclined her head deliberately and waited to speak until Old Dewey had served the meal and gone back to the kitchen. When she spoke, her words came smoothly, as though she had rehearsed them.

"It is my wish and my plan to decorate the interior of Thornton, Grandfather."

"Decorate? What the hell's wrong with the way it is?"

"Some of the velvets show wear, as do the carpets. The furniture is old-fashioned, and George and I, being young and expected to entahtain the countryside, need things modern."

The older man glared at her, speechless.

"Besides, the colahs must be changed. All of them."

"For what reason?" demanded Thorne hotly. "These colors are deep and vivid, and the ladies call them jewel-toned."

"They're wrong for me," Eve said steadily. "I have pale gold hair, and my eyes are a delicate blue and my skin the purest white. I am like a fragile, delicate jewel. To display my looks, I require rooms decorated in powdah blue, powdah pink—very delicate—with touches of gold."

"*I never heard such tomfoolery!*" shouted Thorne Wabash. "What do you think you are—a portrait that needs a special light?"

"You've got the idea exactly, Grandfather, suh!" exclaimed Eve. "Oh, I know it doesn't please you, but when you see how this whole house will bloom with delicate beauty—and I know you can afford it. You can afford anything!"

"Afford, hell! Sure I can afford it! But you'll not do it, not in my lifetime! I'm through with catering to female whims, with fixing up houses to display a certain beauty—or lack of it!"

"Suh! Do you imply I lack beauty?"

"I imply only one thing, Mrs. George Drummond. You can spend all you like on clothes—George can buy you a few jewels—but the seating at table and the redecoration of Thornton will never come to pass during my lifetime! I like things the way they are, I'm the master, and they remain as they are!"

Later, in their rooms, George and Eve quarreled violently.

"You let him talk to me as if I were a wench!" Eve accused. "Why didn't you speak up for me? I'm youah wife—youah bride—the mothah of your future sons! You could at least have taken my side about decorating! Instead, you just sat there and ate your ham and grits! Why didn't you take up for me—why?"

"Because he's the master," George told her furiously. "Because if we don't toe the mark with the old man—what do you think I've been doing all these years?—he'll change his mind and leave Thornton to somebody else! Phil, even! And I'm telling you now to keep your mouth shut and do what he wants!"

"And when he dies? Will you let me have my way then?"

"I don't see anything wrong with the house."

"But by the time he—it'll keep running down, the velvet thinnah—the carpets—! You want Thornton to be the showplace of the state, don't you?"

"Certainly."

"Well, then!"

"What you want'd cost a fortune."

"So? It'll be worth a fortune, won't it? To have the finest place in the state! To have it talked about in New Orleans, maybe."

"I won't say yes, and I won't say no," snapped George thinking of the enormous cost, yet wanting the finest home in the world. He wouldn't even give Eve the satisfaction of a half-promise, but went out to inspect the fields.

Eve never gave up nagging George about the house, trying to force him to promise to let her decorate when his grandfather died. And, though he had decided the house could use new things from top to bottom, he'd be damned if he would give her the satisfaction of saying so.

She was at him all the time, wanting this ring or that brooch. She wanted to go to New Orleans, and he refused to take her. She wanted, wanted, wanted.

She looked more faded and plainer to him every day. Almost every night she was ready to try for an heir, and when her monthly time came, she wept in anger and waited impatiently for it to end so they could try again. When they weren't quarreling over the future decoration of Thornton, they were quarreling about both plantations—his and hers.

She still refused to have any name but her own put on her father's plantation when she inherited. George, in turn, refused to agree to have her name put on Thornton when he inherited.

All they did was quarrel and try for an heir—and hate each other.

Chapter Twenty-two

On January 11, 1858, Hester was fifteen, though she told no one. She had grown in height and filled out, making it necessary to let out the seams at the top of her shifts and to lengthen the hems. Every moment of her time in New Orleans, she had inwardly longed for the affection she had lost when she was sold away from Thornton. She missed the kindness of the slaves, the love of her parents. Most of all, she longed for Phil's arms, his lips, his body.

It was now that she began actively to search for him. One afternoon she stole time to run to where the steamboats docked, seeking one of the showboats, but, though she found one tied up for the winter, and people were moving about it, Phil was not among them.

She continued to study every house she passed, taking different routes as she became more familiar with the city, in order to see different homes. She had no plan. She prayed just to see Phil, even at a distance, or, failing that, to see the house in which he lived. Her boldest hope was someday to speak to him, to know that he was well and content, to explain what she was doing with Master Edward and Master Kidd and why.

One day, pretending to be on an errand to the Bennett house, she ventured to stop two black women and ask directions. One woman had heard of the family, but didn't know where they lived. The other knew nothing at all. Hester dropped this practice as both futile and dangerous.

She continued to use different routes, however, watching, always watching, for any sign of Phil. Phil who might be on some showboat tied up at some other city.

Gradually, as she began to feel at home on the streets, she came to love the city and to drink in its beauty and excitement, to gaze at and admire the finely dressed ladies who passed in their carriages. She thought how fortunate they were, like Miss Mildred, to live in and command such luxury, to pay calls in the afternoons, and dine and dance at balls in the evenings. It never occurred to her to want this life for herself; she yearned only for Phil and for books.

She progressed rapidly with her cutting, fitting, and sewing. At one of the dinners Mildred attended, she wore a sparkling silver gown that Hester had designed, though Nell had directed the cutting and helped with the sewing. Nell told Hester that word had come through the grapevine that Miss Mildred had boasted that evening of the young wench modiste she was training, that soon every garment she wore would be designed exclusively for herself.

During this period, too, Hester raced through every new book, every subject Beau Kidd put before her. She always had a book hidden under her mattress; she studied at night, a candle beside her, after Nell was asleep and the Quarters dark. She absorbed what was in the books, worked her sums quickly, and labored to make her handwriting like that of Beau Kidd.

He was in a state of constant amazement over her. "You never forget anything I tell you," he said one day after their time in bed. "That's a quality few students have, even those in college."

"It's that I'm anxious to learn, Master Kidd, sir."

"You're already far ahead of the little girls. By the end of another year," he predicted, "you'll be ready for higher subjects."

His words drove her to more intensive study. Sometimes, as she meticulously cut out a new gown for her mistress, it was hard for her to keep from yawning with weariness from nighttime study, but she did. Nell, who watched the cutting so carefully, would want to know at once why she was sleepy and might even come to her room and discover her with a candle burning and a book open.

All the while, that ache to get some word of Phil was growing in her.

On a March afternoon when Beau Kidd was unusually pleased both with her grasp of sums and her performance in bed, she dressed more quickly than she generally did, in order to gain time to speak with him for a moment. She stood at the door, waiting for him to peer out and make certain no one he knew was walking by before she went out.

When she didn't move aside, he looked at her in surprise. "Why, Hester, what is it?"

"A favor I'd like to ask of you, Master Kidd, sir."

"I don't know whether I can grant it. If I can, I will. Speak out."

"I wonder, Master Kidd, sir, if you know the Bennett family?" she asked, her heart thundering. "Mr. Bennett is an attorney."

"I know of him, though I'm not personally acquainted. Why do you ask?"

"They were kind to me at the plantation, Master Kidd, sir."

"Ah. At—what was the name of it?"

"Thornton, Master Kidd, sir."

"Yes. The plantation where you were born."

"Yes, Master Kidd, sir. Do you know where they live, on what street, in which house?"

"I can find out easily enough. But you can't go calling on white people because they were once kind to you, Hester."

"Oh, I never would, Master Kidd, sir! It's just that I might walk past their house—on the other side of the street, and see it, only."

He gave her a searching look, then, as was his nature, demanded payment for this favor he might do her. "If you'll give me two afternoons in bed—no time out for lessons—I'll find out where the house is and tell you how to get to it," he said.

"Very well, Master Kidd, sir," she agreed, giving up her treasured lessons for knowledge of Phil.

"You consider it a fair exchange? You won't sulk?"

"It's fair, Master Kidd, sir. I nevah—"

"Never, Hester. Sound your r's, always."

"Thank you, Master Kidd, sir. I never sulk."

He studied her, and his firm mouth relaxed. "No. You never do. That's one of your charms. See to it that it remains a part of you."

"Yes, Master Kidd, sir."

He opened the door and motioned that it was safe for

her to leave, and she went, walking quietly, turning the
first corner. She felt like skipping, like running to the
shops, but that would attract attention. Her glowing heart,
her joy that soon she would know where Phil lived and
would see his house, filled her with anticipation.

The very next time she went to Beau Kidd's room, there
were no books out, nor did she expect them. The bed
was open, and Beau was wearing only a dark blue robe.

Burning with the need to know if he had located Phil's
house, she held back the question. She let him undress her
and slowly wind the tignon off her head. When she stood
nude, he cast his robe aside and drew her to him so their
bodies touched. He ran his fingers through her hair.

"Ah, Hester," he murmured, "what a luxury to have a
full hour with you! What a gift!" He bent his head, put
his lips over hers, and kissed her, running the tip of his
tongue between her teeth. Suddenly he withdrew his
tongue and urged her onto the bed.

She lay flat, awaiting his pleasure. He might want her
on her knees; he might start with her sitting on him that
peculiar way, or he might take her from the side as he
sometimes did, or even directly atop her, as Master Edward always did.

"We've time for something new today," he murmured.

He stretched on his back, drew her hand over, and
placed it on his male part. "Take hold," he directed.
"Press me. Embrace me."

She did as he said. He was distended and hard, though
his skin had the quality, almost, of velvet, and this amazed
her. She pressed a bit more firmly, and he moaned. Bewildered, she wondered what he would do next.

"Kiss me!" he whispered. "Kiss me now!"

She let go of him, lifted herself to her elbow, and put
her lips on his. He turned his head aside before she could
complete the kiss.

"Not there, you innocent! Kiss where you held me!"

Her insides seemed to lurch. She couldn't do it. This
wasn't natural. Phil had been natural, and Master Edward. Even the overseer, in his cruel and violent passion,
had been natural.

"Hester," Beau Kidd groaned. "Don't make me suffer!
I've waited for this, dreamed of it. It's a part of our
bargain!"

Because of that, because she had made a bargain with
him and this was what he demanded, she gripped him
anew.

"Straddle me," he instructed. "Keep the grip, then kiss."

Dazed, she sat astride his legs, held that velvet stiffness,
and lowered her head. Her lips came onto him, and she
kissed. Her stomach convulsed, and she swallowed, hard.
She couldn't throw up. Not now, not here. Not because
of anything Master Kidd demanded, because he was going
to give her the information for which she so longed.

"Again," he groaned. "From the top to the tip—a string
of kisses."

Sickened, she did as he said. When she miraculously
reached the end and would have lifted her head, he
grasped it on each side and held it in place.

"Take me into your mouth!" he moaned.

Her stomach convulsed again, and her lips parted because of it. Quickly he pushed past them. It was over in
just a moment. And this time she did throw up, using his
slops bucket.

"Here, rinse your mouth," he said, putting a glass of
water into her hand. His tone was patient, even kind.
Gently he guided her, once more, to the bed.

He lay down and pulled her into his arms. "You didn't
like that, not at all, did you, Hester?"

"I'm sorry, Master Kidd, sir," she whispered, somehow
keeping revulsion out of her voice.

"You'll learn to like it," he assured her. "I'll not ask it
often, but let you come into it gradually."

"You never—before—" she dared, frightened and re-
volted.

"Dalton never did that?"

"Oh, no, Master Kidd, sir!"

"He either doesn't want to frighten you, or he doesn't
know what he's missing. There's nothing—peculiar—about
any of the things in which we indulge, Hester. There's no
reason why lovemaking must be in one position and only
one. I've taught you several methods and will teach you
more. You need keep only one thing in mind—whatever
a man does to a woman—or a wench—in bed that gives
them pleasure isn't wrong or unnatural. Our bodies are
made to be enjoyed. Can you grasp that?"

"Y-yes, Master Kidd, sir," she said hesitantly. If Phil

asked the things of her that Master Kidd required, she
might be timid, but she would give him the delight he
wanted.

The rest of the hour, to her relief, was spent in simpler
acts. Once or twice she even felt a flash of that hot, con-
suming pleasure she had known with Phil.

After the second hour-long session, Beau Kidd told
her where the Bennett house was located. On her way
home she went by it. It was on Bienville Street, and she
had passed it many times. It was surrounded by high
walls, and from the opposite side of the street, she could
glimpse only patches of roof. Even the double gate of the
patio was so located that she couldn't get the first look
inside the grounds.

She walked slowly. Was Phil in the great house? Was
he thinking of her, longing for her, even as she yearned for
him? She reached the corner and went on, not retracing
her steps lest she be late getting back to Woodlawn.

Almost daily, she walked past Phil's house. Never did
she see any movement.

It was on a day in April, when she was on her way back
to Woodlawn, that she saw a black girl slip through those
gates, a market basket on her arm. On impulse, she
crossed over and timidly accosted the girl, who was younger than herself, and very black.

She looked up in surprise as Hester approached, stared
at her skin, then, reassured by the tignon, smiled. "You
a new wench around heah?" she asked.

"No," Hester said, her pulse drumming. "I belong to
some people on another street."

"I've belonged to the Bennetts all my life," said the
wench. "Bohn heah. I'm Bev. I go to mahket fo' the
cook."

"Is the Bennett family large?" Hester asked, feeling her
way. "Do you have many people to market for?"

"Jus' the mastah an' the mistress. And the young mastah, when he home."

Hester waited, not daring to ask where the young master went, desperately willing that Bev should tell, of her
own accord.

"You got lots of folks to mahket fo'?" asked Bev.

Hester shook her head. "Just the master and mistress

and the little missies," she said. Let the girl think that she, too, went to buy food. Thus, if she mentioned this conversation, Hester's identity wouldn't be suspected.

"No han'some young mastah at yo' house?" asked Bev.

"No. None."

"They the one at ouah house, when he home."

Cautiously, Hester asked the one question she couldn't resist asking. She managed to frame it as a statement. "Some young gentlemen go abroad," she said.

Bev looked dazed. "Wheah that?"

"They get on a ship and sail to other countries. England and France. Far across the ocean."

"Not ouah young mastah! He travel with whut he call a showboat. He a actah. The showboat, it go up an' down the rivah, an' he *acts*. He got to be awful smart to act. That wheah he is now, and the mistress, she said that next wintah, 'stead of spendin' time at home, he goin' to be in a cold place wheah the rivahs begin."

"Pittsburgh," Hester murmured, then knew she shouldn't have said it. However, she decided, Bev wouldn't remember the name of Pittsburgh, and she herself, now that she knew where Phil was, would rarely come past his house. So even if Bev did tell that a white-skinned wench had known the name of the city where the young master would spend the winter, no connection could be made between herself and Phil. It was vital that she keep any embarrassment away from Phil.

January came again, and Hester was sixteen. Another year went by, and she was seventeen. She had reached her full growth; her love for Phil had grown with her body.

She still wore dark brown, not shifts now, but simple dresses that outlined her breasts. At Mildred's order, she still wore the brown tignon to mark her slave status. She was now designing, cutting, and fitting every garment Mildred and the little girls wore.

She continued to go to bed with both white men and had come to compare them to each other and to Phil. Sometimes, when Edward or Beau was making love to her, she tried to pretend that it was Phil, but the flood of sweet passion she sought escaped her always now and left her throbbing for her beloved.

She went to the riverfront often, seeking showboats.

She came away dejected. Not once did she so much as see
Phil's picture on any of the posters at the boats and thus
had no way of even guessing where he was at any time.

"You've grown up, Hester," Beau Kidd said one day.
They had been through her Latin assignment and had
spent their time in bed. She didn't have to rush now as she
had in the beginning; Mildred expected her to comb the
shops for small, unusual items.

"I'm seventeen," she replied. "I am grown up."

"You're a miracle," he told her. "I'd wager there's not
a white girl, and you could pass for white anywhere, in
all the world as beautiful as you."

"Thank you, Master Kidd, sir. You flatter me."

"Not at all. You're the reason I've stayed on in New
Orleans. You're the reason I haven't long since been
traveling the rivers. I find so much pleasure with you that
every time the urge takes me to leave, I think of the de-
lights in this room and stay on. How long it will last, I
don't know. If you were a white girl, and had a dowry—"
He gestured. "But such is not the situation. When I do go,
Hester, I'll not tell you goodbye—it would hurt. I'll just
go. Please understand."

She inclined her head. She liked him and had come to
understand that his strange ways of making love were a
natural part of him. She had learned to accept them, but
not to like or enjoy them.

"You're talented beyond compare," he went on. "You're
as adept in bed as any whore—better—for you have a
quality of innocence and delicacy that they lack. You're
as solid in education as I am, with the exception of law.
You've absorbed knowledge the way a sponge drinks up
water. And I know, from the dresses I see on Mrs. Dalton
and Francie and Anita, that you've become a modiste
beyond compare. You could set up shop and make a
good living if you could buy your freedom."

They parted at the end of an hour and a half, and that
statement about freedom sang in Hester as she made her
way back to Woodlawn. Some masters did permit their
slaves to work and earn the money to buy their freedom.
They were kind masters, but surely no kinder than Master
Edward.

She kept this idea to herself, and it warmed her and
grew. For the first time she deliberately evaluated her life
and that of all slaves.

The white man had no right, she decided, to buy and sell the black man. The anger that had periodically risen in her since childhood and that she had resisted in order to get along with the masters and to avoid punishment, she recognized as the normal reaction of any human being. She would no longer be ashamed of it.

Because of this changed attitude toward slaves and masters, she chose a day and walked deliberately past Phil's house, moving slowly, trying to see the dwelling hidden by the mass of bushes and trees.

As she neared the small gate that led to the front of the unseen house, a lady appeared from the wealth of trees, laid a gloved hand on the gate, and stepped through. They were face to face, and Hester gazed, her heart at a standstill.

The lady was dressed for the street in dusky rose, a matching bonnet on her exquisite black hair. Her brown eyes swept Hester slowly, warmed, and her lips curved in a smile that made her features, which were beautiful in repose, softer and lovelier than any Hester had ever seen. Hester stopped to permit the lady to pass along the sidewalk first. As she stopped, her own lips went into a natural smile, and they stood, smiling together. Hester longed to beg this lady, who must certainly be Phil's mother, for word of him but held back the impulse.

The lady spoke, her voice clear and soft. "You go first, my dear," she said. "I'm waiting for my maid."

Their eyes, of an identical brown, clung. Then Hester nodded and passed on, her heart, which had been so still, now beating furiously. That she had seen and spoken to Phil's mother she hadn't the least doubt.

Long before she reached Beau's room, she had made up her mind. She would buy her freedom.

Now, for the first time, she waited impatiently for the master to seek her out.

It was almost a week before he did so. She serviced him carefully, slowly, the way he liked. She stroked his chest, down across his belly, almost to his maleness. This always excited him. When he had had her twice and was ready to go, she asked him to wait a moment. He stood, his hand on the doorknob, a pleased and friendly expression on his face.

"I have a request, Master Edward," she murmured.

"Yes, Hester. What is your request?"

"I know that sometimes a master permits a slave to work and buy his or her freedom, Master Edward."

"Meaning that is what you want to do?" he asked, not smiling, but no less kind.

"Yes, Master Edward, sir."

"And how could you pay me fifty-two hundred dollars?" he asked gently. "To say nothing of the thousand and more you've gained in value since you've been at Woodlawn? You've even learned to speak as we do."

"I'd pay for it all, Master Edward, sir. Even the profit."

His eyes looked sad. Even in the candlelight, she saw the sadness.

"By working as a modiste, no doubt, Hester?"

"Yes, Master Edward, sir."

"It can't be, Hester," he said, "now or ever. Not only do I want you in bed, but I've promised the mistress that she can keep you for the sewing. So you won't have false hopes, the fact that you *are* an unexcelled modiste makes it certain that Woodlawn is to be your permanent home."

Chapter Twenty-three

The efforts Edward Dalton had made to beget an heir had been useless. Doggedly, Mildred insisted upon the once-a-month pattern. After some additional attempts to persuade her to increase this to once a week, after enduring her screams, tears, and threats, Edward desisted.

He lost the sense of being followed, persisted in his after-supper walks, and made regular visits to Clio. During periods in which Mildred became fretful and suspicious and resumed her unexpected visits to the brokerage, he took his walk but refrained from going to the Ramparts. It was at these times, which lasted a fortnight or more, that he went to Hester in the deep of night.

In February of 1860, Mildred was again called to Natchez. Both her parents were ill, her mother from her heart, her father with a minor stroke.

"I'll not be here for our next encounter," Mildred told Edward as they prepared for bed. "I expect you to remain the gentleman you've always been while I'm away."

"Yes, Mildred. Yet you're always suspicious."

"Because I know your appetite for a woman! You're worse than most gentlemen, of that I'm convinced."

"Perhaps I need it more," he said quietly. "It could be that if you'd been more generous all these years, things would have been happier for both of us."

"I've two daughters to prove my generosity, Edward Dalton!" She gave him a sharp look, and she frowned. "Heaven help you if you ever betray me! You're mine, my husband. I have no regrets. I grant you sufficient marital rights, and I'm prepared to risk my life for you—again—by becoming enceinte. Need I remind you of that? What more can you ask?"

"Nothing, Mildred, I'm asking nothing."

"Nor am I. I'm only reminding you of my rights."

"You'll lose none of them, my dear," he told her quietly, with a twisted kind of honesty. She had never had the rights of which she spoke, because he had taken Clio into his heart before he married. Guilt touched him. "Perhaps tonight we could try again for the baby," he said. "To make up for the time we'll miss."

"No!" she lashed. "You *know* I'm worried about my parents, know I'm tired and worn out from overseeing the packing, yet you suggest that we—! Absolutely not! I simply will not endure—when I have a journey ahead, the girls to oversee, and responsibilities when I get to Natchez! The—fornicating can wait!"

He caught his breath, then struggled not to smile. He wondered where she had picked up the word, fornicate, and knew that she was set against his touching her or she never would have used it.

She was blushing now, but she was still angry, too angry, at the moment, to blame him for causing her to use a word no lady ever used.

Wearily, he accepted her refusal and got into the bed after she had taken her laudanum, which she measured carefully. "Just enough to help me get off to sleep," she said, as she always did. "Not one drop more, not even tonight!"

It was a relief to have her out of the house. Edward missed the children and the way they came running when he got home. He told Beau Kidd to look on the time his students were away as a paid vacation.

"Enjoy yourself," he said. "I know you'll make the girls study a bit harder when they get back."

"That I shall," Beau replied, and smiled. "All I need do is increase the size of their assignments. They'll catch up quickly."

Assuming that Mildred would be in Natchez close to a month, Edward went to Clio nightly, adhering to his pattern of the long after-supper walk. Though he had to force himself to do so, he left the little house on the Ramparts at nine o'clock, just as he did when Mildred was at home, so that Horace, when he opened the door, knew that the master was back on schedule. There would be no deviation for Mildred to discover, no undue suspicion roused, nothing for her to get hold of.

It was during this time that Clio asked Edward to father another child. "I know, without speaking, that it's against your better judgment," she said, as she lay in his arms one evening. "But I long for a baby, perhaps a little girl."

He kissed her deeply, his passion roused. "We'd only have to give her up, my love," he reminded her. "I can't put you through that again. Or myself. And with a girl, it would be much more difficult, maybe impossible, to establish her as we have the boys. And we'd want her to live white, you know we would."

She wept, pressing her salty lips to his, her naked curves against him. Their lovemaking was hotter, sweeter, than it had been in months, but at the end he made certain she was protected.

Mildred and the girls returned in three weeks. As she moved about the suite, overseeing Docia's unpacking, Mildred announced that her parents were well on the way to recovery.

After Docia had gone, Mildred faced Edward fully, her pale eyes glittering as they bored into his. "And you?" she demanded. "How did you occupy yourself while I was in Natchez? While I was on call to first one sickroom, then the other?"

"The same as when you're here," he half-lied. "I went to business, had my meals at home, took my walk, read a while, was in bed at eleven."

"I'll know soon enough if that's true!" she said, unaccountably vicious.

"If you mean to test me in bed," he retorted, suddenly angry, "let's have a go at it here and now! You notice I'm here, that I'm taking no walk, even!"

"At least you're consistent!" she flared. "You know what I've been through, worrying about Mama and Papa, you know I've had to travel home, a woman alone with two children and a wench. Yet you actually expect—and the very night I arrive! Without even an hour's rest!"

"I'm sorry, Mildred," he said, meaning it. "It's only that in the past—well, you've suspected me and tested me in that manner."

This made her even angrier. "Now you can really wait!" she cried. "I don't care how you suffer from your—your appetites! You'll wait until I'm ready, wait until you're so —so starved—you'll appreciate what you get!"

The following night, though he felt uneasy, even unsafe, he walked through the mild late April night to the Ramparts. He didn't even go into the house, but spoke to Clio at the door.

"I don't know when I'll be able to come to you," he told her. "She's very angry, and when she's like that, she's suspicious of my every move. I'm going to continue my walks, but in various directions. As soon as things settle down, I'll be here."

"Of course, my love," Clio whispered.

"Damn!" he gritted. "I'm not going to do it! I'm coming to you! Let her find out! Let it be in the open! I'm sick of sneaking about like a coward!"

Her hands came onto his. "Nevah a coward, nevah that, my love! You've a position to maintain even now that our boys are safe! Secrecy is best for us. I beg you, do nothing that will lead to her finding out; keep our love the way it's always been! Do this for my sake, I beg of you, love!"

"For your sake? How can it benefit you?"

"If there was to be a scandal, my love, I should suffer for you. No scandal would touch me, but to know that people in this city could look at you and know of me, know that you have a placée, and smile and make jests— that happens. And it would grieve me."

Because he had grieved her enough by sending their sons away and denying her another child, and because he wanted no jests made about her, he gave in. "I'll keep things the way they've been," he promised. "But remember this. Every night I'm deprived of you, every week, is an eternity."

He kissed her lingeringly, then walked home, taking care to arrive a bit early. He found Mildred in their suite, carefully measuring her drops into a glass of water.

In the week that followed, Mildred grew colder toward him. She spoke no pleasant word. She used the carriage a great deal. She took to watching Edward closely when they retired to their suite, and Edward made no move to touch her intimately.

As always, an hour or two after the laudanum helped

her drift off to sleep, she was restless and wakeful. The remainder of the night she seemed only to doze, and when she slept, it was lightly, for she was awake and fretful at the least sound. If Edward turned over in bed, she turned over, plumped her pillow, then sighed. Edward's infrequent visits to Hester, made in the deep of night, were possible only when Mildred, exhausted, took a second, very small portion of drops and fell rather heavily asleep for an hour or more.

"Why don't you take a larger dose when we first go to bed?" Edward asked one night when she had been unusually cold and had stared at him so hatefully he thought she might even fly at him and scratch and claw. "Just a drop or two more at the beginning might put you into a sleep that would last long enough to go into natural slumber," he reasoned.

"Because the doctor warned me!" she spat. "If you take too many of the drops, you become a slave to them, and I'll not let that happen to me!"

"I wish you wouldn't take them at all," he said. "That you'd train yourself to fall asleep naturally."

"You sicken me!" she cried, and flounced into the bathroom, taking her laudanum bottle with her. When she came back, she gave him a stare filled with hate and crawled to her side of the bed. "Well, come on!" she snapped. "Get in! I don't need to lose the effect of my drops!"

Angry, but having no stomach to quarrel, he stretched out, his back to her. He was throbbing with need for Clio, even for Hester.

If she falls asleep fast enough, he thought, listening to her breathe, I'll go to Hester. I should be able to get there and back before the drops wear off.

It was a risk, but his need was urgent, it having been over a week, and his appetite as strong as when he had been much younger. It was past eleven. Mildred was breathing deeply and evenly. She snored a bit. Certainly the house servants were asleep by now; he would be very quiet. He eased out of the bed and out of the room.

Edward was in Hester's cot, their bodies linked and moving, when light glowed on them. Startled, Edward tore away from Hester, swung his feet to the floor, and stood naked.

The light came from a china lamp held by Mildred, whose face was twisted and ugly, almost not to be recognized. "So!" she hissed, her eyes stabbing. "I've caught you, caught you in the act!" She stared at Hester, who was nude. "Slut!"

Edward closed the door so that their voices wouldn't carry. "Mildred," he said, "let me take the lamp. We'll go back to our rooms. I'll explain, as best a man can explain—" He gestured toward the cot, where Hester huddled and trembled. "It isn't her fault."

"I'll not go back to my room, not with you!" Mildred cried in a shrill whisper. She set the lamp on the table. It shone on a folded, flat white cloth, on gleaming scissors, on a pincushion. "I told you what would happen if I ever found out you went to a wench, and now you have gone to one, and it's going to happen."

She bared her teeth at him, like an animal. Her fingers arched into claws; her arms were rigid and shaking from the rigidity.

He gripped her arms, but she wrenched free and stood panting. He waited; if he laid hands on her again, he might hurt her.

"You thought I was asleep!" she hissed. "Well, I didn't take my drops tonight, not one! Because, while you were on your 'walk,' I had a report from my private detective!"

"Detective!" he exclaimed, and remembered how occasionally he had thought he was being followed.

"Yes! I finally hired one! I never trusted those 'walks'! So I hired this man the day after I came home from Natchez, and he found out everything. By following you to the Ramparts just once, he discovered the truth and brought it to me!"

He stared, shocked and alarmed. She bore no resemblance to herself. She looked to be mentally unbalanced, even mad. There could be no reasoning with her. "What did you find out, Mildred?" he asked softly.

"About your octoroon, about Clio Ançoine, and the *two,* mind you, *sons* that you had by her! I know all about your filthy placée and your bastards! And now see how I find you! I felt, I *knew,* all this time that there was something between you and this filthy wench!"

She whirled, caught up the scissors from the table, and came headlong for him, the scissors aimed at his chest. He sprang aside, and she crashed into the door, whirled again, and came at him as if she had never stopped, her face that of a madwoman.

This time he grabbed her wrists, wrenched the right one, and the scissors clattered to the floor. He sensed Hester's darting movement and knew that she had retrieved them and that she was standing against the wall. He held onto the struggling Mildred. She twisted and bit, panted and sobbed, and whispered profanities. He held her strongly, trying not to injure her, yet bring her under control.

Unexpectedly, she went limp. Then as he put his arm around her to lead her back to the house, she tore free and was across the room, going for Hester.

Instinctively, though this was her mistress and she had no right to do so, Hester fought back. The mistress was trying to get the scissors away from her. She had to prevent that, somehow she had to keep this wretched woman from doing what she meant to do.

She fended the mistress off with her left arm. At the same time, with her right hand, she threw the scissors to Edward, but so far to one side he had no chance to catch them.

In one motion Mildred swept them up, turned, and went diving at her husband, the deadly point aimed. Hester jumped onto her back, brought one arm across her throat, and hammered her other arm down on Mildred's arm, trying to knock the scissors from her hand.

But the demented woman, her strength trebled by rage, plowed on toward Edward even as he rounded the table and plunged toward her. They crashed together, Hester with them, and all three fell onto the table. The lamp tipped over, and flames reached for the white material lying there.

Hester kept her arm across Mildred's neck. Edward grabbed for the scissors, which were now open. He seized the blade and tried to wrench the scissors from Mildred, but the razor-sharp metal sliced his thumb to the bone.

Hester hung onto her mistress, fighting to get the scissors. All three of them were sprawled across the table in a struggling mass. They fell in a clump to the floor. Mildred holding the scissors like a knife. Hester got her hand around Mildred's wrist and pulled, but that madwoman strength carried Hester's hand along as Mildred drove the scissors with all her might into Edward's throat. Only then did she let go. Edward lay still, the scissors standing up from his throat, the handle pointing toward the ceiling.

The white material on the table caught fire and blazed into flame.

Chapter Twenty-four

Mildred's screams, her weeping, exultant shrieks, filled the room. She stood at the feet of the husband she had stabbed and keened with joy.

Hester dropped to her knees beside Edward, her hand out to pull the scissors from his throat. Uncertain, she let it fall to her side. It might be the wrong thing to do.

"Master Edward!" she cried, searching his face in the light of the fire. "Master Edward, can you hear me?"

Edward lay motionless, his eyes open and staring. Trembling, Hester put her ear to his chest. She could find no heartbeat. She held her lips near his; she could not feel him breathing.

She had to get him out of this burning room, away from the hoarse screams of the mistress. Still nude, she put her hands under her naked master's armpits and dragged him backward, inch by inch, toward the door. He was very heavy, and her progress was very slow. The flames covered the table now.

Behind her, the door burst open. All the servants of the household, it seemed, were there instantly. Horace and Tench lifted their master and carried him far out onto the flagstones, where they laid him down, then knelt, listening, at his chest. One of them pulled the scissors out.

The women, led by Docia, wrestled their shrieking mistress out of the burning room. At the door, she wrenched away and walked of her own accord, not struggling, not screaming, but still crying out, never pausing for breath.

"I showed him!" she exulted. "He wenched, he deceived me, I showed him! He's dead—dead—dead! He'll never betray me again! I showed him! He wenched, he deceived me—"

Horace and Tench both stood. Someone brought a sheet; others spread it over Edward's naked body. It was then that Hester began to weep, letting the tears run down her face, her neck, trailing onto her breasts. Master Edward, who had been gentle and kind, lay murdered, and she would never again hear his quiet voice.

Now Nell was wrapping a sheet around her, drawing her away from where Edward's body lay. "There, child," she murmured, taking Hester into her arms. "Cry," she soothed. "Let it all come out!"

After the doctor had gone, after the law officers had questioned the slaves and heard Mildred's continued ranting, quiet now, but as demented as at the beginning, they took her away. Mr. Crane, who had been summoned, remained for a time. He assembled all of them in the kitchen. "You're to run the house the way it's always run," he instructed them. "Each of you is to do his regular work. The girls are to know nothing of this tragedy until their grandparents, or some agent for them, arrives."

"What I tell 'em when they ask fo' theah mama and papa?" sobbed Flo, who had been their nurse and now served as their maid.

"Tell them their parents have gone on a trip," Mr. Crane replied.

"How 'bout theah lessons?"

"The tutor will come, as usual. I'll ask him to stay the afternoons, too, to keep them occupied. He'll be only too glad, I'm certain, to take the evening meal with them."

"Who'll plan the meals, suh?" asked Hannah.

"You're the cook?"

"Yes, mastah, suh."

"Then you plan the meals. Serve foods the girls like, and above all, treat them normally, every one of you. Smile, speak in natural tones. Don't get off in pairs and discuss the tragedy. Give the children no cause to sense that anything is wrong. To have their parents suddenly absent is enough. Until their grandparents are with them, they should know nothing of their loss."

Hester, listening to Les Crane, felt the sting of tears in her eyes but held them back. But they lay in her, for the needless death of the master, even for the mistress, who had gone mad and would be put in an asylum. She ached with sympathy for the girls and was miserable over the part that she herself had played in their tragedy.

Beau Kidd, smiling, but with grimness behind the smile, arrived a bit early the next morning. Knowing there would be no afternoon meeting any more, Hester was hovering near the door when he arrived, a piece of new lingerie for Francie in her hands as an excuse for her presence.

She saw him enter and watched the girls as they came rushing from the dining room to greet him. Both talking at once, they told him that their parents had gone on a trip to Natchez.

"But we have to have lessons, anyway!" Francie told him. "Flo said that."

"That's right," agreed Beau. "You're not to fall behind. In fact, we'll work even harder now. I'm staying through dinner every night."

Anita began to jump up and down. "Stories!" she cried. "Will there be time for stories?"

"All the stories you want," he promised. His glance touched Hester, then he looked away. She hurried on up the stairs, disappointed that she had had no chance for a word with him.

She had hoped for advice. But then, what could he advise her other than to do as the other house servants were doing? Discharge her duties, which were few now and must be shared with Nell. There were only the girls left for whom to sew. There was no reason to visit the shops. Everything was in limbo.

Three days later, Henry and Evelyn Vannice, worn and frail, arrived at Woodlawn. Hester managed to get a glimpse of their sad, drawn faces, and her heart went out to them. Unwell and old, their burden was great. Their only daughter had gone mad, had murdered her husband, and was already locked away in an asylum. Edward must be buried, and they had to arrange for that. Their young granddaughters must be told the facts and raised to womanhood with love and attention. They were responsible, also, for the disposition of the brokerage and Woodlawn, along with its staff of slaves.

How can they manage, poor old people? Hester worried. She wished there was some way she could help them,

but she was only a wench. However clever she was in
designing clothes, that talent was of no use to them now.
Later, perhaps, she thought. If they keep Nell and me to
do the sewing.

The grandparents stayed at Woodlawn, occupying a
guest suite. Flo confided that the girls had been told that
both their parents were dead, that they had been killed in
a runaway carriage, and that they were already buried.
The girls walked around the house, weeping.

Shortly after that, Beau Kidd stopped coming to Woodlawn. Hester, anxious to speak to him, dared not leave
the house and go to his room. She did venture to mention
his absence to Flo, who was with the grandmother a great
deal.

"Oh, he gone," Flo said. "He went uprivah on one of
them steamboats, Miss Evelyn say."

Hester was speechless. Though he had warned her he
didn't like farewells, it seemed unbelievable that, after all
they had been to each other, he had left New Orleans
without telling her. But of course he had no valid reason
to take her aside, here at Woodlawn, to speak of anything
at all.

"He went suddenly, didn't he?" she asked Flo.

"I s'pose. Miss Evelyn say the missies don' need a gentleman teachah. Horace say he a rivahboat gamblah, anyway."

Hester turned away and went to Nell's room, where
they sewed, each working on a small, embroidered nightgown. They stitched in silence, waiting, as all the house
slaves were waiting, for events to shape themselves.

Two nights later Les Crane assembled them in the
kitchen. "I've been asked to explain what is going to happen," he told them. "As you know, the girls' grandparents
are in poor health, and this interview would put a strain
on them they don't feel they can meet."

He waited. No one stirred.

"The brokerage is being sold," he continued. "In fact,
I am buying it. Woodlawn will be sold, though its value is
so great it will take a while to find a buyer. This means
that the staff won't be able to stay on and can't be sold
as part and parcel of Woodlawn. It means that each of you
will be sold to a new master, except for Flo. Mr. and
Mrs. Vannice are keeping her for the girls."

He stopped. The house slaves just stood, their faces

solemn and lined with care. Tears shone on some of their cheeks. Nell, who was standing with Hester, gripped her hand.

Hester felt as though she had been hit broadside. She could neither think nor feel. Oh, she felt the hurt from Nell's squeezing hand, but inside her, that was where she couldn't feel.

"Go to the Quarters now," Les Crane said. "Do your usual work tomorrow and the next day—until you're instructed otherwise."

The other slaves moved out of the kitchen, but Hester remained. When Nell tugged at her hand, Hester shook her head and pushed her gently. Nell left reluctantly.

When Hester was the only one left in the kitchen, Les Crane looked at her in surprise. She saw a glimmer of sympathy on his face. Then he asked, and his voice sounded as measured as it had earlier, "What is it, Hester? What do you want?"

"I wish," she told him, her tone diffident, "to make a proposition, Mr. Crane, sir."

"A proposition?" he exclaimed. "What proposition can a slave make?"

"I've become a good seamstress, Mr. Crane, sir," she forced herself to press on. She held her fingers clenched so she wouldn't visibly tremble. "I can design clothes."

"I know. Your master told me how proud his wife was of your ability. But I don't understand to what proposition this could lead."

"I wish to buy my freedom, Mr. Crane, sir. From the estate."

"And how do you propose to do this?"

"As a modiste, Mr. Crane, sir. With my scissors and my needle." Inwardly she flinched at speaking the word scissors, but she clenched her fingers more tightly and stood firm.

He was already shaking his head.

"I'll pay six thousand dollars, Mr. Crane, sir!"

"It would take all your life, Hester. And I have my orders. The Vannices have made their decisions, and I won't intrude on them with an impossible idea. They're returning home immediately and want the house clear of slaves before they leave."

"If Nell and I could speak to Miss Evelyn, Mr. Crane, sir. If we could explain how I design and fit and how Nell sews and embroiders, she might keep us to dress the missies as they grow into young ladies."

"She is fully aware of your talents, Hester," he replied, "and of the talents of each slave in the household. But her health and that of her husband won't permit time for finding individual buyers for you all. Or for reconsideration. Hard as it may be for you, Hester, you're to be sold on the block along with the rest."

Part Three

✖

The Showboat

Chapter Twenty-five

❖

Hester made her move that same night. After the household slept and as the men Mister Crane had hired to guard the slaves on this, their last night at Woodlawn, made their rounds, she dressed. In darkness, she put on a simple brown dress, swooped her hair back to a soft knot, pinned it, and caught up her brown shawl.

She stood at the open door, listening. Her heart beat so loudly it seemed to be all she could hear. The night was black and pierced with tiny stars. A mockingbird called, then quieted.

In the darkness, she saw two shadows meet and merge at the back of the house. They split, going in opposite directions.

It was then that she moved, barefoot, carrying her sandals, across the courtyard, into the bushes, to the very back of the estate. Here, set in the wall, was a small gate used by the gardeners. Praying that it was as well oiled as it had always been, she pulled the handle, the gate swung open, and she was through. But when she would have latched it again, she heard the sound of feet on the flagstones and left the gate ajar and fled.

They pursued her, and without looking back, she sped to the corner, where she turned left, raced faster and turned the next corner. She could no longer hear the feet, but she knew they wouldn't stop; they would never give up.

Zigzagging, running faster still, though a stitch took her in the side, she made for the waterfront and its warren of hiding places, the aisles of stacked good—boxes, bales of cotton, kegs of molasses and sugar, crates—all in endless, straight rows waiting to be loaded on the countless ships at anchor.

Her mind was wild with scraps of thought. Escape. Travel. South. Mammy and Pappy. Master Thorne. Gamble to be bought back. Seamstress. To Master George's wife. North. Modiste. Freedom. A dream only. Phil. Above all, Phil. Impossibility.

Ahead, just ahead, was the waterfront. She slowed and listened. There was no sound of the guards. Maybe, please God, they had lost her. She kept to the shopfronts and the dark, closed grog shops.

Far ahead a watchman with a lantern was making his rounds of the stacked goods. She hadn't known about that. To her right, vessel after vessel rode at anchor. She heard the water slap against the hulls and watched them closely. Most of them had lights, and she could even spot a lone figure on the deck of one here and there.

When the watchman had moved on, shining his lantern down the aisles, she looked back. There was no sign of pursuit, no sound. She edged to the side of the pier and started looking for a vessel that had no light shining directly on the gangway. They all rocked so gently, invitingly—surely she could find one on which to sail far away from New Orleans!

She passed great ships, their masts disappearing into the dark sky, and smaller vessels, and it was these to which she was drawn. There, just a step away, a stern-wheeler moved at anchor, and there was only a small light visible, leaving the gangplank dark.

She was up it and onto the lower deck like a shadow. She moved slowly along a wall, feeling her way, and bumped into a barrel. She felt the barrel and cautiously moved her hand to the top, which was open. Water touched her finger tips, and she withdrew her hand. Just then a man with a lantern rounded the corner of the cabin. He was coming her way. Panic-stricken, she did the first thing that came to mind. She dropped her sandals and then scrambled quietly into the barrel, took a deep breath, and submerged herself in the water.

The water muted everything. She couldn't tell whether the man was approaching the barrel or if he had gone on. She could hear only water in her ears, filling them and making a deafening song of its own.

Slowly, a little at a time, she let her breath out, she had

to. If only it didn't make bubbles! If only the man didn't shine his light on the water!

All her breath was gone, and still she remained submerged. Her ears were roaring. She had to put her nose, just her nose, above water and get air, or her hurting chest, her roaring ears, would burst. Forcing herself to slow steadiness, she tipped her head back, under water, and lifted her face so that only her nose would surface. It was then that something hit her squarely in the face and a man's voice exclaimed.

Unable to stay under another instant, she stood up. Water streamed from her as she took deep, heaving breaths.

"What in tarnation—?" muttered the voice. The lantern now shed full light on her, though she couldn't see the man behind it. "What're you doing in our settling barrel?"

She glimpsed a gourd dipper in his hand and stammered, "S-settling barrel?" She had no idea what he meant; he might have been speaking a foreign tongue. She was vaguely aware that he had hit her in the face with the gourd.

"Drinkin' water—river water we put in the barrel so's the mud'll settle and we can drink it," said the man.

"Oh. I'm sorry!" she whispered, gasping, smothering the need to cough. "I'll get right out of it!"

He gripped her arm, helping her, whispering for her to be quiet. "Don't want to wake the others up," he warned.

Once out of the barrel, she stood, water dripping off her hair, which had fallen down her back, running off her skirt in little streams. She was shivering now, both from the coolness of the night and from fear.

"You've run away, eh?" he demanded. He shone the light into her face. She nodded. "Stagestruck, eh?"

Bewildered, she nodded again. She could see that he was an older man, not very tall. His hair was white.

"Want to join up, eh?"

"Y-yes ma—yes, sir," she whispered. "What am I joining, sir?"

"You must know, or you wouldn't have snuck aboard," he whispered. "I'm Captain Valentine Whitlow, and this is *The Mississippi Magnolia*, Floating Theater of the Rivers, like it's painted on the sides."

In spite of the way he was studying her, he didn't seem to suspect that she was a runaway slave. Maybe Phil

had been right. And Master Kidd. Maybe she could pass
for white. She wished she dared ask him if he knew
Phil. But that she must not do, for it could be very dangerous and would accomplish nothing.

"Come along," the man whispered, taking her arm.

She caught up her sandals, and he guided her along the
deck, around the corner of the wall, up some steps, onto
another deck. He kept walking to what seemed to be a
corner cabin, and here he opened a door and urged her
through it.

This was a tiny bedroom with rose-strewn curtains at
the small windows. A lamp, turned low, burned on a
white-painted dresser. A white, wide-armed rocker stood
on either side of a low table.

There was a bed, and sitting in it was a plump old lady
of sixty, her eyes a dazzling blue against her white hair.
Her mouth was open in surprise.

"This is Mollie, my wife," whispered the captain. "Mollie, this is a girl that's run away from home to join the
showboat. Even drippin' wet—I found her hidin' in the
settling barrel—you can see she's a beauty."

"Did you run away from your ma and pa, child?" asked
Mollie, her voice soft.

"N-no, ma'am. From folks I worked for," Hester half-
lied. Then she crossed her fingers behind her back and deliberately, in desperation, did lie. "I'm an orphan," she
said, wincing at the memory of her parents.

"We don't want to take girls who run from their folks,"
Mollie said, getting out of bed. "I'll get you a towel. Look
at you, Captain Val, lettin' the poor child drip and shiver!
Just look at you!"

Hester wasn't shivering so much as she was trembling.
She rubbed her hair with the towel the captain brought,
wiped her face and neck and arms, all the while fearfully
watching the captain and his wife.

Captain Val wore dark trousers and a green coat with
showy brass buttons. He had a white, gleaming, pointed
beard, thick white eyebrows, and a potbelly. Mollie, who
had pulled a robe around herself, could have been his
twin. Her lips were the exact red of his, and she had the
same round belly. Even in her fear, Hester thought they
were the most entrancing pair she had ever seen.

Now Mollie pushed her behind a wide curtain that
matched the tiny ones at the window. "Get out of them

wet clothes," she whispered. "Dry yourself and put this on." She fumbled among the clothes hanging behind the curtain and thrust a robe at Hester.

As Hester hurriedly changed, she could hear the captain and Mollie whispering. She emerged, belted into the tan robe, rubbing vigorously at her hair with the fresh towel Mollie had passed through the curtain. They had turned up the lamp, and the lantern on the table added its brightness.

"My, but your skin's fair!" Mollie whispered. "And your hair—it looks red!"

"Auburn, ma'am," Hester murmured.

"You join up with us," Captain Val said, "you'll have to wear a black wig—Indian princess—with two long braids. And an Indian dress. Wear 'em all the time. You willin'?"

"Oh, yes!" Hester breathed. Black hair would make her look like someone else.

"We'll have to stain that skin, too," Mollie added.

"You're to be an Indian princess," Captain Val explained in his whisper. "A gen-u-ine Indian princess. Not even the others in the cast'll know you ain't Indian."

"All right," Hester agreed. That would make her disguise even better.

"I'll put you in the afterpiece, the concert we give after the play ends," Captain Val planned. "You can learn to sing and dance, I reckon."

"I know a little," Hester said, thinking of the occasional dance in the Quarters at Thornton and of the singing in the fields. "But not the Indian way," she added honestly.

"We'll learn you. Betty—that's our ingénue—can show you the steps and learn you the songs. Later on, we've got a play with an Indian girl part. We'll work you into that."

"Thank you, captain—ma'am," Hester whispered, her heart lunging at how nearly she had called him "master," both now and earlier. Frightened, she wondered if she could get away with this, if she could really pass as an Indian with members of the cast. And to hide from the kind captain and his wife the fact that she wasn't white.

"Your name, dear," said Mollie. "What is it?"

"J-Jewell," Hester heard herself reply.

"We'll bill you as Pocahontas," declared Captain Val. "That's knowed by everybody, best Indian name there is!

When we get new dodgers made, your picture'll be on 'em, with that name! What you think, Mollie?"

"I think we're going to have a lucky season," she said, and smiled.

He smiled the same way. "What Mollie means is," he told Hester, "that we've got an extry good cast this season."

"Out with you now," Mollie whispered good-naturedly to her husband. "You can bunk in the pilothouse. It's going to take all night to stain this child from her hair to the soles of her feet so's she'll be the color of an Indian! And she's got to dry in sections! I want to get her done and slipped into bed with Betty before we shove off!"

The chubby captain gave his chubby mate an exuberant hug and departed. Her trembling gone, ready for what was to come, Hester turned to Mollie and awaited her ministrations.

Chapter Twenty-six

✠

It was still dark when Mollie led Hester, wearing a beaded Indian dress, her body now a soft tan and a black wig securely in place, to another bed-dressing room much like that which she and the captain shared. "You'll be in here with the ingénue—the girl who plays the second most important female part in the plays," Mollie whispered. "Betty Crawford. She's your age, and a sweet child. You'll get along fine."

"I'm sure we will," Hester whispered back. She took the nightgown Mollie offered and, when the chubby little woman opened the door to the tiny cabin, slipped inside.

She felt her way in the dark, located a table with a chair beside it, laid the folded gown on the table, then sat in the chair. It would be dawn soon. She would not risk getting into bed with the sleeping Betty and perhaps frighten her.

She could hear the girl breathing softly. The boat swayed rhythmically, soothing Hester. Gradually she became so sleepy she couldn't hold her eyes open. She crossed her arms on the table, laid her head on them, and slept.

Hester was so exhausted that when *The Mississippi Magnolia* shoved off, she felt no difference in the movement of the vessel, heard no shouts from pilothouse or deck, heard none of the sounds from other vessels as they set sail, and didn't know it was daylight. Her first awareness was of a soft voice right at her ear, of a hand gently pressing her shoulder. Slowly, she opened her eyes, and at first she didn't remember where she was. Then she lifted her head, saw that this was another tiny bedroom, drapes closed, and it all came back.

"Whatever are you doing in my room—do you speak English?"

Hester turned her head. She found herself gazing at a young, extremely pretty girl with brown, waving, lustrous hair, puzzled blue eyes and very white skin.

"Yes," she whispered. "I speak English. You're Betty Crawford?"

"That's right! And you're—?"

At first she couldn't recall the name Captain Val had given her. And then she did. "I'm Pocahontas," she whispered. "Mollie says I'm to share your room."

"Captain Val and his names!" Betty said, and smiled. "You must have signed on late. You should have gotten in bed—I wouldn't have minded, not a bit!"

Hester smiled back. "You don't mind that I'm—Indian?" she asked.

"Why should I? You're a girl, and I think it'll be fun to be cabin mates! I'll dress, and we'll go to breakfast," she said. "Juliette, that's our big fat black cook, is fierce about being on time for meals."

"I have to learn to sing and dance for the concert," Hester said.

"Oh, that's easy! I'll show you steps, and we'll do them together!" Betty declared. "There's not much to it. I expect Captain Val will have us appear together, you so dark and me so fair. He likes contrasts."

Betty put on a blue dress that matched her eyes, then drew her hair into a large knot, letting a few tendrils curl at her ears. She slid her small feet into white slippers, and she was ready.

Hester moved her toes in her moccasins. Betty didn't recognize the Indian costume as being from the stage wardrobe, and neither, hopefully, would the others. It was brand new, Mollie had said.

Betty led the way out of the cabin. Adjusting her balance to the showboat's movement on the water as it headed upstream, Hester gazed at the wonder of the traveling theater.

The upper deck had an awning, and it gave the great boat the look of a home. There were chairs, tables, and little benches under the awning. From this spot, Hester gazed raptly at the ever-moving Mississippi. It was a wide yellow panorama dotted with vessels; it spread out in front of *The Mississippi Magnolia,* stretched to the sides and behind, forever rushing and later, Betty explained, twisting and turning and doubling back or trying to.

"Sometimes," Betty went on, seeing how impressed Hester was, "the river gets so wide it's like the ocean, and you can't see even the shadow of the other shore. And then it gets so narrow, crooked as any snake, that when the boat goes through the chutes, the willows brush the decks!"

Betty, chattering on, led Hester down to the main deck. Here, not far from where the gangplank had been, stood the settling barrel. Beyond was the forward deck, which looked like a front porch. It had pillars with scrollwork on them, and in a curving space was the ticket window.

Hester peered through at the tiny box office, which held a desk and chair and a wall rack for tickets.

"Mollie sells tickets," Betty said, "and I take them up. We can't look at anything else now—we don't want Juliette on the rampage!"

She went at a run down the main aisle of the auditorium, giving Hester no time to see it, dropped into the orchestra pit, and opened a small door under the stage. Here, huge crossbeams were so low they had to stoop as they made their way to the long table, at which a number of people were assembled.

Hester saw that, between the dining room and kitchen, an opening with a shelf on each side made possible the quick serving of meals. Juliette presided over the wide, black stove. She was bawling a stream of orders and abuse at a skinny yellow Negro, who jumped at her command and was obviously her husband.

Captain Val, resplendent in a bright green coat with brass buttons, tapped on his water glass with a spoon for attention. Even before he spoke, Hester felt every eye on her and burned. She hoped the redness wouldn't show through the stain.

"Folks!" Captain Val sang out. "This here is Pocahontas, a gen-u-ine Indian princess I took on last night! She'll perform in the concert and later in a play. She can meet all of you as we eat and afterwards, one at a time, so's she can remember what name goes to what face!"

Hester ventured a glance around the table. There weren't so many people, not really, but they seemed, in her state, to be a horde. They all nodded, and one or two smiled. She didn't know, for she dropped her eyes after nodding back, if any of them suspected she wasn't really Indian.

"Here," Captain Val said, taking her arm, "sit by Velda Rose, with Betty on the other side. Velda is our leading lady. She's got every farmer and villager on the rivers in love with her!"

"Yes, do please sit with me," murmured Velda Rose in a clear, rather light but pleasing voice. "I've never known an Indian girl before."

"I've never known actresses before," Hester managed. "I hope you don't mind if I—stare at you."

"Notice how well Pocahontas speaks," said Captain Val. "She went to a mission school and speaks perfect!"

Hester dared not look at him lest she somehow betray herself, but she marveled at his quick mind and inventiveness. Mission school, indeed! she thought, as she kept her gaze on Velda Rose.

"Look all you want!" Velda said, suddenly peevish. "That's all the yokels do! I should be glad you want to, though. Our fine leading man doesn't know I'm alive!"

"Now Velda, honey," Mollie said.

"He's so young, so inexperienced in life—"

"You can teach him life, Velda!" laughed a man with flaming red hair. "My guess is he'd be worth teaching!"

Hester saw that when the red-haired man spoke, Betty seemed to be entranced.

Because she had been given permission to do so, Hester studied Velda. She had platinum hair, very heavy and thick, worn twisted like molten silver and wound around her head. Her eyes were silver, the shade of her dress, and her skin, like Betty's, was very white. Apparently she worked at keeping it so, for she had a wide-brimmed hat hanging from the back of her chair. Her features were chiseled and lovely, her lips thin and set, now, in lines of discontent. If she smiled, she would be beautiful.

The meal was eaten mostly in silence. Show people, Phil had once told Hester, had to keep late hours because of night performances and the concert afterward. These people apparently had to get up early for breakfast if they wanted the hot, delicious food Juliette served. Hester glanced through to the kitchen again and noted with what intensity Juliette was now frying more pancakes. Inwardly, she smiled. On this showboat, the performers, if they were tired, probably took an afternoon nap.

As they left the table, the red-haired man, who was dressed in the latest fashion, introduced himself to Hester. "Ralph Strickland here," he said pleasantly. "I play the Toby—the G-string—any comedy part. And I play the villain, have to double, make some quick changes. I also double on alto."

Hester, who knew from Phil what that last meant— playing an instrument as well as acting—shook hands with the actor. He was in his early thirties, a bit under six feet tall, with a strong, manly build. His eyes were blue-green and blazing. His features were almost handsome, his skin lightly tanned, with freckles and a dimpled chin.

"I'm happy to meet you," she murmured.

"May I take you on a tour of our auditorium?" he asked.

"That's a wonderful idea!" cried Betty, her eyes on Ralph. Hester couldn't miss the girl's adoration.

"And I'll go along!" declared a woman, whose voice would have been melodious if it hadn't been so taut. She slid her arms through Ralph's left arm and hugged. "I'm Marge Strickland, sweetie, Mrs. Ralph Strickland. I play character parts and double on the piano."

Marge Strickland looked a bit older than her husband. Her figure was almost voluptuous. Her hair was black, tightly upswept, topped by a cluster of curls. Her eyes were brown and snapping.

It was obvious that she was aware of Betty's infatuation with Ralph. Her jealousy showed in the way she clung to him. She appeared possessive and overloving, giving the impression that her marriage was perfect, but Hester, sensing the underlying fierceness, knew this was not the case.

As the group started away, a youth of not more than nineteen attached himself to them. "I'm Billy Myers, juvenile lead opposite Betty," he told Hester. "Mind if I come along?"

"Of course not," Hester replied, liking him instantly. He was short and slight but had square shoulders. He was tanned, his hair a mass of brown ringlets, his eyes a beautiful green. His features were open and his nature so friendly it seemed to reach out and touch everyone.

"I also double on cornet," he added proudly. He turned

to Betty, who was looking bleakly at the way Marge Strickland continued to hug Ralph's arm. "Betty," he asked, "is it all right if I walk with you?"

Suddenly Hester knew that he was in love with Betty. And she knew further, from Betty's careless assent, that she was scarcely aware that Billy existed.

They filed out of the kitchen, Hester feeling surprisingly at ease. She, a runaway wench, was fully accepted by these white people, and it felt wonderful. She was guilty over the deceit, but still she enjoyed being treated as an equal.

They moved up through the orchestra pit and onto the stage. This was not set up for a play yet, but was a clutter of furniture.

"When we set the stage," Ralph explained, "we put the extra furniture off in the wings. And these," he continued, leading to a row of doors at the back of the stage, "are our bed-dressing rooms, each with a door to the deck and a door to backstage."

"Pocahontas is sharing my room," Betty said.

"These," Ralph went on, ignoring Betty and motioning to painted sections of scenery standing up against the walls, "are the sets. When we put one up, the others are hidden from the audience by the way the set in use angles onstage."

He led the way to the apron at the front of the stage and pointed out the row of oil lamps set into the floor. "Footlights." He gestured, indicating lamps bracketed to the green and gold walls of the auditorium and to those in the great brass chandelier in the center. "One hundred lamps!" he informed Hester. "One of the best showboats Marge and I ever played!"

Captain Val came puffing out of the pit and joined them. "Stealin' my thunder, eh?" he joked. "I heard that about the lamps, but I'll just call attention to them rows and rows of seats, all green and gold plush—five hundred of them. That ain't counting the upper boxes." He gestured to the balcony stairs. "Seat another hundred. Niggers, mostly, in the balcony, that's natural. White folks pay extra to sit in the boxes up there, of course."

Suddenly Hester hoped fiercely that no one would suspect her of being a wench. She liked these show people, who amazed her. There was Betty's manner, for instance, no different toward her than had been Jewell's manner

back at Thornton. Or Nell's, at Woodlawn. Mollie Whitlow, too, was easy and natural with her. All of them were
warm toward her; even the standoffish leading lady was
civil. People are people, she reflected, when they meet as
equals. A small thrill coursed through her; it was wonderful, this being equal, even though it had to be temporary.
For she knew she must leave the show upriver someplace,
before her secret was discovered.

Suddenly Billy Myers said, "Lines or no lines to learn, I
vote we take Pocahontas to meet our leading man! He
can't get mad; the room's as much mine as his!"

"I agree!" said Betty, with the first animation she had
shown since Marge had latched onto Ralph's arm.

"Fine idea!" shouted Captain Val. "He's goin' to put his
eyes out if he don't rest 'em!" He stomped across the
stage to the rear, the others following.

He knocked on the door, and they waited. The door
opened and there, script in hand, stood Phil!

Chapter Twenty-seven

For an instant, Hester forgot her disguise. She stared, her numb lips apart, waiting for him to cry out her name.

"We brought our new cast member to meet you, Phil," Captain Val said. "This is Pocahontas."

Phil barely looked at her as he acknowledged the introduction the captain proceeded to make.

Thank God! she thought.

She couldn't take her eyes off Phil. He was the same, but different. He had grown up, had become a man, and his blonde hair with the touch of gold seemed thicker. He was more handsome, his build broader. Here was the boy of her dreams become the man she could never have.

Even as the sight of him flamed through her, she murmured acknowledgment and caught his brief smile that included all of them. Next his look went to the script in his hand, and it was evident that that was where his interest lay.

Her heart surged. He didn't know her! He accepted her as an Indian girl! Nor was his preoccupation with the papers in his hand rudeness; he was simply anxious to do the job for which he had been hired.

"How are you doing with your lines?" Betty asked.

"I'm on the last role," he said. "By tonight I should have it learned in the rough, then begin to make certain I have it word for word."

"You're the quickest study I ever met, Bennett," remarked Ralph.

"He is that," agreed Captain Val. "Takes me a week to learn a part, and mine are shorter."

Betty, excited over Phil's unprecedented speed, put her

hand on Ralph Strickland's free arm. "Isn't it wonderful?" she exclaimed. "To learn five leading parts in—why, it's almost a whole play in twenty-four hours!"

Marge angrily pushed Betty's hand off her husband's arm. "Don't paw Ralph!" she snapped. "He hates it!" She returned her own hand to his other arm, hugging him more tightly.

Ralph gave Betty a warning glance. He put his arm around Marge's waist, and she cuddled to him. Betty's face went blank, and Hester noted a slight trembling of Betty's lower lip. Hester felt a chill and uneasiness, for she was reminded of Mildred Dalton's jealousy, which had ended in murder. Firmly she pushed this thought out of her mind.

Immediately she was filled with a more pressing worry. Please, she thought, don't let Phil recognize me! Maybe he wouldn't; maybe luck would stay with her. After all, she, too, had grown up and matured. Her old dreams that he could buy her vanished; she was wiser now. Even without the disguise, she was nothing like the fourteen-year-old Hester he had once thought he loved. She now spoke properly and even walked differently, moving with the trained grace that Master Kidd had taught her.

After a little more chatter at Phil's door, the party broke up. Phil went inside, and Hester followed the others to the pilothouse, which, they declared, she must see.

At the very top, on the third deck, they entered the glass-windowed space. A tall, very thin man in dark trousers, a blue coat with brass buttons, and a blue pilot's cap on his sandy hair was at the wheel, squinting ahead, turning the wheel slightly.

"This is Sam Janas, our pilot," Captain Val said. "Sam, Pocahontas is our Indian girl, the one I told you about last night."

Sam grunted, and his mouth twitched in what passed for a smile. He gave Hester a fast look, then looked again at the river. "Charlie'll be here any time, cap'n," he said. "He's still low 'bout not gettin' to be leadin' man. I promised to let him take the wheel a bit."

"Fine," approved Captain Val. "Here he comes now."

Hester looked toward the steep, short steps that led to the pilothouse. The engineer was young and handsome and wore his clean, rough, engine-room clothes with an air.

He was young—about twenty, Hester thought. He had time in which to become an actor.

Captain Val performed the introduction. "Pocahontas, this is Charlie Greathouse, best engineer *The Mississippi Magnolia* ever had." Suddenly he slapped his leg and grinned. "I had an idea hit me! Charlie, you're so dark and so brown from sun and weather, by the time we've played two or three places, I'll add you to Pocahontas's act. You'll make a fine Indian brave, and you can play the male Indian part in that play with an Indian girl. It ain't but a walk-on, but it's a start. From that I'll move you up to villain, take some of the load off Strickland."

Charlie's face broke into a wide grin. Rendered speechless by the captain's announcement, he shook hands with Hester, mumbling something she couldn't understand.

"Now watch, Pocahontas," Sam said. "This is the best place to see the river from. And it gives you the feel of how fast this stern-wheeler is pushin' us upstream."

Hester, her pulse still fast over the encounter with Phil, gazed out over the river. They were well away from other craft now and had this part of the stream to themselves. The paddle wheel turned in the water, pushing them against the current, making splashing sounds, keeping up a song of churning water. As far as she could see, there was the river.

Betty, who had lost her sparkle entirely, made the first move to leave. Billy Myers tried to detain her, but she was sweetly determined. "We've all got to sew," she told him. "Mollie mentioned it at breakfast, remember? All the women, that is, of course. We've got to make two more Indian dresses for Pocahontas."

They left the pilothouse and went to the middle deck, where Mollie and Velda were cutting a garment from heavy tan material. The men scattered, making for the auditorium, discussing one of the sets that needed paint. Hester, Betty, and Marge joined Mollie and Velda. Hester had the sudden, firm feeling that all the members of the troupe, even Sam Janas and Charlie Greathouse, thought she had run away from home, be it Indian or white. She wondered if that was what Phil would think.

"Sit and sew, girls!" Mollie said cheerfully. "We've got to make these Indian dresses for Pocahontas to wear all the time. The one she's got on is her costume."

They sat together, stitching on the dresses. They were

simple Indian shifts very like the ones Hester had worn at Thornton, except that these were fringed, and Marge and Mollie were going to brighten them with beadwork. Betty elected to make headbands and stitched the first one without speaking, then began to sew beads on it. She never spoke a word and looked quite pale, Hester thought.

Hester sewed along with them, careful to make her stitches the way they made theirs, some of which were too long and many of which were uneven. She dared not risk calling attention to her natural talent for sewing; if dodgers were posted for a runaway slave who was an expert seamstress, it could put suspicion on her.

As she worked, listening to the others talk idly, her mind dwelt on Phil. Disguised though she was, utterly changed from the Hester of long ago, so Indian-looking that even she could find no resemblance to the old Hester in the mirror, there was always the chance that Phil would recognize her.

He was doing work he loved, she thought, traveling with a showboat, acting. She dared not risk his recognition, the reawakening of his love, which would endanger his present career and his entire future life, ruin it because of her, a runaway wench!

Had he, after all, recognized her today? Was he remaining quiet until he could get her alone? Her panic flared, then lessened. No. There would have been some sign. A stare, puzzlement, astonishment, even open joy. Instead, he had scarcely noticed her, thinking only of the lines he had yet to learn.

Or had he changed? Had he, after all, recognized her and chosen not to reveal it? Her heart fell, and she told herself that that was better than having him determined to tear up his life for her. She was so miserably mixed up she didn't know what to think or what to do.

Stitching, she made a firm decision that she would not remain long with the showboat. While she was aboard, she would watch Phil very carefully. At the least hint that he might be on the verge of recognizing her, she would leave. She needed to earn only a bit of money, enough to exist on while she sought employment as a white girl with some busy seamstress. Thus, away from New Orleans, away from Phil, she could make a quiet life for herself, and someday save enough to buy her freedom. Only then would she be safe from capture as a runaway slave.

Phil brought his script to noon dinner. He apologized and asked permission to leaf through it as they ate, and they laughed and agreed. All but Hester, who dared not draw his attention to her.

There was a rehearsal that afternoon of the first play to be presented at their first stop. Hester sat in the back row watching and listening. Pride filled her at the way Phil moved onstage, at the ring to his voice, at his grasp of the role. If she hadn't known differently, she would have thought he had played this part for a long time. But then she had never been to a play and had no basis for comparison. Still, she thought him better than the others, probably one of the best actors on the rivers.

Her breath shook at the thought that once she had lain in his arms, that once his lips had kissed her, his body had poured its love into her. Her breath trembled a long time before she could get it under control.

Betty, who had to be on and off stage, took her onto the second deck at every opportunity. Here she taught her a sad, sweet song and the simple, slow steps she said composed an Indian dance. After that, while Betty was onstage again, Hester practiced her dance and her song until Betty could rejoin her.

Rehearsal over, Hester sat with Betty on the second deck and watched the river. The streams that emptied into it were green-blue in the late sunlight, olive green far back in the shade. They saw wild honeysuckle winding over black tree trunks and the occasional darting of a bird among them.

From then on, mornings were filled with rehearsal, afternoons with resting in the little cabins and sitting on deck, watching the river, chatting idly, the women often busy with needlework. The stern-wheeler beat steadily upriver, past Natchez, along the borders of Warren County itself and on, ever on.

They sailed into one of the side streams and up it, passing unpainted little cabins the color of the sandy soil on which they stood. They passed a village and upstream from that, sighted a tiny hamlet called Henderson's Point. It looked as though it were asleep, but it was here that *The Mississippi Magnolia* tied up at the wooden pier.

"We'll be here six nights," said Mollie, folding her sewing.

"And every female in the place will be after Ralph," put in Marge Strickland, tight-lipped.

"Or Phil," said Mollie. "He's the handsomest leading man we've had in years. And the best."

Already there were people gathering at the pier, standing in clumps and staring. Children darted about, jumped up and down, and piped shrilly, "Showboat's here, showboat's here!" Captain Val climbed to the top deck in his green, brass-buttoned coat and waved. A few of the grownup watchers lifted their hands in response, and the children waved wildly and squealed.

Hester wondered where the people came from, and how they had gotten to the dock so quickly. The village looked too small to house them. She mentioned this to Mollie.

"They watch for us this time of year," Mollie explained. "Some of them have seen us coming from a distance and made for the pier. Our audiences come from the back country, lots of them. All the spots we play are like Henderson's Point, not on most maps, but with a solid back-country, which means good houses. The showboat's the biggest thing that happens all year."

Only after it was dark did the watchers disperse.

The next morning by eleven o'clock the showboat band had dressed in its green, brass-buttoned coats. The men wore various kinds of trousers, but that didn't matter. Their bright coats and caps were all anybody looked at.

Charlie Greathouse, the engineer, was drum major. Instead of the green cap of the others, he wore a tall fur shako with a strap under the chin. Up the levee Charlie scrambled with his baton, and behind him was Phil with a clarinet Hester hadn't dreamed he knew how to play, Billy Myers with his cornet, Sam Janas with his tuba, and Ralph Strickland with his alto horn. Captain Val came last with his alto horn.

Following them, caught up in the excitement of performing, even for free, were the female members of the troupe, beautifully dressed and made up for the stage, Hester among them. Under her arm Mollie carried a sheaf of playbills announcing the plays to be presented, all of which lauded the talents of the players. The actresses stood with Mollie, bright-eyed, smiling, and professional as the five-piece band struck up under Charlie's baton.

The crowd of locals had grown since the night before. An eager audience, they stood staring at the band and at the showgirls.

Now the band struck up a lively march, and march they did, stepping high, in perfect rhythm. The actresses marched, too, stepping not quite so high, but smiling broadly. Back and forth the troupe marched before their audience, giving them a preview of the wonders to come aboard *The Mississippi Magnolia*. The band played the third tune, not marching, and when that was finished and Charlie had bowed and the onlookers had applauded, Captain Val made his spiel.

"Ladie-ees and gent-lemen!" he intoned, his voice resonant, even in the outdoors. "We are happy to be again in your fair city! *The Mississippi Magnolia* is happy to be back and will present plays for your pleasure and entertainment, for your laughter and your tears. We have drama, ladies and gentlemen, heart-rending drama that will tear your emotions, and we have such comedy as will make you laugh your worries away! We have plays that you will never forget, tragedies that you will recount to your grandchildren, and to their children, mysteries that will bring you to the edge of your seats. . . ."

He went on and on, extolling the beauty of the actresses on *The Mississippi Magnolia*, the handsomeness and manliness of the actors. He described their histrionic abilities, told how he had combed New Orleans, that fair and beautiful metropolis, for the best actors and actresses and had found them. He had done this for the people who came to *The Mississippi Magnolia*, just for them. To bring excitement, change, emotion, and joy into their lives for six nights, six short, glorious evenings.

After the speech, the band played a fourth bouncing number, and then Captain Val got his playbills from Mollie and worked through the crowd passing them out, shaking hands with a remembered acquaintance now and then, drawing the awed admiration of fellow villagers that one of their number knew one of the show folks.

Hester noticed how the girls in the crowd gazed at Phil. Their attention halted at Ralph Strickland, passed over Billy Myers, then centered on Phil. Pride swelled in Hester. It made her happy that these girls, like herself, thought him the handsomest man in the troupe.

After twenty minutes, Captain Val returned to the band, which marched, playing, back to the showboat. The women trailed again, their heads high, smiles flashing.

Hester, trembling a bit from the excitement of being a part of the exhibition and also from relief that Phil hadn't glanced at her once, felt safer to be aboard again. She spent the rest of the day practicing with Betty. Phil, at Captain Val's order, was resting in his room, forbidden to so much as look at a script.

"It's in your head, tonight's part, and all the others," Captain Val had told him for all to hear. "You'll give a fine performance. You, too, Pocahontas. I've watched you and Betty when you didn't know."

That night, wearing her fine Indian costume, Hester went onto the deserted stage, which was set up as a parlor. The curtain was down, but Betty had showed her the peephole, and she put her eye to it.

The auditorium, with its green plush and gilt and the mirrors she had not noticed by day, took on glitter and richness from the hundred kerosene lamps.

She caught her breath. She had never seen anything so grand. The flaming oil flares on tall poles stuck in the clay banks outside to light the playgoers' way onto the showboat were but a dim preview of this. There was an air of excitement among those already seated out there and those coming down the aisles. There was a tense, excited feeling backstage, too, with all the players in costume and makeup, hair in place, sure of their lines and actions.

The band members, dressed in costumes for the play, filed into the orchestra pit and sat down. Marge was at the piano, and they played three numbers. The applause was thunderous, growing in volume as the band left the pit to go backstage.

The curtain went up. Hester stood quivering in the wings, eager to see Phil act before an audience. Velda came onstage, where he was leafing through a book, and they went into each other's arms and kissed. Hester felt a small chill. It was only a play, of course, but it seemed so real! Maybe it was because she knew how Phil's arms felt. But she was proud and excited; he was so handsome and his acting so natural that it seemed he really had become the character he was portraying. She trembled with excitement. Then, lest Phil, in making an exit, see her at close range and recognize her, she fled to the little bed-dressing room and stayed until the play ended.

She could tell the audience liked Phil. When he made his important speeches, they clapped and clapped so that he had to wait before the play could go on. Some people in the audience even stomped their feet on the floor.

Betty came in to change her costume. "Captain Val's making the concert pitch now," she said. "You ready? Listen!" She cracked the door open, and the captain's voice, extolling the acts to come and the presentation of a real Indian princess, reached backstage as well as into the auditorium.

The curtain went up for the afterpiece. Marge and Ralph, made up like low-comedy characters, some of their teeth blacked out, Ralph's flaming hair tousled and standing in points, did a skit. It ended with Marge chasing Ralph offstage with a wooden spoon and the audience, which had paid the extra fifteen cents to see the concert, howled and clapped.

Next, Billy and Betty put on a skit in which two sweethearts had a spat over what they would name their first dog and their first baby. It ended with them parting forever, one making an exit stage right, the other stage left. Then they came flying back into each other's arms and promised to name the baby both names over which they had quarreled, and the dog both names. Again the audience clapped, whistled, and stomped.

Now it was Hester's turn. Marge was at the piano, Captain Val at the drums. It was the first time she had been able to dance to music because, when Betty was teaching her, the cast was onstage rehearsing, and there was no one available to play the music. So she had rehearsed on deck, with Betty humming the music and singing the songs along with her.

At this moment she stood alone, center stage. Her heart felt as if it were in her stomach; her one hope was that Phil would stay in his room, where she had seen him go and that he wouldn't watch her act and recognize her.

She could feel the audience out there, a living, breathing entity. A creature. She forgot it was composed of people; it was a Thing.

She stood swaying to the music, getting the beat of the piano, the drums. She took the first graceful step, the next, and she was in rhythm. Hester danced with the music, whirling slowly, and then she started the song Betty had taught her about an Indian princess lost from her father, the chief, lost from her sweetheart, a brave, lost from her tribe. And as she sang, swaying and dancing, a sadness went through her, and she became Pocahontas, the lost little Indian girl.

At the end of her song, she bowed to the audience and stretched her hands out helplessly to them as Captain Val had taught her, and the curtain slowly went down. The audience shouted, clapped, and cried, "More—more!"

Captain Val trotted onstage and hissed, "Give 'em another bow!" He trotted off, and the curtain rose. Hester gave the bow, still feeling Indian and sad, and the curtain went down, but the clapping continued, then finally dwindled and stopped.

Betty rushed onstage and hugged Hester. Captain Val pushed Betty gently aside and himself embraced his "Indian girl." Mollie was there, too, and Billy, all praising Hester, congratulating her on her first performance. Then Phil emerged, and the entire cast, including Velda and the Stricklands, surrounded him, praising and complimenting him. All but Hester. It was safer for her to hasten to the room she shared with Betty and close the door.

Mornings on the showboat were spent organizing for the parade, which was a daily event, and then going ashore and marching. Afternoons were devoted to sewing and rehearsal of that night's play, the women alternating between the deck and the stage as their roles demanded. Betty did no sewing and Hester very little, for they were working on the new routines Hester must learn for the upcoming performances.

Hester saw Phil only at meals, at which time he talked animatedly enough with the others but, aside from a courteous nod and a direct look now and again, paid no attention to her. This both pleased and troubled her. She was pleased that he paid no attention and troubled to her bones at every direct look.

Sometimes she stared at herself in the mirror. No. She did not look like Hester, she absolutely did not. She looked completely Indian. For one thing, the stain on her cheekbones masked them where her natural alabaster skin highlighted them. And the stain made her nose look some-

what thicker. She did what she could to accentuate the
Indian look. With black pencil, she widened her eyebrows,
lengthened them, and that changed her still more. So
artfully had she done it that she had to get right up to the
mirror to see that it was pencil and not natural eyebrow.

On Thursday, Captain Val decreed there would be no
afternoon rehearsal. "We'll have a quick run-through right
after noon dinner instead," he announced. "Then all of
you relax for a change. No work of any kind. Not even
you, Pocahontas—you learned two songs and dances yesterday. You're under orders to take time off, all of you."

"Ralph and I are going to sleep," Marge announced.
"This week *has* been tiring. We'll appreciate it if it's kept
quiet on the boat. You might, to oblige me, order Juliette
not to bang her pots and pans."

"She'll be done with that by the time our run-through
ends," the captain said.

"Or beginning it for supper!"

"I don't think so, Marge," Mollie soothed. "I'm going
to get the captain to sleep, too."

"I'll have time, at last, to attend to my grooming,"
Velda said, sounding fretful. She gave Phil a reproachful
glance that he didn't even notice. "There's nothing else to
do."

Billy and Phil settled on taking a walk to the north.
"Stretch our legs a bit," Phil said. "Get the kinks out."

"I guess I'll just stay aboard," Betty said when Billy
asked if she wanted to come walk with himself and Phil.

"Should've asked you first," he grumbled. "Made it
sound like—I do everything wrong."

"No, you don't, Billy. I just don't—a walk doesn't appeal to me." She glanced at Ralph Strickland, then away.

Hester said she would sit on deck and watch the river.
"A boat is new to me," she reminded them.

Thus, in early afternoon, they scattered. Hester saw
Betty and Ralph exchange a quick word, but Marge saw
it, too, and interrupted. Ralph went with her to their cabin.

On deck, blessedly alone, with no need to fear being
recognized, Hester sat in one chair and put her feet up in
another. She was more tired than she had realized, for
soon she dozed.

A stiff neck awakened her. She rubbed it, yawned, and
looked around. Some time had passed, but not much. The
streak of sunlight on the water hadn't moved very far.

She stood up, then wandered along the deck, down the steps and gangplank to the shore. She would walk a bit herself, she thought, and work out the stiffness sleeping in a cramped position had caused. It felt good to walk. She saw no villagers, not one, and avoided all houses.

Ahead, in a green field, was a small shed. She would walk that far, then turn around and go back to the showboat. She didn't want to be missed, to stir undue attention. Her footsteps soundless on the planted field, she neared the shed, then went around it, looking for the door. She was curious to see what was kept in it, if anything.

The door was slightly ajar. She pushed, and it swung inward. As it moved, it creaked on rusty hinges, and there was a flurry of movement inside.

Two figures scrambled up, the man adjusting his trousers, the girl straightening her dress. "Oh!" she cried. "I didn't know—I didn't mean—"

"Pocahontas!" cried Betty. "You said you were going to stay on the boat!"

Ralph Strickland came forward, with bits of oats, which were scattered on the floor of the shed, caught in his hair. Frantically, Betty brushed the oats out of his hair, off his clothes, and off her own.

His face was twisted with anger. He seized Hester's arm, hurting it. "You're not to tell Marge, you understand?" he said fiercely.

"Of c-course not!"

"Or anybody else! This is between Betty and me—it's no concern of yours!"

"But Ralph," Betty protested, "maybe this is the time—"

"I'll name the time!" he snapped. "You two come back together. Make it look like you've been for a walk!"

He strode angrily out, and Betty began to sob.

Hester, shocked at what she had learned, was frightened for both Betty and Ralph. She had seen how jealous Marge was, and the tragedy at Woodlawn was still fresh in her mind. Hesitantly, because she was Negro and Betty was white, she tried to warn the other girl. "Since this has happened," she said, "don't you think it would be better not to see Ralph alone again? Jealous wives do terrible things! Please, Betty—be careful—stop while you can!"

"We are careful, we are!"

"That's not what I mean. Ralph is a married man, and you're young and single."

"We can't help that! If only you knew what it's like to be in love! To have to h-hide it from the world!"

A pang went through Hester. Phil. Beloved Phil. She tried, but some of her pain was evident in her voice. "Sometimes there are obstacles to love, Betty," she said as naturally as she would to Jewell or Nell, "things that can't be overcome."

"Not so with R-Ralph!" wept Betty. "All he needs is an excuse to divorce Marge, or even just leave her! The rages he endures, the way she c-claws him. He loves me, only me! We're going to be married! He's promised!"

"It doesn't always work out that way," Hester warned uneasily. "Things sometimes happen—"

"Not with Ralph!" she cried. "Never with Ralph! I believe in him as I believe in God!"

Chapter Twenty-eight

On the last day at Henderson's Point, Phil was sure of every line in every part. Though he had concentrated on the plays so fiercely, he had taken the time, when the showboat passed any landing, to carefully examine the people. Not that he really expected to find Hester thus, but watching for her had become a habit, and he never missed an opportunity to look.

When he visited his parents in New Orleans, he still went to the slave market, and he walked the streets of the city, his eyes roving and quick. His mind told him, as did his father, to give up, that Hester was lost to him, but his heart held its own opinion, and he never ceased to search, indifferent to other girls.

Now that he knew the plays, he let his mind dwell on Hester and on his fattening bank account. He had enough now to pay a substantial amount toward her purchase if her owner, once located, would agree to accept it.

From Hester, his mind unaccountably slipped to the Indian girl. Though he had been so intent on study, he had been aware of Pocahontas, had been impressed, when he glanced briefly at her, by her lustrous black braids and the even, lovely darkness of her skin.

Something about her puzzled him, however. He developed a feeling that he had seen her before, around the showboats in New Orleans, perhaps, or on the streets.

But no. If he had seen her, he would remember. She was not a girl to forget. He wouldn't let himself look at her often because he felt he might be too attracted to her. Her dark beauty, her almost familiar, graceful movements, troubled him, and he kept his eyes strictly away from her. Hester was his love. And one day he would find her. No one else could take her place.

His mind thus set and at ease on this last day, he spied Pocahontas going ashore alone, strolling slowly, every movement one of grace. He was alone on the lower deck, the other troupe members having scattered, and he began to follow the Indian girl, pulled against his better judgment.

It would do no harm to get acquainted with the girl. In fact, it was now time, since he knew his plays, for him to be on friendly terms with all his fellow players. He went down the gangplank and lengthened his steps. It was ridiculous to think he might be attracted to her. She was just a girl, like Betty, like Leloi.

Hester, not knowing that Phil was striding after her, had wandered into the greening field and toward the shed where she had found Betty and Ralph that day.

Suddenly she heard Phil hail her. She stopped, stunned.

"That's it!" he called gaily. "Hold up a bit; we'll walk together!"

She turned, deeply upset that she was going to have to face him at last. It had to come, sooner or later, she thought. Now is the test. If he shows any sign of being about to recognize me, I'll leave the showboat while there's still time.

If he still loves me! the wild thought struck. Her breath twisted, she let it out, then drew it in slowly. He was a grown man; he might have grown out of their sweet young love even as she had grown more and more securely into it.

"Why do you walk the field?" he asked, catching up.

"It's like grass, this crop," she said. "I've walked here before." She dared not look into his face lest she betray herself and lest he recognize her. Her heart was pounding, and her knees were shaking.

"You seemed to be in solemn thought," he said. "Is something troubling you?"

She shook her head. She had so much troubling her. She was a runaway slave, she feared he might recognize her, that she might ruin his life, and she was worried about what might happen to Betty as a result of her illicit love.

"Are you homesick for your people?" Phil asked.

"A bit," she admitted. She was indeed homesick—for

Mammy and Pappy. But he meant her supposed Indian relatives, her tribe.

They walked quietly for a moment. Then she was taken by such a wild, unreasonable impulse to throw herself into his arms and confess her identity that tears came to her eyes. She had yearned for him so long, and here he was, and she dare not speak. Her breath quivered, and he heard it.

They were just outside the little shed at the moment. A compulsion he made no effort to understand moved him to grasp her arms and turn her to face him.

She stood, his dear hands holding her. She dropped her head. No matter how truly she wanted it, he must not look into her face at close range. In spite of her resolution, her breath quivered again, and a tear ran down each cheek, and she wondered, frantically, if the tears would make white paths on her carefully stained skin.

"Lift your face," he said, his voice very low and strained. "Please lift your face. I have got to look at you."

Slowly, very slowly, she raised her chin and met his blue eyes full on. The tears were in the corners of her mouth now, and she tasted them. She waited. His eyes probed hers, wandered slowly over her face, lingered on the contour of cheekbone and nose, followed the penciled line of her brows, studied her lips for a long moment, then came back to her eyes.

"You're Hester," he whispered. "Thank God, I've found you!"

She could no longer look away from him. She drank in the beauty of his eyes. She couldn't lie to him, not to Phil.

"How did you know?" she whispered.

"At first I didn't. I was busy. They said you were Indian. There was this—" He touched one of her braids.

"A wig, Phil."

"Of course. And dark skin—and the tone of your voice —lower."

"I did that—to change it. To keep you from—"

"But your eyes, my darling! Nothing can change those brown, tender eyes! Or those soft, curving lips!" He lowered his head, and right there in the open field, he kissed her long and tenderly, his arms warm about her.

His lips on hers, he whispered, "Let me hear you say it, darling! Let me hear you say, 'I am Hester.'"

"Phil," she whispered, her lips moving against his. "I am. I am Hester."

"We can't stand here!" he exclaimed. "For all at Henderson's Point to see! We've got to have privacy! There's so much to talk about!"

"The shed," she told him, knowing there would be no privacy on the showboat. "It's empty, but it had oats in it before and smells of oats."

"Who cares? Just so we can be together!"

They went into the shed, and he pulled the door closed. A window high up threw dim light over the interior, which had a rough wooden floor with the scattering of oats over it that Hester remembered. He drew her to a spot under the window, and they sat on the floor, embracing. He kissed her again tenderly and gently held her.

"The torment I've been through!" he exclaimed. "Having you spirited away in the night, wondering what happened to you, where you were taken, how you were being treated, unable to find out anything at all! I've searched for you every year, every day, every mile! Tell me what I need to know!"

In his arms, sitting on the floor, she told him first about the coffle. She didn't want to describe the chains or the leg irons because she knew it would hurt him, but he demanded to know. She described traveling in the coffle, sleeping, chained, on the ground, and how she had been taken by boat from Natchez to New Orleans, where she was put in the stockade.

Here he interrupted to recount how he had stopped in Natchez and gone to the slave market looking for her, how he had done the same in New Orleans. "When I'd been to auction after auction in New Orleans, I went back to Natchez, with no better success," he said.

They sat quietly, each hearing the beat of the other's heart. Phil was silent, thinking. "What must have happened," he said finally, "is that I was ahead of you the entire trip. While you were in the coffle, I was on a steamboat. I got to both slave markets before you even reached Natchez!"

She tightened her arms around him. Beloved, frantic Phil! Searching for her so desperately, and she had no way to get to him, to ease his torment!

"Then," he continued, thinking aloud, "while you were being loaded onto the Natchez boat, I was going to the

New Orleans auctions, trying to find you! By the time you were in the New Orleans stockade, I was back in Natchez, attending auctions!"

"Poor Phil! Darling, loyal Phil!" she whispered.

"Not 'poor Phil,' but Hester—beloved, abused Hester! So. It seems you were sold while I was back in Natchez. Go on, tell me the rest. So much time has passed, so much has happened. I want to hear it all, and how you came to be on *The Mississippi Magnolia!*"

Whispering, consumed by shame, Hester told him about being sold to Edward Dalton, cotton broker, of New Orleans.

"We know the family!" interjected Phil. "God! If I had known you were in the same city!"

She told how she had searched for him on the streets and how she had located his parents' house and learned that he had become a showboat actor. She confessed that she had been Edward Dalton's bed wench, that she had traded her body to Beau Kidd for an education.

She felt him stiffen. "I shouldn't have, Phil!" she cried. "I wouldn't have if I'd thought it would make you angry!"

"I'm not angry at you," he said tightly. "But at the bastard who took advantage. Your master, too. I could kill both of them."

He meant it. She recalled how he had fought George for trying to lay hands on her. Now he was a man, determined and strong. He could easily kill anyone who had violated her.

"I couldn't expect Master Beau to teach me without payment," she said firmly. "And he was a splendid teacher. I'm as well educated as you are, Phil."

"I can understand," he said after a moment, some of the tautness gone from his voice. "And once I told you to get an education any way you could."

"You remember!"

"I remember every little thing about you, my darling."

"The Daltons were good to me," she explained. "They permitted me to learn to design gowns and dresses and to fit and sew."

She told of how she had been sent to the shops by Mildred Dalton and how she had hoped to go north and pass as white and earn her living with her needle.

He probed about the men. "How many men did you have to—to—?" he asked.

"Master Dalton, because he owned me, and Master Kidd, for the education."

"No others, white or black? They didn't try to mate you with some stud?"

"Oh, no, nothing like that! There were the two I named. No others."

"How did Kidd—you say he was a riverboat gambler—how did he treat you?"

"Well enough, darling. Do we have to talk about it?"

"I need to know how things were. So I can make up for them. How about Dalton?"

"He was kind, Phil. He didn't come to me often. Only when he couldn't get away from his wife to go to his placée on the Ramparts. His wife—the mistress—was very jealous. She—"

Slowly, careful to leave out no detail, she described that awful night when Mildred Dalton murdered her husband with Hester's scissors.

At the end, Phil was very quiet. "I wasn't in New Orleans at that time," he said at last. "I did hear about the murder, however."

She shuddered, remembering that awful night, and he held her close. "What did you do after the murder, my darling?"

She told how Les Crane had announced that all the house slaves, except the girls' maid, were to be auctioned off. At this, his arms tightened around her. Thus protected, she told how, determined never to stand on the slave block again, she had run. "I ended up in the settling barrel on *The Mississippi Magnolia*," she finished. "Captain Val came for a drink of water, dipped in the gourd, and hit me in the face. He thought I'd run away from home, a white home, to be on the showboat. Then he thought up the Indian act, the Indian disguise, and here I am."

"My sweet precious," he murmured, his palm along her cheek. He brought his lips to hers and stopped, not quite touching. She waited, starved for his kisses now that she had known them once again, but instead of kissing her, he murmured, "If, after what you've been through, my dearest," he said, "my touch is offensive—"

"No!" she protested. "Your touch is heaven! It is I who should be offensive to you after—"

His lips pressed hers, cutting off what she would have

said. She hadn't the will to pull her lips from him, but kissed him in return, long and deeply, ever more sweetly, with burning warmth. Sometime during the kiss, his hand left her cheek and went to her breast, cupping it, and under the material of the Indian garb, her nipple hardened.

Lifting his lips just a bit, he murmured. "It's the other way around, Hester. It is I who should be offensive to you, holding you, wanting—everything. Wanting—it makes me—animal."

"No!" she said fiercely. She pressed to him and felt her breasts crush against him in a sweet embrace of their own.

He moaned. "I want you to know. There's never been another girl in my arms. Only you. Hester, I don't know whether I can wait—"

"You don't have to wait!" she gasped, afire with her own love.

As one, they rose. As one, swiftly, unaware that someone might look into the shed, they stripped away their garments and let them fall. They stepped out of their fallen clothes and into each other's arms. They kissed again, lip to lip, body to body. She felt his hardness and trembled at the raging heat within herself.

"Now, Phil!" she whispered. "Oh, now!"

He lowered her gently to the floor so that she lay on her back, hardly aware of the scattered oats pressing into her skin, and then he lay beside her, one leg thrown over hers. Resting on an elbow, he leaned over and traced kisses along first one penciled eyebrow, then the other. "My Indian princess," he murmured, "my lost love!" He touched the black wig and drew his hand along a braid. "Next time," he said, "the wig won't be in the way; there'll be no need for it!"

She drew in her breath, and it quivered.

He kissed down her cheek, past her waiting lips to her chin, kissed down her neck and between her breasts. He kissed the erect right nipple, took it into the moist warmth of his mouth, and held it. He did the same with the other nipple.

She was moist between the thighs. The burning within her became a flaming torture, and she couldn't breathe. She felt his hardness against her and moaned his name. He kissed on, then, down her belly, into the cluster of auburn hair, through it and on. Down her thighs, her legs, to her toes. He kissed each toe, one at a time, and every kiss sent a sparkle through that dampness and made a tingling at the base of her brain. She rolled her head from side to side, her whole self aflame. "Now, Phil— please—now!"

At her plea he positioned himself over her. Instinctively she parted her legs. His body lowered, and his maleness touched the threshold, gave one strong push and was where it should be, where it must be. Simultaneously they began to move. He thrust excitedly in, then pulled back, and when he did that, she slapped herself fiercely upward, following him. Then he thrust again, spearing, driving her buttocks against the floor, and she moaned with joy. They were gasping now. His movements grew faster; helpless to do otherwise, she matched his speed.

Phil, who had touched no female since Hester when she was fourteen, had no control over his movements. He had no sense of danger, no fear of being discovered, no thought except that this was Hester, that now, this moment, was that for which the world had been created.

He was going fast, so fast the world was whirling, every stroke new, more painfully rewarding than the last. He moved even faster, and still it was not enough.

She was always there, meeting him without fail. His ears began to ring. There was only the spinning of the world, the ringing in his ears, the movement, the heart-stopping movement, the unbearable anticipation.

Then came the sudden cessation, the long, endless clinging, the throbbing that coursed through him, that wracked his body. There was the stillness from her, too, the knowledge that she was holding her breath, that they were touching heaven together.

Afterward, they lay entwined on the floor. He cradled her against him, and she rested there, gasping, feeling him do the same. She listened to their breathing. At last she stirred.

"What is it?" he whispered.

"Could we—again?" Timidly she laid a finger tip on that part of him, and it was turgid.

He groaned and gave a rueful laugh. "Not safe," he said. "We've already run an awful risk. There's your reputation—"

"I've never *had* a reputation," she reminded him.

"You will have, from now on. We've got to get back before we're missed."

She shot up out of his arms, scrambled to her clothes, and began to dress. He did the same.

Before going outside, they checked to see that no one was about. Then they started back for the landing, walking very slowly, because there was so much to talk about. Phil bemoaned the fact that he couldn't keep his arm around her as they went, and she smiled at him lovingly.

She couldn't think; she could only feel. She dreaded the moment when he would begin to speak, for then she would have to think, and that would change the utter perfection of just being together.

Before they had gone twenty steps, Phil said, "We'll be married at once."

"We can't be!" she cried instinctively.

"And why not?" he demanded.

"Phil—Phil! It won't work. It can't. I'm a wench."

"I refuse to let that interfere, my darling. No one knows the wench part. You are now an Indian girl, and you're going to be my wife!"

She was tempted; she wanted it so desperately. But it was impossible. Somehow she had to make him realize and accept that impossibility. "Don't you need a surname to marry, Phil?" she asked.

"Well, yes, you do. We'll make one up."

"The only name I have any right to is Hester. My made-up name, the one I gave Captain Val, is Jewell. He decided on the Pocahontas."

"Then we'll use Kiefer; that's an Indian name. You'll be Pocahontas Kiefer, and then you'll be Mrs. Philip Bennett!"

"Papers, Phil. You have to show papers to get married."

"We'll deal with them. People hereabouts get married. So will we. Then I'll write that Lester Crane, get the letter off on the next downriver boat."

"What purpose will that serve?"

"I'll inform Crane that I know where you are. I'll buy you from the estate. The reward money they've offered for you can be added to the five thousand I inherited from my grandmother; that will cover your price easily. They'll be glad enough to make a deal for you."

"For a runaway wench, darling."

"You're not to speak so. I have the money. They want to clear the estate. It can be that simple."

"The five thousand dollars," she said. "That's for your farm."

"It's never been for the farm. You come first, then the farm."

"It would never work, darling! Someone will discover who I am. I think there's even a law against a white man marrying a black woman!"

"I've done a lot of serious thinking in these years," he told her quietly. "I planned what to do in every conceivable set of circumstances."

"And now you want to marry me as Pocahontas Kiefer, then write Mister Crane and buy me from the estate."

"Precisely."

"And after that, what?"

"As long as we stay with the showboat, you are Pocahontas Bennett. I'll write and have freedom papers drawn up for you. Then you'll be classified, by law, as a free woman of color. When we reach Pittsburgh, we'll leave the show and go further north, up into New York. I'll do what acting I can or any other work, and you can help, if you want, with your sewing. We'll have each other, and in time we'll have our farm."

She gazed at him, dumbfounded.

"It's a sound plan, darling," he said, when she made no comment. "Now that I've found you," he said firmly, "no one is going to take you from me again."

He was still speaking in impossible terms, Hester thought.

"You will go along with it?" he pressed. "You will do things my way?"

"You would only end up hurt," she pleaded. "With your whole future ruined. Because I am, no matter how I look, a Negro wench. It would come out, it would be known, somehow it would."

"I'll not listen to such an argument," he said. "If you don't promise to do it the way I've explained, we'll do it the other way."

"What other way?" she asked, dazed, close to tears. She so longed to go into his arms, to promise him any-thing, everything. But she was as dangerous to his future as the scissors in the mistress's hand had been to Master Edward.

"The only way you leave possible, Hester. For us simply to leave the showboat and disappear together."

"You mean run away together?"

"That's what I mean."

"That's madness!"

"Of course it is, darling. The other is sensible and sound. And it will work. We'll stay in the far north and never come south again."

"I—Phil, darling—I can't—won't!" she cried softly, though it tore her heart.

"What do you mean, 'won't'? After the way we've searched, and now it's possible. I refuse to take no for an answer! You've got to marry me, darling, for both our sakes!"

She stared into his face. She had not known he could look so stern, hard, unrelenting. His jaw was like iron. He was not going to accept her refusal.

"You love me," he said firmly.

Wide-eyed, she nodded. She loved him so desperately she would die for him. Instead, she had to give him up so that he could live a proper life, free to go where he pleased, completely unfettered, with nothing to regret.

"You're as white as any white girl," he insisted. "Correct?"

Her eyes locked to his, she nodded again.

"We'd be accepted as a white couple. Can you deny that?" She shook her head. "And remember, we'd live in the north. All our lives. Would you object to that?" Again she shook her head. "Yet you still think there's a risk."

"Yes, Phil. Yes, darling."

"All of life is filled with risk of one sort or another. If we were, by some crazy chance, found out, we'd go to another country. It's that simple."

It was not simple. She could not be responsible for tearing his life to shreds. She tried to speak but couldn't.

"Hester, dearest love! Please? Promise! Don't torture me!"

His pleading—the tender tone, the love in every word—was almost more than she could resist. He had been true to her for so long. He had searched and had saved his money for the purpose of buying her freedom. This moment all he yearned for, all he had worked for, was within his grasp, and yet, for his sake, she had to deny him.

In spite of her determination, she yearned to fall into

his arms, to promise everything he wanted. She ached to be his wife, to spend her years with him, to lie in his arms and know, again and again, the same wonderful feelings, deep, hot, filled with glory, that she had experienced with him in the shed. Helpless for an instant, she swayed toward him. His arms came out to receive her. Somehow, she managed to step back.

Her face was wet with tears. "It's still 'no,' darling," she sobbed. "I'm a wench—there's no way to take the blood out of my veins! Please, darling, stay with the showboat, other showboats, buy your farm—let me go!"

He stared at her in disbelief.

"If I'd never been sold away from Thornton," she wailed, "none of this would have happened! I'd have been the wench I am, and you would have gone about your life!" She fled, sobbing.

He had reached the edge of the field when her feet touched the gangplank. She had managed to stop crying, but there was no one on deck to see her. She ran to her cabin and closed the door. Betty wasn't there, so she flung herself across the bed and wept.

Chapter Twenty-nine

After she had washed her face and made certain, in the mirror, that tears hadn't streaked the stain, Hester sat at the shelf that served as a desk and wrote Captain Val a note. In it she thanked him for his kindness and said she was going back to her own life, that she had lied about being an orphan. She folded the note and tucked it under the mattress. She had no sooner done that than Betty came in, her face white and drawn. She looked as if, were the wrong word spoken, she would burst into tears.

Not knowing what to do, Hester could only say, "Hello, Betty."

"H-hello," Betty replied. Her hands were shaking. "Where did you go this afternoon? You were gone when I went to sit on deck."

"For a walk," Hester replied, worried that Betty had seen her with Phil. "Did you sit on deck all afternoon?"

"No, I didn't," Betty said, a defensive note in her voice. "Marge Strickland went to sleep, a real, snoring sleep, and Ralph got away from her and took me for a walk. But we went north. We didn't go near that shed, so you needn't get any silly ideas."

"I'm not, Betty," Hester assured her wondering why, if the time with Ralph had been pleasant, Betty's hands were shaking. Or why her lips, usually so pink, were now almost white. Things hadn't gone well, that was evident. Maybe some obstacle had come up to delay Ralph's leaving Marge and getting a divorce. Hester could think of nothing else that could make the girl so white and shaken.

She saw Betty's lips quiver and thought the story of the afternoon was going to come pouring out. Instead, Betty turned on her heel and went to where their clothes hung behind the long curtain. "I'm going to change for supper," she announced.

"But why?" Hester asked, considering this a safe topic. "We just have to get into costume after supper."

"It's for R-Ralph. I'm going to wear the blue silk. He likes me in blue."

"But you're already wearing blue!"

"It's only muslin! Ralph likes the silk, says it makes my eyes bluer!"

"I—see."

Betty whirled, the blue silk in her arms, her face paler than before, and defiant. "What do you care?" she demanded. "What business is it of yours?"

"None," Hester said sadly, "none at all."

She wanted to plead with Betty and implore her to break with Ralph. But filled with her own heartache, she felt she had no right to speak. Clearly, this girl loved Ralph Strickland even as she loved Phil. Her impulse was to take Betty into her arms and comfort her and to seek comfort for herself, but she dared not.

Betty changed into the dress, refusing Hester's offer to do the hooks. Then she sat at the dressing table and applied rouge to her pallid cheeks, colored her lips until they looked as they naturally did, brushed her lustrous hair, and was ready. Much to Hester's relief, she seemed perfectly normal when she said, "Now! Let's go to supper!"

The meal was silent compared to other meals. There was very little chatter, only a laugh or two, and those from Captain Val and Mollie. Velda Rose, looking more beautiful than usual, seemed to be lost in admiration of her ringed hands and her oval fingernails. Hester was in such inner tumult she spoke not a word and dared only glance at Phil.

He was pale and looked stern and determined and spoke only when spoken to. Marge Strickland was openly demanding of her husband's attention, and he gave it freely, calling her "dear" at every turn. Betty, so pale her makeup stood out, chattered, in spurts, to Billy Myers, who was openly delighted and tried to keep the conversation going even when Betty dropped into moody silence. No one ate with appetite, not even Billy, who was so carried away by Betty's attention he forgot the food on his plate. Actually, Hester noted dispiritedly, he ate less than anyone, except for Captain Val and Mollie, who either didn't notice the dejected air at the table or chose to ignore it.

There was standing room only at the last performance on the showboat that night. It was an enthusiastic crowd, and the cast performed with verve and sparkle. Caught up again in the emotions of her song, Hester sang and danced better than she had ever done before.

The audience left reluctantly. The kerosene lamps and the flares were extinguished, and the members of the troupe repaired to their tiny rooms.

Hester undressed quickly and got into the nightshift she had made. Betty, moving as if in some dreadful nightmare, slowly removed her makeup. Her skin was so white it held blue tinges, and her lips were so pale they frightened Hester.

"You don't look well, Betty," she ventured. "Will you let me call Mollie? She has tonics and things."

"I'm p-perfectly well," quavered Betty. "All I need is a night's sleep. You'll see!"

It was Ralph Strickland who was making Betty ill, Hester thought. So long as she loved him blindly and desperately, she would not improve. Unless he married her. But Hester dare not say it; the words would only throw the girl into tears.

Betty lay on one edge of the mattress, Hester on the other. Knowing the other girl yearned for and could not have privacy, Hester did what lay in her power to give it to her. She lay unmoving on her edge of the bed, holding back her own tears, breathing audibly and evenly. Gradually, simulating sleep, she deepened her breathing and slowed it.

Only then did Betty weep, silently at first, then harder, and at last in deep, wracking sobs. Hester forced herself to lie still and tried to figure out what had happened. Had Ralph attempted to convince Marge to agree to a divorce and been violently turned down? Or had Betty and Ralph quarreled? Had she insisted on action, and had he refused on the grounds that he needed more time? Had Betty decided that he had merely been using her?

She wanted to roll over in bed and take the sobbing girl into her arms, but if things were going roughly between Betty and Ralph, even ending, what comfort was there?

The only person who could soothe Betty was Ralph Strickland, and he lay in bed with his wife.

At last Betty fell asleep. Even then, her breath quivered, and she gave a twitch now and again. Cautiously, Hester got out of bed, retrieved the note to Captain Val from under the mattress, stole across the gently swaying floor, and propped it up on the dressing table.

In the darkness, she took off her wig, pulled a brush through her hair, and let it lie on her shoulders and down her back. Careful to make no sound, she put on the brown dress from Woodlawn. Mollie had folded it and the shawl, wrapping the sandals in them, and told her to keep them out of sight, which she had done. She drew her hair back into a knot and pinned it. Later, as she traveled north, she would wash off the Indian stain.

Carrying her sandals, she left the cabin, crossed the deck, went down the gangplank, and up the narrow little street of Henderson's Point. Behind, on *The Mississippi Magnolia,* the troupe slept.

Probably Phil wasn't asleep. He would be thinking of tomorrow, of what he would say to Captain Val about them, and of what he could say to sway her. Suddenly tears ran down her cheeks, but she blinked them away and kept walking, sandals in hand.

She was always running. She had run with her parents, had run from Woodlawn to save herself from the slave block, and was running now, to save Phil from his impossible love. Penniless, for she hadn't yet been paid, she realized it was out of the question, after all, for her to flee north. In this time of dire need, with slave hunters after her, there was no way in which she could use her fine education, either as a modiste or governess. Either job would require at least some money to live on while she looked for work, and even getting a post could lead to her being apprehended, for the Dalton estate would be searching for a white-skinned, auburn-haired wench.

There was only one chance, one place to go, and that was to Thornton, back to her parents and the life to which she had been born. Her parents would hide her at Thornton, all the slaves would hide her, and she'd have a breathing spell. In that time, she'd take joy in her parents and, with their help, slip away one night and take her chances on reaching the north later, when the hue and cry about her had died down. Then she'd get a place as a seamstress and proceed with her original plan to one day buy her freedom.

Phil. He would try to find her, but when he couldn't, he would eventually return to *The Mississippi Magnolia*. She believed this, for he had joined a showboat troupe the other time he lost her.

She had no idea what time it was. The night was very dark. To reach Thornton, she needed to go west and south, but she had no concept of how far. She had asked Beau Kidd to draw her maps of the area where Thornton was located, but he had refused, laughing. "That life is over," he had said. "Forget it."

She did know that she was presently in the north part of Yazoo County, because Captain Val had said so, and that the Yalobusha River, on which the showboat was anchored, flowed out of Warren County into Yazoo, and she knew Thornton was in Warren County.

She walked in that general direction. She was young, and she was strong. Frightened though she was, she could make her way across one county and into the other. When she was away from Henderson's Point, she put on her sandals. Now walking was easier, though she had to step with care so as not to make any sound passing some unseen cabin.

Dawn broke. She walked steadily on, keeping to the river road. The showboat would be shoving off to push further north and east; Hester was still going west and south. The rising sun was behind her.

Phil wouldn't have missed her yet. Most of the troupe slept late on Sunday mornings. Even if Phil was awake now, waiting impatiently to see her, he would think she was sleeping, so he wouldn't be on her trail, not yet. And, if she understood Captain Val at all, he would not set Phil ashore to come racing after her. He would have the note Hester had left. It was no great loss to the showboat for the Indian princess to disappear. But Phil was the leading man, the important one, and Captain Val would use every device to keep Phil from leaving, regardless of what reason he gave.

Please stay, my darling, Hester thought as she made a wide detour to avoid a cabin. Stay with the boat, please, please.

She was very hungry, and she was thirsty. She walked what seemed to her to be another mile, avoiding a second

cabin. On her way back to the road this time, she came
on an isolated garden patch beside a clear, running stream.
There was nothing growing in the patch but green-topped
onions and hot little red radishes, but she ate them hungrily. Then she drank at the cold stream, got to her feet,
and resumed walking again.

She felt a little sick from the radishes, but she would
have to get used to eating whatever she could find. She
had no money with which to pay some farmwife for food;
worse, she dared not present herself to one of them for
fear that word had filtered, even into the back country,
of the runaway wench with dark red hair. She wished now
that she had combed out the Indian wig and worn it
dressed white-girl fashion. But she had had neither the
opportunity, with Betty in the room, nor even the idea
until now.

Despite her circling of houses and cabins and keeping to
the timber when rigs appeared on the road headed for
church services, Hester was overtaken. She had been following a cart track through the timber, eating the few
ripe berries she saw along the way, when from behind her
came the rattle and creak of a vehicle, and a thin, reedy
old voice.

"Mornin' there!" the voice hailed. "Wait up, an' I'll
give ye a ride!"

She spun about, her breath in her throat. She saw a
small, rickety cart pulled by an old, fat horse. On the seat
of the cart was a very old man, deeply tanned, his face so
covered with a network of wrinkles that he seemed to be
wearing a veil. His hair was very white and thin. He was
smiling. She trusted him instantly.

He pulled the rig to a stop, and she climbed up onto the
seat beside him. Shaking the reins, he clucked to the
horse, and it ambled on. The wheels hit a rut, jolted Hester against the old man, and they straightened, laughing.

"That's the way it goes!" the old man chuckled. "Never
know when yer goin' to hit one of them places! I'm Max
Hart. Widower. Live alone. I'm on my way to spend
Sunday with my son and his wife. Eat dinner with 'em
every week. This is a short cut. When I hit the road, I
ain't got but ten mile to go."

"I see," Hester responded. "I'm Jewell—Jewell Kiefer,"
she added recklessly, crossing her fingers.

"New to these parts, ain't ye?"

"This part I am. I'm just passing through."

"Where ye bound?"

"South part of Yazoo County. I've family down that direction."

"Long walk. Couldn't ye git no horse to ride?"

"None to spare, where I started from," she said, and smiled at the idea of a horse aboard *The Mississippi Magnolia*.

Now they turned onto the little main road. "I kin give ye a lift fer the ten mile," Max Hart said. "Others'll do the same."

"I have relatives in the next village," she lied. "They'll take me to where I'm going."

She was amazed at the ease with which the lie passed her lips. But she was doing it for Phil, who would be frantic by now. Suddenly she was overwhelmed by the thought that he might, after all, come chasing in this very direction. She wished the old man would make his horse go faster, even run, to put distance between herself and Phil. But they jogged along at the same easy pace, and she alternately longed for Phil to appear and feared that he would. Her one hope was that he would go in the wrong direction, go north, thinking she had made for a city where she could be a modiste.

Afoot again, keeping to timber, thinking ruefully of the good Sunday dinner she had refused at old Mr. Hart's son's home because she was afraid to stay long enough to eat it, she was overwhelmed by hunger. She ate all the berries she could find as she made her way.

She walked the road all night. Once she saw a rig turning a corner, heading in her direction, saw it by starlight, and plunged into the shallow ditch beside the road. She lay there, scarcely breathing, until the rig had passed and the sound of the horse's hoofs had died away.

She found another hidden garden patch and ate more onions and radishes, as well as some lettuce and some other greens. Not far from that garden, grazing in a pasture, she came on a cow, its udder heavy, a calf busily sucking and butting.

With shaking hands, she moved the calf aside, gripped the teat of the cow it had been sucking, and spoke gently to the cow, who swung her head back as if to see what

was going on. She pulled on the teat the way she had
learned at Thornton, opened her mouth, and shot the
stream of warm, foaming, delicious milk into it. She
milked the cow until her stomach was filled, and then she
went back to the road and continued toward the west and
south.

Her flight fell into a routine. During the day, she began
to hide in woods, searching for and eating berries, then
covering herself with brush and napping. She drank from
streams. By night, she took to the road. She walked at a
good rate and steadily, not permitting herself to run.
She found another cow to milk, then another.

She lost count of the days. Phil, she thought. Where is
he? What is he doing? Thornton. How far do I have yet
to go? How far have I gone? Am I still in Yazoo County?

It was night again. She was trudging the road, her heels
and the tops of her toes blistered. The back of one sandal
had worn so she couldn't walk properly, and this made her
feet hurt all the more. But she maintained her pace; hurting feet meant nothing.

Phil, if he was pursuing her, would travel by day so he
could ask if she had been seen, and so that he could himself see her if he came near enough. As she thought about
Phil, she felt the blister on her right heel break and felt
wetness. She wondered dully if it was bleeding, but she
walked on.

Just then she heard the sound of a trotting horse. It
came from behind. She ran into the ditch and kept going,
making for woods. There was a moon tonight, so that
she had to head for the thickest part of the woods. She
paid no heed to where she went.

"Hold up there!" shouted a man. She knew he had
turned his horse, for she heard the horse's hoofs breaking
dry sticks, making a lot of noise.

She ran headlong and found herself in a soggy, swampy
area. Mud oozed around her ankles, and her breath cut
like a knife. Plunging on, she tried to run faster. As she
did so, she felt a numbing stab in her ankle. She cried
out inadvertently and pitched, face down, in mud. Unknowing, she moaned. She tried to get up but could not.
Her right leg was twisted, and there was numbness in her
ankle.

She heard the horse stop and knew someone had dismounted. She knew that someone was bending over her,

but her brain whirled from flight, from hunger, from fear, from exhaustion, and from the knowledge that she had been captured. She felt herself being lifted.

It was then that her mind went as black and unknowing as the depths of the timber.

Chapter Thirty

Phil didn't sleep at all Saturday night. Before dawn he was on deck, waiting for Hester. He was certain she hadn't slept, either, that she, too, had worried and considered all night long. Surely, now, he could make her see things his way and convince her that her blood would never make any difference.

He watched Sam, Charlie, and Captain Val shove off, and helped a bit. Then he stood at the rail, impatient for Hester to appear, hardly aware that the showboat was moving slowly upstream and had left Henderson's Point far behind. Unseeing, he stared at the black-green of a forest.

The morning wore on. One by one, others of the troupe came on deck, yawning and rubbing their eyes, but no Hester. Even when they gathered at breakfast, Hester had not appeared. Nor had Betty. Which meant that Phil couldn't ask her what was keeping Hester.

Marge sat very close to Ralph, rubbing her face against his shoulder and murmuring. Phil looked away from them. He recalled the looks he had seen Betty give Ralph Strickland, and the immediate possessiveness of Marge. It was just as well that Betty didn't have to watch this if, as he suspected, she thought she was in love with the actor.

At last Betty, wearing too much makeup, slipped quietly into her place. Phil said good morning to her, holding back his anxiety and impatience about Hester. Betty looked so troubled he wanted to give her a moment to compose herself. She looked like she might have been crying.

Maybe Hester had cried all night—maybe she was ill!

Spurred by these thoughts, he asked Betty, before them all, "Where's Pocahontas—still asleep?"

"I d-don't know where she is," Betty replied, her eyes very big as she watched Marge lay her cheek against Ralph's shoulder.

"She's not in your room?" Phil asked. The hairs on the back of his neck stiffened.

"She was when we went to bed, but she's not there now," Betty said. She produced a folded paper and gave it to Billy Myers, who was sitting next to her. "It's for Captain Val, if you'll pass it to him, please."

Phil's body went rigid as the little captain took out his spectacles, adjusted them on his nose, and unfolded the paper. He read what was on it, his lips moving silently within the nest of his white beard.

"Well!" exclaimed Mollie. "What does it say? Don't keep us in suspense!"

" 'Dear Captain Val,' " the old man read aloud. " 'There is no way I can thank you for the kindness and the help you extended to me when you found me hiding in the settling barrel. To repay you in this manner is unforgivable, therefore I don't ask forgiveness.

" 'I love the showboat, love the life. I liked my part in the concerts. And I liked everyone aboard *The Mississippi Magnolia*. But I've since had cause to think. What I've done is wrong, and I must leave, without explanation. With true affection, Pocahontas.' "

Silence momentarily gripped the table.

Phil was stunned. Where had she gone? North—south —where?

"I knew she was a sneak!" cried Marge, her eyes blazing. "All young girls are sneaks! She's not gone, she's hiding on this boat, just to stir us up, to make us search for her! To get attention! You just see if she isn't!"

"She won't be on the boat," Phil said. "But it won't take long to make sure."

Within half an hour every cabin, every deck, the auditorium, the boxes, even the crevices where the scenery flats were stored, had been examined. There was no sign of Hester.

"I'll bet she wasn't Indian at all!" Marge shrilled.

"No," Captain Val told them. "She was just a regular girl, stagestruck like so many of them, prettier than most.

It was my idea to pass her off as Indian, thought it added to the flavor of *The Mississippi Magnolia*."

Drawing the old man to one side, Phil said, "She left us at Henderson's Point, captain, I'm convinced. I suggest we backtrack."

"That would be foolishness, son. Jewell—that's the name she gave me—obviously ran away from home to be an actress. Now she's run away from the showboat to go home. Leave the child be."

"Then put to shore right here," Phil insisted. "Let me off the boat."

"What for? So's you can go lookin' for her?"

"That's it, captain. I'm not free to speak, but there's more to this than meets the eye."

"You knew her before, then?"

"Yes, sir, I did."

"Knew she's white, of course? Not Indian."

"Naturally, sir."

"You in love with her, and her with you? That why she joined up, to be with you?"

"She didn't know I was aboard at first, sir. And yes, I love her."

"Then why'd she run? To get away from you?"

"That's right, sir." Phil faced the captain with pride. "She left because we're from different—social levels. She has the insane idea she's not good enough for me. I mean to find her and make her my wife."

"Your family'd consider her of a lower class, eh?"

"Exactly. That's why, if you won't put me ashore now, the very moment we tie up at Willow Landing, I'll have to go. I hate to leave you this way, to walk out on the show, but when I find her, we'll be right back, if you'll have us, sir. It may not take more than a few hours if I'm lucky."

"You know the plays can go on, wherever you are," said Captain Val. "The show can go on. Every damn play."

Phil nodded, unhappy over what he was doing.

The captain's eyes narrowed. "What if I didn't have Charlie?" he demanded. "Or he didn't know all the male leads? What if your leavin' ruined my business?"

"It's—difficult to say, sir. I'd be honor bound to wait a few days, even a week, so you could replace me."

"It'd take more than a week."

"Then I'd have to stay longer. Sir, to know that the girl you love is on the road alone, that she may be in danger—"

"Danger. What danger?"

"Thieves—gangs—evil men. And she has no money, sir! Not a penny!"

"You won't know where to look—or will you?"

Miserable, Phil met the captain's eyes and shook his head.

After his talk with Captain Val, Phil went to the cabin he shared with Billy and packed. He did it hastily, though there was no need, since it would be nearly dark when they reached Willow Landing. Packing done, he left the cabin and, hearing sounds of rehearsal, made his way to the wings.

The stage was set for Monday night's play. Charlie Greathouse was center stage with Velda Rose in his arms, intoning lines in a clear, flat voice. Captain Val, seated in the front row, stopped him, gave a direction, then told him to proceed.

Phil watched, regretfully, unnoticed by the others, who were intent on rehearsing.

Marge and Charlie had a scene together. Captain Val kept stopping them to drill Charlie, and the rehearsal dragged. Off in the wings, out of Marge's line of vision, Phil saw Betty Crawford and Ralph Strickland in a brief, heated discussion.

Ralph turned from her abruptly and made his next entrance. In a moment, Betty, looking like death, passed Phil, not seeing him, to make her own entrance. He wondered what they had discussed so heatedly.

Time dragged on. Phil had never realized that hours could literally crawl instead of pass with normal speed. Every moment *The Mississippi Magnolia* chugged upstream, he felt he was being carried farther from Hester, and he knew the time before he could find her lengthened.

At last Willow Landing was in sight. Phil, his valises ready to carry down the gangplank, said his farewells to the troupe. Only Captain Val and Mollie knew his reason for leaving the showboat. Puzzled, the troupe assumed he had a better offer elsewhere.

Charlie was getting ready to lower the gangplank when Billy Myers exclaimed, "Betty! You haven't said goodbye to her yet, Phil! I'll go get her!"

"Thanks, but no," Phil said, heading toward the dressing rooms. "Quicker if I go!"

Betty's door opened before he could tap on it. The first thing he saw was blood covering her wrists as she held her hands out to him. The next thing was her terror-stricken face. "Oh, Phil!" she whispered, tears streaming down her face. "I've killed myself!"

Phil pushed Betty back into the cabin and closed the door. He guided her to the lamp on the table, where he examined her wrists. They were bleeding profusely, but the cuts didn't appear to be dangerously deep. Snatching clean towels from the bar above the washstand, he hurriedly wrapped one around each wrist, then held a wrist in each hand, exerting pressure. Blood seeped through the towels. He took them off, refolded them so that a clean portion covered each cut, and applied pressure again.

"Will I d-die?" gasped Betty.

"Of course not," he said, not as sure of himself as he sounded. "Once the worst bleeding is over, we'll bandage them tightly and get you to a doctor."

"No doctor! I d-don't want anyone to know!"

"They'd all have known if you'd killed yourself," he said grimly.

"I didn't want to, not really, not in my heart!" she sobbed. "You fix them, Phil, you put bandages on! I'll w-wear long sleeves until they're well! I'll—oh, God, I don't know what I'll do!"

He unwrapped her wrists and examined them. The blood was only oozing now. "What can I use for bandages?" he asked.

She brought a clean shift, and he tore it in half. She gave him the razor, and he cut the material at intervals, then tore off strips.

"Whose razor is that?" he demanded.

"It's R-Ralph's!" she wept, harder than before. "I s-sneaked into their room while they were onstage and g-got it!"

"To cut your wrists," he said flatly. "Why? Why Ralph's razor? Why did you cut your wrists to begin with?"

"Because I l-love Ralph!" she cried, sobbing so wildly

he could hardly make out her words. "B-because he and I—and now I'm going to have his b-baby!"

Of course, Phil thought. There had been signs all along. The way Betty looked at Ralph, the times she stayed as near him as she could, Marge's exaggerated possessiveness.

"Mollie," he said now, thinking aloud. "Mollie will know how to handle this."

"No! Please, no! You fix it, Phil!"

"I don't know enough to settle a thing like this."

"Ralph and I fell in love at s-sight! He—the third day after we met, we—" She stopped, then continued. "He told me he loved me, that he was going to get rid of Marge because she nags in private and makes love in public, and he was sick of it!"

"That's hardly grounds for divorce."

"Ralph s-swore it was! And nearly every time we were alone together, which was every time he could get away from her, we—and he promised to m-marry me, promised over and over!"

"Then he went back on his promise?"

Still sobbing, she nodded. "Y-yesterday and again today d-during rehearsal!"

"Just what happened?"

"I t-told him about the b-baby yesterday for the first time. And he w-won't do anything about it! He w-won't admit, even to me, that he's the f-father! He says it could have been Charlie or Billy or someone in New Orleans before we shoved off! Or that it could have been Cyrus Milne!"

"You mean the fellow who quit, whose job I got?"

She nodded, weeping.

"How long has Strickland been making love to you?" Phil asked.

"S-seven weeks! But only him! Truly only him, Phil! The whole time we were rehearsing in New Orleans, before you joined us! And since!"

"And now he refuses to leave his wife."

"H-he says she's the only woman for him, the only one who can hold him! And that's the very thing he always said to me! Oh, Phil, tell me what to *do*!"

"There's no point in my facing Strickland with it," Phil said thoughtfully. "Or even the captain. The fellow is absolutely safe because he's married, and you can prove nothing."

"Pocahontas saw us come out of the shed, after——"

"But she's gone. She can't help you. The only thing," he continued reflectively, "I can think of is for you to stay with the showboat until the end of the season. You should be able to hide your—er, condition—until then. Meanwhile, save all your money, take a room in Pittsburgh, and either board your baby out or give it up for adoption."

She began to tear hysterically at the bandages, pushing his fingers aside as he attempted to fasten the first one. "I'd rather die!" she cried. "To see him with that woman every day, to have my baby in disgrace——"

She dived for the razor, and he whipped it up off the table just in time. She was so white that she looked half-dead now. Her body heaved with sobs.

He closed the razor and thrust it into his pocket so she couldn't get hold of it again. He tried to speak, but she sobbed wildly, unhearing, so he gripped her arms and shook her. "We'll work out something!" he told her. "We'll find a way!"

"J-just the two of us?"

"Hopefully. Sit down there. Let me bandage these wrists neatly. Then you put on the long sleeves you mentioned."

She let him work on the bandages. Even though he was torn by his own problem and in an unbearable rush to leave the showboat and begin his search for Hester, he worked carefully. Drawing the bandages tightly, he fastened them by tying narrow strips of material around them, then helped Betty into a dress, assuring her that the ruffled cuffs hid the bandages completely.

When he tried to make her promise not to injure herself again, he ran into trouble.

"Stay with me, Phil!" she pleaded. "As long as you're with me, I can s-stand it!"

"You've got to show up at supper," he said. He carried the lamp from the table to the dressing table, where he set it down. "Be a good girl, now. Fix your face, then go to supper. Lift your chin; pretend to be your usual self. That's what you're going to have to do, you know, to carry out the plan."

"What plan?" she demanded. "I agreed to no plan!

Not that one you talked about, to stay on this boat playing my parts, then Pittsburgh! No! I'll kill myself first, I truly will!"

Her blue eyes were so earnest, yet at the same time so fanatical, he knew she meant what she said and would carry it out. Thinking of Hester running farther and farther from him, he felt caught by circumstances. If he left this desperate girl now, she might very well finish the job she had started; if he stayed with her until he could get her problem solved in some manner, he might well lose Hester forever.

"Don't leave tonight!" Betty pleaded. "I've got to have your help!"

"What more can I do?" he asked. "I've suggested the only way I can think of, and you won't consider it."

"I c-can't! I know I have to do something, but not that! I want to keep my baby! If you'll just sit with me here, and we both think very hard—"

"Can you do something other than act to make a living?" he asked.

She frowned. "Only keep house and cook. And I don't think women living in Willow Landing hire that done. And if they do, they wouldn't hire a showgirl."

Phil agreed. Forcing his mind from thinking of where Hester might have gone, he tried to center it on Betty's dilemma. But his mind was blank. He could think of no way to help her. Then, as a vague idea stirred in him, a rap came at the door, and it was Billy Myers.

Billy stared, open-mouthed, first at Betty, then at Phil. He started to speak but seemed to have lost his voice.

"Relax, Billy," Phil told him, the vague idea suddenly full-blown and alive. "It's bad, really bad, but it's not the way it looks. Betty and I aren't lovers and never have been. Come in. Shut the door."

Even as Billy sidled in, Phil recalled the many fond looks he had seen the young man cast at Betty. He remembered how often Billy had hung around the ingénue, only to have her turn, at the first opportunity, to Ralph Strickland.

"Phil!" Betty protested, on her feet, hands out as if to fend them both off. "No one is to know!"

"It's all right, Betty. It's safe for Billy to know. It'll be good for him to know."

"Know what?" asked Billy.

"You've always been smitten with Betty, haven't you?" Phil asked baldly. "More than smitten?"

"Who wouldn't be?" returned Billy. "She's the prettiest girl I ever saw. And the sweetest." He almost choked on the last word, but he got it out. He was blushing.

"You'd help her if she needed help, wouldn't you?" Phil continued, ignoring Betty's hand on his arm.

"Sure I would!" declared Billy. "I'd beat up anybody did wrong to Betty!"

The picture of the slim juvenile trouncing the well-built Ralph Strickland flashed through Phil's mind. He indulged in a grim mental smile.

And then he told Billy Myers about Betty's suicide attempt and the truth about Betty and Ralph. He made it clear that Strickland refused to divorce Marge and marry Betty and that he even denied being the father of the baby. As he talked, Betty wept.

"Beating's too good for him!" Billy exploded. "I'll kill the bastard!"

"No!" Betty wailed. "Don't kill Ralph!"

"She thinks she loves him," Phil explained, "but in my opinion what she's felt is infatuation. She let him take advantage of her, and now she's in trouble. You calm down, Billy. We don't need a murder on *The Mississippi Magnolia.* That'll solve nothing, just raise another problem and put Betty into the middle of a scandal."

"It can't just be let happen!" Billy stormed. "The baby!"

"I agree. What Betty needs is a husband. A name for her baby. Not a dead lover, with everything coming out in the open and you in jail! How could you help her then?"

As if he had thought of the idea himself, Billy seized on it. "I'll marry you, Betty!" he cried. "That is, if you'll have me! I've been in love with you all this time! I've tried and tried to get you to notice me offstage, but you never did!"

Betty stared at him. A trace of hope came into her eyes as she studied him. Her lower lip quivered. "I'm sorry, Billy," she whispered. "I d-didn't mean to be rude. It was just that Ralph—" Her voice trailed into silence.

"I knew you were sweet on that devil," Billy said heatedly. "And I hated him for it. Then onstage, in our scenes together, you were so sweet and warm in my arms I was beside myself! After the curtain fell, you were different. But nice. You've always been nice to me."

"I knew you were a good man," Betty said. "Even then, I knew."

"Will you marry me—will you? Tomorrow night, after the concert? I'll be a real father to the baby," he continued solemnly, "if you'll have me. If you'll do me the honor."

"I always liked you, Billy," she said honestly. "I liked being in your arms onstage. If R-Ralph hadn't—I might have liked you a lot more, maybe even have fallen in love with you."

"That's enough for now," Billy said, looking both younger and sure of himself. "You liking me and me loving you. I love you so much we can sweep Ralph Strickland right out of our lives. Once we're married and the baby comes and we're a family, you'll love me the way a wife loves her husband, see if you don't."

She looked hesitant. He held out his arms to her, the way he did in one of their onstage scenes. Slowly, she walked to him, and his arms closed about her. Phil saw, with relief, that she snuggled close to him and voluntarily laid her cheek on Billy's shoulder.

"I'm going to love you one day, Billy," she murmured. "I know I am."

Now, Phil thought, relieved for himself, happy for them, now I can leave! Now I can begin my search for Hester!

But when he would have gone, they pleaded with him to stay for their wedding. He told them that Hester had run away and he must find her.

"We understand your hurry," Billy said, one arm around Betty. "But it's soon to be dark, and you can't do much until daylight. We'll move our wedding up—we'll be married tonight!"

Betty nodded, adding her plea to Billy's.

"I really can't wait, much as I'd like to," Phil said.

And then Betty turned, virtually leaping out of Billy's arms. Seeing the look of uncertainty in Betty's eyes, Phil relented. She might change her mind.

Gently he guided Betty back into Billy's arms. "Of course I'll stay," he said.

Part Four

The Refuge

Chapter Thirty-one

She was so hot. She was pursued, caught, tortured.

There was no escape possible. She burned. She could find no comfortable position. Sometimes a cool hand touched her face. Other times a wet cloth passed over her flaming cheeks and along her body, leaving a brief, blessed trail of comfort.

She existed in a well of darkness, of torment, out of which came the touches of comfort. She was aware at times that her head rolled from side to side. There were troubled flashes of memory. Showboat. Phil. Always Phil. Heaviness. Despair. Phil. The burning hotness.

Once, when awareness lasted a bit, she knew that she was in a bed. She knew someone was holding soup to her lips. She felt it trickle down her throat. Another time, there were voices. A woman's voice, low and gravelly, a man's voice, firm and moderately pitched. A third voice—a man's—blunt, rough, but with an edge of gentleness. Somehow, she knew that she was safe, that she would not have to run, not now. She even caught a glimmer of sunlight before the darkness took her back.

The time came when, very weak, she opened her eyes to sunlight streaming across a plain, small bedroom. She was lying in a narrow bed, and she could see a dresser, a wash shelf, a straight chair, and a lamp table. There were snowy curtains at the window, stirring in the breeze.

As she moved her eyes slowly about, a plain-featured woman in a gray dress came into the room. She couldn't have been more than five feet tall, if that, nor weigh over a hundred pounds. In her sixties, she had light brown hair in a knot atop her head, and she was smiling.

"You've come to, child!" she exclaimed, smiling.

"I—yes," whispered Hester. "You've been taking care of me?"

"Me and my man Bud and my growed son Chess! This is my man!" She motioned at the stockily built man who appeared, his wide face kind. His skin was weathered, his brown hair graying, his eyes steady. "Carpenter's our name," continued the woman. "I'm Beulah, and he's Bud, like I said."

"Hello to you, miss," said Bud Carpenter in the firm voice Hester remembered. "You gave us quite a scare, but my Beulah, she's got a gentle hand with the sick, and even at the first there, when Chess carried you in and it looked like you wasn't going to make it, when Beulah took over, you quieted." He smiled.

Hester wanted to smile back, but she was too weak. She lay, not trying to lift so much as a finger, and saved all her strength for words. "How—did I—get here?"

"Chess," called Beulah. "Come here, son."

A young man in his mid-twenties appeared at the foot of the bed. He was stockily built like his father and had strong, almost homely features and light brown hair. "Howdy," he said, in a rough voice with the edge of gentleness. "Glad you came to." He smiled, and it was the kindest smile Hester had ever seen.

She tried to smile back, to speak again, but weakness overwhelmed her, and she could not.

"Chess," Beulah Carpenter related, "found you in the swampland we got on our place, snakebit. Double snakebit. You'd have died if he hadn't heard you cry out and got to work with his knife and sucking out the poison, and getting you home."

It all seemed like a dream. "H-how long—?"

"You been here nigh to two weeks now, and you're still an awful sick girl, got more sickness ahead of you. Child," she went on, lowering her voice to a murmur and laying her palm on Hester's brow, "you're white as the sheets on this bed! Not a drop of color! When you was carried in here, you was dark as an Indian—and with that auburn hair! But the Indian washed off—it was stain. Who were you running from, trying to look Indian—and why?"

Hester, her mind going fuzzy again, but still aware enough not to want these kind people to suffer because they were helping her, fought off the encroaching blackness. Gathering all her fading strength, she began to whisper, and they gathered around her, listening closely.

"Hester—white-skinned wench—from Thornton," she whispered. "Ran away—from—New—New—"

"From New Orleans, child?"

"Yes—to get—Mammy—Pappy—Thornton."

As she sank again into blackness, the last thing she saw was Beulah Carpenter gazing at her, deeply thoughtful. And the last thing she heard was Chess Carpenter, his lips against her ear, speaking quickly, so that she could hear all before the darkness overcame her.

"You're safe here," Chess said. "Our farm is on the Underground Railroad—a network—help runaway slaves go north—called the passengers—we're a way station, with a secret room—in the barn—"

She heard herself moan and felt Chess's hand envelop hers. "You'll get back to Thornton," he promised.

As darkness enveloped her again, it seemed that Beulah Carpenter murmured, "Yes. She must go to Thornton."

As Hester's periods of awareness became more frequent, Beulah Carpenter explained the Underground Railroad to her.

"Some white folks," she said, "in fact, a lot of them, think slavery is wrong and a sin. Some feel this so deep—and me and my man Bud and my son Chess are among them—that we let our houses be put on the network of places that run from everywhere in the South, far as I know, to the North.

"Any slaves that can escape, they find out, through the grapevine, where the nearest way station is, and they come and hide and rest and get directions to the next way station. Lots of them, not all, of course, make it to the North and freedom. We've been on the Underground ourselves for over a year. Bud and Chess built a secret room in the barn, and that's where we let black folks rest. We feed them as long as they need, then we send them on with a supply of food."

"You're kind people," Hester said, remembering how she and her parents had failed in their escape. "And brave."

"I don't know about that," Beulah Carpenter said grimly. "It just goes against the grain. To see human beings bought and sold like cattle, treated like cattle, even abused. Just because they're black and can't do much to help

themselves. What little bit we can do ain't even a beginning to what we'd like to do—it ain't enough. That's why
we don't neighbor much, us being in the Underground."

"You should put me in the barn," Hester said, the significance of being in their house only now penetrating.
"I'm sure there are posters out on me, a reward offered."

"Fiddlesticks! You ain't black! You can pass as our
daughter!"

"That's just the trouble, Mrs. Carpenter. I'm a freak, a
white wench with auburn hair. That could—identify me—"
She still felt too weak to talk.

"Better than having black skin," the older woman said.
"That's a chance we're taking with our eyes wide open.
You've been having brain fever, child, and we ain't putting
you in any barn. Bud and I wouldn't hear to it, and Chess
—he'd let his temper go and shout us down if we even
mentioned it. You just stay in your room when anybody
comes, is all."

Slowly, dreamily, this time, Hester sank into the blackness, the burning fever.

She had periods of awareness during which she did not
have enough strength to open her eyes or move. It was
at these times she wondered about Phil. Where was he
now, what was he doing? Was he searching fruitlessly for
her, on horseback or in a rig, asking at every village, every
cabin? Or was he still on the showboat, staying where she
had pleaded with him to stay? Was he doing that for
love of her, to grant her what she begged of him?

The stronger she grew, the more she dwelt on thoughts
of Phil. At the same time, she came to know the Carpenter family and to respond to their fondness for herself
with fondness in kind.

As her strength slowly built, she walked into the other
rooms of the plain, small house. She felt a little better, a
bit stronger, each day.

Whenever she mentioned Thornton, a quiet came over
all the Carpenter family. They made no objection to her
plan to return there, but a peculiar quiet descended upon
them, and there was a tinge of sadness that lingered until
the subject was changed.

On one point they were adamant. They wouldn't let
her stay in the barn. "We need the secret room for runners," Bud Carpenter decreed. "Never know when they're
going to turn up, and we've got to be ready."

At times like this, Hester felt guilty that she had never told them of being a slave at Woodlawn and of the showboat. But that would bring Phil into the story, and she didn't want to bandy his name about, not even with these dear people.

Weeks passed. Now Hester was strong enough to dry dishes and even make up her own bed. She tried to do more, but the day she took the broom to sweep the kitchen, the older woman gently pulled it out of her hands.

"Later, child, later. You can't hurry getting well, not after what you've been through. Take your time, get back your real strength. You'll need it at Thornton, once you get back there." Beulah turned away and swept vigorously. A moment later, Hester saw her wipe tears from her eyes, then sweep even harder.

"I'm a seamstress, Mrs. Carpenter," she said, to comfort her. "If they take me back at Thornton, I'll probably not be a field hand. I'll be put to designing and sewing— if they keep me."

Beulah muttered something about they would indeed keep Hester, but the rest was lost because the older woman lowered her voice to an angry murmur. Hester hesitated to ask what she had said, and the moment was gone.

That evening after supper as they sat at table over coffee, the men began to discuss the land adjoining their farm. Rumor had it that the land was up for sale.

"What's your thinking on it, Chess?" his father asked. "This here place is free and clear. Want to take out a loan on it and buy that other acreage? It'd double the size of our holdings."

Hester noted the quick, searching look Chess shot at her. She caught her breath, then told herself not to be silly. Chess had no interest in her, none beyond that which he held for any runaway slave. Then she became aware that his parents were looking at her, too, and she blushed.

"How does it sound to you, Ma?" Chess asked.

Beulah Carpenter, a sadness in her eyes, looked away from Hester. "It's up to you, son," she replied. "Whatever you want. I may have to cook a little more to feed you with all that extra work, but that ain't no matter."

"Hester?" Chess asked, turning to look at her.

She was so confused to be drawn into family affairs that she didn't know how to reply. Personally, she thought that for them to double their holdings was wise. She believed that, given the same circumstances, Phil would take out a loan to have twice as much land. "I'm not the one for you to ask," she said carefully. "I'm not experienced in such matters. I'm a runaway wench; I have nothing to say."

"But if you did have something to say," Chess persisted, "if you was part of our family, would you be in favor of getting more land?"

"I'd always be in favor of more land," she replied. "I love land. I was raised on Thornton, and there seems to be no end to the land there."

She dropped her gaze, but not before she caught the fleet expression of worry on Beulah's face, the nod of Bud Carpenter's head, and the bemused look on Chess. She sipped her coffee, regretting her answer; it had been too bold. Kind though they were, they were still white, and she was not.

It was the following noon that the runners came. There were three black men, field hands, and Chess saw them slip into the barn lot. He called his father from the dinner table, and they ran out there. In a moment they came back, excitement in their lowered voices.

"They're from Claiborne County, just to the south of Warren here," Bud announced. "They've had good luck so far—made it from one station to another. All they need is a day's sleep and food. Plus directions to the next station—Henderson's farm. They're in good shape—can make the twenty miles easy during the night."

"Where are they bound for?" asked Beulah.

"Nearest point north where they can be free. Closest point the Underground'll take them to."

"No wives?"

"No wives, no children. They're just three, strong, young black men that want to be free," Bud Carpenter said. "I only wish all the passengers we get could be in as good shape as these."

It was that night, after the runaways had left, still unpursued, each carrying a lunch packed by Beulah and Hester, that Chess asked Hester to sit in the kitchen and talk with him after his parents retired. He was still excited about the passengers they had helped, but he also still had his mind on that adjoining acreage. They sat at the table drinking coffee.

"Hester," he said, speaking low despite the fact that the door leading to his parents' room was closed, "I've got a reason for asking you about that extra land."

"Yes, Mr. Carpenter?" she responded softly.

"You've done it again—called me mister! I've told you. My name is Chess, and you're to use it. Don't give me that slave-girl answer again!"

He was angry. And she was instantly sorry, disturbed that she had angered him. "All right, then—Chess. You were speaking of the land."

"You must know, or at least suspect, that I—like you," he said.

"Of course, Chess. And I like you as much."

"Do you, Hester? That's the big question. If you feel the way I. . . . Hester, I love you."

She gazed at him, not knowing what to say. She was fond of him—what girl wouldn't be? He was kind and dear and lovable. And he had saved her life.

"I know I'm too old for you," he said. "Eight years."

"It's not the eight years, Chess."

"You don't love me—not a bit?"

"That's a hard question, Chess. I like you so very, very much. You're dear and kind and—worthy of any girl in the world."

"If you loved me, we'd buy that land," he said. "If it ain't the eight years, and if you do really like me, what is it? That you couldn't ever love me? Is that the reason?" His eyes were pleading, and his usually determined mouth was actually trembling.

Phil, the agony beat through her, staring into the eyes of this other good and strong man who loved her, too. Oh, Phil! She tore her mind from her beloved and forced it to stay with Chess, who deserved, at the very least, her full attention. She sought an answer to his question— could she ever love him?—and found it.

"I am very fond of you, Chess," she said. "I could, given time, grow very fond of you, indeed. So fond that it would be—I suppose it would be a kind of love. But not the sort of love you offer me."

"You mean a liking—a deep, real liking?"

"More than liking, Chess. Affection. But not the kind you deserve."

With an ache of regret, she knew how his arms holding her in love would feel. Strong and tender and safe.

She had felt them, that awful night he had carried her to safety, and she knew that if she were married to him for fifty years, they would always feel safe. And pleasant. She might, possibly, be content. Except for Phil, who held her heart. And she couldn't hurt Chess by telling him Phil so much as existed.

"Surely," Chess said quietly, "it's not because you're—"

"Yes. It's the blood, too, Chess. An obstacle that can't be overcome."

Swiftly, Chess moved his chair beside hers and put his arms around her. And they did feel safe, warm, and comforting. "I'm asking you to marry me, Hester. To be my wife."

"I'm a wench. It wouldn't be legal."

"You can pass. You know you can."

"Yes."

In his arms, the roughness of his shirt under her cheek, she considered his offer seriously. She felt true affection for him, and since he was a common farmer, marriage to her couldn't ruin his life if the truth came out, as it would that of Phil, who was a gentleman.

"Your parents—?"

"They know I'm asking you to marry me. Pa's in favor."

"And your mother?"

"Ma, she loves you. Acts like there might be other reasons—not the blood—that might hold us apart. It ain't nothing, can't be. It's just a ma hanging onto her son. You know she loves you."

Hester did know this, for Beulah had told her so. And she objected to the blood not at all.

"Neither one of them does, any more'n me," insisted Chess. "Just marry me, Hester, and I'll spend the rest of my life making you glad you done it!"

As she listened, it wrenched Hester to think of belonging to any man other than Phil. Still, marriage to Chess would be safe, it would put an unbreakable barrier between herself and Phil and the harm she would do if she married him anywhere, under any circumstances.

Just as she was about to consent, Chess said, "We wouldn't have but one child, if you want, Hester. Likely it'd be a son."

And as likely it would be black!

She rested, trembling, in his arms, sad with the realization that her own dear babies would forever keep her from the white way of life. "I can't marry you, Chess, dear," she told him. "That son—the blood would show."

"You don't know that for sure!" he argued instantly. "I'm all white; you're whiter than most white girls! Common sense says our son would be white!"

"Chess—Chess!"

"You know how it is on the plantations. When a white master beds a black wench, the baby is mulatto. Then, if that mulatto beds a white, the baby is a quadroon, and some of them, down in New Orleans, they say, you can hardly tell from white! The more white blood that's bred in, the ligher skinned the babies are!"

"But my blood is black, Chess, all black. I'm a freak of nature. I had a brother who died of lockjaw before I was born. He was blacker than black, my mammy said. We could have a mulatto, Chess—one that showed the blood plainly."

"It's a chance, I admit it! But a slim chance!"

"However slim, Chess, dear, I can't take it. Please."

"Then we won't have children! We'll—"

"You must have a son, Chess. You deserve a son. It just can't be by me."

He tried to kiss her, and she drew away at first, then stopped resisting. His lips covered hers and kissed with tenderness, and she returned the kiss because he was so dear to her.

"Change your mind," he pleaded.

"No, Chess, dear Chess. Forever no."

Reluctantly, he let her go. "I ain't taking 'no' for keeps, Hester," he said. "I'll never quit trying."

Chapter Thirty-two

As her strength continued to build slowly, Hester's conviction also grew that she must leave the Carpenters as soon as possible. Chess said no more to her of marriage, nor did he so much as touch her arm in passing, but love was in his eyes every time he looked at her, and Hester became increasingly unhappy that she could not grant him what he wanted.

In her heart, she longed to stay with these kind people forever, to help with the Underground Railroad. But she couldn't stay, not without marrying Chess, which grew more impossible the more she thought about it. Phil, his whereabouts, his activities, were ever in her mind. Hunger for the lovemaking that they had shared grew with her strength. It was even harder to keep her thoughts off him than off Chess, who was in the same house, eating at the same table.

Another pair of runners came and were hidden in the barn. This time three white men arrived in pursuit, made a quick search of the farm, then went on. They did no more than give Hester a sharp glance, revealing only their male interest, and seemed to take it for granted that she was a member of the Carpenter family. When they had gone, she determined to leave for Thornton within the week. She was a danger to the Carpenters, a torment to Chess. Her decision made, the yearning she had had at the bottom of all else for her parents became a force that urged her to be on her way.

The night she meant to tell the Carpenters she was ready to leave, more runners came. It was barely dark, and they were still at table when there was a scratching sound at the back door. They fell silent and listened. The scratching was repeated.

Chess quietly walked to the door. The rest of them sat where they were. Hester was quivering inside. It could be another runner, or it could be one of those men who had looked at her so sharply come back to take her into custody, return her to New Orleans, and collect the reward.

"Yes?" Chess asked in his rough-sounding voice. "Who is it—what do you want?"

"I'se Icky," came a whisper. "Be f'um Claiborne County, mastah, suh. Be lookin' fo' Mastah Bud Carpenter's farm."

"You a runner?" whispered Chess. "I'm a Carpenter. Don't be afraid to speak up."

"I'se a runnah, mastah, suh! Dey tol' me, at de station wheah us cross' into Warren County, dat dey is a station heah, dat de name is Carpenter."

"How many of you are there?" asked Chess.

"Jes' three, mastah, suh. Me an' my woman, Ivy, an' ouah baby, Junior. Junior, he sick, he hongry, he cry a lot. Ivy, she ain' got de milk fo' him."

"Stay under that tree behind you," Chess said. "In the blackest part. We'll see to you fast as we can."

"Yo' he'p us, mastah, suh? Yo' on de Undahground, an' won' turn us in?" came the desperate whisper.

"We'll help," Chess assured him and turned back into the room. Picking up the filled water buckets, he started for the door. Bud Carpenter was lighting a lantern, his movements swift. Beulah was at the stove in a flash, pulling pots forward to heat. Hester, getting up from the table to render any help she might, was dazed at the mercurial change in the room. One moment they had been listening to the whispered conversation at the door, and the next moment everybody but herself was busy helping the runners.

Bud and Chess were out the door and gone before she could have another thought. Beulah was testing the remaining cornpone and stirring the ham hash left in the skillet, making sure it was heated through. "The greens are still bubbling some," she announced. "What them poor souls needs first is a safe place to be, which is our barn, and the next thing is good, hot food, and after that, rest. Sleep."

From the distance came the wail of the baby.

"The milk!" Beulah exclaimed. "Get that biggest jug from the well and bring it in."

Hester ran to do her bidding. She pulled up the jug of milk, which they kept hanging in the well to cool. She ran back to the kitchen, poured some of the milk into a pan, and put it on the stove to heat.

The wail came again. Beulah clicked her tongue. "We've got to get that little fellow's stomach filled so he'll sleep," she muttered. "If he ain't too sick, the milk'll do it. Warm enough extra that the chill's off if he needs more. Then we'll take the rest in the jug. By the time they need more, it'll have been out of the well long enough to take the edge off the coldness so's he won't get a stomach ache."

Bud came back as his mother finished heating the food and Hester was filling a mug with milk. Then she quickly poured the second pan of milk into a pitcher to be used next.

"We'll take the grub to them, Hester and I," Beulah told Chess.

He glanced at what they had to carry. "Too big a load," he objected. "I'll help carry, then come back here and keep watch until you've dealt with them and Pa locks them up."

They went through the darkness to the barn, Chess leading the way and carrying two pots of hot food, Hester following with two containers of milk, and Beulah last, carrying cornpone and the extra milk, some kitchen towels over one shoulder, and a bottle of liniment in her apron pocket.

"Never can tell," she said, trotting along. "I've got rags, too. They get cut up and bruised when they run. My liniment's the best I know. I make it myself."

They walked through the barn and into the adjoining granary, which was half-filled with wheat. Two planks had been installed in one wall so they could be pushed aside as they were now. Beyond them, the floor covered with hay to the depth of two feet, was a tiny, windowless room.

"Don't be scared," Bud Carpenter said to the skinny,

haggard black man who stood drooping in the center of the tiny space. "The women are bringin' you grub. Eat your fill. There'll be more tomorrow, and you can sleep all day, out of sight. When you start north to the next station—twenty miles—we'll furnish you with grub to carry and milk for the baby."

The black man jerked his head toward his equally thin wife, who was rocking a tiny, near-naked, scrawny baby in her arms. It was sucking its fist and making sobbing, jerking sounds, interspersed with thin wails.

"Set down," Beulah ordered the mother. "What's your name?"

"Ivy, ma'am," whispered the woman. Her clothes were dirty and torn, her manner one of utter terror. Her eyes kept rolling, and she rocked her complaining baby faster.

Icky's clothing was in dirty rags, and both he and Ivy were barefoot. There was a large, festering sore across three of the toes on Ivy's right foot, the edges of the sore sending streaks toward her ankle.

"Give the baby to her!" Beulah ordered, gesturing toward Hester. "Put that foot out here and let me—Chess, water!"

After moving one of the buckets to his mother, he left to keep watch and listen for pursuit. Beulah went to work on Ivy's foot, first bathing the ugly sore, then covering it with liniment, waiting, then covering it again.

Icky was beginning to eat, cramming his mouth full.

Hester, holding the baby, which was nothing but bones covered with skin, spooned a few drops of warm milk into his mouth. He swallowed. His mouth opened again. Hester continued spooning the milk into the starving infant's mouth.

Her sore toes bandaged, Ivy ate as ravenously as Icky. While she ate, Beulah soaked the foot bandage with liniment, then covered the first bandage with a dry towel and fastened it.

"You take the liniment with you," she said when she had finished. "Couple of times a day, unwrap the outside towel and soak the inside rags, then put the towel back on. Understand?"

"Yes, ma'am," said Ivy, her mouth full. "Thank you kindly, ma'am."

"We'll lock you in now," Bud Carpenter said after the

couple had finished eating and the baby was asleep. "Can't never tell. Chess has been on guard, but somebody might be on your trail."

"Mastah, suh, dey is! But dey behin' us, 'way behin' when us come heah!" faltered Icky.

"Why didn't you tell us?" demanded Bud. "We could maybe have worked faster!"

"Us skeered, mastah, suh. Mastah in de Undahground, but he a white man! A buck got to be careful whut he say, whut he do—"

"Just be quiet out here," Bud said. He was grabbing up the empty pots, Beulah and Hester helping. Hester ran for the house, and Beulah ran behind her.

Seconds later, Bud was in the kitchen. Chess came in from the outside, and Bud told him of possible pursuit. They sat at the kitchen table, listening, and agreed that it would be too obvious for one of them to be standing around outside should slave trackers arrive. Beulah started washing dishes, using hot water from the kettle on the stove, and Chess went out and brought in their spare bucket, filled with water, then sat back down. Hester dried the dishes as Beulah washed.

"The Negro can be his own worst enemy," Bud growled. "First thing Icky should have done was tell us they were being chased."

"He was afraid, Pa," Chess said. "And he's sickly. They're all afraid."

I'm afraid, too, Hester thought, recalling her own flights.

They had put away the last dish and were going to bed —Bud and Chess planned to take turns standing watch— when there was a hammering at the kitchen door. Bud strode to it.

"Who is it?" he asked, sounding calm.

"Name's Bullard," came a growl. "Got a party with me, five men."

Some dogs yipped, as though they were being held back.

"Won't you come in, Mr. Bullard?" Bud invited, stepping aside. "We were about to retire, but visitors are always welcome. Our name is Carpenter."

A roughly dressed man stomped into the kitchen. He had shaggy dark hair, a short, thick, unkempt beard and thick eyebrows that shelved out over beady eyes. He carried a rifle.

"We're trackers," he said in his growl. "We're lookin' fer three runners." His beady eyes looked all over the room, touched Hester slowly, then slid to Beulah and to Chess.

"I don't know what we can do to help," Bud said. "My wife can give you coffee, mix up some cornpone, and fry up some fatback."

"We've et! There's stations on the Underground everywhere, and we're here first to find out if you've seen them runners, second, to make sure you ain't one of them that's runnin' a station."

Bud spread his hands. "You're welcome to search."

"We'll take the barn first," Bullard said. "Won't do no good, if ye got 'em in the house, to have 'em run. Part of my men'll watch the house; the rest'll search the barn. Our dogs says them runners come onto this place, and our dogs don't lie!"

He stomped out, and Chess, who had relit the lantern, followed. Hester and Beulah flew to the door and peered into the night. They could vaguely make out a group of men. Two figures broke off from the group, and the other three moved, apparently each to some vantage point outside the house. Bud brushed past the women, following Chess, Bullard, and the others toward the barn. The dogs were yipping and howling.

Hester's breath was dry and shallow. Would the trackers find the secret room—would the dogs find it? Now they were closer to the barn, and baying.

It was then that the baby cried. The sound was shrill and piercing. They heard it in the kitchen doorway.

Bullard—he would know. And he would tear the barn apart to get at that innocent baby, to lay his hands on the baby's terrified, fatigued, escaped parents.

Dazed, Hester went onto the back porch and down the steps. Beulah linked arms with her, and they watched the lanterns, the one Chess carried, and the ones belonging to the trackers, go into the barn.

The baby cried again. Then a bellow rose in the night. Bullard had found the secret room.

Somehow, Icky and Ivy eluded them. They came running from the barn, two desperate, sickly figures in the lantern light, Ivy carrying the wailing baby. They went stumbling for the nearest timber.

"Stop!" roared Bullard. "Stop or die!"

Icky and Ivy stumbled desperately on, and a shot rang out. Icky halted in midstride, fell on his face, and didn't get up. Ivy dropped to her knees.

"Icky!" she screamed. "Icky, oh, Icky—he dead!" The baby wailed, on and on, and the kneeling Ivy both hovered over the fallen Icky and rocked the baby jerkily, making it cry even more.

Now everybody was gathered at the one spot. The trackers were all there, and the dogs, held in. Hester, clinging to Beulah, stared unbelievingly as Bullard stooped, flipped Icky onto his back, then dropped to his knees. He put his ear to the slave's chest, kept it there briefly, then stood.

"Dead," he grunted. "Small loss. Had consumption."

He turned his attention to Ivy, who was weeping silently and rocking the screaming baby in her arms. "Stoddard," Bullard ordered one of his men, "shut that sucker up fer keeps. It's got the consumption, too. We got miles to go with the wench. It'd only be in the way"

"No!" shrieked Ivy, clutching the baby. "All he need is milk, mastah! Give him milk, an' he be a fine, strong suckah! Please, mastah—"

Before anyone knew what was happening, the man addressed as Stoddard yanked the baby out of Ivy's arms and raced for the nearest tree. Bud and Chess raced after him.

But Stoddard got to the tree first. Gripping the baby by the ankles, he gave one mighty swing and smashed the baby's head against the tree trunk. The wailing cut off abruptly. Ivy screamed and fell unconscious.

Stoddard flung the dead baby to the ground.

Chess jumped onto Stoddard, going for his throat. Bud threw himself at another man, gouging at the man's eyes. The three dogs, loosed now, ran in and out, yapping and slashing at Chess and Bud, who repeatedly kicked them away.

It was then that Chess felt the rifle prod the middle of his back and that Bud felt one in his belly.

"Don't be damned fools!" Bullard yelled. "We've caught ye with the goods! Ye'll never be able to help in the Underground again! Ye'll be on the list!"

"You were sent to capture these slaves!" Chess shouted.

He stood very still, knowing that the man behind the trigger would not hesitate to pull it. "You weren't sent to kill them!"

"Our orders is catch 'em, dead or alive!" Bullard shot back. "It's the wench they want, only the wench! The other two was sick and goin' to die, anyhow! But the wench, she's a good field worker! What's more, their master don't expect us to lug dead bodies home to 'em!"

Bud glowered.

"Now, Carpenter," Bullard asked him, "you folks goin' to simmer down? We're doin' what we was sent to do. And we aim to finish without you buttin' in. Jest remember —there'll be a rifle on ye the whole time!"

"Get along with it, then," rumbled Bud Carpenter. "Chess, do what they say. They got us cornered."

Bullard guffawed. He muttered to Stoddard, who went at a run for the barn, carrying a lantern. Leaving the barnyard gate open, he trotted into the barn, was gone for a few minutes, then reappeared.

They stood in a group, the Carpenters at rifle point, and waited. In moments, flames licked out of the hayloft, crept, then raced, along the wooden sides of the barn.

Bud and Chess swore and moved to go fight the fire but were stopped by the rifles. Hester seemed to have left her body, to be watching from afar as the fire enveloped the barn. She saw and was glad when first the cow, then the two horses, ran out of the yard and away. Appalled but helpless, she watched two of the trackers scoop up Icky's body and fling it into the midst of the flames. Another tracker seized the slain baby by the ankle and sent the little body flying like some dead, small bird through the night and into the roaring fire. Ivy, who had regained consciousness, was shrieking.

"Put chains on her!" Bullard bellowed. "Fasten her to a tree!"

"Careful of her foot!" screamed Beulah. "It's festering. It needs care, not manhandling! Her masters won't thank you if you bring her back with just one foot!"

"Shut up, old woman!" yelled Bullard. "Or yer house is goin' to look like yer barn does now!"

The barn had become a skeleton of flame. The timbers from which it had been built were still standing, but they were made of fire. The rafters were moving flame. As they watched, the entire barn collapsed to the ground, covering the murdered Icky and his tiny son.

"Now—you Carpenters," Bullard ordered, "into the house! Stoddard, you come, too. I want me a good look at the likes of them."

They filed into the kitchen. Once inside, Bullard gloated, "So—we caught our niggers. And we identified a nest of Undergrounders. And put a stop to their mischief!"

"You can't be sure of that!" Chess gritted. Bud nodded.

"We kin be sure," Bullard retorted. "We turn ye in, yer name an' location of yer place. From now on, even while yer busy on a new barn, ye'll be pestered by every search party lookin' fer runners. Ye'll never be able to hide another nigger. If ye do try it, yer house'll be burnt, same as yer barn."

Stoddard began to laugh. He stared at each of them, then his eyes lingered on Hester. His mouth took on a strange grin.

Sensing something, Beulah moved close to Hester on the left and gripped her hand. Chess, standing on Hester's other side, shifted threateningly. Bullard lifted his rifle, and Chess stood still, his body so tense Hester could feel the tightness of it.

"Bullard," drawled Stoddard, staring at Hester, "remember them posters? 'Bout a white-skinned freak wench with red hair? The one there's a big re-ward out fer?"

He jerked his head toward Hester. Bullard stared, examining her closely. "I see what ye mean," he said. "But it was *red* hair. This hair's more near to the brown side than red."

Chess put his arm around Hester. She leaned against him fully. Her knees would not have held her otherwise.

"This here's my wife, Mary Carpenter," Chess said clearly, his look steady on the slave hunters. "We been married a year. She's carryin' my baby. You don't lay a finger on her."

Beulah let go of Hester's hand, and her own hands moved stealthily beneath the apron she habitually wore. Then Hester felt a circle of warmth as the older woman slipped her own wedding band into Hester's hand. Carefully, Hester put it on behind her back, then brought her hand out, in full sight. She saw both trackers note the wedding band. Glowering but convinced, Bullard and

Stoddard left the kitchen and rejoined the other trackers and dogs. Two of the men dragged Ivy along between them.

Hester saw them yank Ivy and put a chain around one ankle. Oh, please, she thought, as they dragged her out of sight, let it be that the chain isn't on Ivy's sore foot, let it be on the other one!

Chapter Thirty-three

The next morning, the ashes of the barn were gray and cold, a hard rain having fallen during the night. All of them, the three Carpenters and Hester, wandered about the ruins searching, but they had no more than a general idea of where the ashes of Icky and Junior lay. It would take much digging and pushing aside of debris to find even a few bones to bury, which they would do.

The cow came up to be milked, and Bud squatted on his heels to do it, for the milk stool had burned, too. The horses came up, slowly swinging their heads as though they, too, were surveying the spot where once their barn had stood.

At breakfast, Bud announced that he was going to walk to their nearest neighbor, Roy Benson, to tell him about their past Underground activities and what had happened last night. "I think he'll lend me a couple of halters so you and me can ride to the store, Chess, and buy a harness, saddles, an ax, and whatever other tools we can buy."

"I'll go with you, Pa," Chess agreed.

"No," Beulah objected, "I'll go! What are you thinkin' of, Bud, to leave two women alone after last night! Besides, I ain't seen Marcy in a month of Sundays! She'll want to hear about the trouble from a woman, not from a man, who don't bother to put in the little things!"

"What was I thinking of, indeed!" exclaimed Bud. "Chess, you stay home, son. Maybe you ought to stay, too, Beulah. It's a long walk after all the excitement and trouble."

"Piffle, it ain't but a couple of miles to the hill! Then

up the hill and another mile! Can't be more'n three miles
—four, all told! I've heard you say it, many's the
time!"

And so it was settled, Bud and Beulah leaving at nine
o'clock, Bud bemoaning the fact that he didn't even have a
length of rope at the house so he could lead the horses to
the Bensons and ride them back. Beulah, smiling at his
fuming, wrapped two loaves of bread in a towel and carried them carefully, so as not to crush them. She forbade Hester to scrub floors while she was gone.

"You see to it that she don't," she admonished Chess
when Hester smiled, not promising. "Won't hurt for the
dust to build up one extry day."

Chess went to the barn site to check on what parts of
tools—ax head, hammer head, plowshare—might be salvaged. and to look for bones. Hester put away the dishes
after they were dried and tidied the house.

She had a bucket with rags in the water ready to begin
scrubbing when Chess walked in and caught her. "None of
that!" he exclaimed, taking her bucket over to the wash
shelf, where he poured the water into the pan, soaped
his hands with yellow soap, and washed them thoroughly.

"I found one plowshare," he said. "We can clean it up
and sharpen it so it'll make an extry one. But we need a
new one for the heavy work. No bones—not a bone
have I found yet. I'll look again later."

Hester drew a careful breath, straightened her shoulders, and faced his back so that, when he turned from the
shelf, she was looking him in the eye. "Chess," she said as
he dried his hands, "I'd meant to tell all three of you at
the same time, but your ma and pa were so set on this
visit that I . . . Anyway, it's only fair that I tell you
first."

He kept drying his hands, his eyes quiet and serious.
"It ain't a thing I'll want to hear," he said.

"No, Chess, it isn't. But it's got to be said. It's time
for me to be on my way to Thornton. I'm well now, I
have my strength back, and last night we had a demon-
stration of what can happen when a runaway slave is
caught."

"You've got your mind made up."

She nodded.

He turned, hung the towel, then came to Hester, taking

her left hand in his. Beulah's wedding band still gleamed
on her marriage finger.

"You know why Ma insisted you keep this on today."

"Because that man, Bullard, or some other might come
back. To make it look true, what you were kind enough to
say last night. That I'm your wife."

"That, yes. But more. Ma knows how much I want
you." His sober gaze went over her face, as if he must
commit it to memory, as if it were a treasure that, when
taken from him, he could recall in the deep of night. His
lips quivered slightly, and this, along with the love that
emanated from him, wound into her, and she was moved
to go to him, to put out her arms and comfort him.

His arms enveloped her. He held her gently against his
solid, secure body, and she relaxed and let its strength
and safety flow into her. "Hester," he murmured, gentleness covering the natural bluntness of his tone, "let me
show you how it can be!"

She knew she should pull away, but instead, she let his
mouth cover hers and accepted his kiss, which was long
and comforting. Then she returned it tenderly because he
was Chess, because he had saved her life in the swamp
and had saved her again last night, and because he had
need for what only she could give.

Their lips still together, he carried her to her room. He
lay her on the bed, took his lips away, and gently moved
his great hands over her, taking off her garments.

And she let him do this, even helped, because he was
Chess. Because he was love, calm and endless love, with a
necessity in him that could not be denied.

When she was nude, he sighed. Sighed, she knew, with
the love that shone from his dear face, with the privilege
that was to be his. Never taking his gaze from her, he
took off his clothes.

His body, stocky though it was, held the essence of
power. His shoulders were broad, and his muscles were
well defined as he moved toward her.

"Hester!" he whispered. "Little love!"

There was a throb in his voice that touched her deeply.
Only Chess filled her mind; she was aware only of his
strength, his goodness, his contained power.

He stroked her hair, then down along one cheek and
then the other. When he touched her breast, his hand was

trembling, and it was trembling as it went lower. She quivered under his hand, and her arms came up to him and embraced him.

When he entered her, it was with worship, and it was with adoration and worship that he began to move. Twice, in this manner, he took her, and twice she returned his glowing affection, returned it in full measure. And then her heart wept because once again, she had betrayed Phil, because Chess, though he was her dear friend, was not Phil, and because he could never be her dear and only love.

"Hester," he said, stroking her hair, "this is how it would be with us. Marry me, Hester, and I'll be better to you than any man has ever been to any woman."

She stirred against him and touched his maleness, for it was dear to her. In spite of her love for Phil, Chess was precious to her, though in a different manner.

He held her closer. "Does that—touch—mean you'll marry me, Hester?"

"No, Chess, no. Nothing has changed. The babies—"

"How do you know there won't be one from today?"

"It's a chance I must take. If I did bear a mulatto child at Thornton, it would be accepted as another sucker on the plantation."

"Not my child!"

"How else can it be, Chess?"

"You'd let me know, you'd do that much? So I could buy it and raise it free?"

"Yes," she breathed. "Dear Chess, thank you!"

"I won't give you up," he said.

She withdrew, slowly, from his arms, and he let her go. She put on her clothes, and he, seeing that it was truly ended, dressed also. She could feel, in the beat of the silence, that he was determined in some manner to have her for his wife. And she knew this would not come to pass.

"I'll leave at dawn tomorrow," she said.

"How do you plan to get there?"

"Walk. It's not so far."

"Too far. Can you ride bareback?"

"It's the only way I've ever ridden."

"I'll take you."

"You daren't, Chess! If they saw you—I want no trouble! I want to walk up that driveway alone."

"I'll leave you at the start of the driveway. They'll not see me. That's a promise."

Her instinct was to go into his arms again, to kiss him and murmur her gratitude, but she did not. She had hurt him enough with her gratitude, with giving him twice what he would never have again.

Chapter Thirty-four

❋

Phil, driving the rig he had bought at Willow Landing for Hester's comfort in riding once he overtook her, was now nearing Thornton alone. Alone, discouraged, he was exhausted from the long weeks of searching. It was June, and the world about him was a riot of green, of blossom, of growing crops, of darting, singing birds, but he paid no attention to any of these things.

He was on an empty stretch of road where there were no rigs, no horsemen, no houses, even. He let his mind wander back, though his eyes did their habitual roving on the far chance they might yet spy a slender, auburn-haired figure slipping through the timber or across a field or even trudging along the road.

Swiftly, he reviewed his fruitless search. He had bought the rig at Willow Landing and made for Henderson's Point where Hester had left *The Mississippi Magnolia*.

He didn't know, of course, in what direction she had gone, but he was convinced she wouldn't follow the path of the showboat, but would go in the opposite direction. So he drove that route, urging the horse as fast as he could.

At Henderson's Point, he rested the horse and let him drink at a public trough. Here, he asked people who gathered and who recognized him as one of the show people, if they had seen a girl of Hester's description—white, but with dark skin and auburn hair. No one had seen her.

He drove on, heading for the Mississippi because that was the logical way for Hester to go. When she reached that river, she would have to go either north or south. North would lead her to Vicksburg, where she might try

to lose herself, or beyond, if she could manage, into a
northern state. But she would have wilderness to pass
through, and she was on foot and weaponless. Yet, knowing her determination, he dared not skip looking for her
toward the north.

He stopped at every settlement on the way to the Mississippi, stopped at every house and every lone cabin,
making inquiries. Nothing. It was as if she had vanished,
as if the countryside had swallowed her up.

Doggedly, he kept going. He had money left from buying the rig, part of it his salary from *The Mississippi
Magnolia*, part left from the goodly amount he had been
carrying with him since he joined his first showboat so
that he would have ready money should he ever find Hester
and need to make a fast move. Now he spent frugally,
saving every penny he could against the time he overtook
Hester.

At the Mississippi he drove north for a week. The road
grew narrower, eventually becoming a cart track, then
disappearing completely. Trackless wilderness lay beyond.
Hester could never travel that. Nonetheless, he hid his rig
in a growth of trees and rode on north for five days,
bareback, sore and miserable, watching for any sign of a
human being's having passed here. Again there was nothing. He rode back to his rig and turned back the way he
had come.

He stopped at all the places he had stopped at on the
way north, asking again, never finding anyone who had
seen a girl like Hester. Or any girl, traveling either alone
or with others.

Driving south now, he saw posters on Hester, but no
one who could give him word of her. His horse got a stone
lodged in his hoof, and, not having money enough to replace the animal and care for Hester both, he had to
camp out for two weeks, treating the bruise, feeding the
horse on grass, and watering him from the river. He
bought his meals from a hard-faced, suspicious settler
woman, who handed them out the door to him and quickly snatched his money when he paid.

At last he was able to travel again, slowly, for the horse
still favored his foot, but he made a few miles every day.
He asked dozens of questions, and never got the answer he
sought.

At night he lay on a blanket from the rig, crossed his arms under his head, and stared at the stars. One question crossed his mind ceaselessly at night even as it did while he traveled the roads by day: Hester, where are you? Where are you, my darling, what is happening to you?

Maybe she had been captured. Maybe someone had collected the ransom, and she had been sold again on the block. Yet, had she been captured on this southern route, those living near where she had been taken would be full of the story and would probably have related it to him in detail. Eventually, one night as he lay on his back, he thought of what Hester had once cried out. Something about it being better if she had never been sold from Thornton.

He sat up, his pulse racing. That was it! That was the one place she could really hide—Thornton! In the Quarters, with her parents, for none of the Thornton slaves would ever betray their beloved Hester. They had always defended her.

He followed the river to Warren County, pushing the horse as much as he dared. He drove to Thornton, tied his rig at the foot of the driveway, then hurried, keeping out of sight of the big house, to the Quarters.

It was evening, and the hands had come in from the fields and were in their cabins for supper. Walking quietly and swiftly, meeting no one on the paths, Phil made his way to Hester's cabin.

He gave a token knock at the side of the door, then stepped into the kitchen. Lela Belle was stirring something in a pot at the fireplace; Sam was polishing his shoes.

He looked up. "Mastah Phil, suh!" he exclaimed in surprise, getting to his feet.

Lela Belle did not seem surprised. "Yo' bin lookin' fo' Hester!'" she whispered, spoon in hand. "Yo' allus good to her. Yo' thin an' worn! Wheah yo' think she is, Mastah Phil, suh?"

"She hasn't been here?" he asked hoarsely.

Both Lela Belle and Sam shook their heads solemnly.

"You needn't be afraid to tell me!" Phil whispered. "I want to help her to freedom! I swear to you she'll be safe if only you'll tell me she's in the Quarters!"

Big tears rolled down Lela Belle's face. "We swears to

yo', Mastah Phil, suh. De las' we know of ouah Hester was when Mastah Thorne an' Boss Murray throw her into de jailhouse an' de coffle took her away!"

"Yo' know more, Mastah Phil, suh?" implored Sam. "Kin yo' tell us what happen to ouah chile since she was took f'um us?"

Hurriedly, Phil related what had happened to Hester. Both parents were sobbing. Lela Belle was shaking her head; Sam's hands were clutched into fists.

"It was my fault she ran from the showboat," Phil said. "I recognized her and wanted to take her north. and she ran because she thought I'd get into trouble and ruin my life."

"Ouah Hester's like dat," wept Lela Belle.

"I feel that she'll come to you," Phil said, "and that everybody in the Quarters will hide her. But she can't live her whole life that way!" He ached to confide in them, to reveal his love for Hester, but some instinct warned him not to speak.

"Dey'll hide huh!" said the parents together.

"If she does come, I'll be at the big house," Phil told them. "Supposedly I'll be visiting, but actually I'll be waiting for Hester. And the moment she comes, get word to me."

"We'll tell huh yo' heah, Mastah Phil, suh," Sam promised. "But whut she do when we tell, we don' know. She a woman growed now, ouah baby. We won' have no powah ovah huh."

"The power of love," Phil insisted. "She'll at least listen to—or do—what you want. Don't forget. Hester will know how to get word to me."

He left them weeping in each other's arms, then slipped out of the Quarters, walked down the driveway, got into his rig, and shook the reins. "Get up!" he said. "Get up!"

One of the stableboys met him at the front of the house. "Feed the horse lightly at first, water him a bit, then feed him a small amount again," he told the young boy. "He's been underfed for a time, and we've traveled hard. I want him nursed into top shape."

"Yas, suh, Mastah Phil, suh!" said the boy, and Phil gave him a close look in the moonlight. This boy had been playing around the stables, not as big as a quarter-hand, when last Phil was here, and he had grown and changed.

Old Dewey opened the door when Phil knocked. The old fellow greeted him warmly. "They be in the big room, Mastah Philip, suh," he said. "If you'll follow me, please, suh?"

Phil was aware of his travel-stained appearance, and he knew that the trousers and coats in his valise, which Old Dewey would bring in from the veranda, were in need of cleaning and pressing, but he decided it didn't matter. These were his kinfolk.

There was a small group in the room as Old Dewey announced Phil. Thorne Wabash, as slim and erect as ever, faced Phil across the room.

"Welcome," he said sharply, which could mean either that Phil was welcome or that he was not. "I thought you'd joined the stage life."

"For a time, yes, sir," Phil said. He came to the older man and shook hands. "I'm taking a rest. Which has always meant time at Thornton. I apologize for my appearance."

There was movement in the room, and George sauntered over to greet his cousin. He shook hands briefly and muttered, supposedly in welcome.

Eve, her lips tight, her blue eyes snapping with coldness or with hatred—Phil couldn't tell which—advanced on them. She was elaborately gowned in blue, with much lace at the bosom, concealing its flatness. Her golden blonde hair was, as ever it had been, a work of art.

"George Drummond!" she cried, her voice more demanding than Phil remembered it, and filled with ill-concealed venom. "If that isn't just like you, no consideration! The lady of the house greets the guests first!"

"My darling," he said, his tone sharp and as dripping with venom as Eve's, "I do beg your forgiveness! But then! You're not a forgiving person, are you, my love?"

Uncomfortable, wondering why it had come about, Phil recognized that George and Eve hated each other. He bowed over Eve's hand, murmured an apology for his travel-worn condition, and won a frosty smile.

"You'll nevah guess who's heah!" Eve sang out, with no softening of her tone.

Phil turned in the direction she indicated, and there,

at the far end of the room, stood Leloi Roper with her parents. He went to them quickly, shook hands with all three of them, then after a short chat with the parents, drew Leloi to one side.

Her blonde hair looked softer than before, her midnight blue eyes more luminous. Her voice seemed even more pleasant than in the days when the four of them—George and Eve, Leloi and himself—had spent the summer together, and he felt a small thrill of pleasure.

Standing together, they chatted. Phil thought again of how they had been forced by their parents to announce an engagement neither of them wanted, and he wondered that, attractive as Leloi was, she hadn't married.

Old Dewey came in with a tray of drinks and served them. George joined Phil and Leloi. "You can freshen up before supper," he said. "Some of my clothes should fit you. Dewey will see to it."

"That's kind of you, and thanks," Phil responded.

Eve, who had come up, laughed shrilly. "Kind? George Drummond kind?"

"That's enough, Eve," Thorne Wabash snapped, drawn to the group by her needling. She gave him an impudent curtsy and smiled, but there was an edge to the smile. Then she went to stand alone at the mantel, where she sipped at her drink.

Thorne and George drifted to the senior Ropers, and Leloi and Phil remained together talking.

"Remembah when we were engaged?" she asked, laughing.

He nodded, not knowing quite how to respond.

"And how we broke the engagement at the end of the summer? Phil, I met a gentleman that very next winter, a Mr. Elton Sommers, an oldah man, a plantation ownah in Hinds County. I—I've given my heart to him, and we're going to be married Christmas!"

He had barely time to wish her happiness when Old Dewey came to him, bowing, saying there was just time for him to change before supper.

Phil wrote his parents that he was at Thornton and that his Uncle Thorne had extended them an invitation to visit. They arrived on the next boat. Their reunion was affectionate, though the Bennetts were disappointed to hear that Leloi Roper was going to marry another man.

Two days later, Neal and Wanda Bennett requested the use of a carriage to take them to Whitehall so they could extend their good wishes to Leloi. Phil accompanied them, and they descended to the waiting carriage.

Thorne Wabash had gotten there first and was striding back and forth, jabbing his cane onto the driveway at every step, his face redder every second. Phil had seen him angry many times, but in a cold, withdrawn manner. Now he lifted his cane threateningly at the stableboy, who both cringed back and kept hold of one horse's halter.

"I told you yesterday to shine this harness!" he snarled at the boy.

"Mose done do dat, Mastah Thorne, suh! Mose shine an' shine all aftahnoon, an' dis mawnin', too! Mose, he can't make dat harness shine no brightah, Mastah Thorne, suh!"

"I'll be the judge of that!" shouted Thorne, brandishing his cane and making for Mose, who was obliged to stay where he was, cringing.

"Thorne!" protested Neal Bennett, trying to catch the older man by the arm and restrain him. "Cool down! The harness is fine enough! You mustn't exercise yourself—"

The cane lifted and came down over Mose's quaking shoulders. The horses reared, and Bennett seized the halter, quieting them. Phil lunged for Thorne's arm as it lifted for another blow, but he missed, and the cane cracked down again. Mose, sobbing and pleading, clung to one halter, Neal Bennett to the other. The team reared, then quieted restlessly.

As the cane lifted the third time, Phil gripped it hard and forced his uncle's arm down. For no reason, Thorne Wabash fell, striking the driveway face down. Phil knelt and turned him over. Neal and Wanda knelt, too, and Neal put his ear to Thorne Wabash's chest and kept it there.

"Neal," whispered Wanda. "Is he—?"

He nodded. "Saddle up a horse, Phil," he said, lifting his ear and beginning to rub Thorne's wrists. "Ride for Dr. Cline. I think it's too late—that he's—but go."

By the time the old doctor had arrived, they had carried the inert and unbreathing Thorne into the house and laid him on a long sofa, then placed a cushion under his head. The redness was gone from his face now; it looked whiter than any of them had ever seen it, the pallor showing even through his weathered skin. He was obviously dead.

George had ridden in from the fields by this time. He was quiet, watching every move, permitting a pale, silent Eve to cling to his arm.

The doctor made his examination. He asked a few questions, heard about Thorne's fit of rage, and listened to the account of his taking the cane to the stableboy.

"He was gone before he hit the driveway," the doctor said kindly. "Heart. He's been having trouble. I warned him, but Thorne was never one to listen to what he didn't want to hear."

George now drew himself to his full height. Gently, for him, he disengaged his arm from Eve's clinging fingers and started giving orders. The others made no challenge, for it was well known that George Drummond was to be Thorne Wabash's heir.

It was one of his orders, given in the form of a request, that brought his father and stepmother, Seth and Rosalie Drummond, to Thornton.

"I want all family connections present as I take over," he announced when they had gathered. "So there'll be no contest, no question about my rights."

"Thorne never signed the will, then?" asked Seth Drummond, amazed.

"He kept putting it off, said there was plenty of time," George replied. "And I was in no position to insist and bring on one of his rages. He might have disinherited me on the spot."

"You'll have no trouble from your stepmother," Seth assured his son, putting his arm around Rosalie.

She was very pale. "None, George," she agreed. "My father and I have been estranged for so many years that it's almost as if we weren't even related. I waive all natural rights, and you're next in line, after me, being my stepson."

He permitted his stepmother to put her hands on his shoulders and kiss his cheek. The feel of the room lightened. Phil and his parents congratulated George on being master of Thornton, and presently George was smiling and being almost pleasant.

It was during this time that Chess Carpenter parted from Hester at the foot of the long Thornton driveway and went riding off, leading the horse that she had ridden. She watched the stiff, square set of his body for a moment, and then she began to run toward the Quarters, keeping out of sight of the big house.

It was supper time; she and Chess had arrived at this hour deliberately. All the slaves would be in their cabins, and with any luck at all, she could get to her parents unnoticed. Far down one street in the Quarters, someone was moving, and Hester slowed to a walk. She reached her home and slipped across the little stoop and into the kitchen.

Her parents were there, as was Granny Myrtle. They had their backs to the door.

"Mammy!" Hester whispered. "Pappy!"

They spun, their arms open before their eyes could focus. Sobbing, Hester went to them. She was home.

Chapter Thirty-five

✸

Hester had been home now one full day. Granny Myrtle had taken the responsibility of giving out word of Hester's secret presence to every slave. By keeping to the cabin and coming out only briefly after dark, Hester was safe until she decided on her next move.

The slaves were in a subdued panic over their own futures. Master Thorne was buried; Master George was owner of all Thornton properties. This fact affected Hester as seriously, and more so, than it did any of the others. She needed time to think, to weigh, to evaluate her chance at success should she ask Master George to buy her.

Granny Myrtle brought word that not only Phil, but his parents as well, were at Thornton. Lela Belle confessed to Hester they had promised to tell her that Phil was here, wanting to see her.

She knew why Phil was there. He had quit *The Mississippi Magnolia* and had gone searching for her. And he had come to Thornton in the hope she might return to her parents. She dared not see him. Given time, he would go on about his life.

Granny Myrtle was present on this evening on which Hester related what had happened to her after she had left Thornton. Among other events, she told about how she had gotten her education from Master Beau Kidd.

"Lawd, lawd," Granny Myrtle said. "Heah that!"

"It was you who started my learning, Granny," Hester said. "You taught me my first few letters and how to count. My only regret is that I had to pay for my education in the manner I did."

"That don't mattah," Granny said. "A black wench has

got to get what she can, how she can. You done good, Hester! I'm proud of you!"

"We is proud, too," her father murmured. "To know dat ouah lil' girl got de learnin' she so hongry fo'."

Wrapped in the moment's safety, Hester opened her heart completely and told them about Phil, their love, and his determination to find her. She told of the showboat, of how he had recognized her, and how she had run to protect his future.

"He wants to marry me," she finished simply.

They gasped in unison, and she could feel their horror, their fear, and their bewilderment.

"Yo' purty 'nuf fo' Mastah Phil or any man," her father said. "Yo' good 'nuf, too good, fo' any man. But it won' do—dey ain't no way yo' kin marry him, Hester!"

"He says we can go north or go to another country. He says I can pass any place."

"That's right," Granny Myrtle agreed. "But a hidden, mix-up marriage ain't to be thought of! Can't Mastah Phil undahstand that for himself?"

"He sees only that he loves me. It hasn't occurred to him that our children would be dark skinned. And, I'm ashamed to say, that it hadn't come to me until recently."

"Dat right," agreed Lela Belle, and there were tears in her voice. "Yo' brothah what died befo' yo' was born— yo' babies prob'ly all be dat black!"

They sat silent for a time. It was Lela Belle who spoke of Phil again, relating how worried and anxious he had been.

"He does want to help me," Hester agreed, "but as his wife."

"He say yo'd know how to git in touch wif him," Lela Belle said, as she had promised.

"Theah's me," Granny Myrtle reminded them. "I can go to the big house."

"Please," Hester cried softly, "don't let him know I'm here! It can't be kept secret forever, I know that. But I've a thing I must do first, a thing that will force him to drop any thought of marrying me!"

They promised, and Hester nestled in her mother's arms, comforted by her.

"I need to see Master George," she told them finally. "I'm afraid, if I send one of the younger bucks to ask

him to come to the Quarters, Boss Murray will spot him
and get the truth. And I need to see Master George
quietly."

"Boss Murray done lef'," Sam said. "De mastah, he was
lookin' fo' a new ovahseeah when he fall dead."

"It a good thing yo' goin' let Mastah George know,"
Lela Belle said, " 'cause he a devil. He'll find out some
day an' have a mass whippin' fo' evahbody dat hid yo',
an' dat's evahbody in de Quarters."

"I'll go to him," volunteered Granny. "Wouldn't do it
for anybody but you, Hester. Not Mastah George. He
mean as cat dirt. In the mornin' when ev'rybody's in the
fields, I'll go to the big house and tell Mastah George he
needed at Sam and Lela Belle's cabin."

Hester did not sleep at all that night, but lay thinking
of Phil, of Chess, of Edward Dalton, and Beau Kidd.

In the morning she was waiting, dressed in blue calico,
when Granny Myrtle started for the big house. Her parents had already left to begin their work day. As she
waited, Hester examined herself in the mirror. Her hair
was swept back in waves, pinned in its soft knot at the
nape of her neck. The powdery blue of the dress made
her skin look extremely white, her eyes very dark. She
sighed as she wandered into the kitchen to wait. Maybe
Master George wouldn't come.

But he did come, tramping across the stoop in his polished boots and striding into the kitchen. He stopped
abruptly and stared. "So!" he exclaimed at last. "You always did have unmitigated gall! With posters out on you,
a reward offered, you come back to Thornton, bold as ever!"

"It's home, Master George," she replied quietly. "I
ask you now to buy me from the Dalton estate, to let the
reward be part of the purchase price. I assure you I'll be
a faithful slave for all time."

"I understand they want over six thousand. Grandfather
sold you to the coffle for considerably less."

"I'm worth more, Master George. I've been educated,
can speak properly, and can read, write, and figure. I
even know Latin. I can teach your children, when they are
born. I'm a good seamstress—in New Orleans they called
me a modiste. I can design the most chic gowns in the
county for Miss Eve."

"Smart wench, aren't you?" he mocked.

"I wouldn't know, Master George. But I have grown up. I'll be eighteen my next birthday."

His eyes raked her, missing nothing from the shining auburn hair to the curves of breasts and hips.

She stood her ground.

"Why me—why do you want me to buy you?"

"Because you are master of Thornton. Because, to me, Thornton is home. My mammy and pappy are here, and I belong here."

"No other reason?"

"One, Master George. I don't want to go to the slave block, ever again."

"You prefer me to some other master, eh?"

"Yes, Master George."

"I'll buy you, I'll get a letter off to New Orleans today, by hell and damnation, I will! Not as teacher, not as seamstress, for Miss Eve is never to know about you and me. You'll be my bed wench. For now and for always, as long as you keep a shred of that damnable beauty!"

"Not as a bed wench!" she cried angrily. "I'm educated beyond that! I told you!"

"Education be damned!" he snarled. "Think it's made you too good to be a bed wench, eh?"

"I've always been too good for that! Find yourself another wench. Use your mind and see how I can earn back my purchase price a dozen times over, by making gowns for all the ladies in Warren County! Don't throw money away!"

"Money be damned!" he whispered. "I'll bed you as I please, or back you go to the Dalton estate!"

She studied him. He would do it. He would send her to the block. Rage boiled in her, flamed in her cheeks, and she flung up her head so he could see her anger. But he had won. This was what she had half-expected, what she had feared. Distasteful as it was—revolting—it would solve all her problems. She wouldn't struggle against George, much as she disliked him; she would do his bidding. And with the doing, buy Phil's freedom from love for her, buy the privilege of being with her parents, of staying on the land that seemed to be her very blood.

"All right!" she hissed. "You win!"

George lost no time. He shut the kitchen door, then ordered Hester into her bedroom, her girlhood bedroom, and told her to undress.

Her hands trembling, her heart beating rapidly, she unfastened her dress, stepped out of it, and hung it on a hook. As George undressed, he watched her. She stepped out of her sandals and stood in her shift.

Now he was nude. His body was strong and muscular, pleasant enough to look at, Hester thought. His male part stood erect. Going by his body alone, he was no more objectionable than Master Edward or Master Kidd. It was his nature, his cruelty, that roused dislike.

"I said undress!" he snarled.

She loosened the shift, let it drop, then picked it up and laid it across the straight chair.

"Onto the bed!" he snapped. "Flat of your back! Fast!"

Suddenly too weak to remain standing, weak from what was to come and from loathing, she stretched out on her back. He bestrode her, a cruel expression on his face. Reaching out, he yanked at her hair, pulling it, hurting her scalp, as he loosened it. "I want my females, women or wenches, with their hair loose!" he snorted. His male part touched her navel, and he prodded, then snorted again.

"Always play around a bit!" he chortled. "Makes it better! Especially when you get a wench you've always wanted!"

She gritted her teeth. He was pawing through her hair, yanking it hard, letting it fly back, watching it spring into waves, repeating the process, prodding her navel deliberately each time. He kept pulling her hair, so hard now that it felt every strand was being yanked from her scalp. She drew her breath in, held it as long as she could, then exhaled. He was wild in bed, different from the others. They had shown consideration for her feelings; he was concerned only with his own desires.

"Now," he muttered, "for the real fun, the real preparation! Bet you never had anything like what I'm going to show you!"

She moaned.

"So! Anxious, eh?" He grabbed a fistful of her hair and gave it a merciless yank.

And then he began to lick her. He started at the hairline, his tongue going like that of a cat, down her brow, across her nose, her lips, around her chin and down her neck. He licked a trail down the curve of each breast, down to her belly. At the nest of hair, he thrust his tongue into it and pressed, and then, so abruptly she gasped, he lifted himself and stabbed into her. He was like a knife, and every stab caused pain.

"Move, wench—move!" he snarled.

Cords standing out on her neck, she met his onslaught, and it wasn't quite as painful this way. There was less of the stabbing pain, more of relentless pounding. and that she endured. Her teeth were so firmly clamped together that she could feel pain in her jaws. Her ears were roaring. There was one more vicious stab, then George drew back and was still except for intermittent jerks.

Only after that did he withdraw, and then he continued to sit astride her, his buttocks on her upper legs. "You'll learn to like it," he said. "I can tell."

She gazed numbly at him. His expression was almost pleasant, but it frightened her. Once, when they were children, he had looked this way after he had stoned a frog until it lay dead. Not a wicked, triumphant expression, but a calm, relaxed expression. She wondered if causing pain, even death, was the only way he could find peace.

He took her again, and this time the stabbing was worse. And the only way to lessen it, to take off the edge of pain. was to slam against him, again and again.

This time, after he reached the end and lay quiet for a few moments. he withdrew, got off the bed, and stood looking down on her. Then he reached for his clothes and dressed, his mouth in a grim smile. "You're the best I ever had," he told her. "And I'm going to keep it that way. This is to be secret from the big house, secret from my parents, from Miss Eve, from my uncle and aunt, secret from Phil. From the world."

She inclined her head in understanding, got off the bed, and began to wash herself. Let him look. She had no secrets from this beast.

Unexpectedly. his voice became tinged with evil. "Phil, on second thought," he said slowly, savoring each word, "is to know—in time, in time. I'll tell him personally when the moment comes."

She looked full into his eyes. She would not gaze just past them like a proper slave any more. "You wouldn't tell him!" she cried.

His expression didn't change. "I'll make you forget he exists, Hester-wench. And him—the damned fool! Thinking he's in love with you, in love with a nigger bed wench!"

Chapter Thirty-six

After George left, Hester scrubbed herself again, all over, then rubbed her skin with a towel until her skin glowed. She was filled with shame and grief because she was a bed wench and because George, unlike Edward and Beau, was, she knew, innately evil.

Desperately she willed that Phil leave Thornton to search for her, to join another showboat, anything to get him away before George told him she was on the plantation and in what capacity. Slowly she brought herself under control. If Phil found out about herself and George—when he found out—he would really leave and would build his life as it should be.

By the time her parents came for supper, she had the meal ready. She managed to smile and even made a small joke about her cooking, and this kept them from suspecting that anything had gone wrong.

Phil, at this time, was positive that Hester would eventually return to Thornton. He risked no more visits to the Quarters, trusting her to notify him, through Granny Myrtle, that she had arrived. He would not, however, wait indefinitely; if he had no word from her in a reasonable time, he would again seek out Lela Belle and Sam.

It was mid-morning of the day after he had taken Hester that George came to the cabin again. His sharp eyes caught her instinctive shrinking, and he smiled sardonically. "Not today," he said. "There's no time; Miss Eve expects me back within minutes, and I won't do anything to rouse her suspicions. In fact, it's to keep her from getting suspicious, ever, that I'm here."

She waited, not understanding.

"It is possible that she may, at some time, get a look at you in the Quarters," he explained. "She knows, as everybody does, that we sold off a white-skinned wench a few years ago, but fortunately she never did see you. I've told her I've bought you back for breeding and that she's not to mention it. Which she won't do, because she enjoys intrigue. Naturally, I don't want the others at the big house to know, the white folks."

"Why not?" Hester asked. "The house servants will know. The slaves in the Quarters already know."

"I've given orders to the house slaves."

"Very well, Master George."

"My plan goes deeper. I told Miss Eve that I bought you for Proteus."

"P-Proteus?"

"He's a field buck Grandfather bought not long before he died. He meant to use him in the fields, but his main purpose was for breeding. Proteus should get fine suckers on the right wench."

Hester's throat constricted. "And the wench?" she asked.

"You. I told Miss Eve that you and Proteus will jump the broomstick tonight. You'll live in the new cabin Grandfather built for him."

"No! You wouldn't!"

"Why wouldn't I?"

"You wouldn't share your bed wench with any buck, not the master of Thornton!"

He laughed. "It's the safe way, with Miss Eve! I've thought out every angle. I have no intention of losing Rose Hill, no matter what sort of bitch I have to live with to keep it!"

"But to share your bed wench with a field buck," she persisted. Surely, if she could get him to appreciate the significance of that, he would not make her submit to any buck, ever.

"The idea doesn't bother me," he said. "In fact, I want you to produce some really black suckers to keep Miss Eve's mind at rest. If a white one appears, now and again, she'll consider it a freak, like you."

She could think of no more arguments. She stood helpless. "Tonight. At dark. Everybody in the Quarters present." With that he turned on his heel and left.

George found Eve and their houseguests having coffee. He accepted a cup, then spoke of the broom jumping scheduled for that evening, careful to make no mention of a white-skinned bride.

"Broom jumping!" exclaimed his father. "Didn't your grandfather let them have a preacher and get married?"

George took a sip of coffee before he replied, then said, "He did, but not I. Those marriages don't mean a thing. Marry or jump a broom, they still get sold away from each other when the master feels like it. I don't suppose any of you want to go and watch—I have to go, being master—but it'll be boring."

There was a general murmur of dissent, and Eve put her feelings into words. "I'd no more watch that, George Drummond, than I'd watch you breed mules! In fact, I don't know but what it's an insult for you to invite us!"

He apologized stiffly. The others were silent.

Phil drank his coffee, not tasting it, and gazed moodily into his empty cup. Miserably he wondered if, should Hester be captured and forever out of his reach, she might be forced into such a "marriage" as this one tonight. The thought alone was enough to keep him from going along to the Quarters even when George asked him, later, if he had changed his mind.

When Lela Belle and Sam came in from work and Hester told them of Proteus and the broom jumping, they were appalled. "No weddin', no preachah?" cried Lela Belle. "Whut Mastah George thinkin' 'bout?"

"He's changing things, Mammy. I'm his bed wench. He's pairing me with this buck to keep Miss Eve from being suspicious. I'm to have black babies."

Pappy wrapped her in his big arms and stood rocking her.

"Proteus, he a good buck," her father comforted her. "He a good hand. Yo' be sweet to him, he be good to yo' as he know how. It jus' dat he ain' smart, like yo' is."

"I've never even seen him!"

Her mother tried to comfort her, too. "Yo' pappy an' me, we nevah seen each othah 'til de preachah stood us up togethah. It bad now fo' yo', but latah it mebbe be like wif us."

"I can't do it!" Hester cried.

"Yo' got to, baby," her father said. "Dat de only way to be wif us. Mastah George, he sell yo', or he'll whip. He like whippin'."

"Promise yo' jump de broomstick," pleaded Lela Belle. "Don' let no mo' trubble come down on us!"

"De trubble be on Hester," Sam moaned.

"But it got to be," Lela Belle said sadly.

They didn't talk any more. They could hear excitement outside, voices calling about the broom jumping. Proteus's name was heard and even Hester's, for now it was safe because the master knew Hester had come home, and he was broom jumping her with the biggest, strongest, newest buck on the plantation. Hester didn't know how lucky she was; Proteus didn't know what a lucky man he was going to be.

Lanterns hanging from cabin fronts and from trees outlined a clear area where the children played during the day. All the people, including a grim-faced Granny Myrtle, stood in a circle around the edge of the area. The children were pushed to sit on the ground at their feet and stay quiet. Though they were excited about a broom jumping, there was a sadness on all the people that their special pet, their Hester, was being given to such as Proteus, powerful and good worker though he was.

Hester, pale and tremulous, wearing her blue calico, stood in the kitchen with her parents. They were dressed in their best and were wearing their shoes. The three of them waited for the signal that Master George had said would be the moment for Hester to come out. They were dry-eyed. Hester straightened her shoulders. This couldn't be happening, but it was happening. Master George was buying her, and she had wanted that. But he was linking her to Proteus, thus making her pay a double price for being kept on at Thornton.

The great bell that called the slaves from bed in the morning and from the fields at night tolled once. This was the signal.

Hester walked steadily to the door, through it, went into the lantern-lit area and directly to the mammoth, waiting figure at the far side. A faint ripple sighed through the slaves as she passed. She kept her head high, her jaw firm, her hands hanging loosely at her sides.

She reached her towering mate. In his early twenties, he was the biggest man, black or white, she had ever seen. He was well over six feet tall and had a big, powerful build. His shirt strained across his chest, and his thighs threatened to break out of his trousers.

They stared at each other, and he was open-mouthed. Somehow, she kept her face calm as he stared at her. He hadn't known, then, how white she was.

His skin was black and shining and had a red tinge. His head was big in proportion to his body, and his features were as mammoth as his build—a big, spreading nose, thick cheekbones, and wide, very thick lips.

George stepped forward, out of the shadows. He carried a broom. "Hester," he ordered, "stand beside Proteus."

He wasn't even going to introduce them! She moved to stand beside Proteus. She didn't look at him directly, but from the corner of her eye caught the swing of his head toward her and knew that he was still staring. Then she gazed straight ahead, at nothing.

"Pay attention, both of you!" snapped George. "Look at the broom! Now!" George stooped and held the broomstick parallel at the height of their ankles. "Now," he snapped out, "jump—both of you!"

Hester closed her eyes and jumped. She heard Proteus jump as she did.

"Turn!" ordered Master George. They turned, and again he held the broom. "Jump!" he sang out.

They jumped the second time, then George threw the broom aside, and dusted his hands. "That's it," he announced in a carrying tone. "It's done. All of you go to your cabins and straight to sleep. Proteus, take your woman to your cabin and show her what it means to jump the broom!"

Hester tried to catch George's eye, to at least give him a pleading glance, but he turned and went quickly toward the big house, leaving her with her broomstick mate.

The people scattered, afraid to linger, to joke and laugh as they did after a regular wedding. Only Lela Belle and Sam held back, enfolding Hester, kissing her.

Sam told Proteus that Hester was a good girl and that she was used to gentle treatment. "Yo' know whut I means?" he finished.

Proteus, mute, stared without visible comprehension, then grabbed Hester's arm and hurried her down the street to the new cabin. He pushed her through the door, across the kitchen, and into the bedroom. She caught the fresh, clean smell of new wood.

Only in the bedroom did he release her. She was standing within the room, but near the door. He stepped to the middle in one stride and peeled off his trousers, under which he wore nothing. His hard, swollen male organ sprang free and stood at right angles to his belly, the hair surrounding it woolly and thick.

Now Hester stared, appalled. It was like a club, like a log. It was too big, much too big to go where he intended for it to go. A shiver ran down her spine.

He took off his shirt and his boots, and when he was completely naked, he looked at her. His great hand was on his male part, ready.

"Git dem clothes off!" he bellowed, his voice deep as thunder. He came at her, and she backed away, edging toward the door, looking for a chance to run anywhere, just so it was away from him.

Slowly moving from him, she thought, God help me, I'm as black as he is, but I'll not let him use me!

He sprang at her. Grabbing her dress at the shoulders, he ripped it down, off, and tossed it away. He did the same with her shift. Then gripping her nude shoulders, his fingers digging to the bone, he yanked her against his huge, woolly body. His male part prodded, hard and unyielding, and he gave a howl of pleasure.

She twisted, jerked, and raked her fingernails down his wide cheeks, and he laughed. He held her as if she were a fish he had caught from the stream, even while she tore, jerked, and struggled. She gagged at the odor of him. It came from everywhere—from his shining, sweating skin, from his armpits, from low on his body.

Desperate, she brought her knee up and drove it into his groin. He just laughed and grabbed her so hard she struck his chest with a thud. Now the terrible smell was getting all over her, and she fought harder. And the more she fought, the worse she, herself, stank.

She struggled so hard that it was impossible for him to bed her. She would die before she would let him enter her. She would kill him rather than let him defile her, rip her, pour odor into her that she could never be rid of.

She still had her sandals on. Like a flash, she jerked away from him a bit, and brought her foot up to kick him. She missed. This time he didn't laugh. Instead, he slapped her so hard her head rang.

"Don' kick Proteus!" he bellowed. "Yo' mine, an' whut's mine I has!" He yanked her off her feet and threw her across the room. She landed on the bunk, and before she could stir, he was over her, straddling her.

He crawled up her thrashing body until his male part was prodding her face. She twisted and jerked, but he sat on her and with one hand held onto her legs so that she couldn't move.

"Open dat mouf," he growled.

She clamped her lips so tightly they puckered, but he forced her mouth open, and then he rammed himself inside and began a brutal plunging. "Tight!" he howled. "Or I hit yo'!"

Gagging, she obeyed. He rammed deeper, blocking all air. She was going to die. He was choking her to death. With flashes of red behind her eyelids, she did what instinct drove her to do. She bit into him as hard as she could. He howled and hit her, but the impact brought her jaws together harder, and she clamped down and held on. Bellowing like a bull, he began to throttle her. She relaxed her jaws and tried to spit him out.

Just then, he yanked himself free and jumped off her, dancing about, yelling and cursing, holding his part. Coughing, gagging, and spitting blood, she pushed up on the bed.

And then he fell, unconscious, to the floor, and she thought she had killed him.

After Doctor Cline had come and gone, leaving ointment for Hester to put on the stitched area and drops for pain, George was alone in the kitchen with her. There was a white line around his mouth. He gripped her sore arms, digging into them. "You know what you have coming to you," he said.

She nodded. A whipping. Master George would never miss an opportunity to whip.

"Much as you deserve it, I'm not going to put you to the lash," he said.

"Thank you, Master George."

"Oh, it's not that I want to spare you. But Proteus gave you a good beating, and I don't want you marked up. Not my bed wench. And I don't want Miss Eve and the others, especially Phil, to show up at a whipping. He chose not to come to the broom jumping, and I've decided I'm not ready yet for him to know about you. Understand?"

She nodded again.

"You're to nurse Proteus. You're his woman. Nothing has changed."

"But Master George!" she cried instinctively, "in my mouth, and he's so big! He—he'll choke me to death!"

"He'll have his orders. There'll be no more of that."

"Thank you, Master George," she said. It would accomplish nothing to plead with him to free her of Proteus altogether.

He left then, and she moved about the cabin, every inch of her body aching. She stole a moment to go to her parents. All their sympathy was with her, but they, too, looked upon her as Proteus's woman. When she told them what George had promised, they brightened.

"Aftah yo' learn to put up wif Proteus," Lela Belle said, "he not be a bad buck. Yo' kin clean him up, too. Yo'll see."

"He a good worker," her father added. "When he git bettah, I'll talk wif him. Make him undahstand dat yo' used to kind treatment, dat yo' make him a bettah woman if he kind an' easy wif yo'."

"He'll never be able to understand," Hester said unhappily. "It's not in him, the ability to understand. All he'll ever know is what he wants and can get."

"Dat how Mastah George be," Sam said. "It how Mastah Thorne was."

Reluctantly, Hester returned to her own cabin. Proteus was awake and in pain. She gave him some of the drops, and after a time he stopped groaning and slept.

A few hours later she came into the bedroom to check on his dressing. He lay glowering while she examined him, added ointment, and rebandaged him. Her fingers were light and gentle.

He watched every move. "I likes a woman wif fight," he said unexpectedly. "When I git well, no mattah how long

1111111111111111111111111111111

it take, I goin' pay yo' back fo' whut yo' done to me. Yo'll know whose woman yo' is."

"I'll never be your woman, Proteus," she whispered fiercely. "Not once!"

Chapter Thirty-seven

The next morning, having tidied her cabin, fed Proteus, and dressed his wound, Hester waited until the drops she gave him for pain made him fall asleep. Then, taking a kitchen knife with which to cut some of the tougher-stemmed flowers, she made her way past the empty cabins of those at work in the fields, avoiding the blacksmith shop, and ran for her secret place beside the lake. Here she would gather flowers, both for her parents' cabin and for her own. Here she would recapture the memory of joy with Phil; here some measure of peace would come into her and, please God, ease her despair.

She laid her knife at the foot of a tree and went to sit beside the water, to feel the sun on her face, and to think. There must be some way to persuade Master George to release her from being Proteus's woman, there had to be.

Suddenly, from behind her, she heard George's sharp laugh. She sprang up.

He was standing right there, a cruel smile on his face, tossing and catching a folded knife with ease. "Didn't know I was behind you all the way!" he taunted.

"No, Master George," she said. "I—" She gestured toward the kitchen knife. "Flowers. For the cabin. Proteus is tended; he's sleeping."

"Snoring," George said. "It's a good time for me to claim my rights, don't you agree?"

"Yes, Master George," she said, quickly trying to think of a way out. "But I'm—Proteus—marked me up. Which makes me not as—clean—as the master has the right to expect."

He tossed the knife again and caught it. "See this?" he

asked casually. "I brought it for a purpose. If you get any ideas with me as you did with Proteus, I'm prepared to deal with them. This knife is razor-sharp. You're lucky I'm not going to have you whipped."

"I understand, Master George," she said quickly. "But not here, not in this place. Please let it be a cabin, even the jailhouse, where we'll have privacy." She couldn't subject herself to violation here, not in this wilderness room. It would be a desecration.

He laughed, tossed the knife, and caught it. "This will do wonderfully!" he declared. "When Proteus is back in the fields, your cabin will suffice. None of the slaves, even if they see us go in, will dare to talk."

"Please, Master George, the jailhouse!"

"And just why, teasing little wench?"

"I'm not teasing, Master George! It's that somebody—anybody—might come along and see us here! But not in the jail!"

"It'll not take that long," he said. "Not today. It would offend me to see your bruises, so we'll not undress."

He began to unfasten his trousers. "Go on," he ordered. "Lie on your back. Lift your clothes."

She tried to run, but he overtook her in one leap, twisted her arm, and flung her to the grass. He opened the knife and brandished it. "Want me to use it?" he demanded, and bestrode her.

"You know I don't! Please, Master George, it's just that in a cabin or the jail—"

"First, I'd cut those long auburn curls. To the scalp. Then I'd cut behind the ears, enough to leave scars. Is that what you prefer, Hester?"

She shook her head, tears in her eyes, and lay quiet.

Dropping the knife into the grass he reached to push her clothing higher. It was then that she found herself unexpectedly struggling to get out from under him. She pushed at his shoulders with the heels of both hands and wriggled her hips, trying to slip free.

He gave a mirthless laugh, stabbed himself into her body, and began that fast, cutting rhythm. "Move!" he gasped. "Move, wench—*move!*"

Those were the words that Phil, wandering to the spot where he had found love with Hester, heard. Recognizing his cousin's voice, he moved into the edge of the clearing, wondering what unfortunate wench was George's chosen partner. He stood behind a tree, peered around it for an instant, then got a flash of white skin and auburn hair. He sprang across the space, violently grabbed George, peeled him up and off, and threw him, staggering, toward the encircling trees. George, his face blank, trousers open, came up against a tree so hard it jolted the breath out of him, and he leaned there, fighting for balance.

Phil lifted Hester. Trembling, she straightened her dress.

"Close your trousers!" Phil snapped at George.

His blank expression giving way to one of rage, George secured his trousers. The two men faced each other.

"She's mine, you damned fool!" snarled George. "I'm buying her from the Dalton estate. She jumped the broomstick with Proteus last night. Yes—she's the one! She's clear out of your reach!"

"Proteus is not to touch her," Phil said grimly. "You're not to touch her. She's mine."

George gave a snarling laugh. "She bit Proteus half in two. She gave in to me. By what right is she yours?"

"By the right of love!"

George swaggered up and ran a palm over Hester's breast. She shrank; he started to repeat the gesture.

It was then that Phil tackled his cousin, grabbing him at the knee, bringing them both crashing to the ground. They rolled, fists pounding, legs interlocking, bodies straining.

Hester, glimpsing George's knife in the grass, snatched it up. If she could get it to Phil, she thought, he would be able to subdue Master George. She circled them, opening the knife, watching her chance. They broke, stumbled to their feet, and again lunged at each other.

"Phil!" she shrieked, holding out the knife. "Here!"

But it was George who got the knife. He grabbed the knife, then lunged, the blade going into Phil's arm, ripping from shoulder to elbow. Blood sprang out along his shirtsleeve in a thin line as George readied himself for the next attack. Phil, standing his ground, deflected the next attempt, crashing his left fist into George's arm, sending the knife flying. His ripped arm flowed with blood.

George started after the knife, Phil with him. Hester sped for the tree, the one where she had left her kitchen knife, grabbed it up, and ran back to the men.

George had the knife and was stabbing wildly, missing

the mark, for Phil kept on the move, now and again de-
livering a blow with his left fist. "Out of the way!" he
shouted at Hester as she darted in with her knife. She
thrust it into his hand, then darted away.

The fighters, each with a knife now, danced about,
vying for position. Blood covered Phil's arm. He held
the kitchen knife poised in his left hand. George had his
arm drawn back, the knife point aimed for Phil's heart.
They moved at the same instant, and they were a blur of
deadly motion.

When it ended, Phil was on his feet, bleeding. George
lay on the ground, face up, his eyes staring. There was a
reddening trail beginning under his heart, ending above his
hip, where the knife was still sticking. Phil had to yank to
get it out.

Hester drew close and touched Phil. "Phil?" she whispered. "Are you badly hurt?"

"Couple of cuts is all," he said. "George—he's the one
hurt." He knelt beside his cousin, Hester kneeling with
him. Blood began to soak through his shirt. He moaned,
and there seemed to be a bubble of blood on his lips.

"You've killed him!" Hester whispered. "Run, Phil, get
away! Let them think I did it!" Indeed she had done it.
By handing Phil the knife.

"Not a chance!" Phil cried. "Take off your dress, soak
up that blood! I'm going for help!" He left, running, before she could protest.

She did as he said. Clad only in her shift, she cut her
dress with George's knife, ripping it into jagged strips.
She opened George's clothes, saw the width and depth of
the wound from the crude kitchen knife, and sucked in
her breath. She snatched up one of the cloths she had
torn and began to sop away the blood.

Before the blood could again overflow, she packed the
jagged wound with strips of cloth, pushing them against
it firmly. Carefully, she worked one last, wide strip under
his back, up and over, then tied the ends securely to hold
the blood in his body, to hold in the life.

She watched his face. After that first dazed stare, his
eyes had closed. But he was alive; he was breathing in a
shallow, slow pant. Never taking her gaze off him, she collected the knives, wiped their blades on the grass, dug
them into the soil for cleansing, then wiped them on grass

again. There was blood on the grass around George. She
wished she dared moved him away from it but feared even
to try. He's going to die, her pulse beat. He's going to
die, and they'll blame Phil. Phil is the one who will have
to pay!

Help came at last. Seth Drummond pounded up at a
run and dropped to his knees beside his son. He listened
to his heart and spoke his name, but got no response.
Neal Bennett also came, Phil with him, and they knelt, also.

Hester backed away. If any of them noticed her, they
gave no sign, not even Phil. All their attention was on
George.

Two strong blacks appeared. They had a blanket, which
they spread on the ground. On it they placed a thin piece
of wood, and over that another blanket.

Following Seth Drummond's low commands, they all—
the three white men and two blacks—moved the unconscious George onto the litter and carefully carried him toward the big house.

Hester followed, bringing the knives, not knowing what
else to do with them. She followed them all the way to the
big house, uncaring that she was wearing only her shift.

The house slaves were gathered in a shocked, weeping
clump. Miss Eve appeared on the back gallery, took one
look at George from a distance, and swooned. Some of the
house slaves, along with Rosalie Drummond and Wanda
Bennett, who were weeping, carried her inside.

Just then, Doctor Cline appeared. A stableboy, sent to
bring him, had met his rig just down the road.

"Let him lay," the doctor ordered when Seth would
have moved his son into the house. "I don't want him
moved until I look him over."

Hester waited with the others.

"Get the law," Seth ordered Old Dewey. "Send the
fastest buck on the fastest horse."

"Dat be Mose an' de horse he rode fo' de doctah, mastah, suh."

"Tell him!" snapped the father.

Doctor Cline knelt beside George. After taking off the
cloths, he called for clean white rags, then opened his
little black bag and took out a bottle. Carefully, he lifted
George's head and poured liquid into his mouth.

George swallowed, then moaned. A servant ran to the

doctor and handed him the rags he had ordered. Then the doctor began to swab the long wound. Next, he took a big needle out of his bag and threaded medical string through it.

It was then that Seth Drummond caught sight of Hester, still holding the knives, pressing forward to look. He motioned her forward, and she came hesitantly. "What are those?" he demanded. "Speak up, wench!"

"K-knives, master, sir," she stammered, and surrendered them.

"This one is George's," Seth said. "What's the other one?"

"K-kitchen knife, Master Drummond, sir."

"Were you there—did they fight with these?"

"Yes, Master Drummond, sir. To b-both things."

Seth knelt again, the knives in his hand. The doctor was stitching the wound together. George's eyelids were fluttering.

From inside they could hear Eve having hysterics. The voices of Rosalie and Wanda were comforting her. Rosalie appeared at the door, gazed out anxiously at her wounded stepson, then turned back when Eve screamed.

After the doctor finished stitching, he spread a liquid along where he had stitched. George opened his eyes and moaned.

Seth spoke softly. "Son—were you and Phil fighting a duel?"

The doctor now was stripping away Phil's shirt, getting ready to stitch his long arm wound.

Hester held her breath, Phil sat on the edge of the gallery, holding himself still under the doctor's ministrations. George moaned again. Her eyes flew to him; he seemed to be looking at the knives his father held up. Would he lie, even now?

"Duel," George mumbled. "Phil—started, stabbed first—"

"That's not true," Phil said quietly. "It wasn't a duel. It was a common fight. And George stabbed first."

Neal Bennett moved close to his son, belief on his face.

By the time the lawmen arrived, George had been carried upstairs and put into his bed. Because she had had the knives in her possession, Hester was ordered up to the sickroom. The lawmen were beside the bed on one side, Rosalie on the other, and the doctor off in a corner, repacking and closing his bag.

George was conscious. He lay flat, his skin white, and his eyes open. Seth Drummond and Neal Bennett stood at the foot of the bed. Both were pale and solemn.

Hester knew the bedroom was very fine, even beautiful, but she couldn't really see it. All she could see was George, perhaps mortally wounded, in the wide bed and Phil standing erect at a window, chin up, arm in a sling.

"So," the sheriff stated in a hard voice, "you and your cousin were fighting, eh, Bennett?"

"Yes, sir."

"Why should cousins—gentlemen—fight?"

"We've often fought. Since childhood, sir."

"With knives?"

"No, sir. Not with knives."

"But today it was with knives. Why?"

Phil's lips pressed together. He shook his head. He would never answer that; Hester knew he wouldn't.

"George Drummond, what were you fighting about?"

"Just—personal—quarrel," whispered George.

He would never tell, either, Hester thought. Because he didn't want Miss Eve to find out about her.

The sheriff wheeled on her. "Were they fighting over you—a wench?" he demanded.

Her eyes flew first to Phil, then to George.

"Don't—" whispered George, "be—a—fool."

"How did you come to have the knives, wench?"

"I was there—later, master sheriff, sir," she lied. "I saw them on the ground and picked them up."

The sheriff joined the doctor, and they conferred. Producing handcuffs, he returned to where Phil stood. "I'm arresting you for attempted murder," he said. "He's got no chance to live. Once he's dead, you're a killer."

Phil looked numb; George seemed not to have heard. Hester almost cried out the whole truth. As her lips parted, she saw Phil's eyes and the tiny shake of his head. The old rancor burned. Of course. She was only a wench. The law wouldn't take the word of a wench.

"There's no need of those handcuffs, sheriff," Neal Bennett said. "Or to take my son to jail. I'll assume the responsibility that he'll stay here, available."

The sheriff shook his head. "No. Put that good hand up by the one in the sling, young man."

Phil did what he was told. The handcuffs made a loud snap as they locked. The sheriff marched Phil out and downstairs, his father behind them, his mother appearing, weeping and pleading without effect. Outside, Phil climbed into the rig with the other lawmen.

Hester had followed. She saw that one of the lawmen had the knives. Phil sat erect, looking straight ahead; he didn't even know that she was near. The rig drove off, and she watched it become smaller in the distance. Suddenly she was running after it, shrieking. "I saw it all! Master George stabbed first! He tried to murder Phil!"

But no one paid any attention to her. The rig went faster. One of the black men who had helped carry the master was sent to drag her back.

"Yo' pick' up de knifes," he said. "Dat good. Now yo' got a husban' waitin' in yo' cabin. Mastah Seth Drummond, he say yo' tend him."

It was only then, as she turned toward her own cabin, that Hester realized that everyone in the Quarters knew what she had done to Proteus. But it seemed a small matter. All she cared about was that Phil had been taken to jail for possible murder and there was no way she could save him.

Chapter Thirty-eight

All at Thornton knew that George Drummond lay wounded in his bed and that he was dying. And no one knew who would be master after him because his mother, Rosalie, had been like a stranger to her father for so many years that she didn't want anything to do with Thornton.

Those in the Quarters gathered around Granny Myrtle for information. "Miss Rosalie, she won't take Thornton for nothin'," Granny Myrtle stated. "That's why Master George got it without that thing called a will. And Master Phil, he couldn't be master even though he's a blood cousin to George, 'cause he's the killer, and the law is pe-culiar and won't let a killer inherit nothin'. Miss Eve, she'll get Thornton. She's the wife. She's next in line."

Hester was walking along the dark streets of the Quarters, bound for her parents' cabin. She had just endured a foul cursing from Proteus as she carefully spread ointment on his injury and bandaged it. Every time she saw what she had done to him she was sorry, but she knew she would do it again if he came at her in the same manner. If Master George lived, she thought, she would plead earnestly with him to free her from Proteus. She would even offer to jump the broomstick with some other, less animallike man if only she could be rid of Proteus.

It was very dark tonight. Most of the people had gone to bed, but she knew her parents were waiting for her. She went to them as often as she could, despite the fact that they urged her to make her peace with Proteus and predicted that he would tame down.

"Pssst!" came a long hiss. She slowed. The hiss sounded again, and she stopped.

"Come over here," whispered a man. "It's Chess!"

Bewildered, she made her way to the spot.

"Where can we talk?" he whispered.

It really *was* Chess! "A-at Pappy's blacksmith shop," she whispered.

She took his arm, aware of its hard strength, and guided him in silence. Inside the shop they stood in the darkest corner and spoke in whispers.

"What are you doing here?" she asked.

"I told you I'd never give up, Hester. This is the third night I've waited. Ma took a notion to come to the village and board a spell. I don't know why, but she's set on it, and Pa's willin'. Not permanent, though, just for now."

She waited, and he continued. "We heard about George Drummond and that cousin of his, Phil Bennett, in the village."

"Yes," Hester whispered. "Master George is very ill, and Master Phil is in jail."

"That's what Ma said. She's got her reasons for bein' here, and I got mine. I want you to come away with me. Now. Tonight. With the master so sick, nobody's going to be on the lookout to see what you're doing."

"I can't, Chess. Nothing has changed between us."

"Then there's bound to be somebody else," he said reflectively. "Such love as I feel, you couldn't not love me back. Unless there is another man."

"Yes," she admitted, for he deserved to know, now that he had sensed it. "It's Master Phil I love, Chess."

"But he's in jail! He'll be—" He stopped, then said, "Hester, I can give you a future!"

"I'm even married, the slave way, Chess. I'm married to Proteus."

"Who the hell is Proteus?"

"A big black buck. Stupid. And rough."

"Has he—have you—?"

"No. I couldn't. I—bit him—there. Almost in two. He can't try again, not for a long time."

"I'll buy you from Drummond if he lives, from the estate, if he doesn't. Ma and Pa have decided to sell the farm, and I know they'll lend me the money."

"It might not be enough, Chess. My price is six thousand dollars, maybe more. It's a fortune."

"Did Drummond pay that?"

"I believe so. He bought me for his bed wench."

He was silent for a heartbeat. She could feel rage, like heat, emanating from him. At last he spoke. "Then we do like I said. We just—go. North. Tonight. That slave marriage don't count. Or did you have a preacher?"

"We jumped the broomstick only."

"Then it don't count." He put his hand on her arm. "Let's get started."

She held back. If Master George died, she didn't think that Miss Eve would ever keep her—which meant she would have to go on the block again. She would be safer with Chess. But she couldn't run, not with Phil in jeopardy. She had to stay, to know what was happening to him.

Chess argued and pleaded. At last she told him he must leave.

"I must see Mammy and Pappy, then get back to Proteus, or else I'll rouse his suspicion. Please, Chess."

"I'll go," Chess agreed at last. "This time. But I'll not stay gone, Hester. As long as there is you, not legally married, I'll always come back."

She let him kiss her, briefly, and then he was gone into the darkness, and she made her way to her parents' cabin. A deep sadness for Chess wound into her fear for Phil and into her constant terror that George would die, and, because of his death, Phil would be executed.

As the days passed, she grew ever more thoughtful and spoke only when spoken to. She began to lose weight, and her eyes showed that she slept little. Time fell into limbo. There was nothing to do but wait.

Phil Bennett knew every square inch of his tiny jail cell. Seven steps one direction, eight steps the other. It was built of dirty, damp, gray rock. The door was wood and three inches thick, with a small, iron-barred peephole for the benefit of the jailer. One tiny, barred window near the ceiling admitted a bit of light when the sun was high. There was a cot with ropes for a mattress. It did have a pillow, though it was filthy. A bucket for slops stood in one corner. Bugs skittered along the floor and walls.

Phil's meals were passed through the door by a guard, and he sat on his cot and ate whatever was brought. He got bread and water for breakfast, and thin stew with a chunk of bread at night, as well as water.

His greatest fear was that if George died, he would be tried for murder. A murder he had had no intention of committing. He would never have chosen to fight with knives. He had meant to fight George with his fists as they had always fought.

When he thought of George, his blood cousin, lying near death at his hand, tears of regret filled his eyes. When he thought of Hester, which was every moment in which he didn't think of George, other tears, of helplessness and love, filled his eyes, but he would not let them overflow.

Quentin Harrison, his attorney, came to his cell on a regular basis, sent by Neal Bennett. Harrison was the only visitor Phil was allowed to have. He told Phil the same thing at each visit. "I believe your story, Phil. The problem is to get a jury to believe it You'll be charged with murder in the first degree if young Drummond dies. Or with assault with intent to murder if he lives. Unless I can get his attorney—and Spencer Sheridan is a tough old cuss—to persuade Drummond to drop the matter and avoid further scandal."

"George does want to be proper," Phil replied. "He wants to be looked up to and admired. His vanity might possibly lead him to drop the charges—if he lives."

"Let us hope, let us hope. If he lives, we'll have a chance."

"How is George, really?"

"Hanging by a thread. Gangrene. Doctor Cline's trying to clear it up, to keep the wound clean so it can heal."

After each of these talks, Phil was deeply troubled for his cousin and for his own part in this. He became sadder and more dejected. He brooded over George's state; he worried about Hester and what would happen to her if George died and he himself was, as he assuredly would be, tried and executed. What would become of her? What sort of life would she have without him? Would she be sold from man to man, only to be discarded in her old age?

Over and over again, he paced in his cell, thinking and waiting. Waiting to see if George lived or died.

It was on one of his worst days, an hour after Harrison had left, that the jailer gave him a letter. It had been unsealed, and Phil asked about this.

"You know I got to read yer mail," growled the jailer, whose face Phil had never seen. "To be sure you ain't plottin' no jail break. This one passed the test."

Phil took it as the man slid it through the bars, then went to stand under the high window to get what light there was. The letter might be from his parents, there might be good news about George. This paper, however, was unlike the stationery his parents used, and Harrison would have known if George was better.

He unfolded the thick, rough paper and began to read. It was from Hester.

My beloved,

Things go well with me, so do not worry.

Proteus heals, but slowly. I'll never be his wife. Master George is the same, though the grapevine says he may take a turn for the better.

I'm staying at Thornton until I know your fate, my darling. Later, through friends, I'll go North, where I'll work as a modiste.

I'll never marry because it is you I love and be- cause of who my parents are.

Forever, your own
Hester

He read the letter again and again. He read it until his eyes were blurred with tears and he could no longer see. Then, like a desperate animal, he paced his cell. In all the world, there was no hope.

Part Five

Retribution

Chapter Thirty-nine

Again Chess waylaid Hester at night. "Don't be angry," he whispered. "I had to come, just had to!"

"It won't do any good, Chess."

"It ain't what you think. There's a thing eatin' on me that I can't keep secret from you no longer." She waited, puzzled. "It's about the day of the fight between Drummond and Bennett." He paused, breathing heavily, and she knew he was having trouble finding a way to continue.

"Yes," she said. "Go on, Chess."

"I seen it, Hester. I seen the duel."

"But how could you? You weren't even—"

"Oh yes, we was hereabouts, Ma and Pa and me. I snuck around the edges of the plantation, just wantin' to see favorite parts you'd told me about. Mostly, I was tryin' to spot that kind of a wilderness room you said you loved. I found it, but you and Drummond and Bennett was there—I know now who they was—and I stayed hid."

"Then you really saw what happened?"

"I seen 'em fight over you. Seen you try to help Bennett. Seen clear as day that it was Drummond, the dark-haired one, that stabbed Bennett first, not the other way around, like folks say, and like Bennett is accused of."

"Why didn't you speak up sooner?" she whispered. "Maybe they wouldn't have taken Phil to jail."

"I lit out, fast. It was only later I found out the blond one was took to jail. Besides," he continued, shame creeping into his voice, "I figured I could somehow take you away from here if he was in jail, if you believed it was hopeless. It was wrong; I've come to admit that to myself."

"It was so you could get what you wanted!" she accused, her whisper louder, fiercely angry. "No matter what happened to Phil, to an innocent man, no matter how you might have helped him, what you wanted came first!"

"It was that I need you so bad," he groaned. "Because I got to have you, Hester! Without you, I won't have no life at all!"

"You'd take me under *any* conditions?" she whispered, angrier still.

"As God's my witness. I would."

"Even knowing I love Phil?"

"Even that. Because, in time, you'd be fond of me. I know it in my guts."

"I—" she faltered, seeking through anger and despair for truth, "understand your thinking. But it couldn't work out, Chess. Phil *is* my heart. I'd never be anything but a friend to you, even if we were married. Every day of our lives, every time you took me into your arms, every time you made love to me, it would be Phil I was thinking of, yearning for. You deserve better than that, Chess!"

He was silent. They heard a baby cry somewhere in the Quarters.

"You mean all of that," he whispered at last. "You really never · ould change."

"Not even when I was an old lady, Chess. For me, it would always be Phil."

Another silence followed. This time it was Hester who whispered first. "Chess, dearest friend Chess," she said, and touched his arm. She felt it stiffen, but he made no move to her.

"Chess?" she breathed.

"Yes, Hester?"

"If you'd go to Mister Quentin Harrison in Warrenton —he's Phil's attorney—if you'd tell him you saw the fight, that you saw Master George stab Phil—that he was the first one to use a knife—it could save Phil from being executed."

"So you can marry him, is that it?"

"Not that, no."

"The blood. He'd let the blood stand in the way?"

"He wouldn't, Chess," she whispered. "He's like you about it, exactly like you. He wants—wanted—to take me north, or to some other country, and marry me, but I refused then and will refuse if—if he's somehow freed."

"If you love him so, why not do what he wants? In another country—"

"The babies, Chess. The same danger. As with you."

Unexpectedly and suddenly he gave in. "All right. I'll go see this Harrison, if it means so much to you."

"It means everything! To have Phil free—that's all I ask!"

"And me? What about me?"

"You're my dearest friend now," she told him. "You'll be even dearer then. Whether your going to the attorney results in Phil's release or not."

"You've got my word," he muttered.

She put her hand on his arm, and his hand covered it.

"I'll tell Pa and Ma about the duel and me seeing the attorney," he told her. "I keep no secrets from them except—" His finger traced her wedding finger on which she had worn his mother's ring. "That I'll never tell. It belongs to me alone."

"Chess, Chess, I'm sorry."

"You can't help what you feel." He dropped his hand. "I've found out one thing since Ma got so set on coming to Warrenton. Her and Pa knew old Thorne Wabash at one time in their lives, and they say he had a daughter, Rosalie, that he practically threw off the place. They know she's at Thornton now, come when he dropped dead, say she's stepmother to George Drummond, and is helping take care of him."

Hester nodded, though she knew, in the darkness, that he couldn't see. Then she murmured, "She'd naturally stay on when her stepson is so seriously wounded. She must be half out of her mind with worry."

"I reckon. Ma let slip that Thorne Wabash hated his daughter. She must have hated him, too, because Ma says she never come back to Thornton, not once, until now."

Again silence fell between them. They were standing so close their bodies touched. The night throbbed; it seemed to Hester that she could feel the pulsing of Chess's heart.

"Hester," he muttered roughly, "one more thing. Just one. And I'll never ask again."

"Yes, Chess," she breathed and went into his arms and lifted her lips.

Their parting kiss was long, tender, and sweet. It held yearning, and it also held relinquishment.

Chapter Forty

Three days later there was much ado at Thornton. The dying master had taken a sudden turn for the better, the threat of gangrene had vanished, and his wound was now clean and beginning to heal. Doctor Cline pronounced him out of danger.

Phil was released from jail as a result both of Chess Carpenter's long interview with Quentin Harrison and Spencer Sheridan, and the fact that George was not going to die of the knife wound.

Chess had an even longer interview with a judge and the two attorneys. The judge decreed that, should George Drummond be persuaded to drop charges that Phil had attacked him with fists, his cousin would be completely exonerated.

In their attempt to accomplish this, the attorneys escorted Phil to Thornton and into the sickroom. George was propped, half-sitting, in bed. He looked pale. He glared in Phil's direction as he entered the room.

Phil went to the bedside. "I'm sorry I knifed you, George," he said at once. "There's no excuse for my using a knife; I should have stuck to fists."

George said nothing, just glared.

"It's asking too much of a man," Quentin Harrison said, on Phil's behalf, "to use fists when the other party is coming at him with a knife. Especially if he can get hold of a knife himself."

"Knives are outside the issue now," put in George's attorney. "The point now is the fight itself, whether my client is willing to withhold a charge of bodily attack on the part of your client, sir."

Harrison inclined his head. "Your point is well taken, Mr. Sheridan."

"Let me be sure I understand what my cousin is asking," George said, his voice thinner than before, but as sharp. "I don't want to agree to something I may regret."

Harrison spoke. "We all know that your cousin laid hand on you first," he said. "He admits to that. True, Phil?"

"True," Phil replied.

"We know now, for we have a witness to the duel with knives that followed, Mr. Drummond, that you were first to use a knife and that it was a moment before your cousin even got a knife into his hand. Given him by the white wench, we know further."

George remained silent, sullen.

"These are facts, is that not true, Mr. Drummond?" pressed Harrison.

George turned his head and looked in the direction of Sheridan.

"You may admit to that, George," the attorney said.

"Very well!" snapped George. "I admit to the first stab."

"Now," Harrison took up again, "the question is, we repeat, whether you will drop the charge of assault on the part of your cousin."

"Why should I?"

"For the good name of Thornton. Word of the duel has swept the countryside, as you can imagine. Everybody knows that Phil has been jailed and that had you died, he would have been executed."

"The damage is already done," George muttered.

"A great deal, true," cut in Sheridan. "But, as your attorney, with your interests in mind, hear me out. Drop the first assault charge."

"Why? What good will that do? What'll it change?"

"Memories fade. Already, now that word is spreading that Phil is no longer in jail, people are beginning to think it wasn't so serious, after all. In time, they'll pass it off as a youthful misunderstanding, almost a prank. They'll remember, but time will blur the memory until it is all but forgotten. Thornton will still be the leading plantation, Drummond the leading name. No scandal, no gossip."

George scowled. "It goes against the grain," he said at

last, "but it's sound. However," he continued, his voice sharpening, "I demand, Phil, that you and your parents stay on at Thornton until after I'm well. I demand that we be seen in public together as we were before. We'll kill gossip faster that way."

Phil, thin and pale, nodded. "Agreed. In fact, it's a brilliant idea on your part, George."

"Naturally. I'm not master of Thornton for nothing. I know what's best for it. Now, if you'll all leave me, let's start getting things back to normal."

Ten days later, with George able to be about the house with the aid of a cane, Thornton took on its old air of being under the hand of a master. Eve was the main problem. Since George's illness, which she claimed had impaired her nerves and with it her health, she had heard that Hester had been involved in the duel and took out her spite on one and all. She became snappier and more unreasonable every day, but she made no mention of Hester to anyone.

She did, however, fight with George over the least thing. It seemed to him that she was using small matters to provoke fights, building up to some really important battle she had in mind. Daily he regretted being tied to her for life; but daily he reminded himself that, on no account, would he do anything to endanger his future ownership of the plantation that she would inherit.

The moment he anticipated came one morning after breakfast. They had eaten in silence in the sitting room of their upstairs suite.

George decided to put an end to her icy silences, to her frozen, disapproving expression, and to her short outbursts of venom over trivialities. "What's wrong with you?" he demanded.

She sniffed and tossed her chin in an ugly manner.

"You're spoiling for a big fight, so let's have it!"

"It's your duel!"

"We've settled the duel. People are forgetting."

"Pah! Do you think they'll forget that you and Phil were fighting over that white nigger wench?" She spat the words.

George blinked. So. She really had found out.

"Gossip!" he snapped. "Not a word of truth in it!"

"Oh, yes, there is! She gave Phil the knife!"

"Where did you get such an insane idea? If you're going to believe gossip instead of your husband—"

"It's true, and I know it's true!" She glared at him, and he realized that she did know the truth.

"All right, then," he improvised, "we *were* fighting over the wench! I'd come on Phil trying to—" He stopped. "I hope you're lady enough not to force me to say the ugly words."

"Why should you care about her and Phil? What difference would it make?"

"She's the one who jumped the broomstick with Proteus," he said, raising his voice. "I want her bred to a powerful buck, not to my cousin! Isn't that reason enough?"

"I don't see where one time would make any difference!"

"It makes a difference to me! I own that white wench! She's bred where I say, or she's not bred at all!"

"I know she bit him nearly in two!" Eve cried viciously. "I know he can't use—anything—for a long time to come! You'll have to wait for your sucker!"

"Watch your tongue!" he ordered. "Don't lose sight of the fact that you're a lady!"

"I'll speak as I please. She'll bite it clear off next time!"

"No, she won't. When he's healed, I'll warn her that if she doesn't knuckle under, I'll sell her parents down-river."

"Not them—sell her! I want her sold and gone right now! I want her off this plantation! Wipe Thornton clean of all the scandal while you're about it!"

"She's the most valuable wench I own. I've just had a letter from the Dalton estate accepting my offer. Proteus is one of my finest bucks. I'm keeping both of them."

"We'll see!" she screamed. "We'll see! She'll make some mistake—or you will! You'll want to take her the way Phil—"

"Have you ever known me to lower myself by touching a black?"

Her face twisted. "No! And you'd better not start with this one!"

She flounced into the bedchamber and began to dress. George, leaning on his cane only a bit, made his way downstairs. He was scowling.

Damnation! After he was healed, he would have an

already suspicious Eve with whom to deal when he went
to Hester! Before the duel, she had had no suspicion. Now
she was filled with it.

Days passed. Hester was deeply content because Phil
was free. He made no effort to seek her out, and she
sensed this was to avoid causing her even a breath of
trouble.

Phil, on his part, gained weight and color, and his determination to marry her was stronger than ever. He would
wait until George was himself again, then have it out with
him about buying Hester. He pondered arguments to
persuade his father to lend him any money he might need
for the transaction.

His strongest argument, both for George and for his
father, was that the whole countryside knew that he and
his cousin had fought over the white Negro woman. Thus,
as long as Hester remained at Thornton, she would be a reminder of this, and some talk would persist. If Phil, however, bought Hester, then took her to a foreign country
and married her, never to return, the talk would die out.
George's position in the county would be spotless. Neal
and Wanda Bennett need not be shamed before the people
of Warren County or those in New Orleans.

Chess appeared in the Quarters a time or two, just
to speak with Hester. He reported that his mother seemed
to have something mysterious on her mind and that she
wouldn't yet go home to the farm.

It was now that Hester realized that everyone she had
ever known at Thornton, or in Warren County, if the
Carpenters were included, was now gathered at Thornton.
This struck her as odd and, somehow, threatening. She
wanted things to continue as they were—Phil free and
not urging her into wild flight, George up and around,
Chess restraining himself, Proteus unable to molest her.

She realized it couldn't last. Things would change. This
was only a small stretch of calm. It would certainly be dis-
rupted, for there were too many people, too many situa-
tions involved, for it to be otherwise.

It happened the next day.

Old Dewey appeared at Lela Belle and Sam's cabin, at
Hester's, and at Granny Myrtle's. The white lady, Miss
Beulah, who used to be midwife at Thornton, had asked

that certain individuals assemble in the Thornton library an hour from now. She sent word that she had information, startling and true, that all must hear. And the master said to come.

Hester gasped in surprise. Then she warmed with affection for the kindly woman who had saved her life when she was on the run, and looked forward to seeing her again.

Chapter Forty-one

✠

When those from the Quarters—Hester, her parents, Granny Myrtle, and Proteus, edged into the library, it was already filled with people. The room was silent. All were standing, though extra chairs had been brought in.

Dazed, Hester flicked her glance about, wondering what Mrs. Carpenter could possibly have to say. She caught the woman's glance and nodded. Then a lovely lady entered on the arm of Neal Bennett, a lady who had helped carry Eve into the house when she fainted, after George was stabbed.

Hester's breath caught. That lady was also the one she had seen on the sidewalk in New Orleans so long ago! She was Phil's mother, indeed. Their eyes met in recognition, and they nodded slightly and solemnly to each other.

Phil came in last. His look flew to Hester and clung. She gazed back at him as if she could never stop, then tore her look away. He was out of jail. He would live. Nothing else mattered; nothing else could matter. But she felt his continued, steady regard, and her skin grew warm.

"Well," George said sharply, "everybody's here. Sit down, all of you, blacks included. Mrs. Carpenter says this will take some time."

In hushed silence they found seats, then gazed wonderingly about. Hester, sitting on a straight chair between her mother and father, looked slowly over the room, calling a mental roll.

There was the Carpenter family, mother, father, and Chess. Beulah Carpenter was the only one in the room who remained standing. There were the four Drummonds —George and Eve, George's father and stepmother, whom

Mrs. Carpenter had kissed. There was Phil, his eyes on Hester, and his parents. There was Doctor Cline and Mr. Quentin Harrison, Phil's attorney, and a man with high color in his cheeks whom George introduced as Mister Spencer Sheridan, his attorney. And there was Granny Myrtle, Proteus, her parents, and herself. Eighteen of us, she thought. Eighteen!

She noted that Mrs. Carpenter was giving each person a probing look. Finally, she began to speak.

"Years back, twenty and more," she said, her voice low, "my man, Bud, was overseer of Thornton, and I was the white midwife and housekeeper in charge of the house slaves. I had a black midwife, by the name of Manda, who caught most of the suckers, though I helped when she had a hard case.

"I was present when Justine Wabash, the young wife of Thorne Wabash, gave birth. I was also present as housekeeper for two seasons in the Wabash home in New Orleans. I saw some things with my own eyes, overheard others, and was told the rest by Justine herself. That's what I'll start with. . . ."

* * *

Justine regarded herself critically in the long mirror at one end of her boudoir in the lush New Orleans house Thorne had given her. Though she was frowning slightly, she loved the house, and she considered the paved court-yard, which was shaded by magnolia trees and many shrubs, as perfect as heaven.

But at this moment she studied her brown eyes closely. No, it simply was not true. The fact that she was enceinte absolutely did not show in her eyes, no matter what the older ladies said. And her flowing, flame-colored negligee would continue to hide her secret as her body filled out. She looked at her face a long time and was relieved. She was almost three months past her twenty-sixth birthday and appeared, even to her own close examination, not over twenty-two.

She smiled. Thorne would melt; in time he would. She would overcome his propriety, the feeling he entertained that he must behave with reserve, even when they were alone.

Thorne, a handsome man of thirty-five, came into the boudoir at that moment and caught her staring at herself. He stopped behind her and was also reflected, dressed in fine gray trousers and smartly cut coat. "You'll find only perfection, however much you look, my dear," he said. His voice was less sharp than usual. He put out a hand and drew her to stand beside him.

"We make a handsome pair, can you deny it?" he demanded seriously.

Playfully, she cocked her head to one side and regarded the mirror. They were the same height exactly, which was a bit unusual. "We *are* stunning!" she agreed, still playfully. Then, abandoning her gay mood, she whirled to him and put her hands on his shoulders.

"Oh, Thorne!" she cried, managing to keep her tone partly gay. "Love me—hold me!"

Firmly, he put her away. "But why, my dear?" he asked reasonably. "I—er—bedded you last night with—er —appropriate warmth, I believe. Surely you don't—"

"But I do!" she interrupted. "It's as if last night, wonderful as it was, never happened! I'm hungry for more, starving for it! I'm so terribly hungry for you, Thorne, darling!"

When she would have pressed into his arms, he restrained her. "My dear. You are twenty-six years old. You must learn that I can't give in to you on every little point. I'm dressed for the day."

She drew back, tears in her heart. She had so hoped to get him to make love to her this morning, this moment, and then she had planned to whisper to him that she was enceinte. Now she couldn't tell him, not when he was like this. It needed to be confided with love, with tenderness, with mutual rejoicing.

"My dear," he continued, "I don't mean to be unfeeling, though at times you give the impression that I am. But you know better, in your heart. Remember how I've humored you. You hated Thornton—"

"Not 'hated,' darling! I was just bored. It's so quiet there, and there is life and gaiety in New Orleans! There's always a play, an opera, a ball, or some fine restaurant! Don't you see how different it is?"

"Indeed, I do. And you have all those things, true?"

"Yes, Thorne," she said, her tone subdued. "And I

thank you for them. You're a very patient man, darling, to put up with my notions!" All but the one, she thought. All but being generous with his love and accepting the love she had to give.

"So," he said now. "Being older than you by nine years and more settled, I am still perceptive enough to understand your longings. Because of this, I bought you our fine house in the city of your choice, and we'll spend all our winters here, if you choose. Isn't that enough, my dear? That and all the love that's in my heart?"

It was enough. He couldn't give more love than he contained; he couldn't satisfy her greediness.

In spite of the sensible thought she had forced herself to entertain, she cried out again. "The house is wonderful, it's perfect! Life in New Orleans goes beyond my dreams! But I need more, I must have it!"

He looked bewildered. "What is it you want, in the name of all that's holy?"

"For your love to grow! For you to drown me with love!"

"I made you my wife. That doesn't precisely indicate hatred. And you do have my love, Justine."

"If you'll only let it grow, darling! That's what I want—must have! I want to love wildly, hotly, passionately! I want—"

"When you give me a son, Justine, your very—youthful—fires will bank. Our affection will turn into a warmth, and that will last our lives."

"But I need the other, darling! I need to love you as I need for you to love me! We both need the fire, the passion, the burning—we need it now!"

This time, when she pressed into his arms, he set her away sternly. "The subject is closed, Justine. It is beyond me to provide this—hysteria—you demand. We'll continue as we have been. In time, you'll see that I'm right."

Choking back sobs, she almost told him about the baby. And then she did not. She would wait for their next lovemaking, whenever that might be. She would tell him then; perhaps that would be the fuel he needed.

She turned away. Glancing into the mirror, he adjusted his coat. "That artist I spoke of recently," he said calmly, "the one all New Orleans is talking about. You know who I mean?"

"Yes," she replied, trying to keep her voice steady. "I've heard about him at a tea party. Steven Bird, I think his name is. What about him?"

"He's put you on his list."

She spun to face him. "Me?"

"Precisely. I'll hang the portrait over the mantel in the library at Thornton. In the event that I should neglect to mention it later, I want you to be painted in your wedding gown. With perfect detail to the lace and with that diamond"—he motioned at the large stone glittering on her right hand—"visible. Also the diamond wedding band."

"Yes, Thorne," she said, the life gone from her voice.

"You're to pose in this room at the mantel. With red roses in silver vases at either end, the red to match your lips."

"Yes, Thorne," she murmured, "yes, darling."

She didn't want to be painted, but if he loved her enough that he wanted her portrait, wasn't that a spark? Would that flame in him, and in herself, then flare to the shared emotion for which she yearned?

The next month passed swiftly enough. They attended a dance each week, were present at two operas, had dinner in the homes of friends, and entertained in their own dining room.

Justine's natural sparkle made each occasion merry. Only she knew that, under the sparkle, lay a deepening sadness as she came to realize that her husband, though a handsome escort and courteous husband was, basically, a cold man. She schooled herself to be content with his polite admiration and his short, though intense, bedding of her. He never failed to assure her that it had been delightful, but he never held her in his arms afterward.

And still she could not bring herself to tell him of the baby. She would have to tell him soon. She mustn't wait until he saw her condition for himself.

She met Steven Bird, the artist who was in such demand, at a dance. She had finished a waltz with Thorne, and he had told her to wait a moment, that there was someone she should meet. When he returned, he brought with him a slightly built man with flaming red hair.

"Justine, my dear," Thorne said, "this is Steven Bird. Mr. Bird, my wife."

The artist held out his hand, and Justine put hers into it. His fingers closed over hers, and she gasped silently. His touch was like hot coals and sent sparks through her body. This, she thought wildly, is what I tried to rouse in Thorne again just last night, to rouse it in myself—and failed!

Steven Bird bent over her hand and put his lips lightly to the back of it. He straightened, but kept her hand and studied her. His gaze lingered on her lips, which she could scarcely keep from trembling.

"May I have the next dance?" he asked, and even his voice seemed intense to her.

She nodded, feeling as if she would swoon.

He took her into his arms for the dance, which was another waltz. His palm on her back and his right hand holding her left hand were burning hot. "To think," he murmured, "that I've been in New Orleans so long and haven't met you!"

"It is odd," she managed to say. "We—do go out a great deal."

"And I, sadly, do not. I work."

"H-how did you happen to come to this dance?"

"I'd finished a portrait and felt like celebrating. Incidentally," he continued, "I'm ready to do your portrait. Next. Beginning tomorrow, if you like."

At her startled look, he held her closer. "Did I say the wrong thing? If I sounded highhanded, I beg your forgiveness."

"Oh, no! It's that I—well, I'm—enceinte. To have my portrait done now would be impossible."

"That doesn't matter, though I noticed," he confessed.

"How could you? Not even my husband knows! And I chose this gown because of its easy, floating lines! It—"

For the first time he smiled, right into her eyes, setting her heart aflame. She trembled in his arms, and he felt the trembling and held her firmly and closely.

"An artist sees what others miss," he said. "I'll paint you in this gown. No one will ever know, after I'm finished, of your—condition—at the time you posed."

"Thorne wants the portrait in my wedding dress. And so—so do I."

She wanted to escape being alone with this upsetting man whose touch was burning her, but she also wanted to stay. Not that she was in love with him, she couldn't be.

His touch excited her, yes, and attracted her, even. But it wasn't love.

"The wedding gown—it nips in at the waist?" he persisted.

"Oh, yes, way in! I couldn't possibly fasten it now!"

"Very well," he said. "I'll put you first on the list next season. Is that agreeable to you?"

"Y-yes," she stuttered, and was relieved that the dance ended and Thorne claimed her.

Steven Bird didn't ask for another dance, and when she looked out over the ballroom floor, she saw nothing of him. Apparently he had left. She was both relieved and disappointed.

That night in bed, Thorne asked, "Did Bird say when you're coming up on the list?"

"Yes. He did. I was to be next."

"What do you mean, you *were* to be next? Did he let someone buy your rightful turn?"

She snuggled to him, and he let her stay. "Let me put my head on your shoulder, darling," she murmured. "I have something to tell you."

At first she thought he was going to refuse, then he extended his arm, and she lay close to him. "I can't have my portrait done, not this season, darling," she whispered. "I can't get my wedding gown together at the waist. I'm enceinte!"

He was silent. Then he said, "An heir. For Thornton."

"I hope so, for you, darling! I'll take what I get, boy or girl!"

He kissed her on the lips, coolly, then drew back from hers, which were clinging. "Thank you, Justine. You've made our marriage perfect."

She tried to get closer, to tempt him into her body, but he only kissed her again, a shorter kiss this time, then pushed her gently but firmly away. "No more lovemaking until my son is born," he said. "We'll risk nothing that might harm him."

Fighting tears, she turned on her side and closed her eyes. She didn't sleep for a very long time. It occurred to her that she hadn't told Thorne that Steven Bird knew of her condition.

* * *

Everyone in the library was silent.

"Justine told me all this, sobbing in my arms," Beulah Carpenter went on. "Even about her fear of the emotion Steven Bird roused in her. The baby was born and was named Rosalie."

She paused again. They all carefully did not look at Rosalie Bennett.

"Thorne Wabash was disappointed that she wasn't a son, and he didn't pay much attention to her, though he was kind enough in his way. He was sure the next child would be an heir.

"The following winter, with Rosalie learning to crawl and walk, Steven Bird painted Justine in her wedding gown. She suffered the tortures of the damned the whole time. . . ."

* * *

She could hardly stand in the pose he wanted. When he lifted her hand to the mantel so the wedding diamonds would show, his touch ignited again the passion she felt for him.

Even to be in the same room with him was torment, and for that room to be her boudoir, with the bed in the next chamber, was torture. Perhaps, if Thorne would make even his short, intense kind of love to her, these sessions would be bearable. But Thorne had decreed no lovemaking until Rosalie was two. Only then, he theorized, would Justine reach the peak of health after the birth of Rosalie. Only then would he try for the heir he so deeply wanted.

Standing in position at the mantel, she could see Steven's bright red hair on the other side of the easel as he worked. Watching his hair, especially when sunlight touched it, seeing him step back to get perspective, catching his wonderful eyes when he looked at her eyes to paint them, her heart lunged. She was in love with Steven Bird. In love the way she had dreamed of being in love with Thorne and was not allowed to be. Standing in her wedding gown, holding her pose, willing her knees not to quiver, her lips to lie in the half-smile for which Steven had asked, she hungered for Steven's arms, for his lips, for all of him.

At their first sitting, he had said, "I don't mean to be

bold, but there is an—intimacy between the artist and his subject. They look into each other, so to speak. They become friends. I always ask this of everyone who sits for me. May I call you by your Christian name, and will you call me by mine?"

She nodded, her eyes glowing. She could feel her lips tremble, but there was nothing she could do to stop it.

While posing, she would steal a glance at his intense, sensitive artist's mouth and find herself unable to tear her eyes away. Gazing at those lips, she would wonder how it would feel to have them on her own. With a choking sensation, she would look at his shoulders when he turned his back, and imagine how it would be to stand in his arms, her fingers on that supple play of muscle that rippled his shirt as he moved. She thought about his leg touching hers, about his finger tips on her throat, tracing its length, moving on and on, down and down. She tore her eyes free. She had to stop these thoughts. She was the wife of Thorne Wabash. Her loyalty was to him. Her love must be his kind of love—cool, dispassionate, unshaken.

Steven Bird, in turn, privately battled his passionate, wild love for this startlingly beautiful woman, this married woman who had a child. His love had sprung in him that first night when he had danced with her. That night he had wanted to dance cheek-to-cheek, to make a trail of kisses along her brow, to cover her red, passionate mouth with his own in front of all the fine ladies and gentlemen present—her husband, too.

It was fortunate that she couldn't sit for her portrait at that time. Stricken with hot, impatient love, he would not, then, have been able to keep from telling her of it, or to resist pleading that she love him in return. He had not known that love could be so delightful yet so painful and hopeless.

When the time came and she was actually sitting for him, life became a hell on earth. He had to tighten his fingers on the brush to keep it steady and to hold his lips tensely to keep them from spilling out words of love.

He looked at her dark, lovely head with its tiara of white blossoms, at the lace veil falling to her shoulders, and he wanted to tear it off and cast it aside. He painted in the detail of the lace of the wedding gown, aching to rip it to shreds. She was his, she had been created for him. That she was married was no longer of consequence.

Thorne Wabash was the coldest man he had ever met; he would stifle Justine until her heart lost all capacity for joy. But somehow, when he was in her presence, he managed to mask his feelings.

Thorne Wabash never appeared at the sittings.

"Does he—your husband—look at the painting?" Steven asked her one day, removing the cloth with which he draped it.

"No," she replied softly. "He doesn't want to see work in progress, but will view it when it's finished."

If she were my wife, Steven thought hotly, God, if she were, I'd look in on every sitting! I'd watch every brush stroke to make sure the artist was doing her justice.

Constantly he steeled himself against her. And constantly his love grew.

The morning that he signed the portrait, he threw the brush down on the pallet, then dropped the pallet onto the small table that he had used for supplies.

"Finished," he said. "You may look, Justine."

She stood beside him and regarded the portrait closely, though she had looked at it every day when he had finished and gone. She was astonished that this final day had made it look so different; before, it had seemed to be just a picture of herself. Now it was as though she stood, alive and breathing, before herself. She couldn't speak.

"It's you, my darling," he said softly.

The endearment, his tone, the smell of the lotion he wore, wove into her. She swayed, but when he would have steadied her, she caught her balance.

"I don't think—you shouldn't call me darling," she gasped. She was trembling, and she couldn't stop it.

"I'm going to call you darling always," he murmured. And then, fingers gentle, he began to unbutton her wedding dress, and she did not have the strength to stop him. Gently he undressed her. Then he got out of his own clothes. He was breathing fast, and she sensed that he could no more speak than she could.

She couldn't walk into the bedchamber; her knees wouldn't hold her. He lifted her into his arms and carried her, then lowered her to the bed and entered her. Their meeting sent them into instant, flaming passion. Their movements were instinctive, rhythmic from the start. They were melded by the fire of long denied love. At the peak, when they seemed to float above the bed, they cried out. Afterward, they rested in each other's arms, fed and nourished.

"I hope," Steven whispered, "that you won't let the thought of using your—marital bed—torment you."

"No," she murmured. "Thorne actually sleeps in his dressing room now. The bed is mine."

"No longer," he said. "I'll not live without you, my darling."

"And I c-can't live without you!" she whispered.

"Divorce Wabash. Marry me."

"He'd never—that's impossible!"

"Why impossible?"

"I have no grounds, no reason to divorce him."

"Then I'll tell you what we're going to do," he murmured and went on speaking with tenderness and with love.

* * *

In the Thornton library, Rosalie Drummond was weeping. Seth's arm was around her. There were tears in Hester's eyes for the beautiful, unhappy Justine and for Rosalie, the daughter.

"Justine told all to me," Beulah Carpenter continued. "Because divorce was impossible, she ran away to Paris with Steven Bird. She left behind her year-old baby, Rosalie, because she wouldn't take everything away from Thorne."

She stopped, giving them time to digest what she had said.

Hester wiped away her tears. Seeing this, Phil openly came to her. He stood behind her chair, his hands on the back of it.

George broke in impatiently. "I don't see any point to all this!" he snapped. "It's only bringing out old family scandal—"

"Wait!" Beulah cut in. "There's more!" She turned to Rosalie, who had now dried her eyes. "Child, I ain't seen you in so many years I don't know if you've changed."

"I don't think I've changed, Mrs. Carpenter."

"Then, can I tell your part of it now? Can I break my word to you? I'm ready to break my word to your father."

Rosalie's tears welled again, then subsided. She seemed not to know what to say.

"You need to know the end of it, child. All of these folks—there's need for them to know. That's why I came back and asked to speak."

Rosalie, holding back tears, nodded. "Speak," she whispered.

Chapter Forty-two

"Thorne Wabash," Beulah continued, "was a bitter man. For days you couldn't speak to him. What happened struck into his pride, and he never did get over it.

"He divorced Justine, sold the New Orleans house, forbid anybody to mention her name or existence. He never spoke of her once.

"Rosalie was put in care of first one slave, then another. He had forbid them ever to kiss or pet her, just see to her needs. Same way with governesses he brought in to educate her—frequent changes, no kindness or affection to be shown.

"I got up courage and asked him why he was depriving her of affection. He said it was so she'd learn to be like him, clearheaded and sensible, not weak and clinging and demanding constant attention."

He educated Rosalie thoroughly, Beulah explained. The girl had every luxury, including beautiful clothes, but his manner, detached at first, became colder toward her with every passing year. "Because she resembled her mother," Beulah said.

Thus Rosalie grew up without love, for which she yearned. Only Beulah Carpenter gave her a hug now and then, a whispered endearment, and that on the sly. And Rosalie never failed to breathe, "I love you, Mrs. Carpenter! You're the only one!"

Just one kiss on the brow from her remote father would have fed the child's heart. Instead, she had to exist on good service from slaves and teachers and secret hugs from the overseer's wife. Yet despite her cheerless upbringing, Rosalie kept her warm nature and sought always for kindness and for affection.

She grew into a beautiful young woman, and young men in the vicinity flocked to her, much to Thorne's satisfaction. He wanted to marry her off as soon as possible. He didn't particularly care whom she married, so long as he was of a good family. He wanted no repetition of Justine.

He even broke his silence to Beulah Carpenter on that point. "Marriage," he said. "That's what Rosalie must have. She'll get into trouble otherwise. Like mother, like daughter."

When the Millhouse twins came courting, their hearts in their eyes, Rosalie, starved for love, was beside herself with happiness. She could tell that her father was pleased, and this added to her joy. She dared to become more gently gay, softer, tremendously appealing.

Robert and Richard Millhouse were identical twins, twenty years old, nearly six feet tall. They had coal black hair, coal black eyes, and patrician features.

Their voices were strong and merry, like their natures. They were mischievous, inveterate pranksters with one goal—to enjoy life. And they were both attracted to Rosalie.

Usually they came to Thornton together, but one day Robert appeared alone. "Richard sends his regrets," he said gaily to Rosalie, who came down the veranda steps to meet him. "He's feeling lazy. So am I, for that matter, but not too lazy to come see the most beautiful girl in Warren County."

Rosalie laughed, the laugh catching in her throat. "Richard is forgiven!" she cried. "So long as you're here!"

He caught her hands, pulled her to him, his handsome face abruptly serious. "Do you feel that way, blessed angel?" he asked. "That you'd rather see me than Richard?"

"Yes!" she breathed, and it was true because he was holding her in his arms, calling her a loving name, and this had never happened before, in her whole life. Instinctively, she lifted her face, and they kissed, a long, tender kiss.

Abruptly Robert pulled away. "We mustn't be seen, not yet!" he warned. "How about that clearing where you spend so much time? The one among the trees beside the lake?"

"Oh, yes!" she cried and, slipping her hand into his,

began dancing away from the house. "Hurry, before Papa knows you're here!"

At their destination, he lost no time taking her into his arms again. This kiss was longer, and it stirred feelings in her she hadn't known existed.

"Oh, Robert!" she breathed.

"I love you, blessed angel," he murmured, his hand on her breast.

She gasped with pleasure. "And I love you, my darling Robert!" she exclaimed softly. "For now and forever."

"Enough to marry me?" he asked, kissing her again, his hand wandering downward. "To become Mrs. Robert Millhouse?"

"Yes, Robert. Oh, yes—yes!"

"Blessed, beautiful angel!" He kissed her again.

She was choking with love. She pressed closer; there was no way to get close enough.

Suddenly he swung her in his arms, stretched her on the grass, flipped up her dress and her petticoats, and tore away her undergarment.

"Angel, angel,—spread your legs!"

Maybe she shouldn't be doing this, she thought, but it was love. And even Papa approved of her getting married. He had said so, and Robert was going to marry her, so this was just a part of that. Trembling, she moved her legs apart.

Then he was inside her. It hurt, and she almost screamed. But then she did not, because this was Robert, and they were engaged. He moved, and that didn't hurt. When he told her to move up and down, she did, and that began to feel good. In a moment they were going very fast; she was meeting his thrusts with all her strength, and then a warmth spread all through her. Abruptly, Robert was still, but tense, and it was then, as his body gave three or four little jerks, that she felt it, the glory that rose in her to a peak and exploded the way fireworks do in the sky.

"Robert," she murmured, as he pulled her against him and she lay in his arms. This was the first time she had ever been held so, except perhaps when she had been an infant.

Robert chuckled. "How do you know I'm not Richard, blessed angel?" he teased.

She laughed, low. "I know you and Richard play those

identity pranks," she said. "But not about love. You wouldn't play a prank about love, you're too perfect."

"More so than Richard?" he teased. "How do you know that, when we're identical? Our perfection may be identical, too." He held her closer and kissed her.

Before they left the clearing, they made love again.

The next morning Robert brought her a double armload of yellow roses. "Richard wanted to come along," he said, "but I wouldn't have it. I told him you're mine, that we're engaged and need privacy."

She held the roses in her arms, careless of thorns, and smiled into his eyes. "How did he receive the news?"

"Surprised. I told him to get his own wife. I've found mine."

"Do you," she asked shyly, "want to go to the lake again?" It was a bold question; she felt it was unmaidenly but also felt it was his due. He loved her, and yesterday had been the beautiful expression of that love.

"Not now, but this afternoon," he said. "When your father takes his rest. Then I'll come back."

He sat with her on the veranda. They decided to keep their engagement secret for a time—except from Richard—and marry at Christmas or even later. They wouldn't let her father know yet.

"We need our time of courtship before we settle down," Robert declared. "Nobody's going to cheat my angel of that!"

She glowed, looked forward to the afternoon.

When he returned in the afternoon, he brought more yellow roses. His eyes were dancing with mischief. This morning they had been soft, love-filled, adoring. She took the flowers, wondering why he would bring the same kind of flowers again, wondering at the change in his eyes. Knowing how the twins passed themselves off as each other to unsuspecting friends and even their father, the possibility that this might be Richard came to her. She accused him of it.

"My beloved!" he cried, his eyes instantly soft and filled with love. "Richard is at home; I swear it. He and Pa are leafing through some travel books. They invited me to join them, but I had better things to do!"

He kissed her then, full on the lips, his mouth covering

hers, and she was convinced. Only Robert could kiss in such manner.

"Let one of the servants put the roses in water," he said. "I want to get to the lake."

That settled it. Robert would tell no one of the lake, not even his twin.

This time, the clearing being secluded and hidden by trees, he undressed her. Then he undressed himself. He didn't wait to hold her in his arms first, and she missed that. But his hardness told how urgent his need was, and she sank to the grass, to the flowers, and parted her legs.

He speared into her. It didn't hurt, but it surprised her so she caught her breath. Then he began a circular motion, impatiently, almost, and told her to move the same, only in the opposite direction, which she did. She was clumsy at first, but soon she was whirling her hips fast and faster. And again there was the explosion inside, the fireworks and the sparks.

"We'll be married," he said after their second time.

"Yes," she breathed, yet wondered. "You said that yesterday."

"Hmm—so I did. Just don't forget it. You're mine—not Richard's!"

In bed that night she lay curled and smiling. She was loved! She was loved by Robert Millhouse! She frowned slightly. Why had he made love to her in one manner the first time, and in another manner the second? He hadn't explained why, and she had been too shy to ask.

She really liked the first way best. And she liked for him to call her "blessed angel," as he had done earlier, rather than "beloved," as he had done later.

Her head began to whirl. Surely they wouldn't play *this* prank on her, though they had played tricks on her before. They had always confessed quickly, though, and laughed until they rolled on the grass.

Of course it was Robert who had been with her both times. She needn't worry her head about it. Still, the thought kept returning. Sometimes, even now, they came together to Thornton, and if Robert hadn't held her hand and called her "blessed angel," she wouldn't have known them apart.

On another afternoon the twins came to Thornton together, excited, bearing news.

"You've got to be the first to know, blessed angel," Robert said. "Because we're engaged."

"What is it?" she asked, looking from one beaming face to the other.

"Pa," Richard announced, and she knew it was Richard because Robert had spoken of their engagement, "insists that Robert and I make an extended trip to the Continent before we take over the double plantation. We leave tomorrow!"

"But I—Robert—our wedding!" faltered Rosalie, stricken. "We're engaged!"

"You're engaged to both of us," laughed Robert. "We both gave you the love you need, down in the clearing. We both brought you roses. We both courted you. We both want you. But we've got to go on this trip first! Pa would disinherit us if we didn't both go—if one stayed behind just to get married!"

She fell into stunned silence. Instinct had spoken more than once that they were playing a prank on her, and she hadn't listened. At last she choked out, "It really was a prank! Another one of your pranks!"

They confessed, then declared that each wanted to marry her on their return from abroad. She could have whichever of them she wanted. And the other one would be good, and play no more pranks.

Crushed, not knowing now, which of them she loved, she listened to their profuse and heartfelt apologies. They called themselves dastards. They begged her forgiveness.

"We both want you, Rosalie," said Robert—or was it Richard?—"so think carefully while we're gone and decide. Meanwhile, you're to consider yourself engaged to one of us."

"Indeed you are," said Richard—or was it Robert?—"and you're to work on your trousseau. We'll bring you a diamond from Amsterdam, lace from Brussels, gowns from Paris. You'll end up being the luckiest girl in Warren County!"

"In the whole state of Mississippi!" corrected Robert.

Or was it Richard?

Chapter Forty-three

Two months after the twins left, Rosalie found that she was pregnant.

When her father drove to Warrenton one morning, she went running to the overseer's house, to Beulah Carpenter. The older woman was in her kitchen, vigorously kneading bread. One look at Rosalie's face set her to cleaning dough from her hands and wiping them on a towel. Then she enfolded the stricken, silent girl in her arms. "There, there," she comforted. "It can't be as bad as all this!"

"Oh, but it is!" Rosalie quavered, trembling in Beulah's arms. "It's the very worst that can happen to a girl if she's not married!" The trembling increased, though still she didn't weep.

"Tell me about it, darling," soothed Beulah. "I'll help you, no matter what it is."

"You c-can't help me! Nobody can! Not if it's true! And it is true, I know it is!"

"Tell Beulah, little darling. Maybe it isn't true."

Rosalie clung to the overseer's wife, her only friend. "I'm g-going to have a baby!" she choked out.

"Are you sure? Have you missed your monthly?"

Rosalie nodded.

"Sometimes a girl does miss," comforted Beulah. "But before she does, darling, she has to—do certain things—with a man."

"But I've done those things! Over and over! With two men! And I throw up my breakfast every morning!"

The two of them clung together. Rosalie confessed who the men were, and Beulah clicked her tongue because they were across the water, unavailable now that one or

the other of them was so sorely needed. "There ain't but
one thing you can do, child," Beulah said gently. "And
that's go to your father and tell him the whole thing. Now
is the time for the father to step in, when some young
blade has got his daughter into trouble."

It was then, at the inescapable prospect of confessing
to her father, that Rosalie wept long and bitterly in Beulah Carpenter's arms. Then she went home to await her
father's return from Warrenton.

She waited until supper time. During the meal, her
father ordered her to eat her potatoes, saying he didn't
want her so thin that people would think he didn't feed
her, and she had lost weight recently.

It's because of the baby, she thought, surprised that her
father had noticed her enough to see that she had become
thin. She took a deep breath. This was as good an opening
as she would find to tell him. So, no servant being in the
dining room at the moment, she took the plunge.

"I've gotten thin, Papa," she said, her voice steady
though scarcely audible, "b-because I'm pregnant."

Immediately he went into a towering rage. "You—?
Who is the father?" he demanded.

In spite of her determination not to cry, tears ran
down her cheeks. "I d-don't know, Papa," she said.

"Good God!" he exclaimed. "Are you telling me that
you permitted not only one, but—!"

"No, Papa, no!"

"What, then? Explain yourself!"

"Robert and Richard, Papa. They both—!"

"And you were witless enough—like your mother—to
open yourself to both of them?"

"They play tricks!" she sobbed. "I c-can't tell them
apart! Even their own father can't! You can't, you've
said it! And they b-both asked me to m-marry them!"

"And you considered a proposal of marriage—when
the man didn't even speak to me, your father, first, excuse
enough to—?"

"They—he—was so much in love! And I loved him—
them! I—it's impossible to say no to them when they—
they—"

"Didn't you suspect, you little fool? You know their
reputation for pranks!"

"At f-first I thought it was Robert, Papa! They—each

time he *said* he was Robert, and when I did wonder, I—thought I was being disloyal!"

"So you don't know which one is the father. And now they're in Europe, safely out of it! Out of another scrape!"

"They—I'm engaged, Papa! When they come home, I'm to marry whichever one I choose!"

He gestured angrily. "Marry the one you choose with a bastard in your arms!"

"Papa, you never spoke to me so before!"

"Until now, you haven't betrayed your true nature, though I sensed the nature, for me to use the blunt language you deserve!"

She bowed her head, shamed beyond endurance. Shame stopped her tears. "Maybe their father will bring them home, if you speak to him," she managed.

"By the time they could get here, you'll be too far along in your unspeakable condition for the matter to be kept quiet. Everybody will know that Rosalie Wabash has chosen to walk in the footsteps of her mother."

"If they know about my mother! Even I don't know what terrible thing she's supposed to have done!"

"She eloped with an artist, eloped without marriage! God knows what's become of her. Certainly I don't care."

She ached for that unknown mother who, surely, must have been driven to her scandalous action. She must have loved her artist deeply.

"People have forgotten about my mother," she ventured. "They'd forget, in time, that my baby was born too soon after marriage. Please, Papa! Let me marry Robert!"

"Absolutely not. That would mean, among other things, that Barry Millhouse would know of this new disgrace you've brought on me, and he'd laugh up his sleeve because of what his sons got away with, because he'd know about the baby before the county people found out. And it won't be found out, I'll see to that."

"W-what am I to do, Papa?"

"First, keep your mouth closed. Dress to hide your condition, even from the house slaves. Obey me in all matters. I'll keep this hidden so no one ever finds out. As a first step, go to your rooms. Stay there. I'll have Doctor Cline look you over and then circulate word that you're in a decline. That will explain your not being seen these next months. With that as a basis, I'll find a way to accomplish complete secrecy."

In Thorne Wabash's eyes, his daughter was even filthier than her mother. He admitted only the doctor and the overseer's wife to Rosalie's rooms. The house slaves were told that Beulah Carpenter was nursing Miss Rosalie through her decline, which threatened to go into consumption. He swore Beulah to secrecy, and the doctor grunted angrily that of course he would never let anything slip.

Thorne next decided to find Rosalie a husband at once, even if he had to buy one. It was on the heels of this decision that news reached him of the arrival of Seth Drummond, a young widower with a small son, and Neal Bennett, his brother-in-law, to visit Drummond's distant kinsman, Barry Millhouse. A slave boy brought a note to Thornton inviting Thorne and Rosalie to dine at Elmhurst and meet the houseguests. This struck Thorne as a possible means out of his dilemma, and he sat down at once to write an acceptance, which he sent back by the same slave.

Rosalie, though now three months pregnant, was very thin and had not yet begun to show her condition. Thorne ordered her to wear her best gown and to use a bit of color on her pale cheeks and lips.

Rosalie, having been told the purpose behind her attendance at the small dinner party, was reluctant to go. She didn't want to marry just any man who might be willing to take her; she wanted to marry Robert. But what she wanted carried no weight, so she went obediently along to Elmhurst, looking her prettiest.

"It's the widower, Seth Drummond, I'm interested in," Thorne instructed her. "He has a small son, and Millhouse let drop some time ago he had a kinsman who needs a mother for his son. Doubtless this is why you're invited tonight—to be looked over."

Eyes downcast, Rosalie entered Elmhurst on her father's arm. Since learning of her condition, she felt shame at all times, and she made herself as unobtrusive as possible. She did not look up when the men introduced and acknowledged each other.

"Rosalie," Papa said clearly, "Mr. Neal Bennett and Mr. Seth Drummond. Gentlemen, my daughter, Rosalie."

She shook hands with Mr. Bennett in a haze of confusion. She saw only that he was young and personable.

"My dear," her father continued, addressing her as he

had never done before, "Mr. Drummond has a young, motherless son. Perhaps you could have the boy for an afternoon in your rooms and entertain him."

She felt a hand touch hers and looked up into a tanned, strong-featured face. Kindness showed in Seth Drummond's gaze and in his smile.

She smiled back. "I'd be happy to entertain your little son, Mr. Drummond," she said, though she didn't see how her father was going to explain that to the slaves with herself supposedly in a decline.

"Thank you kindly," Seth Drummond said. "And do me another favor?"

"A-anything," she stammered, remembering, her face hot, the favors she had done Robert and Richard.

"Call me Seth. Mr. Drummond is much too formal. We're going to get acquainted during the fortnight I'm here. And there's no time to waste."

Indeed, time was not wasted. The frequent presence of little George Drummond in Rosalie's rooms was explained to the house slaves as being to cheer her up, to help her face the oncoming decline. At the end of a week, Seth Drummond asked Thorne Wabash for Rosalie's hand in marriage and for permission to ask her to become his wife.

She accepted because she must. But also because Seth was kind and gentle. He was a man, not a boy, like the Millhouse twins. And he was quietly, seriously, in love with her.

"He wants to get married right now, Papa," Rosalie told Thorne. Seth had just departed with his son, who had spent several hours with Rosalie.

"Out of the question!"

"But—"

"Seven months from now, or eight."

"But why not now?" she cried, thinking of her baby.

"Because Drummond would never believe your bastard is his, born only six months after marriage. The birth will be kept secret from him for all time. You're never to tell him, understand, not if you're married for fifty years."

"Yes, Papa."

"Swear it."

"I swear. But my baby—what of it?"

"You should have thought of that sooner," he said coldly. "However, I'll do what has always been done in cases where secrecy is imperative. I'll board the child with good people—on a farm somewhere—and see that it gets a start in life. You can ask nothing better, and I advise you not to, or I'll not take the care in situating it I would otherwise take."

Rosalie, devastated that she must give up her baby, wept bitterly. Again, under Thorne's relentless threat, she swore never to tell Seth Drummond she had borne a child out of wedlock.

But at the first opportunity, she told Beulah Carpenter everything.

"This Seth Drummond," Beulah asked quietly, "what sort is he?"

"He's a real gentleman! He's ever so gentle with his little son, and you can tell the gentleness and kindness are real, because the boy runs to him and trusts him."

"He's in love with you, of course."

Rosalie's cheeks warmed. "He says he is. And I believe him. Believing him is different than it was with Robert and Richard. This is real."

"Can you love him, child? He sounds like he deserves a loving wife."

"I hope to love him," Rosalie replied thoughtfully. "I believe a kind of love will come because he *is* so kind and gentle, so thoughtful of me. He's going to New Orleans and buy us a house and refurbish it, then come back here for the wedding. In eight months."

"You'll correspond with him?"

"I've promised. But Papa forbids me to tell him I'm supposed to be in a decline. He's afraid Seth might come rushing to see me if he thought I was ill, and then he'd find out the truth. He's made Seth promise not to come see me at all, to wait for the wedding. Seth didn't like that, but he agreed."

Beulah Carpenter nodded thoughtfully. "It may work," she said. "The only thing I hate is deceiving Seth Drummond. He's going to be your husband for life. One day he must know, regardless of your papa, darling, and anything he's forced you to swear. One day this man you're marrying has the right to know the truth."

Chapter Forty-four

Rosalie gave birth on a dark, stormy night, with Beulah Carpenter, Doctor Cline, and her father in attendance. All the house slaves had retired to the Quarters, and Thorne Wabash himself carried up buckets of hot water.

A woman in the Quarters was also giving birth, her pains, at Thorne's order, having been induced by the black midwife when Rosalie felt her first twinge. The woman was shrieking with pain, and Manda, working over the laboring mother, kept waiting for the arrival of the white midwife, for she needed her help. She had sent a man to the overseer's house long ago, and the overseer had said his wife was busy at the big house and would come as soon as she could.

Rosalie arched her back as a cutting pain sliced through her body. She fought it, sweat pouring over her face.

There was movement around her; there were voices. Why didn't they help her, these people, whoever they were? Why didn't they see she couldn't breathe, that she couldn't bear the hurting?

"Bear down, Rosalie, bear down—push!" Dr. Cline kept saying. "Do it now, and it'll be over. Take a deep breath, then bear down—"

Mrs. Carpenter said it, too. "Bear down, darling—bear down hard as you can!"

She pushed her shoulders against the mattress, gripped hands that reached out to her, and pushed with all her strength. Still the voices told her to bear down.

At one point, she screamed. A hand clapped over her mouth.

"No noise!" snapped her father. "Not one sound out of you, Rosalie!"

"For God's sake, Thorne," Dr. Cline said. "She's in labor, hard labor. What if some slave does hear her scream? They'd think she was having a nightmare!"

Nightmare. She was having a nightmare, and the world wanted her to bear down.

"Bear down, darling," urged Mrs. Carpenter again. "Bear down so your baby can be born—so it can get into the world and breathe."

And then, the real pain tore into her. She had no control over it; instinctively she began to push, straining, sweating, clinging again to the hands that had reached out to her.

"She's really bearing down now," said the doctor. "It shouldn't take long. There—here comes the head—the shoulders—it's a girl!"

She thought she heard a thin wail, but before she could ask anything, she was sinking into blessed darkness where there was no pain, no bearing down, no trouble of any sort. Only blessed relief.

When she regained consciousness, Mrs. Carpenter was gone. Only Thorne and Doctor Cline were with her.

"My baby," Rosalie said faintly. "Did I have my baby?"

"You had it," Thorne snapped. "It was stillborn."

Her eyes went to the doctor, who looked angry. "Was it a girl?" she asked. "I thought I heard you say—"

"It was a girl," the doctor said grimly. "A beautiful little girl."

"There's no need to make it worse than necessary," snapped her father. "She knew she couldn't keep it, anyway. You knew."

The doctor said nothing. Rosalie wondered, dimly, if he was angry, or if it was her own fatigue, her sore and bleeding body that made her think it.

"Mrs. Carpenter will tidy the room, doctor," Thorne said. "She'll be back in a moment. I'd like you to come to the library with me—if you've finished here."

"I've finished. Be back tomorrow. And I want to see you privately myself."

In silence they went out, leaving Rosalie alone. She

wept for her dead baby for a while, then, drained, fell asleep, still weeping.

In the library, it was the doctor who spoke first. "You've got no right to play God, Thorne Wabash," he said. "For you to board the child out—people do do that, and with good results I'll admit, but for you to tell her it was stillborn—"

"It'll keep her from pining over it and wanting to know where it is. It would have solved a problem if it *had* been stillborn. It's only trash."

"It's a beautiful baby with a *soul,* Thorne. It's—"

"A female. All females are trash. And this one is also illegitimate."

"She's a nice baby. She—"

"Trash. I'll dispose of her as trash. Doctor, you took your oath. You're sworn to secrecy."

"If any harm comes to that baby, if you mean to kill her, oath or no oath, I'll—"

"You must think I'm a devil! The child will have care. It'll come to no harm. You have my word."

The doctor gave Thorne a searching glance, then picked up his black medical bag. "As I said, I'll be back tomorrow. And every day for a while. Your daughter had a very difficult delivery. I had to sew her up. She needs close attention."

"Mrs. Carpenter will give it to her," Thorne said, then hurried the doctor on his way as he himself had something that needed to be done.

Even as the doctor's rig went down the driveway, instantly blotted from sight in the raining darkness, Thorne took the steps three at a time and hurried to his own bedchamber. Here Mrs. Carpenter, white-lipped, was holding the newborn child in her arms. It was wrapped in a square of white blanket, and it made no sound.

"Quiet, sir," Mrs. Carpenter warned. "She's asleep."

"Wrap it in oilskin," he ordered. "I've a piece ready on the table there. And a coat for each of us."

"You're not going to take her into the rain, sir? She's only just been born! She—"

"It'll be safe. Won't take but a few minutes. You're coming with me, and later I want your husband to join us in the library. I have a proposition for you both."

Wearing oilskins, Mrs. Carpenter carrying the baby, they stole down the stairway and through the kitchen to the back door. Here Thorne Wabash paused.

"You gave Manda her orders about the wench and her sucker?" he demanded. "You made certain she got it through that thick skull what she's to do, and how?"

"Yes, sir. It's all set up. If the timing is right, and I think it is, it'll all go the way you planned."

They went into the night and hurried to the Quarters, their heads down against the driving rain. They came to the cabin where the woman had been giving birth, opened the door, and entered. They stood there, water streaming from them. Mrs. Carpenter was careful to keep the baby covered and out of sight of the black man who sat slumped in a chair, his head in his hands.

Seeing them, the man, his face twisted with worry, sprang to his feet. "Mastah!" he exclaimed. "Dey sumpin' wrong! Manda, she keep de suckah in de bedroom—she keep de new mothah 'sleep wif laudanum. I 'bout to go crazy, mastah, suh!"

"Manda!" called Thorne.

The inner doorway was filled with a massive black woman.

"Everything worked out?" Thorne demanded of her. "All over with?"

"Yas, mastah, suh. An' de mothah, she jus' wakin' up," Manda said proudly.

Thorne Wabash went into action. He sent the man outside, rain or no rain, to fetch a bucket of water, though water wasn't needed. Then he motioned Mrs. Carpenter to give the sleeping baby girl to Manda, which she did, first removing the wet oilskin.

He stood in the doorway and watched Manda put the infant into the arms of the woman on the bunk. The woman smiled tiredly, held the bundle to her, lifted a corner of the blanket, and gazed in awe. Then she put her lips to the tiny head.

While the woman's attention was diverted, Manda took the blanketed, newborn male sucker from a pallet, wrapped the oilskin Thorne gave her around it, and scurried outside and away. Then Mrs. Carpenter left to go and get her husband, as requested.

Thorne hurried Manda, with her little burden, to the

jailhouse. "You'll spend the night here," he told her. "In the morning, before dawn, a coffle will come along with a nursing wench in it. The man in charge is waiting word from me. I'll send a buck. All he'll know is that I've got a midwife to sell. You and the sucker will be taken down-river and sold."

Manda began to blubber aloud and plead. Thorne pushed her into the jailhouse and locked the door.

By the time he got back to the house, the Carpenters were waiting in the library. Beulah said she had looked in on Rosalie, who was asleep.

"Crying in her sleep," she added grimly.

"She'll get over that," Thorne said, just as grimly.

He then laid his proposition before the couple. "You know, Bud, of what's happened here tonight," he began.

Carpenter frowned, but nodded. "My missus has told me."

"In return for your silence," Thorne continued, "I propose to give you money to buy the farm you want, elsewhere in the county."

The Carpenters sat, stunned. They looked at each other. "If we stay quiet," Carpenter said, "then your plan will work, is that it? And your daughter, she'll marry the widower and have a good life?"

"Precisely. Further, her child will never suffer, but grow up where it was born. I don't know what more a man could do under the circumstances than I'm doing."

"You might let us take the baby," Beulah said. "We'd raise her as our own, with our son. He's eight now, and would like a little sister. We'd love her."

"The answer is no. The matter is settled—if you agree to take the farm and hold your silence. If not, I'll have to dismiss you and sue you if you spread gossip. All of which, I'm certain, will not happen. Also, I need you to stay here long enough, Mrs. Carpenter, to nurse Rosalie back to health."

They accepted, though reluctantly. Bud Carpenter went back to the overseer's house, Thorne Wabash repaired to his chamber and went to bed, and Beulah Carpenter tiptoed to Rosalie, who was still weeping in her sleep.

Thorne Wabash stretched out comfortably on his mattress. Now he had closed every lip. Now there would be no scandal. He smiled to himself as he drifted into slumber.

Late the next afternoon he made his traditional call on the new mother in the Quarters. Traditionally, too, he named the baby.

The mother was sitting up in the bunk, holding her baby. She lifted away the blanket so that the master could see her.

He gazed for a few seconds, his face impassive. Then he lifted his eyebrows. "Lela Belle," he exclaimed, "what freakish trick have you played on us? First, only one sucker which died, for years, and now—what rarity rides your blood? She *is* healthy and beautiful, for all that. I'm well pleased."

He paused thoughtfully, then said, "Her name will be Hester."

Chapter Forty-five

Hester felt as if she had had her breath knocked out of her. The room and everyone in it seemed to be whirling. She had one flashing impression after another; she felt numb.

She heard Rosalie Drummond cry out softly and saw her turn, her eyes frantically seeking Hester's eyes. She saw her lips tremble and noticed how Seth Drummond kept his arms around his wife, restraining her, murmuring to her, kindness and concern in his face.

Without knowing, Hester, along with all the others, had sprung to her feet, and now Phil had his arm around her for all to see.

Her mother—for how could she think of Mammy any other way—was weeping, and her father, also weeping, had both arms around her. Neal and Wanda Bennett, openly dazed, seemed slowly to be comprehending what they had just heard. Eve, pale and completely aware, hissed at the equally pale George to get that lying Carpenter creature out of Thornton. Chess was dumbfounded. The attorneys stared at each other in shocked, dawning realization. Doctor Cline looked relieved, as did Bud Carpenter. Granny Myrtle began to weep aloud, joyously. Proteus was open-mouthed and uncomprehending.

Then Beulah Carpenter spoke again. "When Hester was brought to our farm, she'd been running from a showboat, also from slave hunters, trying to get to Thornton. She was near death; we loved her on sight. We nursed her, and when she could, she told us who she was—the white-skinned wench at Thornton. My man and I knew then that she was the beautiful baby girl that Thorne Wabash had

352

foisted onto Sam and Lela Belle as their own, selling their newborn boy downriver with the midwife, Manda."

A long moan rose from Lela Belle. She was hushed by Sam.

"Look at Hester!" Beulah Carpenter demanded. "Look at Rosalie Drummond! See for yourselves how alike they are! There are differences, but if you look well, you'll see the similarities.

"Only Bud and I knew," said Beulah. "And Doctor Cline. All these years. Even our son Chess didn't know until now!"

Hester's ears were ringing. If Phil hadn't been holding her, her knees would have buckled. Filled with all she had heard, all she had seen, she still could not believe it. Nothing so stupendous could happen, not to her!

She cried this out. "It isn't that way, it can't be! It can't be true! I'm only the white-nigger wench Hester! I'm not—" She broke off, she couldn't speak the words.

"It *is* true, Hester," Doctor Cline spoke up. "You are the granddaughter of Thorne Wabash. You are Rosalie Drummond's daughter; I brought you into the world. You're a white girl, one hundred percent white. And, if Rosalie, who is the rightful heir to Thornton, wants no part of it, you are next in line and will be its mistress."

"Rosalie doesn't want it," said Seth Drummond, still holding his wife. "She knew only unhappiness here. Despite the oath her father forced her to take, she confided the whole story to me on our wedding night. More than once, I've held her in my arms and comforted her as she wept over the baby she believed to be stillborn."

"She can't have Thornton!" George cut in. "I'm the master! I inherited!"

"Thorne never signed the will," Attorney Harrison said quietly. "Everything will go to Hester." He looked at his fellow attorney, who nodded agreement.

George stood pale and stiff, Eve pinching his arm. She whispered to him, ordering him to do something to change matters. Dazed, he stood silent and unmoving.

Hester's two sobbing mothers went over to her, and she clung to them. They pressed her close, then released her into Phil's arms. Their tears dwindled, and they managed, for the sake of their beloved daughter, to smile a bit.

"Now, my stubborn darling," Phil murmured, "every obstacle is gone! You can't say no again!"

She smiled at him, felt George's angry stare and realized suddenly that actually he was her stepbrother because Rosalie, her blood mother, was his stepmother. On the heels of that, the thought struck her that she would use Thornton as a way station on the Underground Railroad. She was almost certain she could persuade Bud and Beulah Carpenter to return to Thornton as overseer and to run the station. Chess, she realized, thoughts streaming through her mind so quickly she could hardly grasp them, would go back to the farm, alone and lonely. And she would free her slaves, all those who would go. She would try to get Mammy and Pappy to live in the big house but knew they would refuse.

Suddenly Phil was announcing that he and Hester would marry the next day. When consulted, the attorneys agreed that the broomstick jumping had no validity.

"To say nothing of the fact," added Attorney Sheridan, "that it's against the law for white and black to marry."

Phil turned and kissed Hester long and tenderly, for all to see, after which he stood with one arm around her, his strength seeming to flow into her.

Suddenly Hester saw the room as beautiful. She felt joy rising in her. She was white, and this meant that she really could marry Phil tomorrow.

And that was the most important thing in all the world.

ABOUT THE AUTHOR

SALIEE O'BRIEN has been writing for as long as she can remember, and publishing stories since the age of fourteen. She was lured away, while in her twenties, by community theater and radio broadcasting; but they couldn't keep her from her first love—writing. Stories began appearing in a wide range of magazines: *Saturday Evening Post*, *Collier's* and *Blue Book*. Novels followed, and in abundance. They include *Farewell the Stranger*, *Too Swift the Tide*, *Heiress to Evil*, *Bayou* and, most recently, *So Wild the Dream*. *Black Ivory* is her ninth novel published under the pseudonym Saliee O'Brien. Ms. O'Brien is married and lives in Florida.

BRING ROMANCE INTO YOUR LIFE

With these bestsellers from your favorite Bantam authors

Barbara Cartland

☐	12785	LIGHT OF THE MOON	$1.50
☐	12792	THE PRISONER OF LOVE	$1.50
☐	13036	A NIGHTINGALE SANG	$1.50
☐	12576	ALONE IN PARIS	$1.50

Catherine Cookson

☐	13279	THE DWELLING PLACE	$1.95
☐	10358	THE GLASS VIRGIN	$1.50
☐	13170	KATIE MULHOLLAND	$1.95

Georgette Heyer

☐	13239	THE BLACK MOTH	$1.95
☐	11249	PISTOLS FOR TWO	$1.95

Emilie Loring

☐	12946	FOLLOW YOUR HEART	$1.75
☐	12947	WHERE BEAUTY DWELLS	$1.75
☐	12948	RAINBOW AT DUSK	$1.75
☐	12949	WHEN HEARTS ARE LIGHT AGAIN	$1.75
☐	12945	ACROSS THE YEARS	$1.75

Eugenia Price

☐	13682	BELOVED INVADER	$2.25
☐	12717	LIGHTHOUSE	$1.95
☐	12835	NEW MOON RISING	$1.95

Buy them at your local bookstore or use this handy coupon for ordering:

THE LATEST BOOKS
IN THE BANTAM
BESTSELLING TRADITION

Barbara Cartland

The world's bestselling author of romantic fiction. Her stories are always captivating tales of intrigue, adventure and love.

☐ 12572	THE DRUMS OF LOVE	$1.50
☐ 12576	ALONE IN PARIS	$1.50
☐ 12638	THE PRINCE AND THE PEKINGESE	$1.50
☐ 12637	A SERPENT OF SATAN	$1.50
☐ 12273	THE TREASURE IS LOVE	$1.50
☐ 12785	THE LIGHT OF THE MOON	$1.50
☐ 12792	PRISONER OF LOVE	$1.50
☐ 13311	THE BRIDGE OF KISSES Ruck cond. Cartland	$1.50
☐ 13566	IMPERIAL SPLENDOR	$1.50

Buy them at your local bookstore or use this handy coupon for ordering:

Barbara Cartland

The world's bestselling author of romantic fiction.
Her stories are always captivating tales of intrigue,
adventure and love.

☐ 13570	THE POWER AND THE PRINCE	$1.50
☐ 13556	LOVE IN THE CLOUDS	$1.50
☐ 13035	LOVE CLIMBS IN	$1.50
☐ 13036	A NIGHTINGALE SANG	$1.50
☐ 13126	TERROR IN THE SUN	$1.50
☐ 13446	WOMEN HAVE HEARTS	$1.50
☐ 13579	FREE FROM FEAR	$1.75
☐ 13832	LITTLE WHITE DOVES OF LOVE	$1.75
☐ 13907	THE PERFECTION OF LOVE	$1.75
☐ 13827	BRIDE TO THE KING	$1.75
☐ 13910	PUNISHED WITH LOVE	$1.75

Buy them at your local bookstore or use this handy coupon:

Bantam Book Catalog

Here's your up-to-the-minute listing of over 1,400 titles by your favorite authors.

This illustrated, large format catalog gives a description of each title. For your convenience, it is divided into categories in fiction and non-fiction—gothics, science fiction, westerns, mysteries, cookbooks, mysticism and occult, biographies, history, family living, health, psychology, art.

So don't delay—take advantage of this special opportunity to increase your reading pleasure.

Just send us your name and address and 50¢ (to help defray postage and handling costs).

BANTAM BOOKS, INC.
Dept. FC, 414 East Golf Road, Des Plaines, Ill. 60016

Mr./Mrs./Miss _____
                    (please print)

Address _____

City _____ State _____ Zip _____

Do you know someone who enjoys books? Just give us their names and addresses and we'll send them a catalog too!

_____

Mr./Mrs./Miss _____

Address _____

City _____ State _____ Zip _____

_____

Mr./Mrs./Miss _____

Address _____

City _____ State _____ Zip _____

FC—9/76